THE ILLUSTRIOUS HOUSE
OF RAMIRES

Eça de Queirós

THE ILLUSTRIOUS
HOUSE OF RAMIRES

*Translated from the Portuguese, with an afterword
by Margaret Jull Costa*

A NEW DIRECTIONS PAPERBOOK

Published by arrangement with the Dedalus Press, London. Originally published in Portuguese as *A Ilustre Casa de Ramires* in 1900.

The translator would like to thank, as always, Maria Manuel Lisboa and Ben Sherriff for all their help, advice, and support.

Manufactured in the United States of America
First published as a New Directions Paperbook (NDP1376) in 2017
New Directions books are published on acid-free paper

Library of Congress Cataloging-in-Publication Data
Names: Queirós, Eça de, 1845–1900, author. | Costa, Margaret Jull, translator.
Title: The illustrious House of Ramires / Eça de Queirós ;
translated from the Portuguese by Margaret Jull Costa.
Other titles: Ilustre casa de Ramires. English
Description: First American paperback edition. | New York : New Directions
Publishing Corporation, 2017.
Identifiers: LCCN 2017000397 | ISBN 9780811226028 (alk. paper)
Subjects: LCSH: Authors—Fiction. | Aristocracy (Social class)—Fiction. |
Portugal—Fiction. | GSAFD: Humorous stories.
Classification: LCC PQ9261.E3 I613 2017 | DDC 869.3/3—dc23
LC record available at https://lccn.loc.gov/2017000

10 9 8 7 6 5 4 3 2 1

New Directions Books are published for James Laughlin
by New Directions Publishing Corporation
80 Eighth Avenue, New York 10011

THE ILLUSTRIOUS HOUSE
OF RAMIRES

I

In his slippers and wearing a light linen jacket over his pink cotton shirt, the Nobleman of the Tower had been working since four o'clock in the afternoon, in the heat and silence of a June Sunday. Gonçalo Mendes Ramires—known to everyone as the Nobleman of the Tower both in his own hamlet of Santa Ireneia and in the neat, handsome neighbouring village of Vila Clara, and even in the nearby town of Oliveira—was engaged on writing an historical novel, entitled *The Tower of Dom Ramires*, which he intended for publication in the first issue of *Annals of Literature and History*, a new journal founded by José Lúcio Castanheiro, an old friend from his student days in Coimbra, where they'd both attended meetings of the Patriots' Club held at the house of the Severinas.

The bright, spacious library was lined with heavy rosewood shelves filled with stout tomes from convent and court, dusty and grave in their calfskin bindings; the room, with its blue-painted walls, looked out over the garden through two large windows; one had a velvet-upholstered window seat, while the other broader window opened onto a balcony, where one could breathe in the sweet scent of the honeysuckle twining about the iron balustrade. Bathed in the strong light flooding in from the balcony stood his desk—a vast affair with turned legs—covered by a faded red damask cloth and cluttered with several thick volumes of *Genealogical History*, the whole of Bluteau's *Portuguese and Latin Vocabulary*, sundry issues of *Panorama*, and, on one corner, a stack of Sir Walter Scott's novels, serving as a pedestal for a vase of yellow carnations. Seated in his leather chair, scratching his head with a quill pen and looking pensively down at the sheets of foolscap paper on the desk, Gonçalo Mendes Ramires always had the inspiration for his Novel there before him—the Tower, the ancient Tower, looming square and dark above the lemon trees that had grown up around it, a sturdy survivor from the old fortified manor house, the celebrated Solar de Santa

Ireneia, seat of the Mendes Ramires family from the middle of the tenth century; ivy now filled the crack—still clearly visible—in one wall, and, silhouetted against the blue of the June sky, were the battlements and the turret with its deep arrow slits and iron grilles.

As even the heir to the Cidadelhe family, that stern genealogist would admit, Gonçalo Mendes Ramires was definitely Portugal's most authentic nobleman, scion of its oldest family. Few lineages, even those dating from the same period, could trace their ancestry by the purest of male lines back to those shadowy gentlemen who, between the Douro and the Minho, had defended both castle and lands against the French barons who, along with the Burgundian hosts, had assailed them, brandishing both flag and cooking-pot. The house of Ramires marched on, and, always maintaining that same pure male line, from the son of Count Nuno Mendes, that giant of a man Ordonho Mendes, Lord of Treixedo and Santa Ireneia, who, in 967, married Dona Elduara, the Countess de Carrion, daughter of Bermudo the Gouty, King of León.

Older than the so-called County of Portugal and equally robust, the Solar de Santa Ireneia had grown in strength and reputation, resisting both cruel fortune and time. And at every important stage in the History of Portugal, there was always a Mendes Ramires who stood out for his great heroism or loyalty or for his nobility of mind. One of the most courageous of the line, Lourenço—whose soubriquet was the Butcher, and who had shared the same wet nurse as Afonso Henriques (with whom, before being dubbed a knight, he had kept an all-night prayer vigil in Zamora Cathedral)—had fought at the Battle of Ourique, where Jesus Christ had also put in an appearance, nailed to a cross ten *covados* high and borne aloft on golden clouds. At the siege of Tavira, Martim Ramires, a brother of the Order of Santiago—after smashing down a fortified door with his axe and forcing his way in among the slashing scimitars that cut off both his hands—clambered to the top of a tower, his two wrists spurting blood, shouting gaily to his Captain, Paio Peres, 'Sir, Tavira is ours! For Portugal and for the King!' Locked up in his Tower, with the drawbridge raised, and the barbicans bristling with archers, Old Egas Ramires, having decided that the presence of an adulteress would sully the purity of his house, refused to welcome King Fernando and his mistress, Leonor Teles, when they were travelling in the North of the country and indulging in merrymaking and hunting. In Aljubarrota, Diogo Ramires, the Troubadour, defeated a troop of crossbowmen, slew the Governor of Galicia, and it was thanks to him and no one else that the royal standard of Spain fell, the same standard in which, once battle was done, his brother-in-arms, Dom Antão de Almada, had wrapped himself and, singing and dancing, carried it to the Mestre de Avis. Two more Ramires, the aged Sueiro and his grandson Fernão, fought magnificently on the walls of Arzila, and Afonso V, standing before the old man's body—where it lay, pierced by four arrows, in the castle courtyard beside the body of the Count de Marialva—dubbed both his son the Prince and Fernão Ramires knights, while murmuring tearfully, 'May you prove to be as good as these men lying here!' Then Portugal took to the seas! And it was rare for any fleet or battle in the Orient not to include a Ramires or two, with one man in particular entering tragic maritime legend, Baltasar Ramires, a noble captain in the Persian Gulf, who, at the time of the wreck of the *Santa Bárbara*, donned his heavy armour and stood erect on the forecastle, leaning on his sword, and silently went down with his sinking ship. In Alcácer Quibir, two Ramires, who never left the King's side, both went proudly to their deaths; the youngest, Paulo Ramires, the royal standard-bearer, was neither injured nor wounded, but, not wishing to live when his King was dead, grabbed an axe and mounted a riderless horse, crying, 'Go, my tardy soul, and serve thy master!' and charging into the Moorish hordes, he disappeared forever. Under the reign of the Spanish Felipes, the Ramires withdrew sulkily to their estates, where they hunted and drank. With the Braganças, another legendary Ramires appeared, Vicente, governor of arms in Douro and Minho for King João IV; he invaded Castile, destroyed the Count de Benavente's Spanish troops and took Fuente Guiñal, presiding over the furious sacking of that city from the balcony of a Franciscan convent, where he sat in his shirtsleeves eating slices of watermelon. However, as the nation declined, so did the noble race of Ramires. Álvaro Ramires, a favourite of King Pedro II, was a thug and a bully: he wrought havoc in Lisbon, kidnapping the wife of a tax inspector whom he'd ordered to be beaten to death by black slaves, setting fire to a gambling den in Seville where he had lost a hundred doubloons, and ending up as the commander of a pirate ship in the fleet of Murad the Ragged. In the reign of King João V, Nuno Ramires shone at court, shod his mules in silver, and ruined the family by paying for endless sumptuous masses, where he sang in the choir wearing the habit of a brother of the Third Order of St Francis. Another Ramires, Cristóvão, president of the Committee for Good Conscience and Order, acted as go-between for King José I and the daughter of the prior of Sacavém. Pedro Ramires, the chief excise officer, was famous throughout the kingdom for his vast girth, his jokes, and his feats of gluttony in the Palace of Bemposta alongside the Archbishop of Thessalonica. Inácio Ramires accompanied King João VI to Brazil as his chamberlain, became a slave-trader and returned home with a trunk full of pieces of gold, which was then stolen from him by an administrator, a former Capuchin monk; he later died on his estate after being gored by an ox. Gonçalo's grandfather, Damião, a liberal man of letters devoted to the arts, disembarked with King Pedro IV in Mindelo, composed the Party's bombastic proclamations, founded a journal, *The AntiFriar*, and, when the Civil Wars were over, dragged out a rheumatic existence in Santa Ireneia, wrapped in a thick woollen greatcoat while he translated into Portuguese—with the help of a lexicon and some snuff—the works of Valerius Flaccus. Gonçalo's father—sometimes a supporter of the Regeneration Party and sometimes of the Progressive Historical Party—lived in Lisbon in the Hotel Universal, wearing out his shoe leather going up and down the steps of various Ministries and of the Mortgage Bank, until a government minister finally appointed him Governor of Oliveira, purely in order to banish him from Lisbon because the minister's mistress, a chorus girl at the Teatro São Carlos, had taken rather too much of a shine to him. *Our* Gonçalo failed his third-year university exams.

That was the year Gonçalo Mendes Ramires made his debut as a writer. A fellow student of his, living in the same house, one José Lúcio Castanheiro—a very pale, very thin young man from the Algarve, who wore enormous blue-tinted spectacles, and whom Simão Craveiro used to call 'Castanheiro the Patriot'—had founded a weekly publication entitled *The Nation*, 'with the lofty intention (as the advertisement put it) of reawakening, not only among the student population, but throughout the land, from Cabo Sileiro to Cabo Santa Maria, a love—long gone cold—for the beauty, grandeur and glory of Portugal!' Consumed by this idea, 'his Idea', and feeling it was not just his vocation but almost his mission, Castanheiro, with the stubborn fervour of the apostle, ceaselessly proclaimed in the bars and cafés of Coimbra's Rua da Sofia, as well as in the University cloisters and the smoke-filled rooms of his friends—'the necessity, damn it, of reclaiming tradition! Of dragging Portugal, damn it, out of the mire of Foreign Influence!' When the journal managed to appear on three consecutive Sundays, and actually did publish studies crammed with italics and quotations on 'The Unfinished Chapels of Batalha Monastery', 'The Capture of Ormuz', and 'Tristão da Cunha's Embassy to Rome', it was immediately hailed as a new dawn, still somewhat pale, but no less certain for that, and as a National Renaissance. Warmed by that patriotic flame, a few good souls from the academic world—especially Castanheiro's housemates, or, rather, the three with the necessary scholarship and intelligence (because as for the other three, one knew only how to use his fists, the other was a guitarist, and the third was a real prize-winner)—went on to search the Library, scouring fat, previously unread tomes by Fernão Lopes, Rui de Pina and Azurara for great feats and legends—'purely Portuguese, purely ours (as Castanheiro urged), and guaranteed to rekindle the nation's sense of our heroic past!' Thus the Patriots' Club came into being, meeting in the house of the Severinas. And it was then, one Sunday after lunch, that Gonçalo Mendes Ramires—a very pleasing youth, always elegant and immaculate in his gown and polished shoes, a fair, slim young man, with porcelain white skin and fine, smiling eyes always quick to fill with tears—presented to Castanheiro eleven sheets of paper entitled *Dona Guiomar*. In this he recounted the ancient story of the castellan's wife who, while her bearded, heavily armoured husband was away at the wars battering with his poleaxe at the gates of Jerusalem, she, one moonlit May night, welcomed her curly-haired page-boy into her bare arms and her bedchamber. Then winter came roaring in, and her husband returned, even more heavily bearded and now carrying a pilgrim's staff. The castle steward, an inquisitive man with a sardonic smile, told him of the betrayal, of the stain on his purer than pure name, honoured throughout the Peninsula! Alas for the page-boy! Alas for the lady! The bells soon tolled their death knell! The executioner, wearing a scarlet hood and leaning on his axe, stood in the castle courtyard between two blocks covered in black cloth. And at the tragic end of *Dona Guiomar*, as in all such stories and ballads, their graves were dug outside the castle walls, and two white rose trees sprang up, and the wind entwined both scents and flowers. And yet (as José Lúcio Castanheiro remarked, pensively stroking his chin), there was nothing in *Dona Guiomar* that stood out as 'purely Portuguese, purely ours, sprouting up from the Portuguese soil and the Portuguese race!' Then again that sad love affair *had* taken place in the much-disputed Portuguese territory of Ribacôa; the names of the knights involved, Remarigues, Ordonho, Froilas, Gutierres, had a delightfully Gothic ring to them; every line resonated with authentic cries of 'Zounds, sir!' 'Thou liest, cur!' 'Page, bring me my dark bay horse!' and all this vernacularity was filled with hordes of stableboys in snow-white tunics, mendicant friars with their faces hidden in the shadow of their cowls, stewards carrying bulging leather money bags and manciples carving gleaming sides of pork. The Novel, in short, marked a salutary return to national sentiment.

'Besides (added Castanheiro), our friend Gonçalo writes in a terse, manly style, full of archaic colour, yes, wonderfully archaic colour! It reminds me of Herculano's *The Fool* or *The Cistercian Monk*! Dona Guiomar could be from anywhere, from Brittany or Aquitaine, but the Portugueseness of the steward and even the husband are plain to see, they're Portuguese to their very fingertips, hailing from somewhere between Douro and Cávado. Oh, yes, when Gonçalo immerses himself in our past, in our chronicles, Portuguese letters will at last have found a man with a real sense of the soil, of our race!'

Dona Guiomar filled three pages of *The Nation*. That Sunday, to celebrate his entry into the world of Literature, Gonçalo Mendes Ramires bought supper for the other members of the Patriots' Club and for a few other friends too, and there, as soon as they had devoured the chicken cooked with peas, and when the breathless waiters at the Camolino were replenishing the bottles of Colares wine, he was acclaimed as 'our very own Sir Walter Scott!' He, for his part, modestly announced that he was going to write a two-volume historical novel based on his own family lore, starting with a sublime early exploit by Tructesindo Mendes Ramires, Sancho I's friend and standard-bearer. Given the detailed knowledge of clothes and furnishings that he had revealed in *Dona Guiomar*, not to mention his own ancient lineage, Gonçalo seemed, temperamentally, to be the perfect candidate for restoring the historical novel in Portugal. He had a mission, and he immediately began striding up and down the streets of Coimbra, his cap pulled pensively down over his eyes, like someone busily engaged on reconstructing a whole world. That was the year he failed his exams.

When he returned for his fourth year, the Patriots' Club no longer filled Rua da Matemática with its former ardour. Castanheiro had graduated and was now vegetating in Vila Real de Santo António; with him went *The Nation* and the zealous lads who had scoured the library for the chronicles of Fernão Lopes and Azurara; and abandoned by the apostle who had so inspired them, they fell back on the novels of Georges Ohnet and, in the evenings, resumed their games of billiards in the bars in Rua da Sofia. Gonçalo was a changed man too, in mourning for his father, who had died in August; he had grown a beard, and although he was the same affable, gentle soul he had always been, he was more serious now and somewhat averse to suppers and nights out on the town. He took a room in the Hotel Mondego, where he was waited on by Bento, an old servant from Santa Ireneia, complete with white tie, and his preferred companions were three or four lads studying Politics, who often leafed earnestly through the Parliamentary Records, were *au fait* with certain plots and intrigues in Lisbon, proclaimed the need for 'positive direction' and 'long-term investment in the rural economy', considered the University's irreverence for Dogmas to be a piece of despicable, Jacobin frivolity, and, even when strolling in the Choupal by moonlight or along the belvedere known as the Penedo da Saudade, they would hold ardent debates about the two party leaders—Brás Vitorino, the new man behind the Regeneration Party, and the Baron de São Fulgêncio, the old leader of the Progressive Historical Party. Leaning more towards the Regenerationists, because the Regeneration Party traditionally represented for him ideals of conservatism, cultivated elegance and generosity, Gonçalo began to frequent the local Regenerationists' Club, where, at night, sipping a cup of black tea, he would urge 'strengthening the authority of the Crown' and 'further colonialist expansion!' Then, in the spring, he sloughed off all that political seriousness and stayed up into the early hours at Calomino's, consuming huge platefuls of *bacalhau* to the sound of plangent guitars. He no longer mentioned his great two-volume novel and either withdrew from or forgot his mission to revive the historical novel. It was only during the Easter of his fifth year that he took up his pen again, this time in the *Gazeta do Porto*, in which he published two acerbic letters addressed to his fellow countryman, Dr André Cavaleiro, whom São Fulgêncio had appointed Governor of Oliveira; indeed, so personal and rancorous were the letters, they even made fun of 'His Excellency's bushy black moustache'. He had signed the letters 'Juvenal', as his father had before him, when he had published political articles from Oliveira in that same *Gazeta do Porto*, where he had friends, one of whom, Vilar Mendes, a distant relative, was editor of the foreign news section. But when Gonçalo read out loud to his colleagues at the Regenerationists' Club those two resounding blows that would 'knock Senhor Horseman off his horse!', one serious young man, the nephew of the Bishop of Oliveira, could not conceal his surprise.

'But Gonçalo, I always thought you and Cavaleiro were close friends! If I remember rightly, when you arrived in Coimbra for your first year, you lived in his house in Rua de São João. Don't the Cavaleiros and the Ramires enjoy a traditional, almost historic friendship? I hardly know Oliveira myself, I've never actually been there, but I understand that Cavaleiro's estate shares a boundary with Santa Ireneia!'

And Gonçalo screwed up his face, his smooth, smiling face, and declared tartly that Corinde did not share any boundary with Santa Ireneia, that between the two estates there ran a stream, appropriately named the Coice, the Kick; and that Senhor André Cavaleiro, more horse than horseman, was the vile creature who grazed on the other bank!

The bishop's nephew applauded this riposte, exclaiming: 'Very funny, sir!'

A year after graduating, Gonçalo went to Lisbon to sort out the mortgage on his Praga estate, near Lamego, on which the tithe of ten *réis* and half a chicken owed to the Abbot of Praga was causing unspeakable hold-ups on the Board of the Mortgage Bank; but he went, too, hoping to get to know his party leader, Brás Vitorino, to show his loyalty and submission to the party line, and to pick up a few tips on how to become a politician. One night, when he was returning from supper with the Marchioness de Louredo, his ancient 'Aunt Louredo', who lived in Santa Clara, he bumped into José Lúcio Castanheiro in the Rossio; Castanheiro was now working for the Treasury, in the department dealing with National Heritage. Thinner and gaunter than ever, his spectacles even larger and darker, Castanheiro still burned, as he had in Coimbra, with the flame of 'his Idea': 'the resurrection of a sense of Portugueseness'! Expanding his plan for *The Nation* to be something worthy of the capital city, he was now devoting all his labours to the creation of a fortnightly review, seventy pages long, with a blue cover, and entitled *Annals of Literature and History*. On that soft, warm May night, as they strolled together around the dried-up fountains in the main square, the Rossio, Castanheiro—who was carrying under his arm a roll of paper and a fat folio bound in calfskin—first recalled the jolly gatherings in Rua da Misericórdia, then lambasted the dearth of intellectual life in Vila Real de Santo António, before returning eagerly to 'his Idea', begging Gonçalo Mendes Ramires to let the new journal publish the Novel he had spoken of in Coimbra, about his ancestor Tructesindo Ramires, Sancho I's standard-bearer.

Amused, Gonçalo confessed that he had still not begun that great work!

'Ah,' murmured Castanheiro, stopping in his tracks and fixing him with hard, dark, disconsolate eyes. 'So you didn't carry on? You lost faith in the Idea?'

He gave a resigned shrug, accustomed now, in the course of his mission, to these fallings away from the patriotic cause. He would not even allow Gonçalo, humbled by his friend's pure and constant show of Faith, to make excuses or carry on about the laborious task of drawing up an inventory of the house following his father's death.

'No, that's it. *Procrastinare lusitanum est.* Start work this summer. For the Portuguese, my boy, summer is the season of good fortune and bold exploits. Nuno Álvares was born in the summer in Bonjardim! The Battle of Aljubarrota was won in the summer! Vasco da Gama reached India in the summer! And this summer, our Gonçalo will write his sublime little Novel! Besides, the first issue of the journal is only due out in December, probably on the first of the month. So you have three whole months in which to bring back to life an entire world. I mean it, Gonçalo! It is a duty, a solemn duty, especially among the young, to work for the *Annals*. Portugal, my boy, is dying from a lack of national pride! We are dying miserably from the disease of being insufficiently Portuguese!'

He stopped and waved one thin arm, like the lash of a whip, as if hitting out at the Rossio, the City, and the whole Nation. Did Gonçalo know the secret behind this sinister state of affairs? The worst among the Portuguese despised their country, and the best knew nothing about it. The remedy? To reveal the real Portugal, to popularise Portugal. Yes, dear friend, we must blazon abroad the name of Portugal, so that everyone knows it, at least as well as they know James' Cough Syrup! So that everyone embraces it, just as they have embraced Congo Soap! So that its heroes and their exploits—even its defects—will be known and embraced and loved, down to its very cobblestones! This was his aim, the greatest task one could possibly undertake in this drab period of our History, and that was why he had founded the *Annals*. To bellow forth, to thunder out the name of Portugal, to shout it from the rooftops, to announce the unexpected news of its greatness! And it was especially incumbent on the descendants of those who had made the Kingdom to undertake the pious work of remaking it. How? By reviving Portugal's past, its traditions, damn it!

'Take your family, for example. Throughout the history of Portugal, there has been a long beautiful line of Ramires. Even that judge who, one Christmas, ate two suckling pigs at a sitting! He was merely a belly, but what a belly! There was in that belly a heroic vigour that was evidence of a race, a race that, as Camões put it, went beyond mere human strength. Two suckling pigs, damn it! It's quite moving really. And the other Ramires men, the ones who fought at Silves, at Aljubarrota, at Arzila, those who went to India! And the five valiant men, about whom you may not even know, who died at the Battle of Salado! Breathe life back into those men and reveal their marvellous heroism and their sublimely unbending will, both of which provide a superb lesson for the young. It's bracing, damn it! A new awareness of our former greatness would shake up our feeble, flabby acceptance of remaining small and insignificant! That is what I mean by reviving the past. And if you were to do that, Ramires, how chic that would be! How chic, damn it! A nobleman, the greatest in Portugal, who, in order to reveal his country's heroic past, does not even have to leave his house, all he has to do is consult his thousand-year-old family archives. It's just amazing! And you don't have to write a long novel ... A long, involved novel wouldn't really fit with the review's militant nature. A short story will do, twenty or thirty pages. Of course, we can't actually pay you anything right now, but then you don't need the money! Besides, it isn't a matter of money, but of social renewal ... In Portugal, literature carries all before it. I know that in your last year in Coimbra, you were involved with the Regenerationists, well, my friend, your Novella could lead us all to Parliament! It is the pen, not the sword, that rules kingdoms. Think about it. Though I must say goodbye now, because I still have to make a legible copy of this article by Henriques about Ceylon. You don't know Henriques? Of course you don't. No one does. Well, whenever the great Academies of

Europe have some question about Ceylonese history or literature, they call for Henriques!'

He hurried off, still clutching the roll of paper and the fat volume, and Gonçalo caught a last glimpse of him in the lit doorway of the Tabacaria Nunes, waving one thin, apostolic arm at a very plump man, wearing a vast white waistcoat, who drew back in alarm at this rude interruption of his quiet enjoyment of the soft, warm May night and a large cigar.

The Nobleman of the Tower returned to the Hotel Bragança, impressed by and pondering the Patriot's idea. He found everything about it deeply seductive, and it suited him down to the ground; yes, contributing to a substantial seventy-page journal like that, in the company of learned writers, university teachers, former ministers, even councillors of state, and making clear his ancient lineage, older than the Kingdom itself, made popular in a tale of heroic beauty, in which the proud, courageous Ramires soul would be shown to full effect, as would his serious academic turn of mind, his noble bent for erudite research, all this would appear just at the moment when he was hoping for a career in Parliament and politics! And the actual work itself, the essential nature of the ancient Ramires family, the archeological resurrection of medieval life, having to fill a hundred sheets of foolscap with powerful prose, none of this frightened him. No, because, fortunately, he already had that 'work', cut out of good cloth and skilfully stitched together by his Uncle Duarte, his mother's brother (his mother was born into the Balsas family of Guimarães), who, in his years of idleness and imagination, from 1845 to 1850, between graduating from university and qualifying as a lawyer, had been a poet, and the weekly journal *The Bard*, published in Guimarães, had included a short poem of his in blank verse, *The Castle of Santa Ireneia*, which he had signed with the initals D. B. The castle in the title was Gonçalo's castle, that most ancient of mansions of which all that remained was the dark tower among the lemon trees in the garden. And the poem sang, with romantic grace, of a noble episode in which Tructesindo Ramires, Sancho I's standard-bearer, had done himself full justice during the squabbles between Afonso II and his siblings. That copy of *The Bard*, bound in morocco leather and bearing the Ramires coat of arms—a black goshawk on a scarlet ground—had remained in the family archive as yet one more example of the Ramires' heroic history. And often, as a child, Gonçalo, having been taught by his Mama, would recite the opening lines of the poem, so harmonious in their melancholy:

> *In the pale evening light, among the leaves*
> *That Autumn was slowly yellowing . . .*

It was precisely this, his remote ancestor's sombre exploit, that Gonçalo Mendes Ramires had had in mind when his supper companions and fellow supporters of *The Nation* had proclaimed him their 'very own Sir Walter Scott', and when he had decided to write a modern novel of epic realism in two stout tomes, creating a rich and colourful study of the Portuguese Middle Ages. Now it would, with delicious ease, provide him with the basis for the brief, sober, thirty-page Novella required by the *Annals*.

He opened the window of his hotel room. And leaning on the balcony, finishing his cigar, in the soft, drowsy May night, before the silent majesty of the river and the moon, he savoured the thought that he would be spared the laborious task of poring over chronicles and tedious folios. Yes, Uncle Duarte had done all the historical groundwork, and with great thoroughness and skill too. The Solar de Santa Ireneia, with its deep moat, its barbican tower, its keep, its dungeon, its beacon and its standard; the huge figure of old Tructesindo, with his long, wild ancestral hair and beard spilling over onto his coat of chain mail; the Moorish servants in leather tunics, digging the irrigation ditches in the orchard; the lay brothers sitting around the fire, mumbling fragments from *The Lives of the Saints*; the young page-boys playing at soldiers—all these things came vividly to life in Uncle Duarte's poem! He could still recall certain episodes: the jester being beaten; the banquet with the stewards opening barrel upon barrel of beer; Violante Ramires' journey to the convent of Lorvão . . .

> *By the Moorish fountain, among the elm trees,*
> *The cavalcade comes to a halt ...*

The whole passionate, barbarous plot, the fierce fights in which family feuds were settled at knife-point, the heroic words spoken by lips of iron—all this was there in his uncle's sonorous, balanced lines ...

> *Hear me, Monk! The house of Ramires,*
> *Stone by stone, would crumble into dust*
> *Were a bastard's abject foot to cross*
> *Its yet pure, unsullied threshold!*

All he had to do was transpose the fluid formulae of the Romanticism of 1848 into his own terse, manly prose (as Castanheiro had described it) with its excellent touch of archaism, reminiscent of Herculano's *The Fool*. Was that plagiarism? No! Who had more right to the memories of the historic Ramires family than he? The resurrection of the old Portugal, so beautifully captured in *The Castle of Santa Ireneia*, was not the individual work of Uncle Duarte, but of all the Herculanos, Rebelos, Academies and of erudition in general. And, besides, who would know about that poem now, or even about *The Bard*, that slender weekly journal published over a period of five months fifty years ago in a provincial town? He hesitated not a moment longer, utterly seduced by the idea. And while he was undressing, having first gulped down a glass of water and bicarbonate of soda, he was already chiselling out the first line of the story, in the lapidary style of *Salammbô*. 'It was a winter's night in the Solar de Santa Ireneia, in the vaulted room of the keep ...'

The next day, he sought out José Lúcio Castanheiro in the National Heritage department, rather hurriedly, since, after a meeting at the Mortgage Bank, he had promised to go with his cousins, the Chelas, to see an exhibition of embroidery in Livraria Gomes. And he announced to the Patriot that he would definitely send him the Novella for the first issue of the *Annals*, and that he had already chosen the title: *The Tower of Dom Ramires*.

'What do you think?'

José Castanheiro, in his alpaca jacket, held two scrawny arms up to the vault of the narrow corridor in which he met him and exclaimed:

'Wonderful! *The Tower of Dom Ramires*. Tructesindo Mendes Ramires' great deed as told by Gonçalo Mendes Ramires! And in the self-same Tower too! In the very Tower where old Tructesindo did the deed; and seven hundred years later, in that same Tower, our Gonçalo tells the tale! Now that is what I call reviving the past!'

Two weeks later, back at Santa Ireneia, Gonçalo dispatched a servant with a cart to Oliveira, to the house of his brother-in-law, José Barrolo, the husband of Gracinha Ramires, with orders to bring back the whole wonderful classical library that Barrolo had inherited from his uncle, the Dean of the Cathedral, the complete set of *Genealogical History*, and (he added in a letter) 'any books that you find bearing the title *Chronicles of King So-and-so ...*' Then, from his own dusty shelves, he disinterred the novels of Sir Walter Scott, various issues of *Panorama*, Herculano's *History*, *The Fool* and *The Cistercian Monk*. Thus provided for and with a thick pile of foolscap ready on his desk, he began rewriting Uncle Duarte's poem, intending initially to transpose to a chill December morning—as being more in keeping with the harsh feudal life of his forebears—that glittering cavalcade of damsels, monks and men-at-arms whom Uncle Duarte had set against the gentle, autumnal melancholy of the plains of the Mondego:

> *In the pale evening light, among the leaves*
> *That Autumn was slowly yellowing ...*

However, since it was June at the time, and the Moon was waxing, Gonçalo decided instead to take advantage of the sensations of heat and moonlight and leafy groves of trees, and to place, right at the very beginning of the Novella, the vast, dark Solar de Santa Ireneia in the silence of an August night and beneath the glow of the full moon.

And, with the help of *The Bard*, he had already blithely filled two whole pages, when an argument regarding his tenant, Manuel

Relho, who worked the land for a rent of eight hundred *mil-réis*, came to disrupt those early stirrings of the Nobleman of the Tower's fresh, new inspiration. For many orderly, well-behaved years, Relho had made a habit of getting blissfully, slowly drunk each Sunday, but since Christmas, he had begun to indulge in wild, noisy drinking bouts three or four times a week, during which he would beat his wife and generally disrupt the peace by standing, drunken and dishevelled, in the street, stick in hand, defying the whole village. Finally, one night, when Gonçalo, having finished his tea, was seated at his desk laboriously excavating the ancient foundations of the Solar de Santa Ireneia, Rosa the cook suddenly started screaming, 'Help, help, save us from Relho!' And above the noise of her screams and the barking of the dogs, came the sound of first one stone, then another, striking the library's venerable balcony! Gonçalo immediately considered grabbing his pistol, but just that afternoon, his servant, Bento, had taken the one and only ancient weapon in his possession down to the kitchen for a general clean and de-rust. Alarmed, he ran to his bedroom, locked the door, and, in his haste to barricade himself in with the chest of drawers, caused glass bottles, a tortoiseshell box and even a crucifix to fall to the floor and break. The shouting and barking in the courtyard died away, but that night, Gonçalo did not budge from his well-defended refuge, smoking cigarettes and thinking dark thoughts about Relho, whom he had always previously forgiven and treated kindly, but who had now stoned the windows of the Tower! Early the next morning, he summoned the local alderman; still trembling, Rosa showed him the red marks on her arms left by Relho's fingers; and Relho, whose lease was due to end in October, was dismissed from the farm, along with his wife, his few belongings and his bed. Another farmer from Bravais, José Casco, who was respected throughout the parish for his serious nature and his astonishing strength, immediately came to ask Gonçalo if he could rent the land around the Tower. However, following his father's death, Gonçalo Mendes Ramires had decided to increase the rent to nine hundred and fifty *mil-réis*, and so a crestfallen Casco went back down the steps. He returned the next day and studied every inch of the land, crumbling the soil between his fingers, scrutinising the stable and the cellar and counting the olive trees and the vines; finally, visibly panting with the effort, he offered nine hundred and ten *mil-réis*! Gonçalo refused to give way, certain that his price was a fair one. José Casco returned again with his wife; then, one Sunday, he brought both his wife and a friend, and spent a long time slowly scratching his clean-shaven chin, taking a few suspicious turns around the threshing-ground, the vegetable plot and the granary, all of which made that June morning unbearably long for the Nobleman, who was sitting on a stone bench in the garden, underneath a mimosa tree, reading the *Gazeta do Porto*. When an ashen-faced Casco came and offered him nine hundred and thirty *mil-réis*, Gonçalo threw down his newspaper, declaring that he would rather farm the land himself and show just what could be done with some up-to-date knowledge, phosphates and machinery! The man from Bravais then gave a deep sigh and agreed to pay nine hundred and fifty *mil-réis*. In time-honoured fashion, the Nobleman shook the farmer by the hand, and the farmer went into the kitchen to drink a large glass of wine and wipe away the anxious sweat drenching his brow and his powerful neck.

However, as if hampered by all these worries, Gonçalo's creative flow dried up and became no more than a slow, turgid trickle. When he sat down at his desk that afternoon, ready to describe the *salle d'armes* in the Solar de Santa Ireneia on a moonlit night, all he succeeded in doing was slavishly turning Uncle Duarte's flowing lines into rather insipid prose, with no interesting modernising touches to lend a lordly majesty or a nostalgic beauty to the thick walls where the moonlight, slipping in through the barred windows, set the tips of lances and the crests of helmets sparkling. And from four o'clock onwards, in the heat and silence of that June Sunday, he laboured long and hard, driving his pen on as if it were a very slow plough cutting through stony ground, only to furiously cross out the one flabby, inelegant line he did manage to write; and sometimes angrily, loudly kicking off his morocco leather slippers, then putting them on again, sometimes sitting inert and resigned to the sense of sterility overwhelming him, he stared out at the

Tower, that most difficult of Towers, black among the lemon trees and against the blue sky, all encircled by the peeping flight of the swallows.

Finally, feeling utterly discouraged, he threw down his disastrously stubborn quill and tossed his precious copy of *The Bard* into a drawer, which he then slid shut.

'It's no good, I can't write a thing. It's the heat! That and spending the whole morning waiting for that brute Casco to ...' Glumly scratching the back of his neck, he reread his last grubby, scribbled line:

'"... In the broad, high-ceilinged room, where the pale, broad rays of moonlight ..." "Broad" and "broad"! And those pale rays, those eternal pale rays! And the wretched castle, so complicated to describe! And old Tructesindo, who I just can't seem to get at all! In short, a complete disaster!'

He sprang to his feet, knocking over his leather chair; then he stuck a cigar between his teeth and stormed out of the library, slamming the door behind him, filled by a sense of the immense tedium of the work, of the confusing, tangled world of the Solar de Santa Ireneia and of his huge, iron-clad ancestors with their ringing voices, as hard to grasp as coiling smoke.

II

Yawning and adjusting his baggy silk trousers to stop them slipping down, Gonçalo—afflicted by a slight ache in the small of his back and having spent the whole day lounging on the blue damask sofa—slouched languidly across the room to peer out at the Chinese lacquer clock in the corridor. Half past five! He considered going for a walk along the shady road to Bravais, just to clear his head. Or perhaps he should pay a visit (as he had been intending to do since Easter!) to old Sanches Lucena, who, in the General Election in April, had once again been elected deputy in the constituency of Vila Clara. The journey to Feitosa, Sanches Lucena's estate, would mean an hour's ride though, and that could prove uncomfortable with that nagging pain in his lower back, which had come on the previous evening, after he had taken tea at the club in town. Undecided about what to do, he was walking slowly along the corridor in order to call Bento or Rosa and ask them to bring him some lemonade, when, in through the open verandah windows, came a loud, metallic voice, which grew louder the more jocular the tone, filling the whole courtyard with the hollow regular rhythm of a hammer hammering:

'Oh Senhor Gonçalo! Oh Senhor Gonçalo! Oh Senhor Gonçalíssimo Mendes Ramires!'

He instantly recognised the voice of Titó, or António Vilalobos, his distant relative and old friend from Vila Clara, where that excellent, stout fellow of old Alentejo stock had moved for no other reason than his bucolic fondness for the town.

For eleven years now he had filled the place with his imposing limbs, the slow thunder of his booming voice, and with his idleness, which overflowed onto benches, street corners, the doorways of shops and taverns, sacristies where he would sit arguing with the priests, and even into the cemetery where he would spend time philosophising with the gravedigger. His brother—eldest son and

heir of the Cidadelhe family (the aforementioned genealogist)—
who had provided Titó with an allowance of eight *moedas* just to
keep him away from Cidadelhe, from his own grubby harem of
country lasses and (it was hoped) from the somewhat perverse task
on which he had now embarked, namely, *The Real Inquisition*, an
enquiry into the bastard lines, sundry sins and illegitimate titles of
the noble families of Portugal. And Gonçalo had loved Titó, that
kindly Hercules, ever since his student days in Coimbra, seduced by
his prodigious strength, his incomparable ability to drink a whole
barrel of beer and devour a whole lamb, and, most of all, by his supreme independence of mind, backed up by the very large cane he
carried and by that allowance, those eight *moedas* safe in his pocket,
which meant that he feared nothing and wanted nothing either on
Earth or in Heaven. Gonçalo leaned over the balcony and shouted:

'Come up, Titó! Come upstairs while I get dressed. You can have
a glass of gin and then we can walk to Bravais together.' Seated on
the edge of the round, waterless pool in the centre of the courtyard
and looking up at the great house, Titó—his broad, frank, sunburned face framed by a thick, reddish beard—was slowly fanning
himself with an old straw hat:

'No, I can't, I'm afraid. But listen, do you want to come and have
supper at Gago's with me and João Gouveia? Videirinha's coming
too and bringing his guitar. We've got ourselves a huge mullet,
an enormous one, that I bought this morning for five *tostões* from
a woman on the coast. Cooked by Gago himself! What do you
think? Gago's going to open a new barrel of wine from the Abbot
of Chandim. It's a local wine and very good stuff indeed.'

And Titó very delicately tweaked his own ear to indicate that
he knew what he was talking about. Gonçalo, still pulling on his
trousers, was unsure.

'My stomach's been a bit delicate lately. And ever since last night
I've had a pain in my kidneys or my liver or my spleen or one
of those organs! I was planning to have nothing for supper but
some chicken broth and a bit of broiled chicken. Oh, but what the
hell—tell Gago to prepare me just a small piece of roast chicken ...
Where shall we meet? At the club?'

Titó stood up and positioning his straw hat on the back of his head, said:

'No, I'm not going to the club tonight. I have a lady to see. Meet me by the fountain between ten and half past. Videirinha will be there with his guitar. Between ten and half past. Don't forget! And I'll order a little roast chicken for the gentleman with the bad back!'

And with that he walked with bovine slowness back across the courtyard, pausing by the bush growing next to the door to pick a rose, which he then stuck in the buttonhole of his olive-green velvet jacket.

Gonçalo had immediately decided not to bother with supper at home, convinced of the benefits of fasting until ten o'clock, after a brisk walk to Bravais and along the Riosa valley. And before going back into his room to get dressed, he called for Rosa the cook, but neither she nor Bento responded—for he had bellowed out Bento's name too—in the heavy silence of those shadowy paved depths, under the great vaulted ceilings, which were all that remained of the old palace, restored by Vicente Ramires after his campaign in Castile, but later put to the torch by King José I. Then Gonçalo went down two of the worn stone steps and thundered out another cry that echoed round the Tower—now that the bells no longer worked. And he was just about to continue on into the kitchen, when Rosa appeared. She had gone out into the garden with Crispola's daughter and hadn't heard him.

'I've been calling for about an hour! But you and Bento are nowhere to be found! It's simply to say that I won't need any dinner tonight. I'm going to eat in Vila Clara with friends.'

Standing in the echoing depths of the corridor, Rosa looked most alarmed. 'But, Senhor Doutor, aren't you going to eat anything at all until late in the night?' The daughter of a former gardener at the Tower, she had grown up there and was already the cook when Gonçalo was born, and she had always addressed him as 'young master' or even 'my dear' until he left for Coimbra and became, for her and for Bento, Senhor Doutor. And the Senhor Doutor should, at the very least, have a little chicken broth, which she had been slowly cooking since noon and which smelled positively divine!

Gonçalo consented—for he never disagreed with any decision made by Rosa or Bento—and was already going back up the steps, when he demanded to know about Crispola, a poor widow who, with a whole troupe of starving children to feed, had fallen ill with a terrible fever at Easter time.

'She's much better, Senhor Doutor. She's out of bed now, that's what her daughter told me. But she's still very weak.'

Gonçalo came down another step, leaning on the banister so as to immerse himself more deeply in that sorry tale.

'Listen, Rosa, if the little one's still there, poor thing, why doesn't she take home the chicken I was going to have for dinner. And the broth too. Yes, let her take the whole panful! I can just have some tea and biscuits. Oh, and send Crispola ten *tostões* as well. No, make that two *mil-réis*! But don't just send her the chicken and the money without a word. Say that I hope she continues to make a steady recovery and that I'll drop in soon to see how she is. And tell Bento to bring me up some hot water!'

Standing in his bedroom in his shirtsleeves before a vast mirror supported by two gilded columns, he studied, first, his tongue, which, he thought, seemed somewhat furred, then, fearing some sign of a bilious attack, the whites of his eyes. He ended up contemplating his 'new look', for he had shaved off his beard in Lisbon, preserving only a light, curly brown moustache and a small goatee that made his slender, aquiline, still creamy-white face seem even longer. He despaired, however, of his hair, which, although attractively wavy, was very thin, and, despite all the pomades and treatments he used, his parting was growing ever higher and now began almost in the middle of his clear brow.

'It's so unfair. I'll be bald by the time I'm thirty ...'

He remained standing at the mirror, otherwise pleased with what he saw and recalling what his Aunt Louredo had said in Lisbon, 'Dear boy, a bright, handsome lad like you shouldn't go off and bury himself in the provinces! There are no nice young men in Lisbon. We need a good Ramires here!' No, he wouldn't bury himself in the provinces, beneath the ivy and the melancholy dust of inert objects, like his Tower! But how could he possibly afford an elegant life in Lisbon, among his historic relatives, with his remaining income of only one thousand eight hundred *mil-réis*, which was all that was left once he had paid off his father's debts! And he was really only interested in living in Lisbon if he had some political position—a seat in Parliament, influence in his Party, a slow, certain climb to Power. And what he had so sweetly dreamed of in Coimbra during conversations with friends at the Hotel Mondego now seemed so remote as to be almost unattainable, hidden behind a high, harsh, impenetrable wall, in which there was not a single door. Besides, how could he become a deputy? There would be no General Election for a while, now that the ghastly Baron de São Fulgêncio and the Historicals were firmly entrenched in power for another three whole years. And even if there were a by-election, what chance would he have, given that, ever since his student days in Coimbra—albeit lightheartedly and merely because it was the elegant thing to do—he had always been a Regenerationist, whether in the club at Couraça, in his letters to the *Gazeta do Porto*, or in his passionate diatribes against the governor, the hateful Cavaleiro? Now all he could do was wait. Wait and work, trying to gain some social substance, wisely building a modest political reputation on the strength of his vast, historic name; and weaving a precious web of ever-wider political alliances from Santa Irenéia to Terreiro do Paço in Lisbon. Yes, the theory was splendid, but how did one go about acquiring real substance, reputation and political allies? 'Work as a lawyer, write for the newspapers!' had been the friendly, throw-away advice from his party leader, Brás Vitorino. Work as a lawyer in Oliveira or even in Lisbon itself? No, he couldn't, not with his innate, almost psychological horror of legal proceedings and paperwork. Set up a newspaper in Lisbon as his fellow resident at Coimbra's Hotel Mondego, Ernesto Rangel, had done? That was an easy enough task for the adored grandson of Senhora Dona Joaquina Rangel, who had ten thousand barrels of wine stored away in cellars in Vila Nova da Gaia. Battle away as a journalist on a newspaper in Lisbon? During the weeks he had spent in the capital, with all his time taken up by the Mortgage Bank and his cousins, he hadn't managed to establish

any kind of lasting, useful relationship with the big Regenerationist papers, *A Manhã* and *A Verdade*. The truth was that, in the wall
separating him from wealth and success, he had found only one
small chink, tiny but hopeful—the *Annals of Literature and History*,
with its team of professors, politicians, even a minister, and even
an admiral, that dreadful bore Guerreiro Araújo. Yes, he would
appear along with his Tower in the *Annals*, revealing his rich imagination and broad knowledge. Then, climbing up from Invention
to the more respectable terrain of Erudition, he would write an article (the idea had come to him on the train back from Lisbon!) on
the *Visigothic Origins of Public Law in Portugal*. Naturally he knew
nothing about the Visigoths or those Origins, but he could simply
cobble together an elegant summary from the wonderful *A History
of Public Administration in Portugal* lent to him by Castanheiro. Then
leaping from Erudition to the Social and Pedagogical Sciences,
why shouldn't he compile an excellent, statesmanlike *Reform of
the Legal Education System in Portugal*, in two sizeable instalments?
Thus he would advance, building and shaping his literary pedestal, keeping close to the Regenerationists, until they got back into
power, and then the triumphal arch he was hoping for would open
up in that wall. Standing in the middle of his room in his long
johns, his hands on his hips, Gonçalo Mendes Ramires concluded
that he really must make haste and write his Novella.

'But how am I going to finish it? It's so bogged down, stuck fast,
its liver completely shot?'

Bento—an old man with a dark, clean-shaven face and beautiful,
curly white hair, and always looking clean and fresh in his cotton
jacket—entered slowly, carrying a jug of hot water.

'Bento, did you find a glass bottle containing some white powder
in the suitcase I brought back from Lisbon or in the trunk? It's an
English remedy given to me by Dr Matos ... the label is in English,
with an English name, "fruit salts" or something ...'

Bento bowed his head, closed his eyes and thought deeply. Yes,
in the bathroom, on top of the red trunk, there was a bottle containing some powder. It was wrapped in an ancient sheet of parchment, like the paper in the archives.

'That's it!' cried Gonçalo. 'When I went to Lisbon, I needed to take certain documents with me because of that wretched business in Praga, and in all the confusion, I took from the archives that perfectly useless piece of parchment. Fetch it for me will you, but be careful with the bottle!'

First, though, Bento painstakingly fastened his master's agate cufflinks and laid out on the bed a jacket and a pair of neatly pressed trousers made of light cheviot wool. Still gripped by the idea of the articles he would write for the *Annals*, Gonçalo was standing at the window, leafing through *A History of Public Administration in Portugal*, when Bento returned with the roll of parchment, from which dangled a lead seal on a tattered bit of ribbon.

'The very thing!' exclaimed Gonçalo, throwing the book down on the windowsill. 'I wrapped the bottle in that roll of parchment so that it wouldn't get broken. Unwrap it and put it on the chest of drawers. Dr Matos recommended that I take it with warm water on an empty stomach. It fizzes as if it were boiling, but it cleans the blood and clears the head. And I am in great need of a clear head! You have some too, Bento. And tell Rosa to try it as well. Everyone takes fruit salts now, even the Pope!'

Bento had very delicately unwrapped the bottle, spreading out on the marble top of the chest of drawers the stiff parchment on which someone's sixteenth-century writing lay wrinkled and yellow and dead. Buttoning on his collar, Gonçalo said:

'And to think I took it with me to sort out that business in Praga! A parchment dating back to the time of King Sebastião ... All I can make out is the date, fourteen hundred, no, fifteen hundred and seventy-seven. On the eve of the voyage to Africa. Oh well, it kept the bottle safe.'

Bento, who had now taken out a white waistcoat from the drawer, cast a sideways glance at the venerable piece of parchment.

'It must have been a letter from the King to one of your ancestors ...'

'Of course,' murmured Gonçalo, looking at himself in the mirror. 'Probably promising him something good, something big. Having a king used to mean having an income too. Now though

… Ouch, don't pull the buckle so tight! My stomach's been terribly distended these last few days. Now, of course, the whole institution of the monarchy is wearing rather thin, Bento.'

'So it would seem, sir,' Bento remarked gravely. 'Even *O Século* is saying that kings are on the way out, and it could happen any day. That's what it was saying just yesterday. And *O Século* is usually pretty well-informed. I don't know if you read it or not, but in today's paper there's an account of Senhor Sanches Lucena's birthday party, and the fireworks and the banquet they held at Feitosa.'

Lying on the damask sofa, Gonçalo held out his feet so that Bento could lace up his white boots.

'Sanches Lucena is a complete idiot! What *is* the point of that man—who's sixty if he's a day—what is the point of him being a deputy, spending months at a time in Lisbon, or in Frankfurt, and thereby neglecting his lands and that lovely estate of his. And all for what? So that he can occasionally grunt a "Hear, hear" in Parliament. He should give up his seat to me. I'm brighter than he is, I have no vast estate to keep up, and I enjoy living in the Hotel Bragança in Lisbon. I really should visit him though. Tell Joaquim to have my horse ready at around this time tomorrow, so that I can go to Feitosa and visit the wretched creature. And I'll wear the new riding outfit I brought from Lisbon, with the long gaiters. I haven't seen Dona Ana Lucena for more than two years now, and she's a very pretty woman!'

'While you were in Lisbon, they rode past in a carriage. They even stopped, and Senhor Sanches Lucena pointed up at the Tower, showing it to his lady wife. She's very beautiful! She was carrying a gold lorgnette on a long handle and a long gold chain too …'

'Bravo! Soak that handkerchief in eau de Cologne, will you? My head feels so heavy today. Dona Ana was a farm labourer, wasn't she? A country girl from Corinde?'

Holding the bottle of eau de Cologne suspended in mid-air, Bento stared in astonishment at his master:

'No, sir! Senhora Dona Ana Lucena is of very low birth indeed. She's the daughter of a butcher in Ovar. And her brother went on the run because he killed the blacksmith in Ílhavo.'

'So, to sum up,' said Gonçalo, 'a butcher's daughter with a brother on the run *and* a beautiful woman with a gold lorgnette. Yes, she definitely deserves my new riding outfit!'

In Vila Clara, at ten o'clock, on one of the stone benches around the fountain, beneath the Judas trees, Tító sat waiting with his friend João Gouveia, the local administrator. They were both silently fanning themselves with their hats, enjoying the cool and the dark and the slow murmur of the water. The town hall clock was striking half past ten when Gonçalo—who had been delayed at the club over a longer than usual game of *voltarete*—finally arrived, announcing that he was famished, in the grip of 'the famous Ramires hunger', and hustling them off to Gago's, not even allowing Tító to visit the tobacconist's to buy a bottle of 'very old and very good' Madeira brandy.

'There's no time for that! To Gago's—now! If not, in my wild Ramiresian hunger, I'll gobble one of you up!'

However, no sooner had they set off than he stopped, folded his arms and, looking vastly amused, asked the administrator about *his* Government's latest astonishing feat, for *his* Government, *his* Historical friends, *his* honourable friend São Fulgêncio had named—as Governor of Monforte—none other than António Moreno! António Moreno, always so rightly known in Coimbra as *Miss* Antónia Morena! Truly, the country couldn't sink much lower than that! To complete the whole harmonious picture, they really should, and with all urgency, appoint Joana Salgadeira as procurator general to the Crown!

João Gouveia, wearing a smart frockcoat and a bowler hat set at a jaunty angle, was a small, very dark, very scrawny man, with a moustache as stiff as a brush, and he did not disagree in the least. As an impartial civil servant, serving the Historicals just as he had the Regenerationists, he always greeted with impartial irony the appointment to the juiciest government posts of any young graduate, Historical or Regenerationist. However, when he heard about this appointment, he had almost thrown up! António Moreno, civil Governor of Monforte! The same man he had so often come across in his room in Coimbra dressed as a woman in a peignoir open at the front and with his pretty little face caked in rice powder! Taking Gonçalo's arm, he recalled the night when a very drunk José Gorjão, in a top hat and carrying a pistol, had demanded the equally drunk Father Justino to marry him and Antoninho before an image of Our Lady of a Good Death! But Titó, who was impatiently waiting, twirling his cane, declared that if they had time to linger in the street talking about politics and other such indecencies, then he would go to Brito's and buy that bottle of brandy. Gonçalo, ever the joker, detached himself from João Gouveia's arm and galloped off down the street, his hands together as if he were holding the reins of a particularly high-spirited horse.

And in Gago's upper room, at the top of the tavern's steep, narrow stairs, they enjoyed a very jolly, very tasty supper at the end of a long table lit by a couple of oil lamps. Gonçalo—who declared himself miraculously cured after his walk to Bravais and the excitement of the card game, where he had won nineteen *tostões* off Manuel Duarte—began with a plate of fried eggs and sausages, devoured half the mullet, laid waste to his invalid's portion of roast chicken, cleared a whole plate of cucumber salad, and finished off with a couple of blocks of quince jelly; and throughout these noble labours, and with no visible change to his creamy-white complexion, he downed an entire pitcher of Alvaralhão wine, because, much to Titó's displeasure, he had dismissed the Abbot's new wine after just one sip. Videirinha appeared just as they were finishing. He was an assistant pharmacist and a poet, famous in Vila Clara as a guitarist and for his love poems and patriotic verses, which had been published in the local paper in Oliveira. Having already dined that evening, along with his guitar, in the house of Comendador Barros—who was celebrating the anniversary of his knighthood— he would accept only one glass of Alvaralhão, in which he dissolved a cube of quince jelly, 'to help it slide down more easily'. At midnight, Gonçalo insisted that Gago put more wood on the fire and boil them up some coffee, 'as strong and fierce as you can make it, Gago, a coffee capable of awakening talent even in Comendador Barros'. This was the divine hour of guitar music and *fado*. Videirinha had already withdrawn to the shadows, clearing his throat, tuning his guitar, and perching in an appropriately melancholy pose on the edge of a tall bench.

'Sing, *Soledad*, Videirinha,' Titó said, thoughtfully rolling himself a plump cigarette.

Videirinha gave a deliciously mournful rendition of *Soledad*:

> *When you go to the graveyard,*
> *Soledad, ay, Soledad...*

He finished the song to loud applause, and while he was again tuning his guitar, Gonçalo and João Gouveia, elbows on the table and smoking their cigars, discussed the sale of Lourenço Marques to the English, a deal done surreptitiously by the present government (at least according to the Opposition press, who, naturally, were atremble with outrage). Gonçalo was equally outraged! Not by the sale of the colony, but by the sheer impudence of São Fulgêncio! That this fat, bald man—the sacrilegious son of a priest who later became a grocer in Cabecelhos—should exchange for filthy lucre— and simply so that he could stay in power for another two years—a piece of Portugal, a piece of their own august land, land trodden by such heroes as da Gama, Ataíde, and Castro, and by his own ancestors, this was an abomination that called for a violent response, even a revolution, and for the House of Bragança to be buried in the mud of the Tejo! Munching his way through some toasted almonds, João Gouveia remarked:

'Now be fair, Gonçalo, you know perfectly well that the Regenerationists would ...'

Gonçalo gave a superior smile. Ah, if the Regenerationists were ever involved in such a grandiose undertaking, that would be quite different. Firstly, they would never commit the indecency of selling Portuguese land to the English! They would negotiate with the French, the Italians, with other Latin races, our brothers, then all those round, ringing millions would be used to improve Portugal—intelligently, honestly, wisely, but that ghastly bald man, São Fulgêncio ...! Having talked himself dry, he called for some gin, because Gago's brandy was positively poisonous!

Titó shrugged:

'Look, you wouldn't let me buy that bottle of Madeira brandy, so you'll have to put up with it. And the gin here is even more poisonous. Not even good enough for the blacks in Lourenço Marques that you're so keen to sell off. Call yourself Portuguese, and yet you're happy to sell your own country. You should ban such conversations, Mr Administrator.'

Mr Administrator, however, declared that he *would* allow them and unreservedly too, because he, like the Government, would sell off Lourenço Marques, Mozambique and the whole of the East Coast of Africa! He'd auction them off in big chunks! Yes, he'd have the whole of Africa put up for sale and going under the hammer in Terreiro do Paço! And did his friends know why? Based on the sound principle of strong management (he half-stood up at this point, one arm aloft, as if he were addressing Parliament), based on the sound principle that any owner of distant lands, which he can't fully develop because he lacks either money or workers, should sell them off so that he can mend his own roof, till his own land, buy in new stock, and enrich the good earth beneath his feet. Besides, Portugal had a whole fertile province to cultivate, irrigate, work and sow—the Alentejo!

Tító boomed out his disdain for the Alentejo, as being a place of thin, bad-quality soil, where, apart from a few leagues of land around Beja and Serpa, you'd never be rewarded however hard you worked, why, you only had to scratch the surface to find granite beneath.

'My brother João has an enormous estate there, which brings him in, what, a mere three hundred *mil-réis*.'

João Gouveia, who had worked as a lawyer in Mértola, protested angrily that the Alentejo had indeed been abandoned, thanks to centuries of neglect by imbecilic governments, but it was good, rich land, as fertile as you could possibly want!

'You only have to look at the Moors, but why go that far back? Only days ago, Freitas Galvão was telling me ...'

Then Gonçalo Mendes, who had spat out the gin, pulling a face, also weighed in, sweepingly dismissing the whole of the Alentejo as an unfortunate illusion!

Leaning over the table, João Gouveia was shouting:

'Have you ever been to the Alentejo?'

'I've never been to China either, but ...'

'Well, then you have no right to talk. There's the wonderful vineyard that João Maria planted ...'

'And that yields him about a hundred barrels of vinegar, not wine. But elsewhere, it's just leagues and leagues with not a ...'

'It's the breadbasket of Portugal!'

'More like a barren wilderness!'

Above this tumult, Videirinha continued to pluck away at his guitar in solitary ardour, carried along by the sorrowful words of a *fado* from Ariosa, weeping over a pair of dark eyes, the twin mistresses of his heart:

> *Ah, those dark eyes of yours*
> *Will be the ruin of me ...*

The oil in the lamps was burning down, and Gago, when ordered to bring some candles, appeared in his shirtsleeves from behind a cotton curtain, his sly, humble features wreathed in smiles, to remind the gentlemen that it was past one o'clock in the morning. João Gouveia, who hated late nights, which were bad for his throat (his tonsils were highly flammable), pulled out his watch in great alarm. Quickly buttoning up his frockcoat, getting his bowler hat on slightly askew, he tried to chivvy along slow Titó, because they both lived at the other end of the town—Gouveia opposite the Post Office, and Titó in a narrow street nearby, in a house that had once been home to Oporto's executioner, a man who had been found there, knifed to death.

Titó, however, would not be moved. With his walking stick under his arm, he beckoned Gago over to the shadowy far end of the narrow room, to discuss in whispers the tricky business of buying a rifle, a superb Winchester rifle, which had been pawned by the son of Guedes, the notary public from Oliveira. And when Titó finally got downstairs, he found the Nobleman of the Tower and João Gouveia were standing at the door of the tavern, in the sleeping, moonlit street, and grappling as ever with the thorny topic of the Governor of Oliveira—André Cavaleiro!

It was always the same argument, very personal and very intense, but at the same time vague, with Gonçalo demanding that, please, for the love of God, they should not, in his presence, even mention the name of that Senhor Cavaleiro, the Horseman or, rather, the Horse, that ridiculous despot wreaking havoc in the district! And with João Gouveia, very stiff and starchy, his bowler hat still more askew, speaking up for his friend Cavaleiro's superior intelligence, declaring that he had brought cleanliness and order to the area, a Hercules cleansing the Augean stables of Oliveira! The Nobleman began positively bellowing with rage. And Videirinha, his guitar on his back, was pleading with his friends to go back into the tavern so as not to disturb the peace.

'Especially since Dr Venâncio's mother-in-law, poor thing, lives just opposite, and has been in bed since yesterday with a bad pain in her side.'

'Well, people shouldn't go spouting such vile rubbish! How can you, Gouveia, say that Oliveira has never had a governor like Cavaleiro? I'm not just saying that because of my father. He's been gone for nearly three years now sadly—and I agree he wasn't good at the job. He was too weak and ill by then, but we've had the Viscount de Freixomil. We've had Bernardino. You've worked with them both. They were proper men. But that Horseman of yours ... The first condition for a governor is not to be ridiculous. And Cavaleiro is like something out of a comedy! That long troubadour hairstyle of his, that hideous black moustache, and the languid look in his eyes, like some lovesick lover, and his great protruding belly and his bla-dee-bla-bla-bla! Pure farce! He's stupid—and his stupidity begins in his hooves and rises steadily upwards. The man's an animal. And a scoundrel to boot.'

Standing rigid in the shadow of the vast Titó, like a stake planted in the ground next to a tower, Gouvéia was biting into his cigar. Then, wagging his finger, he said in cool, cutting tones:

'Have you quite finished? Well, you listen to me now, Gonçalinho. In the whole of the Oliveira district, and I mean *the whole district*, there is no one, absolutely no one, who can even remotely rival Cavaleiro in intelligence, character, manners, knowledge and political nous!'

The Nobleman of the Tower fell silent, stunned. Then shaking his fist in unruly, arrogant scorn, he said:

'Those are the views of a mere subaltern.'

'And those are the words of a rude lout,' roared the other man, drawing himself up, his small, prominent eyes ablaze.

Between them appeared Titó's arm, thicker than a plank and casting a shadow on the pavement:

'Now, boys, what is all this nonsense? Are you drunk? And you, Gonçalo ...'

But in one of his typically generous, lovable, infinitely seductive impulses, Gonçalo was already apologising, admitting he had been a brute:

'Forgive me, João Gouveia, I know perfectly well that you're defending Cavaleiro out of friendship, not because you're dependent on him, but what do you expect? Whenever people mention that Horse, I don't know, maybe it's by some kind of contagion, but I start neighing and kicking.'

With absolutely no rancour— because he was full of fond admiration for the Nobleman of the Tower—Gouveia immediately forgave his friend, tugged hard at his frockcoat and merely remarked that 'Gonçalinho is a dear boy, but sometimes there's a sting in his tail.' Then, taking advantage of Gonçalo's submissive mood, he began glorifying Cavaleiro again, albeit in more sober tones. He recognised certain weaknesses, yes, that rather prim manner of his, but what a heart the man had! Gonçalinho really should consider ...

The Nobleman again rebelled and, drawing back and holding up his hands, said:

'No, you listen, João Gouveia! Why is it that, upstairs at supper, you didn't eat any of the cucumber salad? It was delicious, even Videirinha had some. I myself had seconds and finished the lot. Why didn't you? Because you have a physiological, visceral horror of cucumber. You and cucumber are incompatible. There would be no reasoning you out of that, no subtle arguments could persuade you to eat cucumbers. You can't doubt that cucumbers are an excellent thing, since so many good people love them, but you can't touch the stuff. Well, Cavaleiro is to me what cucumber is to you. I simply can't stand the man. No amount of dressing and no amount of reasoning could disguise him. I find him loathsome. I can't stomach him. He makes me want to throw up. So listen...'

Then, yawning, Titó again intervened:

'All right, I think we've had more than enough of Cavaleiro! We're all basically decent people and what we need now is to go our separate ways. I've enjoyed both a lady and some excellent mullet tonight, and now I'm exhausted. It'll be morning before we know it!'

Gouveia was horrified. Oh dear God, he had a nine o'clock meeting of the census committee tomorrow! To dispel any lingering ill feeling, he embraced Gonçalo. And as the Nobleman walked down to the fountain with Videirinha (who on these late nights in Vila Clara always accompanied him home along the road to the Tower), João Gouveia, hanging on to Titó's arm, turned to quote a wise saying 'by some philosopher or other':

' "It isn't worth letting bad politics spoil a good supper." Was it Aristotle who said that?'

And even Videirinha, who was once again tuning his guitar and preparing to sing a solo descant to the moon, murmured respectfully between muted chords:

'It really isn't worth it, Senhor Doutor, it really isn't, because politics is white today and black tomorrow, and then, puff, it's nothing at all!'

The Nobleman shrugged. Politics! When he slandered Senhor André Cavaleiro of Corinde, it wasn't the Governor of Oliveira, that figure of authority, he was deriding, no, what he loathed was the man himself, that fake with the languorous eyes! Between them existed one of those deep grudges that once, in the days of Tructesindo, would have had them at each other's throats, spears at the ready, backed up by their two respective bands of men. As he walked, with the moon high above the hills of Valverde, and while

Videirinha's guitar strummed out the slow, sad *fado* of Vimioso, Gonçalo was piecing together the story that had rushed in to fill his unoccupied soul. The Ramires and the Cavaleiros were neighbours, one owned the old Tower in Santa Ireneia, older than the Kingdom of Portugal itself, the other owned a well-kept, profitable estate in Corinde. And when, as a lad of eighteen, he was still at school immersed in his tedious pre-university studies, André Cavaleiro (who was, by then, in his third year as an undergraduate) already treated him like a real friend and, in the holidays, he would ride over to the Tower every afternoon on the horse his mother had bought him; and often, beneath the trees in the garden or out walking near Bravais and Valverde, he would confide in Gonçalo—as if Gonçalo were the older man—telling him of his political ambitions, his plans for his life, which he envisaged as being utterly devoted to the State. Gracinha Ramires was in the flower of her sixteen years and, even in Oliveira, people would refer to her as 'The Rose of the Tower'. At the time, Gracinha's English governess, kindly Miss Rhodes, was still alive, and she, like everyone else at the Tower, was an enthusiastic admirer of André Cavaleiro, charmed by his friendly manner, his long, wavy, romantic hair, his large, gentle, languid eyes, and the ardent way in which he would quote from Victor Hugo and João de Deus. The same weakness softened both her heart and her principles, which bowed down before sovereign Love, and she allowed André to hold long conversations with Gracinha beneath the Judas trees on the *mirador* and even for them to exchange letters at the fountain as it grew dark. Cavaleiro would dine at the Tower every Sunday; indeed, the old steward Rebelo had with great effort and much muttering saved up a thousand *reis* for the young mistress' trousseau. Gonçalo's father, then civil governor of Oliveira, was always so busy—as deep in politics as he was deep in debt—that he only appeared at the Tower on Sunday mornings, and he heartily approved of the match, because in his already complicated life, sweet, romantic Gracinha, with no mother to watch over her, was simply another problem, another thing to worry about. André Cavaleiro was not, like him, from a family with a long, long history, pre-dating the Kingdom, nor did he have the rich blood of the

Visigoth kings flowing in his veins, but he was from a good family, the son of a general, the grandson of a judge, with a perfectly legitimate coat of arms on his palatial house in Corinde, and the heir to plenty of fertile land, all of it unmortgaged ... And, as the nephew of Reis Gomes, one of leaders of the Historicals, and a member of the Historical Party since his second year at university, Cavaleiro was clearly heading for a brilliant career in politics and government. And, besides, Gracinha was madly in love with his glossy moustaches, his broad shoulders—like those of a well-brought-up Hercules—and the proud, impressive way he puffed out his chest. She, by contrast, was tiny and fragile, with shy, green eyes that grew moist and languid when she smiled, with clear, porcelain skin, magnificent hair, darker and more lustrous than the tail of any warhorse, hair that came down to her feet, and in which, sweet and tiny as she was, she could wrap her whole body. Whenever she saw the couple strolling together along the paths in the garden, Miss Rhodes (whose mind had been stuffed with mythology by her father, a professor of Greek Literature in Manchester) could not help but think of 'powerful Mars in love with graceful Psyche'. Even the servants at the Tower marvelled at the lovely couple they made. Only the young man's fat, bad-tempered mother, Senhora Dona Joaquina Cavaleiro, disapproved of her son's frequent, courtly visits to the Tower, for no sounder reason than that she 'didn't like the look of the girl and wanted a homelier daughter-in-law'. Fortunately, when André Cavaleiro enrolled for his fifth year at university, the disagreeable old woman died of dropsy. Gonçalo's father received the key to the vault and Gracinha went into mourning; meanwhile, as Cavaleiro's housemate in Rua de São João in Coimbra, Gonçalo wore a black armband on the sleeve of his gown. In Santa Ireneia, it was assumed that the splendid André, set free from his Mama's stubborn opposition to the match, would ask Gracinha for her hand as soon as he graduated. However, the moment the graduation ceremony was over, Cavaleiro shot off to Lisbon, because there were to be Elections in October, and his uncle, Reis Gomes, the Minister of Justice, had promised to get him elected deputy of Bragança.

And so André spent all that summer in Lisbon, before moving

on to Sintra, where his dark, languorous eyes set many a heart fluttering, and finally, to Bragança, where his almost triumphal arrival was greeted with fireworks and cries of 'Long live Minister Reis Gomes's nephew!' In October, Bragança 'bestowed on Dr André Cavaleiro (as the local newspaper put it) the right to represent it in Parliament, a man of such vast literary knowledge and magnificent oratorical powers…' He returned then to Corinde, but on his visits to the Tower, where Gonçalo's father, Vicente Ramires, was recovering from gastric fever, which had only exacerbated his longstanding diabetes, André would no longer, as he used to, eagerly lead Gracinha off into the silent shade of the garden, but chose to stay in the blue living room, talking politics with her father, who was confined now to his armchair, a blanket over his knees. And in her letters to Gonçalo in Coimbra, Gracinha was already bemoaning the fact that André's visits to the Tower were no longer so sweet or so intimate, 'preoccupied as he always is now with becoming a deputy'. After Christmas, André returned to Lisbon for the opening of Parliament, fully prepared for his new job, accompanied by his servant Mateus, by a beautiful mare he had bought in Vila Clara from Manuel Duarte, and two boxes of books. Miss Rhodes declared that, as befitted a hero, Mars would only return to claim his Psyche once he had performed some noble feat, his maiden speech in the House, for example, 'some beautiful, flowery speech'. When Gonçalo returned to the Tower in the Easter holidays, he found Gracinha looking pale and troubled. The letters from André, who had long since made that beautiful, flowery maiden speech, grew shorter and less passionate by the week. And the latest one (which she showed to Gonçalo in secret), written in the Chamber itself, had consisted of a few hastily scrawled lines, saying that he had a lot of committee work to do, that the weather was lovely, that there was to be a ball that night held by the Count and Countess de Vilaverde, and concluding by sending her much love and signing himself 'your ever-faithful André'. That same evening, Gonçalo unburdened himself to his father, who, still in his armchair, was growing steadily weaker.

'I think André is behaving appallingly towards Gracinha, don't you agree?'

Vicente Ramires barely moved, managing only a gesture of sad defeat with a hand grown so thin that his signet ring kept slipping off.

The parliamentary session closed in May, the moment for which Gracinha had been waiting, eager for those politicians 'to stop talking and have a holiday'. Yet, almost immediately—when Gracinha was in Santa Ireneia and Gonçalo in Coimbra—they read in the newspapers that 'the talented deputy André Cavaleiro has set off for Italy and France, on a long journey that is to be part holiday and part study'. Just like that, without a word to his chosen one, to his almost-fiancée! This was an outrage, a vile outrage, which once, in the twelfth century, would have brought all the Ramires men, accompanied by horsemen and foot soldiers, thundering down upon the Cavaleiro estate, leaving every roof beam scorched black by flames, and every serf hanged. Mortally ill and wasting away, Vicente Ramires simply murmured, 'The cad!' In Coimbra, Gonçalo bellowed with rage, swearing that, one day, he would slap the scoundrel's face! Miss Rhodes consoled herself by dusting off her old harp and filling Santa Ireneia with mournful arpeggios. And it all ended with Gracinha—so griefstricken that, for weeks, she didn't even bother to comb her hair—shedding secret tears while she sat alone beneath the Judas trees on the *mirador*.

And even after all these years, whenever he remembered his sister's tears, Gonçalo was once again filled with such keenly renewed rancour that he struck out with his stick at the bushes growing in the ditches, as if he were beating Cavaleiro's back! He and Videirinha walked on then by the Portela bridge, with the fields spreading out on either side, and from there they could see Vila Clara, white in the moonlight, all the way from the Convent of Santa Teresa, next to the fountain, to the new wall around the cemetery on the hill with its slender cypresses. In the valley, equally bright in the moonlight, stood the small church of Craquede, Santa Maria de Craquede, the remains of the old monastery in which there still lay, in their rough granite tombs, the mighty bones of the Ramires. Beneath the arch of the bridge, the slow stream flowed gently on over the pebbles, whispering in the darkness. And be-

guiled by that sweet, nostalgic sound, Videirinha quietly strummed
his guitar and sang:

Why these complaints?
Why these sighs?
As if I were dead,
And you would ne'er see me again!

And Gonçalo plunged back into his memories and the sad events
that ensued. Vicente Ramires had died one August afternoon, painlessly, sitting in his armchair out on the balcony, his eyes fixed on
the old Tower, murmuring to Father Soeiro, 'How many more
Ramires will that Tower see living in this house and in its shadow?'
Gonçalo had spent all of what remained of that summer in the dark
office, with no one to help him (for the steward, good old Rebelo,
had also been summoned by God), reading document after document, and discovering just what dire straits the household was in,
reduced to a revenue of only two thousand three hundred *mil-réis*
brought in by rents from Craquede, the land in Praga, and the two
oldest estates, Treixedo and Santa Ireneia. When he returned to
Coimbra, he left Gracinha in Oliveira, in the house of a cousin,
Dona Arminda Nunes Viegas, a very kindly, very wealthy lady,
who lived in Terreiro da Louça in a vast mansion full of intricate
family trees and portraits of her ancestors, where she, dressed in
black velvet, sat on a damask-upholstered sofa, surrounded by her
paid companions, who busied themselves with their spinning as
she read and reread her beloved chivalric novels, *Amadis of Gaul*,
Leandro el Bel, *Tristan and Blanchefleur*, and the *Chronicle of Emperor Clarimundo*. It was there that José Barrolo (who owned one
of the finest houses in Amarante) met Gracinha Ramires and instantly fell in love, conceiving for her a profound, almost religious
passion, quite unexpected in that plump, indolent, apple-cheeked
young man, so lacking in intellect that his friends called him 'José
Bacoco'—'José the Dimwit'. Barrolo had always lived in Amarante
with his mother and knew nothing of Gracinha's failed romance,
which had never been spoken of outside the wooded confines of
the Solar de Santa Ireneia. And under the tender, romantic aegis

of Dona Arminda, engagement and marriage sweetly and swiftly followed just three months later, after a letter from Barrolo to Gonçalo, in which he declared that so great was his affection for his cousin Graça, for her many virtues and other fine qualities, that there were not words enough in the dictionary to describe it. The wedding was a lavish affair, and after a brief filial visit to Amarante, the newlyweds (at Gracinha's request, for she did not want to live far from her beloved Tower) 'built their nest' in Oliveira, on the corner of Largo d'El-Rei and Rua das Tecedeiras, in a mansion that Barrolo had inherited, along with a great deal of land, from his uncle Melchior, Dean of the Cathedral. Two years passed gently and uneventfully, and it was at the end of Gonçalo's Easter holidays, spent in Oliveira, that André Cavaleiro was appointed governor, and ostentatiously took up his post with a display of fireworks and a band playing, with the governor's residence and the Bishop's Palace all lit up, and the arms of the Cavaleiro family traced on coloured transparencies illuminating the Café da Arcada and the treasury! Barrolo was quite a close friend of Cavaleiro and admired his talent, his elegance and his political success. However, Gonçalo Mendes Ramires, who held absolute sway over Barrolo, soon persuaded him not to visit the new governor, not even to greet him in the street, and, out of familial duty, to share the rancour that existed between the Cavaleiros and the Ramires! An astonished, uncomprehending José Barrolo submissively agreed. Then one night, in their bedroom, as he was putting on his slippers, he mentioned Gonçalo's 'eccentric behaviour' to Gracinha:

'And for no reason either, when Cavaleiro has caused no offence at all, over something as trivial as politics! I mean, a delightful fellow like André! And we could have had such fun together!'

Another peaceful year passed. Then that spring, in Oliveira, where he had stayed on for Barrolo's birthday celebrations, Gonçalo began to suspect, to sense, to discover an unspeakable infamy! That arrogant man with the blackest of moustaches, Senhor André Cavaleiro, had, with proud impudence, begun courting Gracinha Ramires again, silently and from afar, with long, languorous, yearning looks, with the intention of having as his mistress that great noblewoman, that Ramires, whom he had spurned as a wife!

Gonçalo was so absorbed in these bitter ruminations as he walked along the white road, that he strode straight past the door of the Tower, and did not even notice the small green door at the corner of the house, with its three steps. He was about to continue along by the garden wall, when Videirinha, who had stopped, his fingers resting silently on the strings of his guitar, called to him, laughing:

'Surely you're not going to walk to Bravais at this hour, are you, Senhor Doutor?'

Gonçalo turned, abruptly awakened from his thoughts, and feeling for the key among the small change in his pocket, said:

'I didn't even notice. But how beautifully you played tonight, Videirinha! In the moonlight, after supper, I couldn't hope for a more poetic companion. You really are the last of the Portuguese troubadours!'

The pharmacist's assistant—the son of a baker from Oliveira—felt the friendly, natural way in which that Nobleman treated him—shaking his hand in the pharmacy in front of his boss, Pires, and in front of the bigwigs in Oliveira—as a real honour, almost a coronation, one that was always new, always a delight. Moved, he struck a loud chord:

'To finish then, Senhor Doutor, here is the greatest of ballads!'

This was his most famous song, the *Fado of the Ramires*, a sequence of heroic verses celebrating the legends of that illustrious House, verses he had spent months polishing, assisted in this happy task by old Father Soeiro, the Tower's chaplain, archivist and font of knowledge.

Gonçalo pushed open the green door. In the corridor, next to the silver candlestick, a dim lamp was sputtering out, its oil exhausted. And stepping back into the middle of the road and giving a last ardent 'diddle-om' on his guitar, Videirinha gazed up at the Tower, which, high above the vast roof, thrust its battlements and its dark turret into the luminous silence of the summer sky. Then to the mournful, sighing melody of a Coimbra *fado*, he addressed the final, glorifying verses to the Tower and to the moon:

Who can look on you and not tremble,
Tower of Santa Ireneia,
So silent and so dark,
Ah, so silent and so dark,
Tower of Santa Ireneia!

He paused to thank the Nobleman, who was inviting him to come up and join him in a reviving glass of gin, but then immediately resumed his song, happily ignoring the offer, caught up, as ever, in the pleasure of his own verses, in the magic of those legends, while Gonçalo disappeared, playfully bowing to the troubadour and apologising for 'closing the castle door':

Ah, there you stand, so strong and proud,
A story in every stone,
Tower, older than Portugal herself,
Tower of Santa Ireneia!

And he had just launched into the verse about Múncio Ramires, otherwise known as The Wolf, when, up above, a light came on in a window open to the cool of the night, and the Nobleman appeared on the balcony, smoking a cigar, to enjoy the serenade. Videirinha waxed more ardent still, his voice almost breaking with emotion. Now it was the verse about Gutierres Ramires, in Palestine, on the Mount of Olives, standing outside his tent before the cheering barons, who saluted him with their unsheathed swords, as he refused the dukedom of Galilee and ownership of the lands of Israel. He really could not accept those lands, however Holy, even those of Galilee ...

For he had land already in Portugal,
The lands of Santa Ireneia!

'Very droll!' muttered Gonçalo.

Waxing still more enthusiastically, Videirinha sang another verse, one he had composed that very week, about the funeral of Aldonça Ramires, St Aldonça, who was carried on the pallet bed on which she had died from the convent of Arouca to the estate of Treixedo, borne on the shoulders of four kings!

'Bravo!'cried the Nobleman, leaning out over the balustrade. 'Wonderful! But four kings are too many, Videirinha!'

Elated and holding his guitar aloft, Videirinha launched into another, older verse, about the terrible Lopo Ramires, who, though dead, had risen from his tomb in the monastery of Craquede, mounted a dead horse and galloped all night across Spain in order to fight in the Battle of Las Navas de Tolosa! He cleared his throat and, more tearfully still, attacked the tale of the Headless Man:

There he goes, the dark silhouette ...

Gonçalo, however, hated that particular legend, the silent headless figure wandering on winter nights along the battlements, his head in his hands. He drew back and stopped that endless chronicle:

'Time for bed, Videirinha. It's dreadfully late, past three o'clock! But, listen. Titó and Gouveia are dining here on Sunday. Why don't you come along too, and bring your guitar and a new song, something a little less grim, all right? *Buona sera!* Goodness, what a beautiful night!'

He threw down his cigar, closed the window of the 'old room', lined with those sad, blackened portraits of the Ramires, which he, when he was little, used to call his 'ugly granddads'. And as he walked down the corridor, he could still hear in the distance, ringing out across the silence of those moonlit fields, the exploits of his ancestors set to music:

Ah, there in the midst of battle,
Beside our royal Sebastião,
The youngest of the Ramires
Standard-bearer to the King ...

Once he had undressed, blown out his candle and hurriedly made the sign of the cross, the Nobleman of the Tower fell asleep. But his room filled up with shadows, and there began a terrible, troubled night. André Cavaleiro and João Gouveia, dressed in chain mail, burst through the wall, mounted on vast, hideous, oven-roasted mullets! And slowly, winking one evil eye, they attacked his poor stomach with their lances, making him moan and writhe about on his mahogany bedstead. Then, in the middle of Vila Clara, it was

the terrifying figure of that same dead Ramires, his bones rattling
inside his armour, and King Afonso II, both baring their wolfish
teeth and dragging him furiously off to fight in the Battle of Las
Navas. He resisted, digging in his heels, calling out for Rosa, for
Gracinha, for Titó! But King Afonso dealt him such a blow in the
kidneys with his iron glove that he hurled him from Gago's tavern
all the way to the Sierra Morena onto the battlefield itself, which
glittered and trembled with pennants and lances. Then his Spanish
cousin, Gomes Ramires, the Master of Calatrava, leaned down from
his black horse and plucked out the last few hairs from his head,
to loud guffaws from the whole Saracen host and to the wailing of
his Aunt Louredo, who had been carried there on a float borne on
the shoulders of four kings! Finally, exhausted, unable to find rest,
with dawn creeping in through the chinks in the shutters, and the
swallows cheeping away in the eaves, the Nobleman of the Tower
finally threw off the sheets, leapt out of bed, opened the windows
and took a deep delicious breath of the silence, the coolness, the
greenness, the peace and quiet of the garden. But he had such a
thirst on him, a desperate thirst that left his lips dry and cracked.
He remembered then the famous fruit salts recommended by Dr
Matos. He snatched up the bottle, ran to the dining room in his
nightshirt and, gasping, put two heaped spoonfuls of the stuff into
a glass of Bica Velha water and downed the fizzing brew in one.

'Oh, what a relief, what a blessed relief!

He finally went back to bed, where he instantly fell asleep again,
only this time, he found himself far off, among the tall savannah
grasses of Africa, beneath whispering palm trees, surrounded by
the spicy aroma of brilliant flowers springing up amidst golden
pebbles. At midday, Bento, concerned at the lateness of the hour,
wrenched him from this state of perfect bliss.

'I've had the most dreadful night, Bento! Nightmares, terrors,
noises, skeletons ... I blame the sausage and eggs, and the cucumber, especially the cucumber! It was that fool Titó's idea! Anyway,
in the early hours, I drank some of those fruit salts, and now I feel
absolutely fine, have never felt better! I almost feel capable of doing
some work. Bring a cup of strong green tea up to me in the library.

Oh, and some toast.' And moments later, in the library, wearing a flannel dressing gown over his nightshirt and taking slow sips of tea, Gonçalo sat by the balcony, rereading the last, feeble, scribbled line of his Novella, the one about the broad rays of moonlight pouring into the broad, high-ceilinged room. In a sudden flash of insight, his mind filled with all kinds of interesting descriptive details of the castle on that summer night—the points of the sentinels' spears glinting silently on the walkway behind the battlements, the sad croaking of the frogs on the muddy banks of the moat ...

'Excellent!'

He slowly drew his chair up to the desk, again consulted his uncle's poem, and with a wonderfully clear head, and with images and words bubbling up like water suddenly bursting from a dam, he launched into that section of the first chapter set in the *salle d'armes* of Santa Ireneia, where old Tructesindo Ramires was talking to his son Lourenço and his cousin Dom Garcia Viegas the Wise, about preparations for war ... War! Why? Were Moorish horsemen riding lightly through the wooded hills on the frontier? No! Alas, 'in that free and Christian land, noble Portuguese spears would soon clash one against the other!'

God be praised! His pen was once more flowing freely! And, paying close attention to the pages he had marked in a volume of Herculano's *History of Portugal*, he confidently set about painting a picture of the period in which his Novella was set, during the disputes between Afonso II and his siblings over the will left by their father, King Sancho I. At the beginning of the chapter, the Princes Dom Pedro and Dom Fernando, stripped of their inheritance, are wandering France and León. With them is the Ramires' powerful cousin, Gonçalo Mendes de Sousa, the magnificent head of the Sousa family. And now, in their respective castles in Montemor and Esgueira, the Princesses, Dona Teresa and Dona Sancha, were denying Afonso's sovereignty over the towns, castles, lands and monasteries so generously bestowed on them by their father King Sancho I. Before his death in Coimbra, Sancho had begged Tructesindo Mendes Ramires, his milk-sibling and standard-bearer, whom he himself had dubbed a knight in Lorvão, to defend to the death his best-beloved daughter, the Princess Dona Sancha, mistress of Aveiras. And he had sworn this at the King's deathbed, where that victor of the Battle of Silves, now dressed in sackcloth like a penitent, lay expiring in the arms of the Bishop of Coimbra as the hospital prior held the lamp. Then came the bitter quarrel between Afonso II—fiercely jealous of his authority as King—and the proud Princesses, egged on in their resistance by the monks of the Temple and by the prelates to whom King Sancho had bequeathed vast swathes of the Kingdom. And so the royal troops returning from the Battle of Las Navas de Tolosa laid waste to Alenquer and the areas around other castles. Then Dona Sancha and Dona Teresa appealed for help to the King of León, who, with his son, Don Fernando, marched into Portuguese lands to bring succour to 'the suffering maidens'. At this point, with proud elegance, Uncle Duarte, in *The Castle of Santa Ireneia*, asked Sancho I's standard-bearer:

> *So, old man, what will you do?*
> *If you join your flag to that of León*
> *You betray your promise to the living King*
> *And if you leave the Princesses undefended*
> *You betray your oath to the dead King!*

However, as stoutly portrayed by the Nobleman of the Tower, this problem did not trouble the heart of the loyal, doughty Tructesindo. That night, the moment he received Dona Sancha's call for help from the brother of the *alcalde* of Aveiras (who came to him disguised as a mendicant friar) he ordered his son, Lourenço, to be at Montemor at first light and to bring fifteen lancers, fifty of his own foot soldiers, and forty crossbowmen. He, meanwhile, would give the alarm, and in two days, would enter the field with all his kith and kin, as well as a stronger force of liegemen and archers, to join his cousin, the great Sousa, who was currently in the vanguard of the Leonese troops coming down from Alva do Douro.

At break of day, the Ramires standard—the black goshawk on a scarlet ground—stood outside the bolted gates and, beside it, on the ground, tied to the flagstaff with a strip of leather, glittered the old family emblem—the large, deep, highly polished cooking pot. The whole castle was filled with servants rushing frantically about, taking down helmets from walls and dragging clanking chain-mail vests over the flagstones. In the courtyards, the armourers were sharpening spears and padding greaves and cuisses with oakum. In the pantry, the provisioner was mustering enough food to last for the two hot days of marching that lay ahead. And all around Santa Ireneia, in the sweet afternoon air, Moorish drums—their drumming muffled in the woods, *ba-da-dam, ba-da-dam*, or louder on the hilltops, *ra-ta-ta, ra-ta-ta*—were summoning all the mercenaries and foot soldiers who owed allegiance to the Ramires.

Meanwhile, the *alcalde*'s brother, still disguised as a mendicant friar, had returned to the castle of Aveiras and lightly crossed the drawbridge, bearing the good news that help would soon be at hand. And here, to brighten this gloomy scene of imminent war, Uncle Duarte, in his little poem, had introduced a rather gallant touch:

From the girl filling her pitcher at the well,
The friar stole a kiss, and cried Amen!

But Gonçalo was unsure whether he should sully the description of that magnificent armed offensive with a priestly kiss, and he was still pensively chewing on his quill when the door to the library creaked open.

'The post, sir.'

It was Bento with the newspapers and two letters. The Nobleman only opened one, which bore the wax seal of the elaborate Barrolo arms, pushing aside the other on which he recognised the hateful hand of his tailor in Lisbon. Then bringing his fist down hard on the desk, he cried:

'Oh no, what date is it today? The fourteenth?'

Bento was waiting with one hand resting on the door handle.

'It won't be long before it's my sister Graça's birthday. I completely forgot. I always do. And I haven't even bought her a present. What's to be done?'

However, the previous evening, Manuel Duarte, playing cards at the club, had announced he was escaping to Lisbon for three days to sort out a job for his nephew in the Public Works department. Gonçalo still had time to rush to Vila Clara and ask Manuel Duarte to buy him a pretty white silk parasol with lace trimmings.

'Senhor Manuel Duarte has really excellent taste! Tell Joaquim not to saddle the mare. I won't be going to visit Sanches Lucena after all. But then, when will I make that wretched visit? I've been meaning to go for three whole months. Oh well, the lovely Dona Ana won't age much in two days, and old Lucena won't die either.'

And the Nobleman of the Tower, who had decided to risk the playful kiss, took up his pen again and rounded off the chapter with an elegantly harmonious sentence:

'The furious girl shouted, "Be off with you, you villain!" And, whistling, the mendicant friar left her, striding nimbly along the path in his sandalled feet, in the shade of the tall beeches, while throughout the cool valley, as far as Santa Maria de Craquede, the Moorish drums beat on in the sweet afternoon air, *ba-da-bam*, *ra-ta-ta*, summoning the Ramires troops ...'

III

Over one long week, during the hottest part of the day, the Nobleman of the Tower worked hard and fruitfully. On that particular morning, after ringing the bell in the corridor, Bento had twice pushed open the library door, informing his master, 'Lunch is ready and it's getting cold.' Gonçalo merely grunted a 'Yes, I'm coming …' without looking up from the page before him or taking his pen off the paper, the nib flowing ever onwards like a light keel through calm waters, so eager was he to finish his first chapter before lunch.

Ah, but the sheer effort of writing that dense, difficult chapter, with the whole vast Castle of Santa Ireneia to construct, and an entire period of Portugal's vanished history to condense and hone into robust shape; with the Ramires troops to equip, ensuring that all the saddlebags were full of food, that not so much as a crossbow bolt was missing from the boxes, all of which had to be loaded onto the backs of the mules! Fortunately, the previous evening, he had already moved Lourenço Ramires' soldiers out of the castle— helmets and lances glittering and the standard fluttering in the breeze—and off on their way to bring aid to Montemor.

And now—at the conclusion of the chapter, night had fallen, the curfew bell had been rung, the beacon lit in the barbican tower, and Tructesindo Ramires had gone down to the ground floor of the castle to take supper—from outside the gates came three loud blasts on a bugle announcing the arrival of some nobleman. Without even asking his master's permission, the steward let down the drawbridge, its iron chains creaking, to fall with a hollow clatter onto the stone supports. The person arriving in such haste was Mendo Pais, a friend of Alfonso II and the head of his council; he was married to Tructesindo's oldest daughter, Dona Teresa, the one whose flowing locks, long white neck and light, bird-like step had earned her the title in the Ramires family of the Royal Egret. The Lord of Santa Ireneia ran out into the courtyard to embrace his beloved son-in-law, 'a burly knight, with reddish hair, and the snow-white skin of the Visigoths ...' Hand in hand, they went back into the vaulted room lit by torches fixed to the walls by roughly fashioned iron rings.

Taking pride of place was the heavy oak table, surrounded on all sides by benches, except at the head of the table, where, before a coarse linen cloth set with tin plates and gleaming mugs, stood the seignorial throne—with its crude carving of a goshawk—on which Tructesindo had slung his sword and his silver-damasked belt. Filled now with pine twigs, no fire burned in the vast, soot-blackened fireplace behind the throne, with its mantelpiece adorned with shells, bottles of leeches and two bunches of palms brought from Palestine by Gutierres Ramires the Traveller. To one side of the fireplace, a falcon, still in full feather, dozed on its perch; and below it, on the flagstones, on a bed of reeds, two enormous hounds were also sleeping, snouts resting on their paws, soft ears limp on the ground. In one corner a barrel of wine rested on oak trunks. Between the iron grilles covering two narrow slits in the wall, a monk, his face hidden by his hood, was sitting on a large wooden chest, reading a parchment scroll by the light of a guttering candle. Thus Gonçalo furnished that gloomy Afonsine hall with details stolen from Uncle Duarte, Sir Walter Scott and various stories published in *Panorama*. Ah, but the effort involved! And, having placed on the monk's lap a folio printed in Mainz by Ulrich Zell, he had to cross out the whole of that erudite sentence when, thumping the table, he remembered that the printing press had not yet been invented when his ancestor Tructesindo was alive, and that the learned monk would have had to make do with 'a yellowing manuscript'.

And pacing the echoing flagstones, from the fireplace to the door covered by a leather curtain, Tructesindo, his long white beard spilling over his folded arms, was listening to Mendo Pais, who, as a friend and relative, had journeyed there unaccompanied and armed only with the short sword and saracen dagger hanging from the belt he wore about his grey woollen tunic. Mendo Pais had arrived covered in dust, having travelled in haste from Coimbra to beg his father-in-law, in the name of the King and of the oaths of loyalty Tructesindo had sworn, not to take sides with the Leonese and with the Princesses. And he set out all the arguments brought against them by the learned notaries of the King's council: the resolutions drawn up by the Council of Toledo, Pope Alexander's Papal Bull, the ancient Visigothic Code! Besides, what wrong had their royal brother done to his sisters for them to summon the Leonese hosts to the lands of Portugal? None! King Afonso had denied the Princesses neither authority over nor revenue from the castles and towns bequeathed to them by King Sancho. The King's sole concern was that not an inch of Portuguese soil, whether uncultivated or inhabited, should lie outside his royal command. They called him mean and grasping, but had he not handed over to Dona Sancha eight thousand gold *maravedis?* And how had his sister shown her gratitude? By allowing the Leonese to cross the border and capture the beautiful castles of Ulgoso, Contrasta, Urros and Lanhoselo! Instead of fighting alongside the Knights of the Cross at the Battle of Las Navas, Gonçalo Mendes, the head of the House of Sousa, had placed himself at the service of the Princesses, and was, like a Moor, laying waste to Portuguese cities from Aguiar to Miranda! And the renegade standard with its thirteen roundlets sable had already been seen flying above the hills of Além-Douro—and, hot on its heels, now came the wolfish pack of Castros! All of this represented a very real threat, and, worse, it came from Christian soldiers fighting against the Kingdom, giving Moors and Muslims free rein in the South! How could the honourable Lord of Santa Ireneia, who had so staunchly helped to create the Kingdom now be a party to its destruction, to helping monks and rebellious princesses to the very finest of its lands! Thus spoke Mendo Pais, pacing furiously up and down and becoming so overheated with effort and emotion that twice he filled a wooden bowl with wine and drank it down in one gulp. Then, wiping his lips with the back of one trembling hand, he said, 'Yes, by all means, go to Montemor, Senhor Tructesindo Ramires, but go with a message of peace and goodwill to persuade Dona Sancha and the other Princesses to do the honourable thing and once again swear loyalty to the person who is now their father and their King!'

The great Lord of Santa Ireneia stopped pacing and, frowning, fixed his son-in-law with a hard look, his eyebrows as bushy and white as brambles on a frosty morning.

'I will go to Montemor, Mendo Pais, but I will go there to offer my blood and the blood of my men so that justice shall be done to those who deserve justice.'

Angered by this heroic stance, Mendo Pais said:

'What can be sadder than that the good blood of good men should be spilled merely out of vile revenge? Know this, Tructesindo Ramires, in Canta-Pedra, Lopo de Baião the Bastard, is waiting with a hundred lances to block your way!'

Tructesindo raised his huge head and gave a laugh so clear, so proud, that the hounds uttered a fearsome growl and the falcon woke up on its perch and slowly stretched one wing.

'That is good news indeed, and raises my hopes still higher! But tell me, sir, do you bring me such cheering news in order to intimidate me?'

'To intimidate *you*? I know perfectly well that you would not be intimidated if the Archangel Michael himself descended from Heaven bearing his flaming sword aloft and with all the heavenly host behind him! But I married into your family, and although I will be of no help to you in this battle, I nonetheless wanted to give you due warning.'

Old Tructesindo clapped his hands to summon his servants:

'Let us have supper then! Come and dine with us, Brother Múnio! And you too, Mendo Pais. And for the moment, forget your fears.'

'I will! After all, what possible harm could come to you from a hundred lances coming to meet you on the road—or even two hundred?'

And while the monk was rolling up his parchment scroll, Mendo Pais approached the table, slowly unbuckling his sword belt:

'Only one thing weighs on me, which is that on this day, you, my own father-in-law, will be at war with the Kingdom and with the King.'

'My dear son and friend, I may be at war with the Kingdom and with the King, but I will be at peace with my honour and with my soul!'

This proud, loyal cry did not appear in Uncle Duarte's poem, and when this unexpected burst of inspiration came to him, the Nobleman of the Tower threw down his pen, and gleefully rubbing his hands, cried:

'There's talent for you!'

He finished the chapter there and then. He was exhausted, having been at his desk since nine o'clock, reliving with great intensity, and without his breakfast, the magnificently energetic exploits of his powerful ancestors! He numbered the sheets of paper and carefully locked his copy of *The Bard* away in the drawer. Then, standing at the window, his waistcoat unbuttoned, he boomed out those final words in a gruff, grave voice, just as Tructesindo would have done, 'I may be at war with the Kingdom and with the King, but I will be at peace with my honour and with my soul!' And he really did feel stirring within him a true Ramires soul, a twelfth-century Ramires soul, sublimely loyal, truer to his word than a saint to his vows, and, in order to remain true, blithely forfeiting wealth, contentment and life!

Then Bento, who had given one last desperate ring of the bell, flung wide the library door:

'It's Pereira, sir. Pereira is downstairs in the courtyard, wanting to speak to you, sir.'

Gonçalo Mendes frowned impatiently at being thus dragged down from the heights where he had breathed the same air as the noble spirits of his ancestors:

'Oh really! Pereira, you say, but which Pereira?'

'Pereira, Manuel Pereira from Riosa, the Brazilian.'

Pereira was a farmer with land in Riosa, and was nicknamed the Brazilian because he had inherited twenty *contos* from an uncle who had travelled the rivers of Pará selling goods to the natives. With the money, Pereira had bought land, taken on the lease of Cortiga, the famous home of the Counts of Monte-Agra, wore a fine frockcoat on Sundays, and had sixty votes on the parish council.

'Tell him to come up and we can talk over lunch. And set another place at table.'

The dining room, with its three glass doors opening onto a covered verandah, was still adorned—an inheritance from his grandfather Damião (the translator of Valerius Flaccus)—with two beautiful Arras tapestries representing *The Expedition of the Argonauts*. A vast mahogany cabinet was home to a splendid, albeit motley collection of porcelain from Japan and India, while the still lavish, gleaming remnants of the celebrated Ramires silver—which Bento was constantly, lovingly cleaning and polishing—were displayed on the marble-topped sideboard. However, Gonçalo, especially in Summer, always lunched and dined on the bright, cool balcony, where the floor was covered in matting and the lower halves of the walls were decorated with fine eighteenth-century tiles, and where, in one corner, there was a wickerwork sofa, piled with damask cushions, where one could enjoy a leisurely cigar.

When Gonçalo went in, carrying his as yet unopened morning papers, Pereira was waiting for him, leaning on a large scarlet parasol, staring pensively out at the estate, which stretched as far as the poplar trees on the banks of the stream called Coice and the rolling hills of Valverde. He was a stiff old man, all skin and bone, with a broad, dark, ugly face, tiny blue eyes, and a sparse, already white beard that straggled down over a huge collar held in place by two gold studs. A man of property, accustomed to the city and to dealing with people in authority, he shook hands with the Nobleman of the Tower and nonchalantly accepted the chair drawn up for him at the table, which was dominated by two tall antique cut-glass jugs, one full of lilies, the other of *vinho verde*.

'So what fair wind brings you to the Tower, my friend? I haven't seen you since April!'

'It's true, sir, not since that great thunderstorm on the Saturday before the Election!' said Pereira, stroking the handle of his parasol, which he held between his knees.

Ravenously hungry and eager for his lunch, Gonçalo rang the small silver bell on the table, then, laughing, said:

'And I assume that as surely as rivers flow down to the sea, your votes, my friend, went, as usual, to the eternal Sanches Lucena!'

Pereira laughed too, a pleasant laugh that revealed his very bad teeth. Well, the constituency did, after all, belong to Senhor Sanches Lucena, who was a wealthy man, decent, knowledgeable and always ready to help. And since he had, in April, also received the backing of the Government, not even if Our Lord Jesus Christ were to return to Earth in order to stand for the seat of Vila Clara, not even He could dislodge Senhor Sanches Lucena!

Wearing a glossy black jacket over his splendid apron, Bento was approaching slowly with a dish of scrambled eggs, when the Nobleman, who had now unfolded his napkin, immediately scrunched it up again and threw it down in disgust:

'This napkin has been used before! How often must I tell you, I don't mind a napkin that's torn or darned or patched, but I want it white and clean every morning and smelling of lavender!'

Then noticing Pereira discreetly shifting his chair away from the table, he said:

'Aren't you having any lunch, Pereira?'

No, the Nobleman was most kind, but he would be dining with his son-in-law in Bravais that evening, to celebrate his grandson's birthday.

'Bravo! Congratulations, friend Pereira! Give your grandson a kiss from me. But surely you'll have a glass of *vinho verde*.'

Gonçalo examined the scrambled eggs only to reject them, demanding 'a proper family lunch', always a delicious, lavish affair, beginning with a thick soup made from bread, ham and vegetables, which had been his childhood favourite and which, as a boy, he used to call 'the big bowl'. Then, buttering a cracker, he said:

'Well, frankly, Pereira, your Sanches Lucena does the constituency no good at all! True, he's an excellent fellow, respectable, generous, but silent, absolutely silent!'

Pereira slowly dabbed at his hairy nostrils with a red handkerchief rolled into a ball.

'He knows his business, he thinks prudently ...'

'Yes, but those prudent thoughts don't emerge from his brain!

Besides, he's really old, Pereira. How old is he now? Sixty?'

'Sixty-five. But he comes from sturdy stock. His grandfather lived until he was a hundred. I knew him when he was still running the shop ...'

'What shop was that?'

Screwing his handkerchief into a still tighter ball, Pereira expressed his surprise at the Nobleman's ignorance of Sanches Lucena's origins. His grandfather, Manuel Sanches, had been a linen merchant in Oporto, in Rua das Hortas. And he married an extremely handsome girl, who was always dressed up to the nines.

'I see,' broke in Gonçalo. 'That's all very praiseworthy. People who grow rich and rise up in the world, I mean. And I agree with you, Pereira, that the constituency should send a man like Sanches Lucena to Lisbon, a man with land, roots, interests, a name, but he should also be a man with talent, with pluck. A deputy who, in important matters, in moments of crisis, stands up and carries the Chamber with him! And in politics, Pereira, it's the man who shouts loudest who gets the most done. Look at the road to Riosa, for example! It's never got further than the drawing board, but if Sanches Lucena was the kind of man who would shout a little louder in Parliament, your carts would be creaking down that road right now.'

Pereira shook his head sadly.

'You may be right. We do need someone to speak up for that road to Riosa. Yes, perhaps you're right.'

The Nobleman had fallen silent, concentrating on the delicious-smelling soup served up in a tureen and garnished with sprigs of mint. Then Pereira drew his chair closer, gripped the edge of the table with hands that half a century of working the land had made black and hard as roots, and explained that the reason he had dared to trouble the Nobleman, even interrupting his lunch, was because they would be beginning to cut some timber over near Sandim that week, and before other such matters got in the way, he wanted to talk to him about renting the land belonging to the Tower.

Gonçalo paused, spoon in mid-air, a look of pleased astonishment on his face:

'You want to rent the land around the Tower, Pereira?'

'Yes, that's what I wanted to talk to you about. Now that Relho has been dismissed ...'

'But I've already spoken to Casco about it, José Casco from Bravais! We pretty much agreed a price some days ago, no, more than a week ago now.'

Pereira scratched his sparse beard, slowly, deliberately. That was a shame, a great shame ... He had only found out on Saturday about the upset with Relho. If it wouldn't be breaking a confidence, how much rent was he intending to charge?

'There's nothing confidential about it, old man! I'm charging nine hundred and fifty *mil-réis*.'

Pereira took his tortoise-shell snuffbox from his waistcoat pocket and inhaled a large pinch of the stuff, meanwhile staring down at the floor. That was a great shame, especially for the Nobleman. Still, if he'd given his word ... It really was a shame, though, because he genuinely liked the land; he had considered approaching him in June, and even though times were hard, he might be able to offer one thousand and fifty or even one thousand one hundred and fifty *mil-réis*!

In his excitement, Gonçalo forgot about the soup, and his slender face flushed scarlet at the prospect of such an increase in rent, and of renting the land to such a wealthy man too, a man with money in the bank and who was, to boot, the best farmer in the area!

'Are you serious, Pereira?'

The old farmer set the snuffbox firmly down on the tablecloth:

'Sir, I would not joke with you about such a matter. It's a serious offer, and I can have the contract drawn up as soon as you like, but since you've already reached an agreement ...'

He had picked up his snuffbox again and was resting one large hand on the table prior to getting up, when Gonçalo, nervously pushing away his plate, said:

'Listen, I haven't given you all the details of my discussions with Casco. You know how these things are: Casco came, we talked, I asked for nine hundred and fifty *mil-réis* and a pig at Christmas-time. Initially, he agreed, then he said no. He came back with a friend, then he came back again with that same friend, his wife, his godson and his dog! Then he came again on his own. He walked around the land, measuring it and sniffing the earth; I think he may even have tasted it. You know what Casco's like! Then, finally, one afternoon, he gave in and agreed to the nine hundred and fifty *mil-réis*, but no pig. I gave way on the pig. We shook hands, drank a glass of wine, and he said he'd be back shortly to sort out the lease. I haven't seen him since, and that was nearly two weeks ago! He's probably changed his mind, gone back on his word. In short, I have no firm agreement with Casco. We simply had a conversation in which we established, as a basis, a rent of nine hundred and fifty *mil-réis*. I hate matters being left so vague, and I was already thinking of looking for someone better.'

Pereira was scratching his chin uneasily. When it came to business deals, he liked absolute clarity. He had always got on well with Casco. And he would not for all the world want to interfere in an agreement made with Casco, who could be violent and quick to anger. So to avoid any subsequent unpleasantness, he wanted to be quite clear. If no contract had been signed, fine, but hadn't the Nobleman and Casco both given their word?

Gonçalo Mendes Ramires, who had rapidly finished his soup and filled his glass with wine to calm himself, shot Pereira an almost stern look.

'What a question! If I had given Casco my word, the word of Gonçalo Ramires, do you think I would even be discussing renting the land with you now?'

Pereira bowed his head. This was true. In that case, he would make his offer. And since he knew the property and had already made a valuation, he would offer the Nobleman one thousand one hundred and fifty *mil-réis*, but no pig. He would not keep the family provided with milk, vegetables or fruit either. The Nobleman, being a bachelor, didn't really need it. An ancient household like the Tower, however, inevitably swarmed with servants and other hangers-on. They all took their share, they all abused their situation. Anyway, that was his offer. Besides, the orchard and the vegetable patch provided enough for the Nobleman and even for his staff. Both the orchard and the vegetable patch required a little more care too, and he, out of love for the Nobleman and simply for his own pleasure, would sort it out and leave it immaculate. As for any other conditions, he accepted those set out in the old lease. They could sign the contract next week, on Saturday. Was it a deal?

After a moment during which he blinked nervously, tremulously, Gonçalo held out his hand to Pereira.

'Yes, let's shake on it. You have my word.'

'And may the good Lord bless it,' added Pereira, leaning hard on his parasol in order to get to his feet. 'So, we'll meet on Saturday, then, in Oliveira, to sign the contract. Will you be signing it or will Father Soeiro?'

The Nobleman was thinking.

'No, it can't be Saturday. I will be in Oliveira on Saturday, but it's my sister's birthday …'

Giving a fond smile, Pereira once again revealed his bad teeth.

'Ah, and how is Senhora Dona Maria da Graça? I haven't seen her for ages! Not since last year, at the procession of the Stations of the Cross in Oliveira. An excellent lady and always so friendly! And Senhor José Barrolo? Another truly excellent person. And that estate of his, Ribeirinha! It has the best land for twenty leagues around! Beautiful! His neighbour André Cavaleiro's estate, Biscaia, is nothing in comparison, it would be like comparing a thistle to a cabbage.'

The Nobleman of the Tower was peeling a peach and smiling.

'Nothing of André Cavaleiro's is any good, neither his land nor his soul!'

Pereira seemed surprised. He imagined that the Nobleman and Cavaleiro were still close friends. Not as regards politics, but privately, man to man.

'What me and Cavaleiro? No, we're not close politically or otherwise. He's a horse, and a contrary one at that.'

Pereira did not respond, staring down at the tablecloth. Then, summing up, he said:

'So that's all arranged then, we'll meet on Saturday, in Oliveira.

And if it's all right with you, we can call in and see the notary Guedes and get everything signed and sealed. You, of course, will be at your sister's house …'

'Yes, come over at three o'clock, and we can talk to Father Soeiro about it.'

'It's been an age since I saw Father Soeiro too!'

'The ungrateful wretch hardly ever comes to the Tower now. He's always in Oliveira with my sister, who is the apple of his eye. Can I not even tempt you to a glass of port, Pereira? All right, until Saturday then. And don't forget to give your grandson a kiss from me.'

'I certainly won't, sir. How could I? And please don't get up. I know the way, and I'll pop into the kitchen for a chat with Rosa. I've known everyone here at the Tower since your father, God rest him, was living here. And I always hoped to have the pleasure of one day seeing the land around here cultivated the way it should be!'

Over coffee, with the newspapers lying forgotten beside him, Gonçalo was still savouring that excellent deal. Two hundred *mil-réis* more in rent. And with the land around the Tower being cultivated by Pereira, whose agricultural expertise and love for the soil had transformed the barren lands of Monte-Agra into a marvel of wheatfields, vineyards and vegetable plots! Besides which, he was wealthy enough to be able to pay in advance. And the fact that such a canny, careful man as Pereira should be so eager to rent the land was further proof of the Tower's worth. He almost regretted not having wheedled more out of him, say, one thousand two hundred *mil-réis*. Anyway, it had been a very profitable morning! And there really was no written agreement binding him to Casco. They had merely had a conversation about the possibility of him renting the land, a possibility to be discussed in more detail later, on the new basis of a rent of nine hundred and fifty *mil-réis*. And how foolish it would have been for him, out of some scrupulous sense of respect for a vague conversation, to have turned down Pereira and stuck with Casco, a mere labourer, the sort who scrapes a living from the soil, leaving it poorer with each year that passes, depleted and drained.

'Bento, bring me my cigars! And tell Joaquim to have the mare saddled and ready for half past five. I'm going to Feitosa! Today's the day!'

He lit a cigar and returned to the library. He immediately reread that magnificent last line, 'I may be at war with the Kingdom and with the King, but I will be at peace with my honour and with my soul!' Ah, in those words lay the soul of the Portuguese as they used to be, with an almost religious devotion to their word and their honour! And still holding the sheet of paper, he stood on the balcony, looking out at the Tower, at the dusty arrow slits with their iron grilles, at the sturdy battlements, still intact, and around which a flock of pigeons now fluttered. On how many mornings, in the cool of dawn, had old Tructesindo leaned on those battlements, then new and white! All the land round about, whether cultivated or not, would doubtless have belonged to the great man. And Pereira, who, at the time, would have been either a tenant or a serf, would only have dared to approach his master on his knees and trembling. He would certainly not have offered him a resounding one thousand one hundred and fifty *mil-réis*. Then again, of course, Tructesindo would not have needed the money. Whenever the money chests were growing empty, and his dependents were beginning to mutter about not being paid, the great man could always raid the ill-defended granaries and wine-cellars of the nearby villages, or, at a bend in the road, he could ambush a steward returning from collecting the royal rents or a Genovese peddler of knicknacks, his mules laden with merchandise. Underneath the Tower (or so his father had told him), lay the dark feudal dungeon, now full of rubble, where you could still see the chains fixed to the pillars and, on the vaulted roof, the ring from which the victims of *strappado* would be hung, and the holes in the flagstones where the rack had once stood. And in that dank, silent cave, stewards, peddlers, clerics and even members of the bourgeoisie from other towns would have howled and screamed beneath the whip or on the rack, until, as they lay dying, they gave up their very last *maravedi*. Ah, how much pain and torment had it seen, that romantic Tower of which Videirinha had sung so sweetly in the moonlight?

Then suddenly, with a shout, Gonçalo snatched up a volume by Sir Walter Scott and flung it pitilessly, like a stone, at the trunk of a beech tree. He had spotted Rosa the cook's cat climbing up, claws gripping the branch, back arched, to raid a blackbird's nest.

When, that evening, the Nobleman of the Tower, elegant in his new riding outfit, polished leather gaiters and white suede gloves, stopped outside the door of Feitosa, an old man in ragged clothes, with shoulder-length hair and a long, straggly beard, immediately got up from the stone bench where he was eating some slices of sausage and drinking from a gourd, to inform him that Senhor Sanches Lucena and Senhora Dona Ana had gone out for a ride in the carriage. Gonçalo asked the old man to ring the bell for him. And handing a visiting card to the young servant who opened the elaborately gilded wrought-iron gate on which the letters S and L were intertwined above the coronet of a count, he asked:

'Is Senhor Sanches Lucena well?'

'Yes, sir, he's a little better now ...'

'Has he been unwell, then?'

'Yes, sir, three or four weeks ago, he was gravely ill.'

'Oh, I'm so sorry. Please do tell your master how very sorry I am to hear that.'

He summoned the old man who had rung the bell, intending to reward him. And, intrigued by the man's long beard and hair, like that of some beggar out of a melodrama, he asked:

'Do you beg for alms locally?'

The man looked up at him with bleary eyes, reddened by the dust and the sun, but cheerful too, almost contented.

'I sometimes visit the Tower too, sir. And thanks be to God, they treat me very well there.'

'The next time you visit, tell Bento ... you know Bento, don't you?'

Of course he did, and Senhora Rosa too.

'Well, tell Bento to give you some trousers! The ones you're wearing now are barely decent.'

The old man smiled, a slow, toothless smile and looked proudly down at the filthy rags flapping about shins blacker and barer than branches in winter.

'Yes, they're a bit the worse for wear, but Dr Júlio says they suit me like this. Whenever I go by his house, he always takes my picture with his camera. Just last week in fact. He even took one of me with chains on my wrists and with me holding up a sword. He said he was going to show it to the Government.'

Laughing, Gonçalo spurred on his mare. He was thinking now of riding a little further on to Valverde, then coming back via Vila Clara, hoping to tempt Gouveia over to the Tower to share the meal of spit-roasted goat to which he had already invited Manuel Duarte and Titó last night at the club. However, as he crossed Cruz das Almas, where the lovely, poplar-lined road to Corinde meets the hill leading to Valverde, he stopped, noticing, in the distance, over towards Corinde, the seemingly confused encounter of a wagonload of wood, a butcher's cart, a gesticulating woman wearing a scarlet headscarf and mounted on a donkey, and two farm labourers carrying hoes. Then, suddenly, the whole conglomeration broke up—the woman trotting away on her donkey and disappearing behind some trees; the cart jolting off amid a small cloud of dust; the wagon proceeding on its creaking way to Cruz das Almas; and the labourers heading down across a haymeadow to another field. The only person left on the road was a man, apparently helpless; he had his jacket slung over his shoulder and was limping slowly, painfully along. Curious, Gonçalo rode over to him.

'What's wrong? What happened to you?'

Resting all his weight on one leg, the man looked up at Gonçalo, almost fainting, his face contorted with pain and running with sweat.

'A very good afternoon to you, sir! What else could it be, but one of life's misfortunes!'

And still wincing, he told his tale. For some months he had had a sore on his ankle, which refused to heal, despite the application of poultices, myrtle powder and special charms ... And he was just walking over to Dr Júlio's place, to repair some steps for a friend of his who had malaria, when, bam, a rock came loose and struck his bad leg, scraping the skin, grazing the bone and leaving him in the sorry state he found himself in now. He had even torn off his shirt tail to staunch the bleeding before binding up the wound with his scarf.

'But you can't possibly walk like that, man. Where do you live?'

'In Corinde, sir. My name's Manuel Solha from the hamlet of Finta. I'll get there somehow or other.'

'And what about all those people who were here just now? Could none of them help you? There was a cart and two great strapping men ...'

A sudden movement, a stubborn attempt to put weight on his injured leg, made the man cry out. Yet he still managed to smile, even though the pain had left him gasping for breath. What did the Nobleman expect? We all have our lives to live, although the girl on the donkey had promised to go to Finta to tell his people. And perhaps one of his boys would ride over on the mare he had bought at Easter, and which, alas, was also lame!

The Nobleman of the Tower immediately jumped lightly down from his horse.

'One mare is as good as another, so here's mine ...'

Solha stared at Gonçalo open-mouthed.

'Good Lord, sir. You mean I should ride while you walk?'

Gonçalo laughed.

'Look, with all this talk about who's walking and who's riding, all this "please, sir" and "no, sir", we're losing precious time. Get into the saddle, keep your seat and off you go to Finta!'

'No, sir, I can't do it. I'd rather stay here and starve, with my wound going bad on me.'

Gonçalo stamped his foot authoritatively.

'Up you get! And those are orders. You're a mere labourer with a hoe, and I'm a graduate from Coimbra University. I know what I'm doing and I'm the one giving the orders.'

Submitting at once to this dazzling display of Superior Knowledge, Solha silently grabbed the horse's mane, respectfully put one foot in the stirrup, helped by Gonçalo, who, without bothering to

'It must be two years, Senhora, since I had the honour …'

But Sanches Lucena let out a cry:

'Sir, you have blood on your hand!'

Startled, the Nobleman looked down. There were two dark red stains on his white suede glove.

'Oh, it's not my blood. It must have happened when I helped Solha onto my horse with his injured foot …'

He tore off the soiled glove and flung it into the weeds growing up behind the stone bench. Then, still smiling, he went on:

'No, I haven't had the honour of meeting you, Senhora, since that ball put on by the Baron das Marges in Oliveira, his famous Carnival Ball. Yes, that was more than two years ago, when I was still a student. I remember that you were splendidly dressed as Catherine of Russia …'

And even while he enfolded her in the gaze of his fine, affectionately smiling eyes, he was thinking, 'She's certainly a gorgeous creature, but so vulgar. And that voice!' Dona Ana also remembered the ball.

'You're mistaken, kind sir. I wasn't dressed as a Russian, but as an Empress.'

'Yes, yes, the Empress of Russia, Catherine the Great. And so tastefully dressed too, such a lavish costume!'

Sanches Lucena slowly turned his gold-rimmed spectacles on Gonçalo, wagging one long, pale finger.

'And *I* remember that your sister, Senhora Dona Graça, was dressed as a peasant from Viana. Oh, it was a wonderful party, wasn't it, but then Marges always takes such pains over everything. And you know, I haven't spoken to your good sister since. I've only glimpsed her from afar at mass.'

Besides, he spent little time in Oliveira now, even though he had a house there and servants and stables, because, whether it was the fault of the air or the water, he didn't know, but life in the town simply didn't seem to suit him.

Gonçalo's ears pricked up.

'Oh, really, sir. What's been the trouble?'

Sanches Lucena gave a bitter smile. The doctors in Lisbon

remove his white gloves, carefully supported Solha's other bandaged, bloodstained foot.

Then, once he was in the saddle, Solha gave a sigh of relief.

'All right?' asked Gonçalo.

The man merely murmured the name of Our Lord, in gratitude and astonishment at such kindness.

'This is the world gone mad, sir, with me up here, riding your mare, and you, the Nobleman of the Tower, walking along below!'

Gonçalo made light of the matter. And to pass the time, he asked about Dr Júlio's estate, where major works were being carried out and a vineyard planted. Then, since Manuel Solha knew Pereira the Brazilian (who had considered renting Dr Júlio's land), they talked about that intelligent man, and about the wonders of his house, Cortiga. Relaxed now, sitting upright in the saddle, enjoying this easy conversation with the Nobleman of the Tower, Solha forgot about the wound and the pain, which was diminishing. Beside him, attentive and smiling, the Nobleman walked briskly along in the white dust.

Thus engaged, they approached Bica-Santa, one of the most famous places in that lovely area. There the road, cut out from the hillside, grows wider to form an airy terrace, and you can see the whole valley of Corinde, so rich in farmhouses, trees, wheatfields and streams. And that hill, thick with oak trees and moss-covered rocks, is home to a celebrated spring, whose waters, in the days of King João V, were said to be a cure for stomach ailments; so revered were its waters that a devout lady from Corinde, Dona Rosa Miranda Carneiro, had ordered a marble tank to be built and for the water to be channelled from on high so that it now beneficently flows through a bronze spout, beneath the image and protection of Santa Rosa de Lima. Around the tank are two long curved stone benches, shaded by the oak trees' spreading branches. It provides a quiet retreat where people can pick violets, enjoy a picnic, and on Sunday afternoons, ladies from the surrounding area come as a group to listen to the blackbirds and enjoy the view over the bright, verdant, well-populated valley.

However, before it reaches Bica-Santa, close to the village of

Serdal, the Corinde road bends sharply, and it was there that the mare pulled up short, obliging the Nobleman of the Tower, unsure of Solha's horsemanship, to grab hold of the reins. A carriage suddenly appeared, a caleche upholstered in blue and drawn by a pair of horses covered in white netting to keep off the flies. Sitting very erect in the driver's seat was a moustachioed coachman, wearing a uniform with a scarlet collar and a hat with a yellow hatband. Gonçalo was still holding the mare's reins, like a helpful muleteer on a dangerous path, when he spotted old Sanches Lucena sitting on one of the stone benches next to the spring, a blanket over his knees. Beside him, a footman was crouched down, using a clump of grass to clean the boot that Dona Ana was holding out to him, leaning forward slightly as she caught up her linen dress with one hand and rested her other gloveless hand on her slender waist.

The disconcerting sight of the Nobleman of the Tower tugging at the reins of his mare, while a labourer in shirtsleeves sat happily ensconced in the saddle, shattered the sleepy peace of Bica-Santa. Sanches Lucena stared goggle-eyed, as did his glasses, and curiosity brought him suddenly to his feet, craning his neck, his blanket slipping onto the grass. Quickly withdrawing her boot, Dona Ana adopted the dignified pose one would expect of the mistress of Feitosa, and, as if it were a sceptre, grasped the gold handle of her gold lorgnette, which hung on a gold chain. Even the footman smiled in astonishment at Solha.

However, with his usual nonchalant elegance, Gonçalo immediately greeted Dona Ana, enthusiastically shook Sanches Lucena's startled hand, and gaily congratulated himself on such a fortunate encounter! He had just come from Feitosa, where, much to his dismay, he had been informed by a servant, who was doubtless exaggerating, that the deputy had been unwell. So, how was he? He looked the picture of health!

'Isn't that right, Dona Ana! A perfect picture of health!'

With a slight coquettish turn of her head—which sent a soft tremor through the white feathers on her red straw hat—she said in a slow, deep, affected voice that made Gonçalo cringe:

'Sanches' health, thank heavens, is much improved.'

'Yes, it is a little improved,' murmured the thin, hunched old man, drawing his blanket back over his knees. 'Thank you for asking.'

Then—so ablaze with curiosity that a blush almost covered his waxen features—he fixed his glinting glasses on Gonçalo.

'Forgive me, sir, but what are you doing here on the road to Corinde, on foot and with a farm labourer mounted on your horse?'

Smiling, especially at Dona Ana, whose wonderfully dark, deep, liquid eyes, so serious and reserved, were also awaiting an answer, Gonçalo explained what had happened to the poor man, whom he had found on the road, in terrible pain and dragging his injured leg.

'So I offered him my mare. And if you will allow me, I must arrange for him to continue his journey.'

He went back over to Solha, who, intimidated by the presence of the master and mistress of Feitosa, at first sat hunched on the saddle, hat in hand, as if trying to appear smaller, and then made as if to take his feet out of the stirrups in order to dismount. Gonçalo, however, told him to ride straight to Finta and send one of his sons back with the mare to Santa-Bica, where he intended to linger a while with the deputy. And when Solha set off, turning round in the saddle and bowing madly, as if propelled reluctantly onwards by the Nobleman's friendly smiles and waves, Sanches Lucena gave voice to his astonishment.

'Well, really! The last thing I expected to see was Senhor Gonçalo Mendes Ramires walking to Corinde, holding the reins, while a labourer rode beside him on his horse. It's the Good Samaritan all over again, only even better!'

Gonçalo laughed and sat down on the bench next to Sanches Lucena. He was sure that the Good Samaritan could not have deserved such a favourable mention in the Gospel simply for offering his donkey to an ailing Levite; he must have done far more virtuous things than that. Then smiling at Dona Ana, who was seated on the other side of Sanches Lucena and peering, with majestic slowness, through her lorgnette at the trees and the spring with which she was already more than familiar, he said:

couldn't agree. Some said it was his stomach, others his heart, but there was clearly something amiss with some vital organ. And he suffered such terrible bouts of pain. Fortunately, with God's grace, a sensible diet and plenty of milk and rest, he hoped to survive for a few more years.

'Of course you will!' cried Gonçalo gaily. 'But don't you think that perhaps spending time in Lisbon, in Parliament, engaged in politics, the murky world of politics, might be too tiring, too agitating...'

No, on the contrary, Sanches Lucena always felt rather well in Lisbon, better even than at home, at Feitosa. Besides, Parliament was a distraction, and then too he still had friends in the capital, a very select circle of friends, of course...

'I'm sure you know one of these excellent people—a relative of yours, Dom João de Pedrosa.'

Gonçalo knew neither the man nor the name, but he nevertheless murmured politely:

'Ah, yes, Dom João...'

And stroking his white whiskers with one bony, almost transparent hand, on which glittered a sapphire signet ring, Sanches Lucena went on:

'And not just Dom João either. Another of our friends is a close relative of yours too. We've often spoken of you and your house, for he also belongs to the first rank of nobility—Arronches Manrique.'

'Such a dear man, so charming, so amusing!' added Dona Ana, with an enthusiasm that caused her chest to rise and fall, her tight bodice emphasising the youth and perfection of her figure.

Gonçalo had never heard of that high-sounding name either, but he didn't hesitate to say:

'Oh, yes, of course, Manrique. But you know, I have so many relatives in Lisbon and I go there so rarely. And what about you, Senhora Dona Ana...'

Sanches Lucena, however, was still relishing this conversation about noble relatives.

'Naturally, you have many historic family connections in Lisbon, indeed, you are, I believe, the cousin of the Duke de Lourençal...

Duarte Lourençal! As a supporter of Dom Miguel, or perhaps out of habit, he doesn't use his title, but he's still the legitimate Duke de Lourençal, and represents the House of Lourençal.'

Smiling attentively, Gonçalo had unbuttoned his jacket and was feeling for his old leather cigar case.

'Ah, Duarte, of course. Yes, we are cousins, at least he says we are and I believe him. But I understand so little about family trees! In fact all the noble families of Portugal are so mixed up that we're all related in some way, not through Adam, but through the Visigoths. And what about you, Dona Ana, do you prefer life in Lisbon?'

Then, realising that he had taken out a cigar and distractedly bitten off the end without asking her permission, he said:

'Oh, forgive me, Senhora. I was about to smoke without even asking if you ...'

She nodded, lowering her long eyelashes:

'The gentleman is perfectly at liberty to smoke. Sanches doesn't smoke, but I rather like the smell.'

Gonçalo thanked her, repelled by her coarse, affected tones, and the awful way she addressed him in the third person, but all the while thinking, 'What beautiful skin! What a lovely creature!' And Sanches Lucena continued inexorably on, again wagging one thin finger:

'The person I know best, though, is not Senhor Dom Duarte Lourençal, for I have not yet had that honour, but his brother, Senhor Dom Filipe. An estimable gentleman, as you no doubt know. And such a talented cornet-player too.'

'Really?'

'You mean you've never heard your cousin, Senhor Dom Filipe Lourençal, play the cornet?'

Even the lovely Dona Ana grew animated at this, the languid smile on her full lips, as red as ripe cherries, revealing her small, white, gleaming teeth.

'Oh, he plays wonderfully well. Sanches loves music, and so do I. But, of course, here in the village, there are so few ...'

Gonçalo flung down his match and exclaimed with genuine enthusiasm:

'Oh, but you should hear my friend, Videirinha—he plays the guitar sublimely.'

Sanches Lucena was bemused by both the name and its vulgarity. But Gonçalo said simply:

'He's a great friend of mine, from Vila Clara. José Videira, the pharmacist's assistant.'

Sanches Lucena's glasses grew even rounder with amazement.

'A pharmacist's assistant, the friend of Senhor Gonçalo Mendes Ramires!'

Yes, they had been friends ever since they were at school together. Videirinha even used to spend the holidays at the Tower with his mother, who was the household's seamstress. Such a genuine, good-hearted lad. And a real genius on the guitar.

'He's written a terrific ballad entitled *The Fado of the Ramires*. The music is from a well-known Coimbra *fado*, but he wrote the words, which are all about my ancestors, their legends and other doubtless apocryphal stories. And it's just brilliant. He was at the Tower just a few days ago, Titó was there as well.'

Sanches Lucena was equally taken aback by this childish name. 'Titó?'

The Nobleman laughed:

'That's our nickname for António Vilalobos.'

Then Sanches Lucena opened wide his arms, as though some beloved person had just appeared on the road before him:

'Oh, António Vilalobos! Why, he's one of our best and most loyal friends! An excellent gentleman! He favours us with a visit almost every week.'

Now it was the Nobleman's turn to be astonished—Titó had never once mentioned this friendship—not at Gago's or at the Tower or at the club—when the name of Sanches Lucena was being bandied about during their political discussions.

'Oh, so you know ...'

Dona Ana, who had suddenly sprung to her feet and was now bending down to pick up her glove and her parasol, reminded her husband how cold it could get in the late afternoon, with the mist rising up from the warm valley:

'You know how bad it is for you. And it's not good for the horses either, standing there all this time.'

And Sanches Lucena immediately, fearfully, drew from his pocket a thick white silk scarf to wrap around his neck. Fearful for the horses too, he rose unsteadily from the bench and gave a weary wave to the footman to pick up the blanket and tell the coachman to get ready. Then, bent and leaning heavily on his stick, he walked back over to the balustrade that separated the road from the steep drop down into the valley. And he confessed to Gonçalo that this was his favourite walk in the area. Not just because it was beautiful—for its praises had already been sung by 'our own dear Cunha Torres'—but because he could sit there on the stone bench, enjoying an unimpeded view of all his lands.

'You see over there, beyond that wood, as far as the plain and the hill behind it, where that big yellow house is, and beyond the pine forest, well, that's all mine. The pine forest is mine too. Over there, from the line of poplars onwards, beyond the flood plain, that's mine as well. The land by the little church belongs to Monte-Agra, but further on, past the oak copse and on up the hill, that's all mine too!'

The thin, pale finger, the bony arm sticking out from the sleeve of his black cashmere jacket, reached out over the valley. The pastures, the fields of rye, the heath, it was all his. And behind that scrawny, broken figure, with his hat pulled well down on his head, his silk scarf wrapped about his protruding ears, stood Dona Ana, as slender and healthy and clear as a marble statue, a dreamy smile on her greedy lips, her magnificent bosom filling with pride; she was accompanying this long enumeration, her lorgnette fixing on each pasture, pine forest and field, and thinking, 'It's all mine!'

'And over there, behind the olive grove,' concluded Sanches Lucena respectfully, 'that is all yours, Senhor Gonçalo Mendes Ramires.'

'Mine?'

'Yes, yours, sir, or rather, your family's. Don't you recognise it? The road to Santa Maria de Craquede runs behind the windmill.

That's where the tombs of your ancestors lie. Another of my favourite walks. Just a month ago, we paid a long visit to the ruins, and I was most impressed. The ancient fragment of cloister, the great stone tombs, the sword hanging from the vault above the central tomb. It's really very moving. And I thought it quite beautiful, a sign of real filial respect on your part, to have that bronze lamp kept burning day and night.'

Gonçalo smiled and mumbled a response, because he had no memory of a sword and had never ordered anyone to keep the lamp burning. However, Sanches Lucena was now asking a particular favour of Senhor Gonçalo Mendes Ramires, which was to give them the honour of driving him back to the Tower in their carriage. Gonçalo hurriedly declined. No, really, he couldn't. He had arranged with the injured man to wait there for his mare to be returned.

'My footman will wait here and bring your mare to the Tower.'

'No, if you'll forgive me, I would prefer to wait. I'll take the short cut via Crassa afterwards, because Titó is expecting me at the Tower at eight o'clock.'

Standing in the middle of the road, Dona Ana urged her husband to hurry up, reminding him again of the imminent cold and damp of night. Resting one bone-thin hand on his sunken chest, Sanches Lucena still insisted on telling Gonçalo that this had been an unforgettable afternoon for him.

'Because I have seen a truly rare sight: Portugal's greatest nobleman walking along the road to Corinde, leading his horse, while a labourer sat astride it!'

Helped by Gonçalo, he finally climbed awkwardly into the carriage. Dona Ana was already installed among the cushions, holding in her hands, like a sceptre, the gleaming handle of her gold lorgnette. The footman also took up his position at the rear and folded his arms; then the luxurious caleche, along with the horses' gleaming white harness, plunged beneath the outspread branches of the beech trees, into the silence and darkness.

'What a bore!' exclaimed Gonçalo, regretting the waste of such a lovely afternoon. Sanches Lucena was simply unbearable, such a name-dropper and so proud of his 'select circle' and of all his possessions—ogling them over hill and dale! His wife was undeniably a splendid piece of flesh—as befitted a butcher's daughter—but she hadn't a smidgen of grace or soul. And her voice, dear God, what a voice! Such pedants, such sycophants. All he wanted now was to get his mare back and gallop home to the Tower, where he could vent his feelings on Titó—that apparently intimate friend of Feitosa—and his disgust for all things Sanchesian.

The mare soon arrived, ridden at a fast trot by Solha's son, who, when he saw the Nobleman, immediately dismounted, bowing and blushing and stammering his thanks, hat in hand, saying that his father had reached home safely and asking Our Lady to repay him for his kindness.

'Yes, all right, all right. Give my regards to your father and wish him a swift recovery. I'll send someone over to ask how he is.'

Then he leaped onto his horse and galloped off down the easy path to Crassa. However, when he reached the Tower, he found one of Gago's boys with a message from Titó, saying that he could not dine with him that night at the Tower because he was leaving for Oliveira that week!

'What nonsense! I'm leaving for Oliveira too, but I'm still having supper tonight! He could even go with me in the carriage. What was Senhor Dom António doing when you left him?'

The boy thoughtfully scratched his head.

'He came to our house so that I could bring you the message, sir. I think he must be going to a party, because he went into Cosme's shop to buy some firecrackers.'

These unexpected firecrackers filled the Nobleman with intense envy.

'And do you know where the party is?'

'I don't know, sir, but it must be quite a do, because Senhor João Gouveia ordered two big plates of rissoles from the cook.' Rissoles! Gonçalo felt as bitter as if he had been betrayed.

The ingrates!

Then he thought of a delightful way to have his revenge.

'Well, if you see Senhor Dom António or Senhor João Gouveia later today, be sure to send them my regrets, and tell them that I'm holding a big party at the Tower tonight, with lots of ladies present, including Senhora Dona Ana Lucena. Don't forget, will you?'

Gonçalo ran up the stairs, laughing at his own brilliance. That night, though, at nine o'clock, after a slow, tedious supper with Manuel Duarte, he went into the portrait gallery, barely lit by the gilded lamp in the corridor, to fetch a box of cigars. Happening to glance out of the open window, he saw a man down below in the shadows cast by the poplar trees, prowling around and spying all about him. When he looked more closely, he thought he recognised Tito's powerful shoulders and bovine gait, but it couldn't possibly be him. The man was wearing a hooded jacket. Feeling curious, he tiptoed over to the balcony, but the figure had already headed off down the road, vanishing under the trees along a lane that ran past the Mirandas' place to emerge further on in Portela, next to the first houses in Vila Clara.

IV

The Barrolos' sumptuous house in Oliveira (known since the beginning of the century as the Casa dos Cunhais—the Corner House) raised its noble façade with its twelve balconies on Largo d'El-Rei; it was positioned between a solitary little alleyway that led to the barracks and Rua das Tecedeiras, a steep, narrow cobbled street, made still narrower by the house's long garden on one side and by the old wall of the Santa Mónica convent on the other. On that morning, just as Gonçalo—driven by Torto in the Tower's caleche—was entering Largo d'El-Rei, who should be coming up Rua das Tecedeiras—clip-clopping proudly and elegantly over the cobbles on a horse with a thick, glossy mane—but the governor, André Cavaleiro, in a white waistcoat and a straw hat. From inside his carriage, Gonçalo saw Cavaleiro's dark, long-lashed eyes glancing up at the wrought-iron balconies. Gonçalo struck his knee, muttering, 'The cad!' When he got out at the rather dwarfish main door (looking as if it had been crushed beneath the weight of the Sá family's vast coat of arms), he was so filled with indignation that he did not even notice the effusive greetings of the old porter, Joaquim, and left behind in the caleche the presents he had brought for Gracinha—the box containing the parasol and a basket of flowers from the Tower covered with silk paper. Once upstairs in the parlour, to which José Barrolo had immediately hurried when he heard the clatter of carriage wheels in the silent square outside, he immediately gave full vent to his feelings, angrily flinging down his dustcoat onto a leather armchair.

'It seems that I cannot even visit this town without coming face to face with that Cavaleiro creature! And he's always in the square, right outside the house! It really is confounded bad luck. Can't the moustachioed fool find somewhere else to parade that pathetic nag of his?'

José Barrolo, a plump lad, with curly, reddish hair, a fine fair moustache, and a face as round and red as a beautiful apple, said innocently:

'What do you mean "nag"? It's a magnificent horse, a lovely thing that he bought from the Baron das Marges!'

'Well, he's a hideous ass riding a very pretty horse. They should both stay in the stables where they belong or else be put out to pasture!'

In his astonishment, Barrolo opened wide his large, pink mouth, revealing a set of superb teeth. And suddenly, stamping on the ground, bent almost double, he burst into helpless, hopeless laughter that made the veins in his neck swell.

'Oh that's a good one! I'll have to tell that to the chaps at the club. A hideous ass riding a very pretty horse! And both to be put out to pasture. You're on very good form today, Gonçalo! I can see it now, both of them, the governor and his horse, with their snouts in the grass. Excellent!'

He bounced around the room, joyfully slapping his fat thighs. Somewhat placated by this celebration of his wit, Gonçalo said:

'Let me embrace you, brother-in-law, if my arms are long enough. And how's the family? How's Gracinha? Ah, here comes the lovely flower now ...'

And there she was, with her light, delicate, girlish air, her magnificent hair hanging down loose over her lace peignoir; she ran excitedly over to her brother, who folded her in a warm embrace and planted two loud kisses on her cheeks. Then, drawing back, he declared that she was looking even prettier—and plumper too.

'No, you really are looking plumper, and perhaps even a little taller. Do I have a nephew on the way? No? Not yet?'

Gracinha blushed and smiled the languid smile that made her greenish eyes grow still moister and sweeter, more tender.

'It's up to her!' cried José Barrolo, swaying from side to side, his hands in the pockets of a double-breasted jacket that seemed only to emphasise his large thighs. 'It's definitely not the fault of the master of the house. But she just can't make up her mind!'

The Nobleman of the Tower scolded his sister:

'We need a boy-child. And without one—since I'm never going to marry, because I'm simply not the type—well, that will be the end of both our families, the Barrolos and the Ramires. The extinction of the Barrolos would do the world a favour, frankly, but once the Ramires are finished, Portugal will be finished too. Therefore, Senhora Dona Graça Ramires, hurry up; in the name of the nation, we need a son and heir! A very fat heir, whom I intend to call Tructesindo!'

Barrolo protested, horrified:

'Turtesinho? No, if that's going to be his name, I'm having nothing to do with it!'

Gracinha put a stop to all these playful jests, wanting news of the Tower, of Bento, of Rosa the cook, the vegetable garden and the peacocks ... Still talking, they went into the next room, which, furnished with Indian sideboards and heavy, gilded armchairs upholstered in blue damask, had three balconies looking out over Largo d'El-Rei. Barrolo rolled himself a cigarette and demanded to know all about Relho and the ensuing uproar. He himself had been engaged in a dispute with a tenant on his Ribeirinha estate, over the felling of some pine trees, but that Relho business had really been something.

Firmly installed in one corner of an ample blue sofa, and lazily unbuttoning his pale woollen jacket, Gonçalo said:

'No, it was all very straightforward. Relho had been almost permanently drunk for some months, then, one night, he just exploded, threatening Rosa with a rifle. I, of course, went downstairs and an instant later, there was no Relho, and peace and quiet were duly restored.'

'But didn't the alderman come with his men?' Barrolo asked.

Gonçalo gave an impatient shrug.

'The alderman? Yes, but he only came afterwards, for legal purposes. The man had left by then, driven away. And, as a result, I've rented the land to Pereira, Pereira from Riosa.'

He recounted the details of this excellent deal, which had been brokered over lunch on the verandah, washed down by a couple of glasses of *vinho verde*. Barrolo was impressed by the amount of rent and was full of praise for Pereira. Could Gonçalo not come up with another Pereira for the Treixedo estate, which had such fertile land, and yet was so badly managed!

Perched on the edge of the sofa, her long, freshly-washed, rosemary-scented hair hanging loose, Gracinha was observing her brother tenderly:

'And is your stomach any better? Are you still having those suppers with Tító?'

'Oh, that wretch!' exclaimed Gonçalo. 'He promised days ago to come and have supper at the Tower, and Rosa even prepared a delicious spit-roast goat for him, and then he didn't turn up. I think he'd been invited to some wild orgy somewhere, complete with firecrackers. In fact, *he's* coming to Oliveira this week as well. Oh, and yes, did you know he was best friends with Sanches Lucena?'

He then gave a gleefully exaggerated account of the meeting at Bica-Santa, his horror of the lovely Dona Ana, and his unexpected discovery that Tító was a regular visitor to the Lucena household.

Barrolo recalled that, one afternoon in June, before St John's Eve, he had spotted Tító outside the main gate of Feitosa, walking a small white lapdog.

'But what I can't understand is your horror of Dona Ana. Good heavens, the woman's gorgeous! The way she walks, those big eyes of hers, her embonpoint ...'

'Hold your tongue, you libertine!' cried Gonçalo. 'How can you bring yourself to praise such a cut of meat when beside you sits your wife, the loveliest of all Gracinhas!'

Gracinha, who was not in the least jealous, laughed, saying that she quite understood José's admiration for Ana Lucena, who really was most striking, very beautiful indeed!

'Yes,' agreed Gonçalo, 'in the way that a fine-looking mare is beautiful. But that voice of hers, so affected, so coarse. And the lorgnette and her manners in general, all that, "Of course the gentleman may smoke", or, "No, the gentleman is quite mistaken". It's just ghastly.'

Pacing up and down in front of the sofa, his hands in the pockets of his smoking jacket, Barrolo was muttering:

'Sour grapes, Gonçalo, sour grapes!'

The Nobleman gave his brother-in-law a fierce look:

'Not even if she came to me on her knees, in her nightdress, with two hundred *contos* from Sanches Lucena on a silver platter!'

Smiling and red as a peony, Gracinha uttered a scandalised 'Oh!' and clapped her brother on the back. He pulled her playfully towards him:

'Let me kiss you on the cheek again, to purify myself. You see, even thinking about Dona Ana leads people to have brutish thoughts. Anyway, you were asking about my stomach. Yes, it's still a little out of sorts. And some days it's worse than others, especially after that spit-roast goat and Manuel Duarte's drunken company. Do you happen to have any Vidago water in the house? You do? Well, José, would you be an angel and have them bring me a nice cool bottle of the stuff? And could you ask someone to bring me up the wicker basket and the cardboard box I left in the caleche, and have them put in my room. But don't unwrap them. It's a surprise. And have them bring me some hot water too. I need to change my clothes. There was so much dust on the road!'

And when Barrolo hurried plumply off, whistling, Gonçalo said:

'You two make a splendidly harmonious couple. And you really do seem to have filled out. I honestly thought I was going to have a nephew. Whereas Barrolo seems slimmer and lighter on his feet.'

'Well, he walks more now and rides too and doesn't tend to drop off to sleep after supper so much.'

'And what about the rest of the family? Aunt Arminda? The Mendonças? And what's happened to that saintly man Father Soeiro?'

'He had a slight attack of rheumatism, nothing serious though, and now he's fine. He spends all his time in the library at the Bishop's Palace. Apparently, he's writing a book about bishops.'

'Yes, I know, a history of the cathedral in Oliveira. Well, I've been working hard too, Gracinha. I'm writing a Novel.'

'Really?'

'A short Novel, a Novella, for the *Annals of Literature and History*, a journal founded by a friend of mine, Castanheiro. It's about an event from our family's past, about an ancestor of ours, Tructesindo, long, long ago.'

'What fun, and what did he do?'

'Oh, some truly dreadful things, but it's all terribly picturesque. And I describe the House of Santa Ireneia in the twelfth century in all its glory! It's a beautiful reconstruction of old Portugal, and especially, of the old Ramires family. You'll love it. There are no romances, only wars; no, there is one romance from the remote past, involving one of our ancestors, Dona Menda, although I'm not even sure she really existed. Interesting, eh? I still want to get into politics, you see, but first I need to get into the public eye, to get my name known ...'

Gracinha was smiling sweetly at her brother, charmed as ever.

'Have you any ideas about how to do that? Aunt Arminda still insists you should become a diplomat. Only a few days ago, she was saying, "Ah, Gonçalinho is so handsome and from such a noble family, he really belongs in a big embassy somewhere!"'

Gonçalo slowly levered himself out of the vast sofa, rebuttoning his jacket.

'I do have an idea actually, something I've been thinking about for a while now. Perhaps I got the idea from an English novel I'm reading, *King Solomon's Mines*. It's really interesting. I can recommend it. Yes, I'm considering going off to Africa.'

'Oh, Gonçalo, no! To Africa?'

The butler came in bearing on a tray two bottles of Vidago water, both uncorked. Quickly, to get the benefit of the 'fizz', Gonçalo filled an enormous cut-glass tumbler with the water. So delicious! And when Barrolo returned, saying that he had carried out all His Excellency's orders, Gonçalo said:

'We'll talk about it more over lunch, Gracinha! Now, I'm going to have a wash and change my clothes. I'm so itchy from all that dust!'

Barrolo accompanied his brother-in-law to his room, one of the brightest and most spacious in the house, the walls lined with canary-yellow creton, and with a balcony that looked out over the garden and two windows that gave onto Rua das Tecedeiras and the old trees growing in the garden of the convent next door. Gonçalo impatiently took off his jacket and shook out his waistcoat:

'You look splendid, Barrolo! You've lost a few pounds, which must be the pounds Gracinha has gained. If you carry on like that, you'll be the perfectly balanced couple.'

Standing before the mirror, Barrolo was stroking his waistline, a delighted smile on his face:

'Yes, I do believe I have lost weight. My trousers feel looser.'

Gonçalo had opened the exquisite chest of drawers with gilt handles where he always kept some clothes (even two tailcoats), to avoid having to bring luggage back and forth between there and the Tower. And he was cheerily advising Barrolo to continue 'the slimming process' for the sake of the future Barrolic race, when down below, in silent Rua das Tecedeiras, the hooves of a pedigree horse came clattering over the cobbles.

Immediately suspicious, Gonçalo ran to the window, still holding the clean shirt he was unfolding. It was *him*! It was André Cavaleiro, reining in his horse, as it gracefully, loudly picked its way over the uneven cobblestones. Gonçalo turned to Barrolo, his face aflame with anger:

'This is pure provocation! If that shameless Cavaleiro rides past these windows one more time on that wretched nag of his, I'll douse him with a bucket of dirty water!'

Barrolo peered anxiously out.

'He's probably going to visit the Lousadas. He's very good friends with them now. I often see him riding past, but that's where he's going.'

'He can go to Hell for all I care! Do you mean that, in the whole town, this is the only road that leads to the Lousadas' house? Twice in half an hour! The insolent cur! That great hairy head of his *and* his moustaches will get a good dousing of soapy water, or my name's not Ramires and I'm not my father's son!'

Barrolo was nervously pinching the skin on his neck, troubled by these rancorous words that so spoiled his peace. On Gonçalo's insistence, he had already reluctantly broken off with Cavaleiro, and now he could foresee some quarrel—some scandal—that would turn all Cavaleiro's friends against him, excluding him from the club and from the sweet pleasures of the town's cafés, which would make Oliveira even more tedious than his estates in Ribeirinha or Murtosa in their awful solitude. Unable to contain himself, he risked saying what he always said:

'Why all this fuss, and about something as trivial as politics?'

Gonçalo put his glass down on the marble-topped washstand so hard that it almost broke.

'Politics! What has politics got to do with it? You don't go throwing dirty water over governors because of politics. Besides, he isn't a politician, he's just a scoundrel, and what's more ...'

He went no further, but merely shrugged and fell silent, and poor dim-witted Barrolo stared at him open-mouthed, for whenever he saw Cavaleiro passing the house, he saw only 'the fine horse' or 'the shortest route to the Lousadas' house'.

'Right,' Gonçalo said, 'off you go. I need to get dressed. Leave that moustachioed fellow to me.'

'I'll see you shortly, then. But if he rides past again, no horseplay, eh?'

'Only justice—by the bucketful!'

And he closed the door on a resigned Barrolo, who walked off down the corridor, sighing and regretting Gonçalinho's quick temper and the disproportionate rage provoked by politics.

While he was furiously soaping himself before getting dressed in equally angry haste, Gonçalo pondered Cavaleiro's intolerable, scandalous behaviour. The moment he arrived in Oliveira, Fate had decreed that he would find, wheeling about beneath Gracinha's windows, that man with his great mop of hair mounted on that nag of his with its equally thick mane. What he found most depressing was that he could see in Gracinha's poor, tender, weak heart a stubborn remnant of love for Cavaleiro, deeply buried, yes, but still alive, and which could easily spring into life again. And in the idle town of Oliveira, there was no other strong feeling to protect her, neither her husband's superior love nor the delight of a baby in its cradle. Her only defence was pride, a certain religious respect for the name of Ramires, and fear of that small, nosy, gossipy town. Her only salvation would be to leave the town altogether and shut herself away on one of Barrolo's estates, Ribeirinha or, even better, Murtosa, with its fine woods, its moss-covered convent walls, and a village nearby where she could play the part of the beneficent chatelaine. But Barrolo would never agree to give up his card games at the club, his friends at the Tabacaria Elegante, or Major Ribas' banter.

Overwhelmed by heat and by emotion, Gonçalo opened the balcony doors. Below, on the small tiled garden terrace, edged with flower pots, Gracinha, her hair still hanging loose over her peignoir, was talking to a very tall, very thin lady wearing a sailor's hat decked with poppies and holding in her arms a large bunch of roses.

It was his 'cousin', Maria Mendonça—the wife of José Mendonça, who had been to school with Barrolo in Amarante and was now the captain of the cavalry regiment stationed in Oliveira. She was the daughter of a certain Dom António, the owner (now Viscount) of the Severim estate, and obsessed with noble family connections and origins, she always managed to find a tenuous link between the vaguely aristocratic Severim estate and all the noble houses of Portugal, especially to her great glee, with the great House of Ramires; indeed, as soon as the regiment arrived in Oliveira, she had begun addressing Gracinha familiarly as 'tu' and addressing Gonçalo as 'cousin' with the particular intimacy of those with superior blood in their veins. She also cultivated close friendships with some wealthy Brazilian ladies resident in Oliveira, and even with the widow Pinho, who owned a draper's shop and, who, according to local gossip, kept Maria's two small children supplied with trousers and jackets. She was also on intimate terms with Dona Ana Lucena, both in the town and in the country. Gonçalo, however, enjoyed her wit, her sharpness, the mischievous vivacity that made her positively crackle, like a log on the fire aflame with good cheer. And at the sound above of the stiff window creaking open, she looked up with bright, intelligent eyes, and it was, for both of them, a moment of fond surprise:

'Cousin Maria! What a pleasure to arrive and open my window and find you waiting there!

'For me too, cousin Gonçalo. Why, I haven't seen you since your return from Lisbon. And that moustache makes you look even handsomer.'

'People do say that I'm extraordinarily handsome now, positively irresistible! I would even advise cousin Maria not to come too close—you might catch fire.'

She let her arms, and the heavy bunch of flowers, hang disconsolately by her sides.

'Oh dear, then I am lost, because I have just this moment promised cousin Graça that I will come and dine with you tonight! Gracinha, you'll have to put a screen between us!'

Hanging over the balustrade, delighted by cousin Maria's playful comments, Gonçalo cried:

'No, don't worry, I'll put a lampshade on my head so as not to dazzle anyone! And how is your dear husband and the little ones? How is the whole noble flock?'

'Oh, surviving, with a little bread and by the good grace of God. Anyway, I will see you later, cousin Gonçalo. And remember, be merciful!'

And he was still delightedly laughing when cousin Maria—after exchanging a few whispered words with Gracinha and planting two hasty kisses on her cheeks—had, with her usual slender elegance, disappeared through the French doors. Gracinha proceeded slowly up the three marble steps from the little terrace into the garden. From the balcony, through the web of branches and along the avenues of box hedges, Gonçalo could still see her white peignoir and her long loose hair, gleaming in the sunlight like a cascade of jet. Then the glossy black hair and the white lace vanished beneath the laurels flanking the path that led to the gazebo.

Gonçalo still did not move from the window, vaguely filing his nails and peering suspiciously out from behind the curtains, his mind full of something akin to dread lest Cavaleiro should appear again on his wretched nag, now that Gracinha had plunged into the greenery at the far end of the garden, near the cosy gazebo—an eighteenth-century imitation of a miniature Temple of Love—that looked out over Rua das Tecedeiras. However, no sound broke the silence beneath the long shadows cast by the trees either there or in the convent opposite. And at last, he decided to go downstairs, ashamed of his espionage and convinced that his sister would not show herself to Cavaleiro, and certainly not like that, with her hair hanging loose over her white peignoir.

Then, just as he was closing the door to his room, he found himself in the arms of Father Soeiro, who grasped him fondly and respectfully about the waist.

'Oh, Father Soeiro, how could you be so ungrateful!' cried Gonçalo, affectionately patting the chaplain's plump back. 'How could you be so cruel? You haven't visited the Tower for a whole month! Gonçalinho, I see, no longer exists for you now, only Gracinha ...'

With his small, meek eyes almost brimming with tears, eyes that seemed still darker in the context of his fresh, pink, chubby face and his head of white-as-cotton hair, Father Soeira was clearly touched, folding his hands over his woollen cassock, from which there peeped one corner of a red-checked handkerchief. It had certainly not been for lack of wanting to that he had failed to visit the Tower, but there was his work at the Bishop's Palace, and then that minor bout of rheumatism, and besides Senhora Dona Graça had been expecting a visit from the Nobleman for days and days now ...

'That's all right, then,' said Gonçalo gaily, 'just as long as your heart has not forgotten the Tower.'

'Ah, as if it could!' murmured Father Soeiro, full of grave emotion.

And as they walked along the blue-painted corridor, adorned with coloured engravings illustrating the battles of Napoleon, Gonçalo gave him a summary of all the Tower news.

'There was, as you know, Father, that whole scandalous business with Relho, which has actually turned out to be a blessing in disguise, because, just a few days ago, I rented out the land to Pereira, for one thousand one hundred and fifty *mil-réis*.'

Pausing before taking a pinch of snuff from a silver gilt snuffbox, the chaplain stood staring at the Nobleman in amazement.

'You see, sir, that is how rumours start. Because here, the story is that you had reached an agreement with José Casco, José Casco of Bravais. In fact, over lunch on Sunday, Senhora Dona Graça ...'

'Yes,' the Nobleman broke in, his fine features flushing red.

'Casco did come to the Tower and we did talk. First he wanted it and then he didn't. You know what Casco's like. Anyway, it was all left rather up in the air, and nothing was decided. And when, out of the blue, Pereira appeared with his proposal, I felt under no obligation to Casco, and, as you can imagine, I gladly accepted the offer. A big increase in the rent and with Pereira as the lessee. You know Pereira, don't you, Father?'

'Oh, he's certainly very capable,' agreed the chaplain, awkwardly scratching his chin. 'There's no doubt about that. And he's an excellent fellow. And if, as you say, no firm agreement had been reached with Cas ...'

'Pereira's coming to Oliveira next week,' said Gonçalo, interrupting him. 'If you could warn the notary Guedes, then we can get the papers signed. The conditions are the usual ones. I think there's one new clause needed concerning vegetables and a pig. But you're sure to receive a letter from Pereira.'

And as they went down the stairs, Gonçalo smoothed his moustache with a perfumed handkerchief and joked with the chaplain about the *Fado of the Ramires* and his collaboration with Videirinha. Father Soeiro had certainly furnished Videirinha with some wonderful legends, but he had perhaps gone a little too far with the one about Saint Aldonça, with four kings carrying her coffin on their shoulders!

'That's far too many kings, Father!'

The good chaplain protested, immediately grave and serious, in his love for that song glorifying the House.

'You'll forgive me, sir, but it is entirely accurate. Father Guedes do Amaral describes just that in his *Ladies of the Court of Heaven*, a very rare and beautiful book that Senhor José Barrolo happens to have in his library. The author doesn't specify which kings, but he definitely says there were four of them ... "On the shoulders of four kings and accompanied by many counts." José Videira said he couldn't include the counts on account of the rhyme.'

The Nobleman laughed as he hung the straw hat he had brought down with him on a hook at the bottom of the stairs.

'So the poor counts were lost on account of the rhyme! But it's a lovely *fado*. I've brought a copy with me for Gracinha to sing at the piano. And another thing, Father, what do people here have to say about the governor, Senhor André Cavaleiro?'

The chaplain shrugged, carefully unfolding his vast red-check handkerchief.

'As you are aware, sir, I know nothing of politics. Nor do I frequent cafés, which is where people discuss politics, but he does appear to be popular.'

In the corridor, a fat footman with bushy red side whiskers rang the bell for lunch. Gonçalo had not seen the man before, and, assuming he was new to the job, he informed him that Senhora Dona Maria da Graça was still at the bottom of the garden.

'She has just come in, Senhor Dom Gonçalo,' the footman said. 'She even asked me to ask Your Excellency if you wanted a glass of *vinho verde* from Vidainhos with your lunch.'

Of course he did! Then, smiling, Gonçalo said:

'Father Soeiro, would you tell that new footman not to bother with the *Dom*, I am, thank God, just plain Gonçalo!'

The chaplain murmured that, in documents from the First Dynasty, all the Ramires men still appeared with the title *Dom*. When Gonçalo stopped by the door leading into the dining room, the old man, with his scrupulous, reverent respect for ceremony, bowed and waited for the Nobleman to go first.

'Please, Father Soeiro!'

But the chaplain, with deep respect, said:

'Please, sir, after you ...'

Gonçalo drew back the door curtain and gave the chaplain a very gentle push:

'Father Soeiro, it is stated in the documents of the First Dynasty that saints never follow behind sinners!'

'You give the orders, sir, and always so charmingly too.'

At about three o'clock one afternoon, following Gracinha's birthday, Gonçalo was returning with Father Soeiro from a visit to the library in the Bishop's Palace, when he heard Titó's loud voice issuing from the parlour, rumbling around the blue room like slow thunder. Quickly pulling back the door curtain, he shook his fist at the huge man occupying one of the large gilt armchairs, with his new boots and their gleaming studs planted firmly on the floral rug.

'You wretch! How dare you just abandon me like that, without a flicker of conscience, after I'd had a delicious spit-roast goat especially prepared for you, cooked, what's more, on a cherry-wood spit. And why? Simply in order to attend some base orgy complete with rissoles and firecrackers!'

Titó's look of cosy beatitude remained unchanged.

'I had no option. I met João Gouveia at the fountain that afternoon, and only then did we remember that it was Dona Casimira's birthday, which is utterly sacred!'

Barrolo was always fascinated by and envious of those suppers in Vila Clara, those 'wild nights' with guitar accompaniment that often went on into the small hours. And looking up brightly from the corner of the table where he was carefully crumbling tobacco into a Japanese box, he asked:

'Who is Dona Casimira? You two know some very rum types in Vila Clara. Go on, who is she?'

'Oh, she's a monster!' cried Gonçalo. 'A vast matron, round as a barrel, and with a horribly bristly chin. She lives next to the cemetery in a hovel that stinks of lamp-oil, where this gentleman and other people in positions of authority go to play cards and flirt with floozies wearing short red jackets and with their hair all over the place. Hardly the kind of place one can speak of decently in the presence of Father Soeiro!'

The chaplain, who had discreetly withdrawn into the shadows between the fringed satin curtains and an imposing Indian cabinet, merely shrugged and smiled, as if he were perfectly accustomed to hearing about even the most heinous of sins. And Titó painstakingly corrected the Nobleman's grotesque sketch.

'Dona Casimira may be fat, but she's very clean. Why only today she asked me to buy her a new sitz-bath while I'm in town. The house doesn't smell of lamp-oil and it's behind the Convent of Santa Teresa not the cemetery. The floozies are her nieces, two very jolly girls who enjoy a laugh and a joke. And Father Soeiro could, without fear ...'

'All right, all right,' Gonçalo cried, interrupting him. 'They're delightful people! But let's forget about Dona Casimira, who will now have a new sitz-bath for her nether regions. No, let us pass on to yet another of Senhor António Vilalobos' infamies!'

But Barrolo insisted, full of curiosity:

'No, no, tell us about the birthday party, Tító. I bet you had a high old time of it.'

'No, it was a quiet little supper,' Tító said, with all the seriousness he felt was due to his friends' party. 'Dona Casimira provided us with some delicious roast chicken served with peas, and João Gouveia brought a dish of rissoles from Gago's, which went down very well indeed. Then, after fireworks in the garden, Videirinha played his guitar, and the girls sang. So, not a bad night at all.'

Gonçalo waited, still irresistibly intrigued by that supper at Dona Casimira's house. Then he said:

'All right, are we done with that? Now to the other still worse infamy. It seems that Senhor António Vilalobos is a close friend of Sanches Lucena, that he visits Feitosa every week, takes tea and toast with the lovely Dona Ana, and keeps his other friends completely in the dark about all these glorious privileges!'

'Not to mention,' declared Barrolo, who was enjoying himself enormously, 'taking someone's fluffy little lapdogs for a walk on the lead!'

Tító shifted his vast bulk in the armchair, drew in his gleaming, studded boots, and slowly stroked his bearded face, which was turning rather hot and pink. Then looking Gonçalo straight in the eye, in an attempt at slyness that only made him blush all the more, he said:

'Have you ever once asked me if I knew Sanches Lucena? No, you never have.'

The Nobleman protested. No, he'd never asked, but whenever they talked politics—at the club, at Gago's, at the Tower—they were constantly bandying about Sanches Lucena's name! Surely the natural, indeed prudent, thing would have been for Senhor Tító to reveal so illustrious a friendship? If only to avoid the Nobleman, or his friends, from insulting Sanches Lucena in the presence of Senhor Titó, who had, after all, eaten his toast!

Titó got up from his armchair. Then, plunging his hands into his jacket pockets and giving a nonchalant shrug, he said:

'Everyone's entitled to his opinion about Sanches. I've only known the man for a few months, but I find him both serious and knowledgeable. As for how he performs in Parliament, that's another matter ...'

Gonçalo declared indignantly that they weren't discussing the merits of Senhor Sanches Lucena, but the secrets of Senhor Titó Vilalobos! Then the new footman, poking his red side whiskers through a gap in the curtains, announced that the local administrator was asking if Their Excellencies were ...

Barrolo immediately abandoned his tobacco-crumbling, crying:

'Senhor João Gouveia! Show him in. Now the whole Vila Clara gang's here!'

From the window where he had taken refuge, and in a voice intended to drown out that importunate conversation about Sanches Lucena and Feitosa, Titó thundered forth:

'Yes, we travelled here together in a really rackety old carriage, and one of the nags even lost a shoe and we had to stop in Vendinha. Not that this was a complete waste of time, mind, because they serve a white wine there that's simply out of this world!'

He was tugging at his earlobe and noisily advising Barrolo and Gonçalo to go to Vendinha and sample a drop of that celestial delight.

'Even Father Soeiro might be tempted to try a glass, however sinful!'

At this point, João Gouveia entered, looking hot and dusty, with a red line on his forehead left by his hat and the heat, and dressed entirely in black—black frockcoat, black trousers and black gloves. Too out of breath to speak, he went silently around the room, shaking the hands of the friends greeting him. Then he collapsed onto the sofa, begging Barrolo to be so kind as to bring him a cool drink.

'I almost went into Café Mónaco, then it occurred to me that the Barrolo household would have far more trustworthy beverages.'

'Of course. What would you like? Horchata? Sangría? Lemonade?'

'Sangría, please.'

And wiping the sweat from his neck and brow, he cursed the dreadful heat of Oliveira!

'Mind you, it seems some people positively enjoy it. My boss, for example—the governor—always chooses to go out on his horse at the hottest time of the day. Even today. He was in the office until noon, then he had his horse brought round and headed off along the road to Ramilde, which is as hot as Africa. I'm surprised his brains didn't fry!'

'Oh, that's easy enough to explain,' said Gonçalo. 'He has no brains!'

Gouveia responded gravely:

'That's all we need: Senhor Gonçalo Mendes Ramires with one of his barbed comments. Don't let's start, please. Your brother-in-law is a completely untameable beast, Barrolo. He can always be relied on to kick.'

Embarrassed, Barrolo made some comment about Gonçalinho never being known to let a politician off lightly.

'Well, you just listen to me,' said Gouveia, wagging his finger at Gonçalo. 'In the office this morning, that same brainless Senhor André Cavaleiro was speaking in the very highest terms of *your* brains!'

Gonçalo retorted very gravely:

'That really *is* all we need. For the governor to prove his own utter absurdity, he only has to consider me an ass!'

'Excuse me!' cried Gouveia, springing to his feet and unbuttoning his frockcoat, ready for a fight.

In his alarm, Barrolo rushed over and placed his hands on Gouveia's shoulders to calm him and persuade him to sit back down on the sofa.

'Now, boys, no politics, all right? And no more bickering about

Cavaleiro. Let's get back to really important matters. Are you having supper with us tonight, João Gouveia?'

'No, thank you. I've promised to dine with Cavaleiro. Inácio Vilhena will be there too. He's going to read us an article he's written for the *Boletim de Guimarães* about some moulds for making martyrs' bones that were apparently discovered during work being carried out in the Monastery of São Bento. I'm curious to know more. But tell me, how is Senhora Dona Graça? Well, I hope. The other person I haven't seen for months is you, Father Soeiro—you never visit the Tower any more! But you seem to be in fine fettle still. What's the secret of your eternal youth?'

In his corner, the chaplain smiled shyly. His secret? Live life quietly, and don't waste it on ambitions or disappointments. For him—praise God—life flowed by very simply and very humbly. And were it not for his rheumatism ...

Then, blushing with embarrassment while uttering these evangelical precepts, he went on:

'But not even my rheumatism is wasted. It comes from God, for reasons he alone knows, and with suffering comes edification, because what we suffer makes us think about what others suffer.'

With blithe incredulity, Gouveia said:

'I have to say that whenever I have a bad throat, I never think of other people's throats! I think only of my own, which gives me quite enough to worry about. And now I'm going to treat it to some of that excellent sangría.'

The footman bent down to offer him the gleaming silver platter laden with glasses of sangría bobbing with slices of lemon. And then they all took a glass, even Father Soeiro, simply to demonstrate to Senhor António Vilalobos that he did not despise God's kindly gift of wine, because Tibullus, even though he was a pagan, was quite right when he said, '*vinus facit dites animos, mollia corda dat*' or 'wine strengthens the soul and softens the heart'.

Draining his glass, João Gouveia gave a contented sigh and replacing the glass on the tray, asked the Nobleman:

'So what's this fantastic tale about a party being held at the Tower, with ladies present, including Dona Ana Lucena? I didn't believe a word of it when Gago's boy found me and gave me the message. Then …'

From his refuge behind the curtains, Tító, who had also just finished his sangria, addressed another question to the Nobleman in his usual booming tones:

'And Barrolo tells me you're planning to head off to Africa? Is this true?'

João Gouveia's shock was mingled almost with terror. To Africa? Did Gonçalo have a job in Africa?

'No, he's going to plant coconut palms, cocoa and coffee!' exclaimed Barrolo, slapping his thigh, vastly amused.

Tító approved of the idea. If he himself could get enough capital together, say, ten or fifteen *contos*, he would go off to Africa as well and trade with the blacks. If, that is, he were only smaller and thinner, because heavily-built men like him require a lot of food and a lot of wine, and would never survive Africa. They'd die!

'Gonçalo would be fine, though. He's lean and tough enough. He doesn't overdo the brandy either, so he's perfectly suited for a career as an African adventurer. And that's a damn sight better than that other career he's so keen on, becoming a deputy! Whatever for? To prowl the corridors of power and kowtow to ministers?'

Barrolo enthusiastically agreed. He couldn't understand Gonçalo's determination to become a deputy either! What could be more tedious, what with all the plotting, the insults in the press, the mud-slinging. Not to mention having to put up with the people who elected you.

'I wouldn't do it even if they appointed me governor afterwards, and gave me a title and hung a medal round my neck, which is exactly what happened to Freixomil!'

Gonçalo listened to all this in smug, superior silence, laboriously rolling a cigarette from Barrolo's newly crumbled tobacco.

'No, you just don't understand. You don't know how Portugal works. Ask Gouveia. Portugal is an estate, a beautiful estate, owned by a partnership. As you know there are commercial partnerships and rural ones. The Lisbon partnership is a political one, which governs the estate called Portugal. We Portuguese divide into two classes: the five or six million who work on the estate or, like Barrolo, live on it and enjoy the view and pay for the privilege; and the thirty or so individuals at the top, in Lisbon, who make up the partnership that receives all the taxes and governs. Well, I would like to run the estate, whether simply because I want to or out of necessity or pure familial habit, I don't know. But to get into the political partnership, the Portuguese citizen needs a qualification, namely, becoming a deputy. Just as you need a law degree if you want to be a lawyer. That's why I'm trying to begin by becoming a deputy, so that I can join the political partnership and govern. Isn't that right, João Gouveia?'

Gouveia had returned to the sangría tray and was already enjoying another glass, not downing it in one, but sipping it slowly now.

'Yes, that's how it works. Candidate, deputy, politician, counsellor, minister, mandarin—certainly a better career than heading off to Africa. After all, they grow cocoa in the Lisbon ministries too, and it's so much shadier!'

Barrolo had meanwhile joined Titó in the window bay—since they were of the same opinion—and was standing with his arm around his friend's imposing shoulder. He said jokingly:

'I don't belong to either of those two factions, but I govern the bits of Portugal that most interest me, the bits I own! And I'd like to see them—São Fulgêncio or Brás Vitorino or any other politicians in Lisbon—try to take control of my land, either Ribeirinha or Murtosa. I'd shoot them first!'

Leaning against the window, Titó was thoughtfully stroking his beard.

'Well, all right, Barrolo, but you still have to pay the taxes they demand—you have to accept whoever they appoint to the local council. And you only have roads if they see fit to make them. Depending on the laws they vote in, you sell your wheat and your wine for more or less of a profit. And so on and so on. Gonçalo is right. The ghastly truth is that those who make the laws also make the biggest profits. My landlord in Vila Clara, the swine, is planning to increase my rent at Michaelmas, on a tiny house that no one wants because the executioner was murdered there, and he still puts in an occasional appearance. Meanwhile, Cavaleiro lives for free in the beautiful Palace of São Domingos, with a coach house, a garden, a vegetable patch ...'

Afraid that Titó's loud proclamation of the privileges enjoyed by Cavaleiro might reignite Gonçalo's wrath, Barrolo held up one hand, trying to hush the giant's booming voice. The Nobleman, however, appeared not to have heard, for he was still listening to João Gouveia, who, sitting slumped on the sofa after all that san-gría, was once again describing his astonishment at meeting Gago's boy by the fountain in Vila Clara and being told about the grand party about to be held at the Tower.

'And when it struck nine o'clock, and Titó had still not turned up for supper at Dona Casimira's, I even began to think that per-haps you really *were* giving a party. Maybe he had received the same message and raced off to the Tower! It was only when he ap-peared at Dona Casimira's, in a short hooded jacket, that I under-stood it was Senhor Dom Gonçalo's little joke.'

The Nobleman was assailed by a strange, unexpected suspicion: 'Titó was wearing a hooded jacket?'

But from his post at the window, Barrolo suddenly gave a ter-rified cry:

'Oh, Heaven help us! The Lousada sisters are coming!' João Gou-veia leapt off the sofa hurriedly buttoning up his frockcoat, as if he were in mortal danger; in his panic, Gonçalo collided with Titó and Barrolo, who, afraid they might be seen, had hastily drawn back from the window; even prudent Father Soeiro abandoned his corner, where he had been leafing through the *Gazeta do Porto*. And like soldiers at an arrow slit in a castle, they all stood peering through a gap in the curtains at the square below, golden in the four o'clock sun. The two Lousada sisters—very brisk and scrawny, both wearing short, beaded, black silk capes and both carrying faded, checkered parasols—were advancing along the far side of Rua das Pegas, casting two sharp shadows on the flagstones.

The two Lousada sisters! Thin and dark and as garrulous as cica-das, they had, for many a long year in Oliveira, been the scrutineers of everyone's life, the spreaders of all malicious gossip, the weavers of all intrigues. And in the whole unfortunate town there was not a stain, defect, cracked teapot, broken heart, empty pocket, half-open window, dusty crevice, figure lurking on a corner, brand-new hat worn to mass, or cake ordered from the Matildes cake shop, that their four piercing, jet-black eyes had not detected, and on which their loose tongues, in their near toothless mouths, had not commented with sibilant malice! They were the source of all the anonymous letters infesting the town; the very devout considered any visit from them to be a penance, a visit during which they would whitter on for hours, gesticulating with their scraggy arms; and wherever they went, they left behind them the beating pulse of distrust and fear. But who would ever dare turn the Lousada sisters away? They were the daughters of the aged and venerable General Lousada; they were related to the bishop; they were powerful figures in the powerful confraternity of Our Lord of the Stations of the Cross. And their chastity was so iron-clad, so ancient and so withered, and so loudly bruited abroad by them, that Marcolino of *O Independente* had nicknamed them 'The Two Thousand Virgins'.

'No, it's all right,' said Tító, sounding immensely relieved. 'They're not coming here.'

Out in the square, next to the railings that boxed in the old sundial, the two sisters were standing, sniffing the air with their dark snouts and scrutinising the little church of São Mateus, where the bells were ringing out for a baptism.

'Oh, no, devil take it, they *are* coming here!'

Yes, the two sisters were bearing down on the door of the Casa dos Cunhais! Panic ensued. Barrolo's fat, fleeing legs bumped into cabinets and pot-bellied Indian jars and almost knocked them over. Gonçalo shouted to the others that they should all go and hide in the orchard. Gouveia frantically searched for his bowler hat. Only Tító, who loathed the sisters and whom they called Polyphemus, withdrew calmly, offering Father Soeiro his strong arm. And the whole terrified band were just about to rush out of the drawing-room door when Gracinha appeared, wearing a cool, strawberry-coloured silk dress and smiling in astonishment at the throng of men hurrying towards her.

'Whatever's happened?'

A muffled cry greeted the poor, unsuspecting lady:

'It's the Lousada sisters!'

'Oh no!'

Titó and João Gouveia fleetingly shook the hand she held sadly, limply out to them. The door bell clanged loudly. And the unruly crowd, with plump Father Soeiro bringing up the rear, slipped into the library, where Barrolo bolted the door behind them, but first, in a moment of inspiration, called out to Gracinha:

'Hide the sangria!'

Poor Gracinha! Perplexed and with no time to summon the footman, she struggled out into the corridor with the heavy tray and deposited it on a bench, knowing that if the Lousada sisters were to see the tray, they would construct a whole horrific tale of 'heavy drinking and drunkenness', which would loom larger over the town than the tower of São Mateus church. She gave a brief, breathless glance at herself in the mirror, smoothed her hair, and then standing very erect, like a gladiator in the arena, she waited for the two terrible sisters to advance.

The following Sunday, after lunch, Gonçalo accompanied his sister to the house of their aunt Arminda Vilegas, who after ordering her usual footbath on the previous evening, as she did every Saturday, had, alas, scalded herself and taken to her bed in fright, summoning to her bedside a council of Oliveira's five surgeons. And in the afternoon, Gonçalo stood smoking a cigar beneath the acacia trees on the Terreiro da Louça, thinking about the Novella he had left behind him at the Tower and about the famous episode in the second chapter that both tempted and frightened him—the fateful encounter between Lourenço Ramires and Lopo de Baião, known as the Bastard, in the valley of Canta-Pedra. Later, as he was walking back to his sister's house down Rua das Velas (because he had promised Barrolo to go for a ride as far as the pine forest at Estevinha, to take advantage of that gentle, misty Sunday), he spotted the notary Guedes, who was just coming out of Matildes cake shop carrying a large box. Gonçalo lightly crossed the road, and the portly, paunchy Guedes, poised on the edge of the pavement on the tips of his tiny polished boots, bowed very low and took off his hat, revealing his bald head with the famous tuft of greying hair in the middle, like the prow of a ship, which had earned him the nickname 'Guedes Ahoy'.

'Please, my dear Guedes, put your hat back on. How are you? Still young and healthy, I see. Excellent. Have you spoken to Father Soeiro? As it turns out, Pereira will only be coming to town on Wednesday.'

Yes, Father Soeiro had dropped in at the office and he really wanted to congratulate the Nobleman on his new tenant.

'Pereira is such a capable man! I've known him for twenty years, and what he's done with the Count de Monte-Agra's land is quite amazing. I remember that land when it was a wilderness, and now it's in tip-top condition! You only have to look at the vineyard he planted. Yes, a very competent man. And how long are you staying in Oliveira, sir?'

'Only a few days. The heat here is just unbearable, but, fortunately, it's a little cooler today. So what's new in politics? Are you still a good, loyal, ardent Regenerationist?'

Pressing the box of cakes to his black silk waistcoat, the notary angrily shook one short, fat arm, and his sudden indignation sent a wave of blood from his neck to his hairy ears, from his shaven face to his head, and up under the brim of his white hat with its black band.

'Who wouldn't be, Senhor Gonçalo Mendes Ramires? Who wouldn't be, after this latest scandal?'

Gonçalo's smiling eyes grew serious. 'What scandal?'

The notary drew back. Hadn't he heard about the governor's—about Senhor André Cavaleiro's—latest act of despotism?

'What do you mean, my friend?'

Seeming to swell and expand, Guedes drew himself up again on the tips of his tiny boots and exclaimed:

'Poor Noronha has been transferred!'

A lady as portly as Guedes, with a thick growth of hair on her upper lip, who was almost bursting out of her rich, rustling Sunday-best silks and dragging by the hand a bawling child, stopped and stared at him, because—with his belly, his box of cakes and his indignation—the worthy man was blocking the entrance to the shop. The Nobleman hurriedly opened the door to the shop for her. Then he asked excitedly:

'No doubt you're on your way home. Well, I'm heading that way too. We can talk as we walk. But which Noronha do you mean?'

'Ricardo Noronha. You must know him. He's the paymaster at the Public Works Office!'

'Ah, yes. So he's been transferred, you say, quite arbitrarily?'

They continued on down Rua das Brocas, and in the silence and solitude of the closed shops, Guedes gave full vent to his anger:

'He's been treated abominably, sir, absolutely abominably! He's been moved to Almodóvar, to the outer reaches of the Alentejo! To a place with no resources, no amusements, and no families!'

He stopped, the box of cakes still pressed to his heart and his little glittering, bulging eyes fixed on the Nobleman. Noronha! An honest, hardworking employee! And with no interest in politics at all. He supported neither the Historicals nor the Regenerationists. He cared only for his family, his three sisters, those three flowers, for whom he was the sole support. He was highly respected in the town and so gifted too. Yes, he was a talented musician. Did Senhor Gonçalo not know? Well, he had composed some lovely pieces for the piano! And he was such an asset at gatherings and at birthday parties. He was also the moving force behind any amateur dramatic productions in Oliveira ...

'Because, as a director, no one can compare, sir, not even in Lisbon. No one! And then he's despatched to Almodóvar, to that Inferno, along with his sisters and their few belongings! To transport the piano would cost a fortune!'

Gonçalo glowed with pleasure.

'An utter scandal! But I'm so glad you told me, Guedes. And does anyone know the reason for his transfer?'

They resumed their slow walk along the narrow pavement, and the notary shrugged bitterly. As always with these despotic moves, the reason given was that it was in the public interest.

'But all of Noronha's friends know the real reason, the true, vile, secret reason!'

'Which is?'

Guedes glanced prudently about him. An old lady came limping past, carrying a pitcher of water, and then the notary whispered darkly into the Nobleman's expectant ear. 'It's because that scoundrel Senhor André Cavaleiro had taken a fancy to the oldest of the Noronha sisters, Dona Adelina—a beautiful young thing, tall and dark and statuesque! And when he's rejected (because the sensible girl, a real pearl among women, realised that his intentions were far from honourable), who does he take his revenge on, out of sheer spite? The paymaster! Off he's sent to Almodóvar with the girls and their few belongings! Yes, it's the paymaster who has to pay!'

'Shameless!' muttered Gonçalo, smiling and delighted. 'What's more,' exclaimed Guedes, holding one fat, trembling hand above his hat. 'Only weeks ago, poor Noronha, in his innocence—for he's a good man, who always tries to please his superiors—had composed a lovely waltz which he dedicated to Cavaleiro! He called it *The Butterfly*, a real little gem!'

Gonçalo could not contain his glee, rubbing his hands together in triumph.

'Yes, utterly, divinely shameless! And hasn't anyone spoken out? Has the opposition newspaper, *O Clarim de Oliveira*, made no mention of it, however glancing?'

Guedes hung his head. Senhor Gonçalo Ramires knew what the people who worked there were like. They were all style—ornate, opulent style—but when it came to making public a really serious case like that of Noronha, they lacked the necessary nerve, the courage. And meanwhile, Biscainho, the editor, had slyly changed his allegiance to the Historicals. Did Senhor Gonçalo Mendes Ramires not know? Yes, that abject creature, Biscainho, had changed sides. Cavaleiro had probably offered him a post somewhere. Besides, how could they prove that anything untoward had taken place? These were private matters, family matters. They could hardly publish a statement from Dona Adelina, a young woman of the highest virtue—and with such eyes too! Ah, if this had happened in the days of Manuel Justino and his newspaper *A Aurora de Oliveira*, he would have printed it on the front page in large letters: '*Civil Governor Attempts to Dishonour the Noronha Family!*'

'Now, Justino was a real man, but the poor man's lying in the cemetery of São Miguel! And despotism, sir, is rampant!'

He was panting, his chest heaving, exhausted by this fiery outburst. In silence, they continued on down to the corner of the newly paved Rua da Princesa Dona Amélia. Guedes stopped at the second door and took out his key, and, still breathing hard, asked if Gonçalo would like to come in and rest.

'No, no, thank you, my friend, I won't, but I'm so very glad we met. This story about Noronha is really shocking, but then nothing I hear about the governor surprises me any more. The only thing that does surprise me is that he hasn't been run out of town, as he deserves to be, with the crowds whipping and booing him! But, be assured, not all the good people are lying in the cemetery. I'll see you tomorrow, Guedes. And thank you!'

Gonçalo ran all the way from Rua da Princesa Dona Amélia to Largo d'El-Rei, as excited as someone who's just discovered a treasure and is carrying it under his cape! And he was carrying that scandal with him, the ripe scandal he had so longed for! That he had been trying to sniff out in order to remove the governor from the loyal town of Oliveira that had greeted him with such pomp! And, by God's mercy, that 'ripe scandal' would also demolish the man in Gracinha's heart, where, despite his earlier crimes, he still lingered like a worm in an apple, burrowing away and spoiling the fruit. And Gonçalo had no doubts about the efficacy of that scandal! The whole town would rise up against that womaniser for sending into cruel exile an admirable civil servant, simply because the poor gentleman's sister had refused to accept his slobbering kisses. And Gracinha? How could she not be shocked and repelled by the thought of 'her' André burning with passion for one of the Noronha sisters, who had spurned his advances? Oh, it really was a *superb* scandal! All that was needed was for it to break, very loudly, over the rooftops of Oliveira and over Gracinha's heart, like a beneficent thunderstorm cleansing the corrupt air. And he would gladly be the one to unleash that storm over the whole of the north of the country. And thus, with a few deft penstrokes, he would be working *pro patria et pro domo*.

Once back at the house, he ran to Barrolo's room—where Barrolo was humming the *Ramires fado* and getting ready for his ride—and shouted resolutely through the door:

'I can't go with you to Estevinha. I have something very urgent to write. And don't come up to see me either. I need to be alone!'

He didn't even respond to his brother-in-law's desolate protests when Barrolo rushed out into the corridor in his long underpants. Gonçalo bounded up the stairs and, once in his room, having quickly removed his jacket and sprayed his forehead with a little refreshing eau de Cologne, he sat down at his desk, where Gracinha always placed some flowers and the huge inkstand that had belonged to their Uncle Melchior, just in case Gonçalo wanted to work. He did not hesitate or make a first draft, for the prose flowed passionately from his pen as he improvised a rancorous letter to the *Gazeta do Porto*, denouncing the governor. Even the title blazed forth: *A Monstrous Assault!* Without actually naming the Noronha family, he described in detail, as if he himself had witnessed it, 'the base, despicable assault by the highest authority in the region on the chastity, peace of mind and honour of a sweet young girl of sixteen!' Then he described the scornful rebuff given by the noble creature to that administrative Don Juan, whose fine moustaches were the wonder of the town! Finally, he came to 'the vile, unspeakable revenge that His Excellency has taken on his hardworking employee (who also happens to be a talented artist), arranging for this disastrous Government to have him transferred or, rather, uprooted and cruelly exiled, along with his three delicate sisters, to the farthest reaches of the Kingdom, to the bleakest and most arid of our provinces, simply because he could not legitimately pack him off to Africa in the filthy hold of a frigate!' He threw in a few gruff comments about Portugal being in its, 'political death throes'. With horror and sadness, he recalled the worst days of Absolutism, with innocence interred in dungeons and the Prince's wild excesses as the only letter of the Law! And he concluded by asking the Government if it would cover up for this agent of theirs, 'this grotesque Nero, who, as that other more famous Nero once did in Rome, tried to carry out his seductions in the very heart of the best families and, motivated by lust alone, stooped to the kind of abuse of power that has always, in all centuries and in every civilisation, been condemned by the just!' Then he signed the letter *Juvenal*.

It was almost six o'clock in the evening when he came down to the drawing room, feeling light and resplendent. Gracinha was banging away at the piano as she tried to master the *Ramires fado*. And Barrolo (who had not wanted to risk going for a ride on his own) was lying on the sofa, leafing through a famous *History of the Crimes of the Inquisition*, which he had first begun reading when he was still a bachelor.

'I've been working since two o'clock!' cried Gonçalo, flinging wide the window. 'I'm exhausted. I have, however, righted a wrong. This time, the Horseman will definitely fall off his Horse.'

Barrolo immediately shut his book and turning and leaning on one elbow, asked anxiously:

'What happened?'

And standing immediately in front of him, Gonçalo snickered and jingled the money and keys in his pocket.

'Oh, not very much. A mere trifle. Or, rather, a truly shameful act, but then to our governor shameful acts *are* mere trifles.'

Beneath Gracinha's fingers, the *fado* dwindled to an uncertain murmur.

Barrolo was waiting, open-mouthed:

'Come on, tell us!'

Gonçalo gleefully revealed all.

'An absolute scandal! Noronha, poor Noronha, persecuted, humiliated, exiled! Along with his family too. Consigned to the Inferno, almost to the Algarve!'

'Noronha the paymaster?'

'Yes, Noronha the paymaster, a poor unfortunate paymaster who has himself been made to pay!'

And with great relish, he unfolded the whole wretched tale to them. Senhor André Cavaleiro was hopelessly in love, aflame with passion for the oldest Noronha sister. He bombarded the young woman with flowers, letters and poems and with his nag's hooves clattering over the cobbles outside her window every morning! It seems he even sent her an old procuress, a bawd, but the girl, who is an angel of propriety, remained utterly unmoved. She didn't even get angry, she just laughed. Over tea, the Noronha household would giggle at the doggerel he had written, in which he called her 'nymph' and 'evening star'. All very sordid and grotesque!'

The poor *fado* broke down on the keyboard into a tumult of harsh, discordant groans.

'And to think I've never heard a word about it,' murmured Barrolo in astonishment. 'Not at the club or at the Café da Arcada ...'

'Well, my friend, the person who heard it loud and clear was poor Noronha, banished to the dark depths of the Alentejo, to that insalubrious place, full of swamps. It's a real death sentence!'

At this mention of Death rising up from the swamps, Barrolo slapped his knee and asked suspiciously:

'But who the devil told you all this?'

The Nobleman of the Tower gave his brother-in-law a scornful, pitying look.

'Who told me? Who told me that King Sebastião died at the Battle of Alcácer Quibir? It's a fact. It's history. The whole of Oliveira knows about it. I was just talking about it to Guedes this morning, but I'd already heard, of course. I almost felt sorry for poor André. I mean, it's not a crime to be madly in love. Yes, madly, hopelessly in love! He even broke down at the office apparently, in front of the general secretary! And the girl in question just laughed. No, the crime, and a horrible one at that, is the persecution of her brother, the paymaster, an excellent worker and very talented too. And the duty of any decent man who values the dignity of public office and of society is to denounce such crimes. I, for my part, have done *my* duty. And rather brilliantly too!'

'What have you done?'

'I have plunged my good Toledo pen into the governor's side right up to the very hilt of the nib-holder!'

Impressed, Barrolo was again pinching the skin on his neck. The piano had fallen completely silent, but Gracinha didn't move from her stool, her fingers lying stiffly on the keys, as if she were oblivious to the large sheet before her on which were set out, in Videirinha's careful hand, the triumphal verses in praise of the bold Ramires men. Gonçalo suddenly sensed in her dumb immobility the pain and disappointment that must be piercing her. Touched by this and wanting to free her from that pain, to perhaps prevent a sob from breaking forth, he ran over to the piano and affectionately patted her poor bent, trembling shoulders:

'You still haven't quite got the hang of that lovely *fado*, have you, dear? Let me sing you a verse in Videirinha's style. But, first, be an angel, will you, and call out in the corridor for someone to bring me a nice cool glass of water.'

Fumbling at the piano, he sang in a rather off-key voice:

Forth onto the battlefield
Rode the four brave Ramires men ...

Gracinha had disappeared soundlessly down the corridor. Then Barrolo, who'd been thoughtfully rolling a cigarette, darted to Gonçalo's side and, leaning close, shared the revelation that had been slowly filling his mind:

'I'm telling you, Gonçalo, Noronha's sister is a real stunner, but I can't believe she would repel any man's advances—and certainly not those of a handsome lad like Cavaleiro. I bet you he's *had* her!'

And with his pink cheeks aglow with admiration, he added:

'The rascal. When it comes to horses and women, there's not a man in Oliveira can touch him.'

V

The latest issue of the *Gazeta do Porto*, with that vengeful letter, was due to break over Oliveira on Wednesday morning, the day of cousin Maria Mendonça's birthday. While Gonçalo (protected by his pseudonym *Juvenal*) was not afraid of having some kind of ugly confrontation with Cavaleiro in the streets of the town, or even with one of Cavaleiro's servile bully boys (for instance, Marcolino from *O Independente*), he nevertheless decided to withdraw discreetly to Santa Ireneia on Tuesday, on horseback, with Barrolo accompanying him as far as Vendinha, where both sampled the white wine recommended by Titó. Then, in order to revisit the memorable places where, in his Novella, Lourenço Ramires and the Bastard of Baião so disastrously crossed swords, he took the road that passes through the orchards of the scattered village of Canta-Pedra and leads eventually to the road to Bravais.

He had ridden past the glass factory at a leisurely trot, and then past the cross, a favourite perch for the pigeons fluttering down from the factory's pigeon loft, when, at the window of a very neat little house surrounded by vines, there appeared a pretty, slender, dark-haired girl, wearing a blue jacket and a cheap embroidered chambray scarf over her thick, wavy hair. Reining in his mare, Gonçalo greeted her with a charming smile:

'Excuse me, young lady, is this the way to Canta-Pedra?'

'It is, sir. When you reach the bridge, turn right and head towards the poplars, then it's straight on from there.'

Gonçalo smiled and said jokingly:

'I would much rather stay here.'

The girl blushed, and as he rode on, the Nobleman turned in his saddle to admire her face looking out from between the two pots of carnations on the windowsill of that neat, whitewashed house.

At that moment, a hunter emerged from a shady path leading off from the main road; he was wearing a jacket and a red beret, had a rifle slung over his shoulder, and was followed by two pointers. He was a handsome, strapping fellow, and everything about him oozed arrogance and conceit, from the tread of his large white shoes to his swaggering walk and silk sash, from his fair side whiskers to the haughty way he held his head. He saw the Nobleman's smile and instantly understood his gallant intentions. He stopped and, slowly, arrogantly, fixed him with his fine, thicklashed eyes. Then he walked scornfully past him, making no attempt to move out of the way of the horse, indeed, he almost brushed the Nobleman's leg with the barrel of his rifle. Further on, he pointedly, dismissively cleared his throat, and the click-clack of his boots sounded even more insolent.

Gonçalo spurred on his mare, immediately cowed by fear, by the wretched shiver that always ran through him whenever he was confronted by any danger or threat, and which irresistibly forced him to withdraw, to retreat, to run away. When he reached the bridge, furious at his own timidity, he again reined in his horse and peered cautiously back at the pretty white house. The strapping young fellow was leaning on his rifle, standing by the window where the dark-haired young woman was still looking out from between the two pots of carnations. And glancing up at the girl, the man laughed, and then, head high and with the tassel on his beret sticking up like a fiery crest, he gave the Nobleman a defiant wave.

Gonçalo Mendes Ramires set off at a gallop along the leafy, poplar-lined road that follows the stream known as the *riacho das Donas*, the Ladies' stream. In Canta-Pedra, he did not (as he had intended to do for the benefit of his Novella) pause to study the valley, the winding stream, the ruined monastery, or, on the hill opposite, the windmill that stands on the blackened stones of the ancient and celebrated mansion known as Avelãs. The sky had been heavy and overcast since morning, and was now growing darker over towards Craquede and Vila Clara. A warm breeze stirred the dry leaves, and heavy drops were already pitting the dust when he, still galloping, reached the road to Bravais.

Arriving back at the Tower, he found a letter from Castanheiro.

The Patriot wanted to know if his *Tower of Dom Ramires* was finally being built for the greater glory of literature, just as the other Tower had been built, in more fortunate times, for the greater glory of arms. And he added a postscript, 'I am planning to put posters on every corner of every town in Portugal, announcing in letters a yard high the long-awaited appearance of that redemptive journal, the *Annals*! And since I also intend to promise people your precious little Novella, I need you to tell me if, in 1830s style, it has a tempting subtitle, such as *Episodes from the Twelfth Century* or *Chronicle of the Reign of Afonso II* or *Scenes from Medieval Portugal* ... I do think we need a subtitle. Just as the foundations of a building give it height and solidity, so it is with subtitles. So, my dear Ramires, put your ferocious imagination to work!'

The Nobleman was delighted by the idea of endless numbers of posters bearing his name and the title of his Novella printed in strident colours, pasted on every corner of every town in Portugal. And that night, to the sound of heavy rain beating down on the leaves of the lemon trees, he again took up his manuscript and resumed where he had stopped, at the sonorous, expansive first lines of Chapter II.

In those lines, in the cool of the dawn, Lourenço Mendes Ramires, with his company of horsemen and foot soldiers, was riding to Montemor to bring succour to the Princesses. However, when he rode into the valley of Canta-Pedra, Tructesindo's valiant son saw the mercenary troops led by the Bastard of Baião, who had been waiting since dawn (just as Mendo Pais had warned) to block their way. And then, in this tale of blood and murder, there appeared, as unexpectedly as a rose growing in the crevice in a fortress wall, a romantic episode, of which Uncle Duarte had sung with such poignant elegance.

Lopo de Baião's fair good looks—like those of a nobleman descended from the Visigoths—were so well-known throughout the region of Entre Minho e Douro, that he was nicknamed The Bright Sun, and that same Bright Sun was passionately in love with Dona Violante, Tructesindo Ramires' youngest daughter. On St John's Day, at the Lanhoso estate, amid the bullfights and jousting, he had met that splendid young woman, about whom Uncle Duarte, in his poem, had written these dazzling, charming lines:

> *A liquid fire burns in those two dark eyes!*
> *Her hair so thick, like lustrous, plaited ebony!*

And she, too, had clearly given her heart to that resplendent, golden youth, who, on that festive day, after his displays of skill in the bull ring, had been presented with two embroidered sashes by the noble mistress of Lanhoso, and, later that night, had at the banquet, danced with extraordinary grace and elegance. However, Lopo was a bastard child of the Baião line, whose quarrels with the Ramires over land and sovereignty had been simmering since the days of Count Dom Henrique, an enmity that had been further fuelled by the disputes between Teresa of León and Afonso Henriques, when, at the council of Barons, held in Guimarães, Mendo de Baião, who took the Count de Trava's part, and Ramires the Butcher, milk-sibling of the young Infante, each threw down the gauntlet. And, true to that centuries-old hatred, Tructesindo Ramires had harshly, arrogantly refused to give Violante's hand in marriage to the oldest of the Baião sons—one of the heroes of the Battle of Silves—who, at Christmas, had gone to the castle of Santa Ireneia on behalf of Lopo, his nephew, and made almost submissive offers of friendship and sweet peace. This rebuff had outraged the Baião household, who were proud of Lopo, even though he was a bastard child, because of the lustre his courage and gallantry brought to the family name. And then Lopo, his heart and pride wounded, and in order both to slake his unquenched desire and to sully the pure name of the Ramires, had attempted to kidnap Dona Violante. It was in the spring, when the meadows around the Mondego were already growing green. The gallant lady, escorted by relatives and by serfs from the family estate, was travelling from Treixedo to the monastery of Lorvão, where her aunt, Dona Branca, was the abbess. Uncle Duarte had put into verse that romantic episode:

> *Next to the Moorish fountain,*
> *There among the elms,*
> *The procession came to a halt ...*

from his shoulder onto his tunic. An arrow had penetrated the hinge of his leg armour and more blood was flowing from that wound, soaking the oakum lining. Then his mighty stallion, its haunch pierced by an arrow, stumbled and fell, its girth strap snapping as it rolled on the ground. Jumping free from his stirrups, Lourenço Ramires found himself surrounded by bristling swords and pikes, while from the hillside, leaning forward in his saddle, the Bastard was roaring:

'Hold him fast and tie his hands!'

Trampling over the bodies writhing beneath his iron-clad feet, the valiant youth, Lourenço Ramires, hurled himself, panting, against the glittering array of weapons, which withdrew and retreated. Lopo de Baião's triumphant cries only redoubled:

'Alive, take him alive!'

'Not as long as I have a soul in my body, villain!' roared Lourenço.

And he threw himself yet more furiously against that human wall, until a sharp stone struck him hard on the arm, leaving it hanging limp by his side along with his sword, which remained attached to his wrist by its chain, as useless as a spindle. The soldiers quickly secured him, some grabbing him around the throat, others beating his stiff legs until they buckled. Finally, he dropped to the ground like a piece of timber, and, bound with ropes, he lay there, motionless, his head bare of helmet and hood, his eyes tightly shut, and his hair a sticky tangle of dust and blood.

Lourenço Ramires, captured! They laid him on a litter made of twigs and branches, having first hurriedly splashed him with cool water from the stream, and the Bastard—using the back of his hand to wipe away the sweat running down his handsome face and golden beard—stood beside him and murmured sadly:

'How this grieves me, Lourenço, for we could have been brothers and friends!'

Thus, with the aid of Uncle Duarte, Sir Walter Scott, and titbits from *Panorama*, Gonçalo pieced together the ill-fated Battle of Canta-Pedra. And with those last words from Lopo, filled with the pain of his forbidden love, he concluded Chapter II, on which he had laboured for three whole days, so immersed in his work

Lopo, who, with his men, had been watching from a hill, suddenly appeared amid the elms surrounding the fountain. However, at the onset of that brief battle, a cousin of Dona Violante, the Master of the Palace of Avelim—an imposing figure—disarmed him and forced him to kneel for a moment beneath the glittering blade of his dagger. Then, with his life intact, but filled with silent rage, the Bastard galloped off, along with the few men who had accompanied him on that audacious assault. And ever after, the rancour between the two families had burned ever more fiercely, until, at the beginning of the war of the Princesses, there the two enemies stood, face to face, in the narrow valley of Canta-Pedra! Lopo had a troop of thirty lancers and more than a hundred crossbowmen from the royal ranks. Lourenço Mendes Ramires had fifteen horsemen and nineteen foot soldiers.

August was drawing to an end, and the long, hot summer months had turned all the grass in the famous pastures yellow, as well as the leaves of the alders and the ash trees growing on the banks of the stream whose meagre waters slipped over the glossy pebbles with a drowsy murmur. On the hill, towards Ramilde, among the still impressive ruins overgrown with brambles, stood the fire-blackened Round Tower, all that remained of the old house of Avelãs put to the torch during the fierce battles between the Salzedas and the Landims, now inhabited by the plangent soul of Guiomar de Landim, the Ill-Matched. On the highest hill, which dominated the far side of the valley, stood the new walls of Recadães, with its sturdy battlements and turret, more suited to a fortress than a monastery, where the monks were peering out of the windows, troubled by the sight of the glittering weapons that had been filling the valley since dawn. The nearby villages were clearly equally troubled, for hurrying up the hill to that holy, walled refuge could be seen a train of people carrying bundles or travelling in covered wagons, and driving along the few cattle they owned.

When he saw such a large company of soldiers waiting in the shade of the ash trees along the banks of the stream, Lourenço Ramires brought his horse and his troops to a halt next to a pile of stones topped with a rough wooden cross. His scout dismounted and under cover of his leather shield, went ahead to reconnoitre, only to return at once, unscathed by arrows or stones and shouting:

'They're Baião's men and men from the royal troops as well!'

So the way ahead was blocked, and their own forces vastly outnumbered. Bold Ramires did not, however, hesitate to advance and engage in battle. Even had he reached the valley alone, and with a fragile hunting lance as his only weapon, he would still have taken on the whole of the Bastard's army. Meanwhile, Baião's commanding officer had come prancing forward on a rather scrawny chestnut horse, his sword held high above his plumed helmet, uttering these words of warning, which echoed round the valley:

'Stop, stop, there is no way through! The King in his mercy has ordered the noble Lord of Baião to spare your lives if you will withdraw quietly and without further ado!'

Lourenço Ramires responded:

'Crossbowmen, fire!'

The arrows whizzed and whistled through the air. Santa Ireneia's few horsemen rode down into the valley, lances at the ready. And beneath the hastily unfurled standard, Tructesindo's son stood up in his iron stirrups and raised the visor on his helmet, so that the enemy could see his fearless face as he hurled proud, angry insults at the Bastard:

'Summon as many villainous followers as you wish, but I will be at Montemor tonight, over their dead bodies and over yours!'

And mounted on his bay horse, which was covered by a chain-mail net adorned with gold, the Bastard raised one iron-clad hand and shouted:

'Go back! Because you *will* return whence you came, you treacherous trickster, but only if I am merciful enough to send your father your body on a litter!'

In Uncle Duarte's poem, these fierce, defiant cries rolled forth in serenely measured lines. Gonçalo fleshed out those lines (feeling the heroism of his ancestors gusting through his soul like a wind blowing in from the open countryside) and immediately brought those two valiant bands together in combat. A huge battle ensued, a great clamour of voices:

'Forward men!'

'To the death!'

'Hold hard for Baião!'

'Victory for the Ramires!'

Amid the thick dust and the general uproar, crossbow bolts and rough clay balls from slingshots whistled through the air. Small groups of horsemen from Santa Ireneia and from the royal troops charged and clashed and arrows pierced flesh to the sound of lances splitting, then both sides retreated, leaving behind, on the churned-up earth, mortally wounded men writhing and screaming, while others, disoriented, staggered off into the shelter of the trees and the coolness of the stream. In the noble heart of the struggle, the rearing horses panted beneath the weight of their chain-mail coats, and the blades of their riders' swords gleamed and clanged as they skewered their opponents' shields; now and then, some stiff, armoured gentleman slipped from his red leather saddle and hit the soft ground with a metallic clatter. Horsemen and foot soldiers, however, as if engaged in a tournament, barely had to cross lances to fell their adversary, who would crumple to the ground, armour and all, amid proud, frenzied cries; but the full brunt of their murderous fury was felt by the opposing hordes, felled by great swords or slain by axes, their metal helmets crushed as if they were clay pots.

Lourenço Ramires cut through Baião's troops and the royal host as lightly as a man scything through green grass. With every onward stride of his sturdy steed, which foamed and furiously shook its halter, he provoked curses and cries of 'Dear God!' as another chest was pierced and arms wheeled in agony. His one aim was to exchange blows with Lopo, but the Bastard, usually so bold and aggressive in battle, had not moved from the hillside that morning, where a circle of lances protected him like a stockade, from behind which he urged on his men with shouts, not blows. In his desperate desire to break through that living wall, Lourenço spent all his energies on bellowing hoarsely for the Bastard to show himself and heaping him with insults, 'Varlet!' 'Knave!' Blood was slowly trickling out from beneath his chain-mail hood and dripping dow

that it was as if the world around him had fallen silent and been plunged in darkness.

A barrage of fireworks exploded in the distance, over towards Bravais, where, on Sunday, they were celebrating the festival of Our Lady of the Candles. After those three days of rain, a coolness descended from the soft, washed-clean sky onto the already much greener fields. And since he still had a good half-hour before dinner, the Nobleman grabbed his hat and cane, and set off just as he was, in his old working jacket, taking the narrow path that ran between the wall of the Tower and the fields of rye where the barbican of Santa Ireneia had stood in the twelfth century.

As he walked along that silent, still damp path, Gonçalo was thinking about his formidable ancestors. They were reemerging in his Novella as such solid, resonant figures! And his confident understanding of those Afonsine souls was proof that his own soul was made of the same mettle, and had been carved from the same fine block of gold. A feeble or degenerate heart would have been incapable of describing such brave souls or such valiant times, and it would have been an impossible task for either good Manuel Duarte or kindly Barrolo to understand still less recreate such august characters as Martim de Freitas or Afonso de Albuquerque. He hoped that any critics who read *The Tower of Dom Ramires* (for Castanheiro had assured him that the Novella would be reviewed in *Novidades* and in *Manhã*) would focus on that particular truth. Yes, that was definitely a point to be emphasised (and of which he would be sure to remind Castanheiro!): that all the noblemen of Santa Ireneia lived on in him, their descendant, if not in the form of heroic deeds, then in the same lofty grasp of what constituted heroism. Besides, living as he did under the reign of the ghastly São Fulgêncio, he could hardly destroy the House of Baião, which had been destroyed six hundred years before by his ancestor Leonel Ramires, nor reclaim Monforte with all its towers from the Moors, certainly not with Antoninho Moreno as Monforte's effete governor! But he could feel the grandeur and the historic legacy of the boldness that had once driven the men of his family to raze to the ground their rivals' houses and to sack Moorish villages; he was bringing them back to life through Knowledge and Art, restoring to modern life those fearless souls—with their hearts, their clothes, their deadly swords and their sublime arrogance—and, therefore, within the limitations imposed by the spirit and opportunities of his own century, he was a good Ramires, a Ramires full of noble energy, albeit mental rather than martial, as befitted an age of intellectual slackness. And the newspapers—always so ready to criticise the decadence of the Portuguese nobility—should, in all justice, state (and he would remind Castanheiro of this too!), 'There is at least one nobleman, the noblest of them all, who, in keeping with the forms and customs of his time, both continues and brings honour to the spirit and tradition of his race!'

These thoughts made him tread still more firmly on the ground once trodden by his ancestors, and as he was thinking them, he reached the corner of the estate wall, where his land was separated off from the pine forest and the scrubland beyond by a steep, narrow lane. All that remained of the once grand, ornate gateway, emblazoned with the family coat of arms, were two granite pillars, covered in yellow moss and closed off to straying cattle by a wicket gate made of hastily nailed together planks, half-eaten away by the rain and the years. Just then, emerging from the deep, shadowy lane came a creaking ox-cart laden with firewood and driven by a pretty young woman.

'A very good evening to you, sir!'

'Good evening to you, my lovely!'

The cart passed slowly by, and following immediately behind it came a tall, dark, thin man, with a shepherd's crook over his shoulder, from which dangled a bundle of ropes.

The Nobleman of the Tower saw at once that it was José Casco from Bravais, but, pretending not to have seen him, he continued along the edge of the pine forest, whistling and flicking with his stick at the flowering brambles in the ditch. The other man though, quickened his pace and disturbed the evening silence of the woods by loudly calling out the Nobleman's name. Heart pounding, Gonçalo Mendes Ramires stopped and managed a forced smile:

'Oh, it's you, José! How are you?'

Casco seemed embarrassed, his chest heaving beneath his faded work-shirt. Finally, untangling the ropes from his crook, he stuck its pointed end in the ground:

'I have always been perfectly clear and honest with you, sir, and I never expected you to go back on your word!'

Gonçalo Ramires slowly, painfully, nobly raised his head, as if he were lifting a great iron block.

'I don't know what you mean, Casco. In what way did I go back on my word? Are you referring to the lease of the land around the Tower? Well, that's news to me. We never actually signed an agreement, did we? You never came to see me again, you vanished ...'

Casco fell silent, too taken aback to speak. Then, with an anger that made his pale lips and his strong, hairy hands tremble as they gripped the end of his crook, he said:

'Are you saying that if we had signed a contract, you wouldn't have been able to back out? But surely a verbal agreement between honourable men is as good as any signature! When I accepted your offer, you even said, "It's a deal!" You gave your word!'

Cornered, Gonçalo adopted the patient air of a benevolent lord of the manor:

'Listen, José Casco, this really isn't the place to discuss the matter. If you want to talk, come to the Tower. As you know, I'm always there in the mornings. Tomorrow, for example, would be fine.'

And he was about to head off into the pine forest, his legs shaking, sweat pouring down his back, when Casco quickly, boldly planted himself in front of Gonçalo, barring his way with his crook:

'No, no one treats me like that! We must speak here and now. You gave me your word!'

Gonçalo glanced anxiously around, hoping someone would come to his aid. No one, only the silence and solitude of the dense forest. Along the lane, dimly lit by what remained of the daylight, the creaking of the cart was growing ever fainter, ever farther off. The high branches of the pine trees were sighing a drowsy, distant sigh. In the woods, the darkness and the mist were growing thicker. Terrified, Gonçalo took refuge in the idea of Justice and the Law, concepts always guaranteed to terrify countryfolk. His lips were dry and tremulous, but, like a friend gently giving advice to another friend, he managed to say:

'Listen, Casco, listen! Matters like this can't be sorted out with angry words. We don't want any unpleasantness, we don't want the law to get involved, because that could lead to a trial and to prison. And you have a wife and small children to think of. Listen, if you feel you have some cause for complaint, then come to the Tower and we'll talk. We'll find some peaceful solution. But no shouting, all right? The local officer might appear and then it would be gaol for you, my man ...'

On that deserted path, Casco suddenly grew in height and breadth, as tall and black as a pine tree, filled with a fury that made his burning, bloodshot eyes bulge.

'Are you threatening me? Not content with doing the dirty on me, now you're threatening me with prison? Devil take it! Before they put me in prison, I'm going to break every bone in your body!'

He raised his crook, but saved by a flash of reason and lingering respect, he shouted through clenched teeth, his head thrown back:

'Run, sir, run, before I do something I regret. Run before I kill you, and that really would be the end of me!'

Gonçalo Mendes Ramires ran to the gate between the old granite pillars, leapt over it and scuttled away like a hunted hare, past the vines growing along the wall! At the far end, next to the maize-field, stood an old granite-built storehouse abandoned to the elements, and now filled with the dense foliage of a wild fig tree that had seeded itself there. The Nobleman of the Tower took shelter in that hiding-place of tree and stone and crouched there, breathing hard. Darkness had fallen over the fields, and with it a serenity in which trees and pastures were gently drifting off to sleep. After a time, encouraged by the silence and the quiet, Gonçalo left his cramped refuge and again, although more slowly now, he began to run on the tips of his white boots over the rain-soaked ground, as far as the spring.

Then once more, he stopped, his chest heaving. And thinking he could see a pale shape among the trees in the distance, perhaps some worker in shirtsleeves, he called out anxiously, 'Ricardo! Manuel! Is anyone there?' The white blur melted into the shadowy foliage. A frog croaked in a stream. Trembling, Gonçalo followed the path along the wall to the corner of the orchard, where he found a locked door, but so old and rickety a door that it swayed on its rusty hinges. He hurled himself furiously against it, with shoulders made suddenly iron-hard by terror. Two panels gave way, and he slipped through the gap he had created, tearing his jacket on a nail in the process. At last, though, he could breathe easily, safe inside the walled orchard beside the Tower, where the balconies of the house stood open to the evening cool; and in the soft light of the newly risen crescent moon, his dark, thousand-year-old Tower seemed still darker and more weighed down with the years.

Taking off his hat and wiping away the sweat from his brow, he went into the vegetable garden, skirting round the bean patch. And he felt a sudden bitter rage at the vulnerable state in which he had found himself, on an estate normally swarming with people and their dependents! Not a single tenant or labourer had answered his despairing cries! Of his five servants, none had rushed to his aid, and there he had stood, utterly helpless, just a stone's throw from the threshing-ground and the barn. If a few men were to go out now with sticks or hoes, they could still catch Casco on the road and give him a good thrashing.

Hearing a girl's light laughter from behind the chicken-run, he crossed the courtyard to the brightly-lit kitchen door. Two boys from the farm, along with Crispola's daughter and Rosa were sitting there on a stone bench, chatting away in the cool shade of the vine trellis. Inside, the fire was crackling, and a delicious smell of soup filled the air. All of the Nobleman's anger rose to the surface.

'What's all this? A party? Didn't you hear me call? I just met a drunk near the pine forest. He didn't realise it was me and went for me with a sickle. Fortunately, I had my stick with me. But I called, I shouted, and nothing! And here you are chatting away, with the dinner still to cook! It's outrageous! If it happens again, you're out on the street, all of you. And if one of you complains, you'll feel the weight of my cane.'

His face was aflame with anger, his bold head held high. Crispola's daughter vanished into the kitchen, where she hid in a corner behind the kneading-trough. The young men stood up and bowed like two ears of wheat in a high wind. And while poor, terrified Rosa was crossing herself and repeating tearful laments about 'these awful things that do happen', Gonçalo quickly calmed down, delighted by the young men's submissive reaction, for they were both strapping lads and their two thick staffs were leaning against the wall within easy reach.

'Is everyone in this house deaf? What's more, the door to the orchard was locked. I had to use force to open it. There's a gaping hole in it now.'

Then, thinking that the Nobleman was criticising the weakness of that rather neglected door, one of the youths, the braver one with reddish hair and a jaw like a horse, scratched his head and offered this excuse:

'Sorry about that, sir, but after Relho left, we did reinforce the door and put a new lock on, a good strong one too!'

'What do you mean, a strong lock!' roared the Nobleman proudly. 'I smashed it and your so-called reinforced door, smashed it to smithereens!'

The other youth, shrewder and more confident, laughed and said flatteringly:

'Good heavens, sir, you must have given it an almighty shove!'

And thrusting out his equine jaw, his companion added:

'Not half! Because that door was really solid, and, like I said, we put a brand-new lock on it too. Why, we only fitted it after that business with Relho!'

This confirmation of his strength by these two strong young men entirely assuaged the Nobleman of the Tower's rage, and he replied mildly, almost paternally:

'At least I'm still strong enough to break down a door, even a new one. What I couldn't decently do was drag a drunk armed with a sickle all the way to the alderman's house. That's what I was shouting for, for you to come and get him and take him there. Anyway, it's over and done with now. Rosa, give these lads another mug of wine with their supper. And maybe next time you'll be a bit quicker on the uptake and come when you're called.'

He was behaving now like a true Ramires from an earlier century, fair and wise, reprimanding his vassals for some misdemeanour, but immediately forgiving them, knowing he could rely on them for future acts of prowess. Then, with his cane over his shoulder like a lance, he climbed the gloomy kitchen stairs. Up in his room, as soon as Bento arrived to help him get dressed for dinner, he began describing his epic adventure all over again, this time adding more terrifying details, which so startled the sensitive old fellow that he stood motionless by the chest of drawers, without even putting down the jug of hot water, the polished boots, and the armful of towels he was carrying. Casco! José Casco from Bravais so drunk that he hadn't even recognised the Nobleman and had set about him with a huge sickle, shouting, 'Die, you pig!' And the master fending off the brute with his cane, leaping to one side so that the sickle struck the trunk of a pine tree instead. Then he had retaliated, brandishing his cane and shouting for Ricardo and for Manuel, as if both were close at hand; and Casco, not knowing what to do, had retreated, stumbling and grunting, down the lane.

'What do you think, eh? If I hadn't taken action, the man could have shot me!'

Dripping water from the jug onto the carpet, Bento stood blinking, bewildered and alarmed:

'But, sir, I thought you said he attacked you with a sickle ...'
Gonçalo stamped his foot impatiently.

'At first, yes, he came at me with a sickle, but he was walking behind his cart, where he almost certainly keeps his rifle. After all, Casco's a hunter and always has his rifle with him. Anyway, I'm safe and well now and back in the Tower, thank God. And thanks, too, to the fact that, fortunately in such situations, I always keep a cool head!'

Then he hurried Bento along because, what with the shock and the physical effort, his legs were positively shaking with fatigue and hunger—not to mention thirst!

'Especially thirst! A nice cool bottle of wine, a bottle of *vinho verde* and one of Alvaralhão, so I can mix the two.'

Bento gave a deep, tremulous sigh, filled the basin and laid out the towels. Then, very gravely, he said:

'There seems to have been a rash of such incidents lately, sir. The same thing happened to Senhor Sanches Lucena up at Feitosa ...'

'What do you mean? What's happened?'

Bento then unfolded the terrible tale that had been brought to the Tower while the Nobleman was away in Oliveira by Rui the carpenter, Crispola's brother-in-law who was doing some work up at Feitosa. One evening, as dusk was falling, Senhor Sanches Lucena had gone down to the belvedere and two workmen, either drunk or up to no good, were passing by on the road; they started picking on the poor old man, making fun of him, prodding him and laughing. Senhor Sanches very patiently advised them to go on their way and to behave themselves. Then, suddenly, one of them, a big fellow, slipped off his jacket and threatened him with his crook! Luckily, his companion stopped him, shouting, 'Don't, he's our local deputy!' The big lad had then fled in terror, while the other man fell on his knees before Senhor Sanches Lucena. But the whole thing was too much for the poor gentleman and he took to his bed!

Gonçalo listened to this story, greatly shocked and absentmindedly drying his hands on the towel.

'And when was this?'

'As I said, sir, it happened when you were in Oliveira. Either the day before or the day after Senhora Dona Graça's birthday.'

The Nobleman threw down his towel and pensively cleaned his nails. Then he gave a soft, hesitant laugh:

'So there is some point in Sanches Lucena being the deputy for Vila Clara.'

And once dressed and having filled up his cigar case (for he had decided to spend the evening in the village, regaling Gouveia with

the day's events), he again turned to Bento, who was putting away
his clothes:

'You say that when the other man shouted, "Don't, he's our local
deputy," the drunk came to his senses and fled. You see, it *is* worth
being a deputy! It's still a position that inspires respect! It certainly inspires more respect than being descended from the Kings
of León, but never mind, it's time for dinner.'

Over dinner, while he drank copious amounts of *vinho verde* and
red Alvaralhão, Gonçalo could not help brooding on Casco's brazen behaviour. For the first time in the history of Santa Ireneia, a
worker from one of the surrounding villages, someone who had
grown up in the shadow of the illustrious House—which, for so
many centuries, had lorded it over mountain and valley—had insulted a Ramires! And violently too, brandishing his crook at him,
right outside the walls of this historic estate! His father used to tell
him that when his great-grandfather Inácio was alive, men from
Ramilde to Corinde would bend the knee whenever the Nobleman
of the Tower passed them on the road. And now there they were
threatening him with sickles! And why? Because he had refused to
lower his rents just to please Casco, a mere upstart! In the days of
Tructesindo, a bold villain like him would have been roasted, like
a wild boar, over a crackling fire outside the castle walls. Even in
the days of his great-grandfather Inácio, he would have been left to
rot in a dungeon. No, Casco could not go unpunished, he'd only be
all the bolder, and when they met again, Casco, in his anger and resentment, would not waste his breath on words, but would immediately reach for his rifle. Not that Gonçalo wanted to inflict any
lasting punishment on Casco; after all, he had two small children,
one of whom hadn't yet been weaned. But he ought at least to be
handcuffed by two policemen and brought before the administrator to stand in that grim room with its view of the prison bars, and
be given a tremendous dressing-down by Gouveia, stern and erect
in his black frockcoat. Only by such tortuous means could Gonçalo
protect himself, because he was not a deputy, and—despite his
native talent and his name, his extraordinary lineage and those
ancestors who had built the Kingdom—he nevertheless lacked the

prestige of a Sanches Lucena, that kind of inestimable prestige that could stop an assailant in his tracks, his weapon frozen in mid-air!

As soon as he had finished his coffee, he told Bento to tell the two lads from the garden, Ricardo and the one with a jaw like a horse, to wait for him in the courtyard, armed and ready. For the Tower still had its own *salle d'armes* in the form of a small dark room next to the archives, which was home to a collection of dented bits of armour, a hauberk, a Moorish buckler, halberds, broadswords, powder horns, an 1820s blunderbuss, and—in among all this dusty, blackened ironware—three clean rifles, with which the gardeners, on the feast of St Gonçalo, would fire off a few rounds in honour of the saint.

Then he slipped a pistol and a whistle into his pockets and unearthed from a cupboard in the corridor a big old walking stick with an ornately carved handle. And thus equipped, warmed by the red and white wine he had drunk, and accompanied by the two young men looking stiff and important with their rifles over their shoulders, he set off for Vila Clara to find Gouveia the administrator. The coolness and quiet of the night was gradually enfolding the fields. The new moon that had brought about the change in the weather was brushing the tops of the Valverde hills like the shining wheel of a golden carriage. The rhythmic tread of the two labourers' heavy, studded boots echoed in the silence. And ahead of them, smoking a cigar, Gonçalo was enjoying this march, in which, once again, a Ramires was walking the paths of Santa Ireneia followed by his own personal troops, his armed vassals.

However, when they entered the town, he discreetly left his escort in Serena's tavern and took the short cut through the market to Simões' tobacconist's shop, where Gouveia usually stopped off in order to buy a box of matches and study the lottery tickets in the window before going to play cards at the club. On that night, though, Gouveia was not there. Gonçalo headed off then to the club, and downstairs, on one of the benches in the billiards room, he found a bald fellow—waistcoat unbuttoned, chewing a toothpick, head jutting forward as he contemplated the solitary moves of his opponent—who informed him that his friend Gouveia was ill.

'It's nothing serious, just a sore throat, but you'll be sure to find him at home. He hasn't left his bed since Sunday.'

Another gentleman, who was stirring his coffee while seated at a table crammed with liqueur bottles, assured him that Gouveia had been up and about that very afternoon, that he had met him at around five o'clock in the Café Amoreira with a woollen scarf round his neck.

Gonçalo hurried impatiently off again, and was just passing the fountain in the square when he spotted Gouveia standing in the brightly-lit doorway of the draper's shop, talking to an enormously fat man in a white coat and sporting a dark, bushy beard.

Raising one finger, Gouveia immediately said to Gonçalo:

'So you know already?'

'What?'

'Haven't you heard, man? It's Sanches Lucena!'

'What about him?'

'He's died!'

The Nobleman stared open-mouthed at Gouveia, and then at the other man, who was, with great difficulty, trying to pull a short, tight glove onto one of his enormous, pudgy hands.

'Good heavens. When did this happen?'

'Early this morning. It was very sudden. *Angina pectoris* apparently, something to do with his heart. Yes, he died suddenly, in bed.'

And they both fell silent, still trying to take in the news of that death, which had shocked all of Vila Clara. Finally, Gonçalo said:

'I was just talking about him at the Tower. And, as usual, none too respectfully either, poor man.'

'Me too!' cried Gouveia. 'Why, I wrote to him only yesterday, a long letter with a request from Manuel Duarte. But it would have been his corpse that received it.'

'That's a good one,' muttered the fat man, still wrestling with the glove. 'The corpse receiving the letter. Yes, very good.'

The Nobleman was thoughtfully stroking his moustache:

'How old was he?'

Gouveia had always assumed he was at least seventy, but, no, he had turned sixty-five in December. But he was completely worn out, a spent force, and of course, he had got married rather late and to a very vigorous woman.

'Yes, there's the lovely Dona Ana, a widow at twenty-eight, with no children and the sole heir to a fortune of two hundred *contos*, possibly more.'

'Not bad,' growled the portly fellow, who, having managed to get the glove on, was now struggling to button it up, the veins in his neck bulging with the effort.

The Nobleman felt constrained by this gentleman's presence, for he wanted to talk openly with Gouveia about the 'political vacancy' that had so unexpectedly opened up in Vila Clara with the abrupt disappearance of their traditional leader. Unable to contain himself any longer, he grabbed Gouveia by the button of his frockcoat and dragged him over into the more private shadow cast by the wall.

'So what's going to happen next, Gouveia? A by-election presumably, but who will be the candidate?'

Oblivious to the presence of the fat man in the white coat, who, now fully gloved, had lit a cigar and come over to join them, Gouveia set out the facts very plainly:

'Well, my friend, since Cavaleiro's uncle is Minister of Justice and José Ernesto is Minister of Home Affairs, the candidate will be whoever Cavaleiro chooses. It's obvious. Sanches Lucena kept his seat in Parliament because he was the party's natural choice. He was the most important person in Vila Clara, and the Historicals' number one man. Since there is now no natural choice for the party, what else can they possibly do but follow Cavaleiro's personal wishes? You know what a regionalist Cavaleiro is, so logically, he'll choose a candidate who he believes will continue Lucena's legacy, someone influential and well established locally. In any other constituency, you might be able to install some made-in-Lisbon deputy, but not here. The new deputy will have to be a local man and pro-Cavaleiro. And believe me, at the moment, Cavaleiro is at a complete loss as to what to do.'

The porcine person with him muttered smugly through clenched teeth, as he puffed away on a vast cigar:

'I'll be seeing him tomorrow, so I'll find out …'

Gouveia though, had fallen silent, scratching his chin and fixing Gonçalo with bright eyes, which shone as if illuminated by a particularly happy idea, almost an inspiration. And he suddenly turned to the other man, who was smoothing his dark beard, and said:

'Well, my friend, that's settled then, I'll see you the day after tomorrow. And I'll send the basket of cheeses direct to the Counsellor.'

He then took Gonçalo's arm, which he squeezed impatiently. And taking no further notice of the fat man, who was rather more prolix in his farewells, he dragged the Nobleman off to the silence of the main square.

'Listen, Gonçalo, this is a splendid opportunity for you! If you wanted, in a matter of days, you could be the next deputy of Vila Clara!'

The Nobleman of the Tower stood stockstill, as if a star had suddenly fallen from the sky into the ill-lit square.

'Listen,' Gouveia exclaimed again, letting go of Gonçalo's arm in order to develop his idea more freely. 'You have no serious commitment to the Regenerationists. You left Coimbra a year ago and are just taking your first steps in public life. You've never really taken sides, apart, that is, from firing off the occasional letter to the newspapers, but that doesn't count!'

'But ...'

'Listen, man! Do you want to get into politics or don't you? Yes, you do. So what does it matter if it's with the Historicals or the Regenerationists? Both are constitutional, both are Christians. The important thing is to get a foot in the door ... And you, unexpectedly, find that door open. What's to stop you? Your private enmity with Cavaleiro? Mere nonsense!'

He made a sweeping gesture with his hand, as if dismissing such puerile notions.

'Yes, mere nonsense! No one died. And deep down, you're not enemies. Cavaleiro is a man of talent and taste. I don't know of anyone else in the area who is more like you in spirit, education, manners and traditions. In a small place like this, there's bound to be a reconciliation at some point, so why not now, when that reconcilation could take you to Parliament! And as I said, as far as finding a new deputy for the Vila Clara constituency is concerned, Cavaleiro will do the choosing!'

The Nobleman of the Tower was almost struggling for breath, overwhelmed by emotion. After a silence, during which he took off his hat and pensively, sadly, fanned himself with it, he said:

'As you so rightly say, Cavaleiro is all about what's local or regional, and so he'll choose someone like Lucena, with money and influence ...'

Gouveia flung wide his arms:

'But that could describe you! Good heavens, you have land here, you have the Tower, you have Treixedo. Your sister is extremely rich, richer even than Lucena. And then there's your name, your family history. You, the Ramires family, have been here, with your estate in Santa Ireneia, for more than two hundred years.'

The Nobleman looked up at this:

'*Two hundred?* More like a thousand, or very nearly!'

'There you are. A thousand years. A family that predates the monarchy or is at least contemporary with it. You, therefore, are more of an aristocrat than the King. Doesn't that put you above Lucena? And you're certainly more intelligent than him. Ouch!'

'What's wrong?'

'It's my throat. It's still a bit sore. I'm not yet completely well.'

And he decided to go straight back home, because Dr Macedo had forbidden any late nights. Gonçalo accompanied him to his door, where, wrapping his scarf more tightly round his throat, Gouveia returned to his theme:

'In the Vila Clara constituency, Cavaleiro decides. Now, Cavaleiro is really keen to choose you and launch you into the world of politics. If you're prepared to hold out a hand to Cavaleiro, the constituency is yours. He's really, really keen to help, Gonçalo!'

'I'm not so sure about that, João.'

'I am.'

And in confidence, in the solitude of the street, João Gouveia revealed that Cavaleiro was eager for an opportunity to resume the fraternal friendship they had once shared. Only last week, he had said (and he quoted), 'Of all the young men of his generation, none has a longer, more assured future in politics than Gonçalo. He has everything, a great name, a great talent, charm and eloquence. He has everything. I'm still as fond of Gonçalo as I ever was, and I passionately want to get him into Parliament!'

'Those were his exact words, my friend! That was just six or seven days ago, in Oliveira, after supper, when we were taking coffee in the garden.'

In the shadows, Gonçalo's face was aflame as he devoured these revelations. Then, slowly, as if candidly revealing the most secret corner of his soul, he said:

'And I still feel as warmly towards Cavaleiro as I once did, and as for certain personal grievances, well, I can let them go! They've grown old, have expired, and are as obsolete now as the quarrels between the Horatii and the Curiatii. As you so rightly say, no one died. Damn it, I was brought up with Cavaleiro, we were like brothers. And you know, Gouveia, whenever I see him, I still feel a mad desire to run over to him and say, "Let's embrace, André, and let bygones be bygones!" And all that holds me back is timidity, yes, timidity. As far as I'm concerned, I'm ready for a reconciliation, my heart is crying out for it. But what about him? Because I've said some very harsh things in my letters to the *Gazeta do Porto*!'

João Gouveia stood still, his walking stick resting on his shoulder, looking at the Nobleman with an amused smile:

'Your letters? What did you say in your letters? That the governor is a despot. A Don Juan? My dear friend, what man doesn't enjoy having the opposition call him a despot and a Don Juan? Do you really think he was wounded by that? No, he was delighted.'

Still troubled, the Nobleman murmured:

'Yes, but I made disparaging remarks about his moustache and his hair ...'

'Gonçalinho, no man is ever going to feel ashamed of his curly hair or his fine waxed moustache. On the contrary, all the women admire him. You're quite wrong if you think you made Cavaleiro look ridiculous. You simply alerted the female readers of the

Gazeta do Porto to the existence of a splendid young man, who also happens to be the Governor of Oliveira.'

And stopping again—this time opposite his house, where the lights were on in the two open windows—he wagged his finger at Gonçalo and gave him one final word of advice:

'Tomorrow, Gonçalo, have Torto bring round his horse and pair, then jump into the carriage and race into town, burst straight into the governor's office with open arms and, without further ado, declare, "André, what's done is done, let us embrace like brothers! And seeing as how there's a vacancy in the constituency, I'll embrace that as well!" And in five or six weeks, you'll be the deputy for Vila Clara, and all the bells will ring out. Do you want to come in for a cup of tea?'

'No, thank you.'

'Remember, get in that carriage and go straight to the governor's office. Although, it might be best to have some pretext ...'

The Nobleman cried out excitedly:

'I do have a pretext—no, I mean, I have a genuinely urgent reason to speak to Cavaleiro and the secretary-general. It's about a tenant of mine. In fact, that was the reason I came looking for you tonight, Gouveia!'

And he quickly rattled off the story of his encounter with Casco, laying it on rather thick so as to make the whole incident seem far more shocking. For weeks, that wretch Casco had been going on at him to let him rent the land around the Tower, but he had already come to an agreement with Pereira the Brazilian and for a far greater sum than the amount Casco had so very grudgingly offered him. Ever since then, Casco had been doing the rounds of all the taverns, muttering dark threats. And that evening, he had emerged suddenly from a dark lane and confronted him, threatening him with his crook! Fortunately, he, Gonçalo, had managed to beat him off with his cane. Now, however, the insult of that crook raised against him hung over his peace of mind, over his life. And if it should happen again, he would shoot Casco as if he were a wild beast. It was, therefore, vital that Gouveia should summon the man, give him a reprimand and lock him up for a few hours.

Gouveia, who had been tentatively feeling his throat as he listened, held up one hand:

'Ah, you need to go to the governor's office for that. They deal
with any cases involving preventive detention. A reprimand isn't
enough for a wretch like him! He needs to be put in prison, just
for a day, say, on half rations. They'll send me an official letter or a
telegram. You're in real danger. There's not a moment to lose. Get
in that carriage tomorrow and off to the governor's office with you.
Even if only for the sake of Public Order!'

And Gonçalo, shoulders slightly bent, yielded to that sovereign
reason: Public Order.

'Yes, João, you're quite right. It is indeed a matter of Public Order. I'll go to the governor's office tomorrow.'

'Excellent,' said Gouveia, giving a tug on the bell-pull outside
his house. 'Give my regards to Cavaleiro. And I promise you we'll
get a huge number of votes, with fireworks and cheering and a
magnificent supper at Gago's. Now you're sure you won't come in
and have a cup of tea? All right, then, good night. And in two years'
time, Gonçalo Mendes Ramires, when you're a minister, remember
this late-night conversation of ours in Vila Clara!'

Deep in thought, Gonçalo continued on past the Post Office,
skirted round the white steps leading up to the church of São
Bento, and then, not even noticing where he was going, set off
along the acacia-lined path that led to the cemetery. And looking
down from that high point, with its panoramic view over the lush
fields stretching from Valverde to Craquede, he felt as if an airy
space full of bustle and abundance had suddenly opened up in
his narrow, solitary, provincial life. A great crack had appeared in
the wall by which he had always imagined himself to be irrepara-
bly enclosed. A very useful crack, through which he could see the
glittering realities of which he had so often dreamed in Coimbra!
However, if he went through that crack, its jagged edges would
certainly snag either his dignity or his pride. What should he do?

It was true that by opening his arms to that brute Cavaleiro, he
was sure to be elected deputy. Given their almost feudal allegiance
to the Historicals, the constituency would unthinkingly embrace

whichever candidate their leader might indolently choose. Such a reconciliation, though, would mean Cavaleiro's triumphant return to the peaceful Barrolo household. Gonçalo was, therefore, selling his sister's peace of mind in exchange for a seat in Parliament. No, for Gracinha's sake, he could not do it. And in the luminous silence of the path, he gave a heartfelt sigh.

The Regenerationists would not have another chance to get into power for another three or four years, and, during that time, he would be stuck in his little rural hole, playing tedious games of cards at the club, idly smoking a cigarette on the verandah of his sister's house, with no career ahead of him, his life stalled and stagnating and gathering moss, just like his crumbling, useless Tower! This was a cowardly dereliction of the holiest of duties both as regards himself and his family name. Soon, his fellow graduates from Coimbra would be getting all the best jobs in all the best companies, many would end up in Parliament thanks to such fortunate vacancies as the one left by Sanches Lucena's death; the bolder or perhaps more servile among them might even end up as Ministers. Only he, who was far more talented, with a far more splendid name, would lie forgotten and complaining by the roadside like a cripple watching the other pilgrims pass him by. And why? Out of some puerile fear of placing Cavaleiro's bold moustaches too close to Gracinha's perhaps too easily tempted lips? And yet that fear constituted an insult, a vile insult to his sister's seriousness of mind, for there was not a woman in the whole of Portugal more serious-minded or purer in thought. That fragile little body—so light that a strong wind might carry her off—contained a truly heroic soul. And Cavaleiro? However seductively he might shake his mane of hair, however languorously he might gaze at her with his long-lashed, liquid eyes, Gracinha would remain as steadfast and unreachable in her virtue as if she were a piece of sexless marble. As far as Gracinha was concerned, Gonçalo could open every door, even throw wide her bedroom door, and leave the two of them entirely alone! She was not, after all, an innocent maiden or even a widow. A strong, spirited husband ruled over the household. And it was entirely up to him to choose who should enter his home and up to him, too, to preserve its tranquillity and modesty. No, his imagined fears about proud, honest Gracinha's frailty were both perverse and absurd, and he should, with a light and happy heart, sweep them away. And standing there in the bright solitude of the path, Gonçalo made a bold, determined, sweeping gesture.

There remained, however, the matter of his own humiliation. For some years now, in writing and in conversation, in Coimbra, in Vila Clara, in Oliveira and in the *Gazeta do Porto*, he had repeatedly attacked Cavaleiro! And would he now, back bent, climb the steps up to the governor's house, murmuring *peccavi, mea culpa, mea maxima culpa?* What a stir that would cause in town! 'In his time of need, the Nobleman of the Tower came, crawled and surrendered.' It would be Cavaleiro's greatest triumph to have the only man in the area who was still on his feet and fighting, thundering out the truth, suddenly throw down his weapons, fall silent and quietly join His Excellency's other sycophantic followers. That would be hard, but, then again, surely the interests of the country were more important! And this reason seemed so utterly admirable that, in the dumb street, he roared out ardently, 'Yes, there's the country to think of!'

Yes, the country! There were reforms to proclaim and to carry out! In his fifth year at Coimbra, he had given a great deal of thought to the public education system, even reshaping the curriculum, eliminating Latin and literature and other such useless subjects, and focussing firmly on industry and the colonies, with the aim of creating a hard-working population of producers and explorers. And when he and his companions discussed their high-flown ideas for the future and shared out the various Ministries among them, it was always agreed that Gonçalo should be in charge of Education! It was precisely because of his potent ideas and his accumulated knowledge that Gonçalo owed it to the nation to serve in this way, just as, in centuries past, the great Ramires men had sallied forth to battle. And it was for the sake of the nation that his pride as a man must give way to his duty as a citizen.

And who knows what might happen? Many years of camaraderie lay between Cavaleiro and the Nobleman, a camaraderie that had merely lain dormant and might be revived by a new encounter, might immediately fold them in a warm embrace, in which their old grievances would vanish, like so much dust. But why waste time imagining and pondering? One overwhelming, inescapable need was emerging, that of going tomorrow morning to Oliveira, to the governor's office, and demanding that Casco be taken into custody. His peace of mind and his intellect depended on it. He would never manage to continue working on his Novella or stroll happily into Vila Clara again, knowing that Casco and his rifle might be lurking around corners and in the shadows. And unless he returned to his ancestors' crude measures and their habit of travelling everywhere with an armed escort, he needed to have Casco tamed and immobilised. He must, therefore, as a matter of urgency, go and see the governor, for the sake of Public Order. And then, when he was standing in Cavaleiro's office, before Cavaleiro's desk, Providence would decide, yes, Providence would decide!

Having taken this decision, the Nobleman of the Tower stopped and looked around him. Borne along on that warm tide of thoughts, he had reached the town cemetery, which glowed white behind the railings, like a sheet spread out before him. At the far end of the avenue bisecting the cemetery—pale in the sad, wan moonlight—a scrawny, wounded, ashen Christ hung, nailed on his high, black cross, looking still more wounded and ashen in all the silence and solitude, with one small, guttering lamp at his feet. All around were the cypresses, the shadows cast by the cypresses, the white gravestones, the small crosses on the poorer graves, a dead peace that weighed even on the dead and, up above, the still, yellow moon. The Nobleman felt a shudder of fear run through him, a fear of that Christ, of the gravestones, of the dead, the moon, the solitude. He raced back down the road until the houses of the town hove into view, then went bowling down the main street like a loose pebble. When he stopped near the fountain, an owl in the town-hall tower was hooting, lending a melancholy note to the dark, sleeping town. Feeling still more afraid, Gonçalo ran to the tavern, where he found his men happily playing cards while they awaited his return. He walked back with them through the town to

Torto's house, to ask him to send his coach and pair to the Tower the next morning at nine o'clock.

Torto's wife gingerly opened the grille in the door and said in a tremulous, hesitant voice:

'Oh, I'm not sure he can, sir. He's already got a job on at nine. Would eleven o'clock be any use to you, sir?'

'No, it has to be nine o'clock!' bellowed Gonçalo.

He wanted to arrive early at the governor's house so as to avoid the curious eyes of the gentlemen of Oliveira, who, after midday, gathered in the square and strolled up and down the arcade.

However, at half past nine, Gonçalo—who had been up until dawn, pacing his room, filled with a tumult of hopes and fears—was still not dressed, but was standing shaving before the vast mirror with the gilt columns. He then went, first, to Feitosa, where he left a note of condolence for the lovely widow, Dona Ana. By noon, he was starving and so stopped for lunch at Vendinha, while the horses rested. And it was already striking half past two by the time he finally reached Oliveira and got out of the carriage at the far end of the main square, outside the imposing door of the former Monastery of São Domingos, which his father had commandeered as his magnificent new offices when he was governor.

At that hour, in the cool shade of the arcade that runs along one side of the square (formerly known as the Praça da Prataria—Silver Square—and now renamed Praça da Liberdade—Liberty Square), Oliveira's gentlemen of leisure, the 'boys', were lounging around in wicker chairs outside Leão's and the Tabacaria Elegante. Gonçalo had cautiously drawn down the green blinds in the carriage, but, in the monastery cloister, which was still furnished with vast benches, he met his cousin, José Mendonça, coming down the steps. The cheerful captain—a slender young man with a trim moustache and slightly pockmarked face—was astonished to see Gonçalo there.

'What are you doing here, Gonçalinho? And wearing a top hat too! Goodness, it must be some very important matter!'

The Nobleman of the Tower bravely confessed. He had arrived that very moment in order to speak to André Cavaleiro.

'Is the illustrious gentleman in his office?' Mendonça drew back, almost horrified.

'Cavaleiro? *You've* come to speak to Cavaleiro? Holy Mother of God! Has Troy fallen?'

Gonçalo blushed and tried to laugh off this remark. No, there had been no tragedy of the epic proportions of Troy, and he was happy to reveal to Mendonça the matter that had brought him to see the august governor. It was about a man from Bravais called Casco, who, furious because he had failed to gain the lease on the land around the Tower, had threatened him and was now prowling the Vila Clara road at night, watching for him, rifle at the ready. And not daring to 'deal out justice' by the hands of his servants, as the Ramires men of old would have done, he was modestly asking the authorities to issue an order so that Gouveia, in keeping with the law and with God's holy commandments, could restrain that impertinent fellow from Bravais.

'So, you see, it's merely a minor matter of public order. Is the great man in his office, do you know? How's your wife, by the way? Well, I hope. Anyway, I'll be dining tonight with the Barrolos—why not join us?'

The captain did not move, but instead idly opened his leather cigarette case.

'What do you think of the latest news about poor Sanches Lucena?'

Yes, Gonçalo had heard about it at the club. Some sort of heart attack, they said. Mendonça lit his cigarette and inhaled deeply:

'Yes, it was very sudden, an aneurysm according to the newspapers. Why, only three days ago, Maria and I had dinner with them. Dona Ana and I even played the arrangement for four hands of the quartet from *Rigoletto*. And he seemed perfectly fine, chatting away and enjoying a glass of brandy.'

Gonçalo adopted a sad, sympathetic expression:

'Poor man. Yes, I met him in Bica-Santa a few weeks ago. A nice chap, charming manners. And, of course, now a vacancy has opened up next to Dona Ana.'

'Not to mention the vacancy in the constituency.'

'Oh, the constituency,' murmured the Nobleman of the Tower with a scornful laugh. 'Frankly, I'd rather have the widow. She's a Venus with two hundred *contos* to her name. Unfortunately, she has a truly hideous voice ...'

Mendonça hastened earnestly to reassure him.

'No, no, in private, she doesn't speak in that affected way at all. She has a really pleasant, natural way of speaking. And what a body, eh? What skin!'

'She must look splendid in black!' concluded Gonçalo. 'Anyway, I'll see you later. Drop in and see us. I must rush. I'm relying now on Cavaleiro's strong arm to save me!'

He shook Mendonça's hand and bounded up the stone steps.

However, the captain, who had set off down Travessa de São Domingos, had his suspicions about that tale of rifles and threats of violence. 'I smell Politics!' he thought. And when, after one slow hour had passed, he returned to the square and saw Gonçalo's carriage still outside the door of the governor's office, he ran to the Café da Arcada and revealed all to the Vila-Velha brothers, who were leaning pensively on either side of the door to the Tabacaria Elegante.

'I bet you can't guess who's visiting the governor? Gonçalo Ramires! Visiting *Cavaleiro!*'

Everyone round about stirred in their worn wicker chairs, as if waking from the somnolent silence and torpor of the long summer afternoon. And Mendonça, wildly excited now, told them that since half past two, Gonçalo Mendes Ramires, in person, had been closeted with Cavaleiro for a very important meeting. So great was the general amazement and curiosity that they all leapt to their feet and peered out from behind the pillars of the arcade to spy on the large balcony above the main entrance, where the governor had his office.

At precisely that moment, José Barrolo, wearing white trousers and a white rose in his lapel, came riding round the corner of Rua das Vendas. And the other gentlemen all hurled themselves on him, in the hope of some revelation:

'Barrolo!'

'Barrolo, come here!'

'Quickly, man, it's urgent!'

Barrolo rode over to the arcade, where his friends gathered round his horse to give him the extraordinary news. Gonçalo and Cavaleiro had been in secret conference all morning! Gonçalo's carriage had been waiting so long that his horses had almost fallen asleep. And the cathedral bells were already starting to ring!

Barrolo jumped down. And asking a boy to walk his horse, he joined his friends and, like them, stood open-mouthed, staring up at the stone balcony, his riding crop behind his back.

'I know nothing about it. Gonçalo hasn't said anything to me,' he said, still astonished. 'True, he hasn't been to town for several days, but not a word! And the last time he was here, for Graça's birthday, he was still raging against Cavaleiro!'

Everyone thought the whole affair 'quite extraordinary'! And suddenly, a silence fell, and a thrill of excitement filled the arcade. The balcony doors had slowly opened and out had stepped Cavaleiro and the Nobleman of the Tower, talking and smiling and smoking cigars. Cavaleiro shot a mischievous glance at the 'lads' down below, huddled in amazement under the arches, but it was only a glance. Then he disappeared back into his office, and was followed by the Nobleman, who, first, leaned over the balustrade to look down at the carriage below. The friends burst into clamorous cheering.

'Hurrah! Peace at last!'

'The War of the Roses is over!'

'Forgotten, along with those letters to the *Gazeta do Porto?*'

'What a turn-up for the books!'

'Gonçalinho will be Oliveira's next administrator, that's for sure!'

'Or something higher still!'

Then they again fell silent. Cavaleiro and the Nobleman had reappeared, so deep in conversation that they stood for a moment, apparently oblivious to the fact that they could be observed on the ample balcony. Then with fond familiarity, Cavaleiro clapped Gonçalo on the back, as if making public their reconciliation to the general wonderment of the square below. And again they vanished, still engaged in a dialogue that brought them back and forth, from the darkness of the office onto the bright balcony, sleeves touching, the smoke from their respective cigars mingling. In the arcade, the group of ever more excited on-lookers grew in size. When Melo Alboim, the Baron das Marges and the local delegate happened by, they were summoned urgently to join the others, where they hungrily, incredulously devoured the news, gaping up at the old stone balcony, which the sun was now gilding with golden light. The large hands on the clock were approaching four. The two Vila-Velha brothers and the other 'boys' withdrew wearily to their wicker chairs. The delegate, who always dined at four and had problems with his digestion, reluctantly left the arcade, begging Pestana, his neighbour, to come to the café later on and tell him all. Melo Alboim, meanwhile, had slipped into his house, which was on the opposite corner of square, facing the governor's office, and from his window, hidden behind his wife and sister-in-law—both wearing white dressing gowns and with paper curlers in their hair—he trained his binoculars on the balcony of the governor's office. Finally, the clock struck four. Then the Baron, unable to contain his impatience, decided to go over to the building and 'sniff out what was going on'.

At that moment though, André Cavaleiro came out onto the balcony again, alone this time, with his hands in the pockets of his blue flannel jacket. And almost immediately, Gonçalo's carriage set off across the square, with the green blinds half drawn down, revealing to the watching gentlemen's eager eyes only the Nobleman's light-coloured trousers.

'He's going to Barrolo's house!'

Barrolo could catch him there, and they all urged Barrolo to get on his horse at once and go home so that his brother-in-law could explain the whys and wherefores of this historic peace agreement! The Baron even held his stirrups for him, and Barrolo trotted eagerly back to Largo d'El-Rei.

Gonçalo Mendes Ramires, however, did not stop at his sister's house, but continued on to Vendinha, where he had decided to dine and allow the horses to rest. Once he had passed the last houses in the town, he raised the blinds and, with his hat off, took a long, delicious breath of that cool, luminous evening air, cooler and clearer and more consoling than any he had ever experienced. He was returning from Oliveira triumphant! He had finally climbed through that crack in the wall and without his honour or his pride getting scratched or torn on the sharp edges. Blessed be Gouveia, canny Gouveia! And blessed, too, be his canny words on the previous evening in Vila Clara!

True, it had been difficult, that first silent moment when he had sat down stiffly, awkwardly on the edge of the chair, next to His Excellency's desk. But he had behaved in a dignified, straightforward manner—'I find myself obliged (he had said) to consult the governor on a matter of public order ...' Looking very pale and nervously smoothing his moustache, Cavaleiro had made the first move, 'I'm only sorry that you have not come to consult me as your old friend.' Gonçalo remained withdrawn and resistant, coldly, sadly saying, 'Well, that is certainly no fault of mine.' And after a silence during which his lips trembled, Cavaleiro had said, 'After all these years, Gonçalo, it would be more charitable not to speak of blame, but simply to remember our former friendship, which, at least as far as I'm concerned, remains unchanged, loyal and deep.' Gonçalo had responded to this touching invocation gently and compassionately, 'If my old friend André still recalls our former friendship, I cannot deny that the flame of that friendship has never entirely burned out in me either.' They both then mumbled a few confused words of regret about life's vicissitudes, and, almost without noticing, reverted to addressing each other familiarly as *tu*! He told Cavaleiro about Casco's clumsy attempt to threaten him. Filled with indignation as a friend and even more so as governor, Cavaleiro immediately telegraphed Gouveia with orders to put the thug from Bravais out of commission. Then he and Gonçalo discussed the sudden death of Sanches Lucena, which had shocked the whole town. They both spoke admiringly of the beautiful widow and of her two hundred *contos*. Cavaleiro recalled how, when visiting Feitosa one morning, he had gone in through the garden gate and found her sitting in a bower of roses adjusting her garter. And what a divine leg she had! And laughing, they both expressed their determination not to marry Dona Ana, despite her two hundred *contos* and despite that divine leg! They had already resumed the familiar forms of address from their days at Coimbra, calling each 'old man' and 'dear fellow'.

And it was, of course, André who mentioned the unexpected vacancy left by the death of the deputy. Sitting back in his armchair, drumming his fingers on the desk, Gonçalo murmured casually:

'Yes, of course, his death must have left you in a very awkward situation.'

Nothing more! Just those words indolently spoken as he drummed his fingers. And Cavaleiro had immediately, hastily, insistently, offered him the constituency, first giving him a long look, as if trying to penetrate his mind and sound him out. Then, in a grave, insinuating voice, he had said:

'If you wanted, Gonçalo, you could put an end to that awkward situation.'

Gonçalo had reacted with surprise and amusement:

'What do you mean, if I wanted?'

André fixed him with his large, lustrous, persuasive eyes and said:

'If you wanted to serve your country and become the deputy for Vila Clara, then there would be no awkward situation, Gonçalo!'

If you wanted ... And faced by his friend's plaintive insistence, so sincere and so deeply felt, he had agreed with a bow, for the sake of his country:

'If I can be of any use to you and to the country, then you can count on me.'

And that was that, he had slipped through that jagged crack in the wall with not a scratch to his pride or his dignity! Then they talked openly, pacing up and down the office, from the document-laden shelves to the balcony doors, which André had opened to let out the lingering smell of some paraffin spilled the previous day. André intended to leave for Lisbon that very night, to talk to the government after Sanches Lucena's unexpected death. And once in Lisbon, he would put forward his dear friend Gonçalo's name as the only possible candidate, utterly safe and solid, given his name, his talent, his influence and his loyalty. And that was the Election over and done with. Besides (declared Cavaleiro with a smile), the Vila Clara constituency was 'his property', as much his as his own private estate. He could, if he chose, elect the stammering, drunken office boy. He was, therefore, doing the nation an enormous favour by introducing them to a young man of such lofty origins and such keen intelligence. Then he added:

'Don't give the Election another thought. Go home to the Tower. And not a word to anyone, apart from Gouveia that is. Just wait there quietly for my telegram from Lisbon. Once you receive it, you will then be the deputy for Vila Clara, and you can safely tell your brother-in-law and your friends, and on the following Sunday, come and have lunch with me at Corinde.'

They embraced each other, an embrace that joined those two separated souls once and for all. Accompanying Gonçalo to the stone steps down to the cloister, André—shyly revisiting the past—gave a thoughtful smile and murmured, 'And what have you been up to lately in that beloved Tower of yours?' And when Gonçalo told him about the Novella he was writing, André sighed nostalgically for the days of Imagination and Art in Coimbra, when he had lovingly chiselled out the first canto of a heroic poem, *The Arzila Border*.

They embraced again, and off Gonçalo went, the new deputy for Vila Clara.

In Parliament, he, Gonçalo Mendes Ramires, would represent all the fields and villages he saw through the window of the carriage. And by God, he would represent them well! His mind was already filling up with rich, fertile ideas. In Vendinha, while he was waiting for them to fry him up some sausage and eggs and two slices of fish, he was considering, as a response to the Royal Speech, the harsh, sombre picture he would paint of our Administration in Africa. Then he would issue a call to the nation, one that would rouse it to action and inspire it to invest some of its energies in that potent land, Africa, where, from coast to coast, they could build a greater Portugal, as their supreme glory and supreme source of wealth! By the time the weary horses pulled up to the Tower, night had fallen, and his head was still buzzing with ideas, vast and vague.

The next morning (a Tuesday) at ten o'clock, Bento entered the Nobleman's room, bearing a telegram, which had arrived in the early hours. Gonçalo assumed it was from the ministry, and his heart gave a joyful leap. It was, however, from Castanheiro, demanding the Novella. Gonçalo screwed up the telegram. The Novella! How could he possibly work on the Novella when he had so much to think about with the upcoming Election? He could not even enjoy his lunch, rejecting dish after dish, because he had to suppress a desperate desire to tell Bento the news. However, once he had impatiently drunk his coffee, he set off to Vila Clara to tell Gouveia. The poor fellow was once more prostrate on his wicker sofa, a poultice pressed to his throat. And all afternoon, in that cramped room with its pale green walls, Gonçalo extolled André's many talents, 'a real statesman, Gouveia, a man of ideas!' praised the current Historical government as 'the only one capable of getting us out of this mess, Gouveia!' and revealed the ambitious laws he wanted to draw up concerning Africa, 'our one great hope, Gouveia!' Gouveia, occasionally checking that his poultice was still warm, now and then interrupted his silence and immobility to murmur feebly:

'And to whom do you owe all this, Gonçalinho? To yours truly!'

When Gonçalo woke late on Wednesday, his first urgent thought was of André Cavaleiro, who, at that very moment, would be having lunch in Lisbon at the Hotel Central (to which André had remained faithful ever since he was a boy). And all day, as he smoked cigar after cigar in the silence of the house and the garden, he followed Cavaleiro on his journey as governor, to the Baixa, to Parliament, to the various Ministries. He would, of course, dine with his uncle, Reis Gomes, Minister of Justice. With them would be José Ernesto, Minister of Home Affairs, an old university friend and political confidant. So this very night, everything would be decided!

'Tomorrow, at around ten o'clock, I'll get a telegram from André!'

No news reached the Tower, though, and the Nobleman spent that slow Thursday at the window, watching the dusty road along which the telegraph boy would come, a fat lad, whom he would recognise at once by his oilskin cap and his gammy leg. As evening fell, he was feeling so unbearably anxious that he sent a boy to Vila

Clara. Perhaps the telegram had been delayed or left on the table by 'that fool Nunes at the telegraph office!' No, there was no telegram. Then he became convinced that Cavaleiro must have encountered some difficulties in Lisbon. And all night, unable to rest and filled with a rising, roiling sense of indignation, he imagined Cavaleiro meekly giving in to the minister's other demands, slavishly accepting as the candidate for Vila Clara an imbecile from some ministry or other, some vulgar party pen-pusher!

In the morning, he scolded Bento for being so late bringing him the newspapers and his tea.

'And is there no telegram, no letter?'

'No, sir, nothing.'

He had clearly been betrayed! Well, then, that dastardly man, Cavaleiro, would certainly never cross the threshold of his sister's house! Besides, what did he care about that mockery of an Election? Fortunately, he had plenty of other ways to prove his worth, ways far superior to sitting in some grubby seat in Parliament! How wretched it would have been, demeaning his talent and his name in the lowly service of fat, bald, ugly São Fulgêncio! And he resolved to return at once to the pure, lofty peaks of Art, and to spend all day on the noble, elegant task of writing his Novella.

After lunch, he managed to make himself sit down and nervously shuffle through some bits of paper. Then, suddenly, he grabbed his hat and again raced off to Vila Clara, to the telegraph office. No, Nunes had received nothing for His Excellency! Then, dripping with sweat and covered in dust, Gonçalo scuttled over to Gouveia's office, only to be told that Gouveia had gone to Oliveira! Some other candidate had obviously been chosen, and his trust roundly abused! He went home to the Tower, determined to take his revenge on Cavaleiro for this affront to his name and his dignity! He spent the whole of a heavy, misty Friday bitterly pondering what form his revenge would take, a revenge that needed to be both very public and very bloody. The simplest and most satisfying method would be to confront him, one Sunday, on the steps of the cathedral as he was coming out of mass, and tweak the villain's fine moustache! When night fell, after barely eating any dinner, he was still so riven with spite and humiliation that he put on his jacket and decided to go back to Vila Clara. Too ashamed to return to the telegraph office, he intended to spend the night at the club, playing billiards, enjoying a cup of tea, and cheerfully reading the Regenerationist newspapers, so that if, later on, people should learn of the trap he had fallen into, everyone would recall his insouciant air.

He went down to the courtyard, where the dark, cloud-laden evening was made still darker by the surrounding trees, and as he was opening the gate, he almost collided with a young lad, who came limping along, panting hard, and who, when he saw him, cried out, 'Telegram, sir!' The Nobleman snatched it greedily from his hand, then ran into the kitchen, where he berated Rosa for the lack of light, and with a match burning his fingers, instantly devoured the long-awaited lines: *Ministry agrees, all settled.* In the rest of the message, Cavaleiro merely reminded him that he would be expecting him at Corinde on Sunday at eleven o'clock, so that they could have lunch together and talk.

Gonçalo Mendes Ramires gave the telegram boy five *tostões* and raced up the stairs to the library, where, by the more reliable light of the oil-lamp, he reread that delicious telegram. *Ministry agrees, all settled.* In his unfettered gratitude to Cavaleiro, he immediately concocted the plan of a superb supper laid on by Barrolo at the Casa dos Cunhais, thus confirming the reconciliation of the two households. And to bring still more honour to this sweet celebration, he would advise Gracinha to wear a modestly décolleté dress in order to show off her magnificent diamond necklace, the last of the Ramires' historic jewels.

'Ah, André, what a gem of a man!'

The Chinese lacquer clock in the corridor grumbled out nine o'clock, and it was only then that Gonçalo noticed the heavy rain falling outside, which he, pacing the library in a great luminous wave of imagined triumphs, had been too absorbed in his own glory to hear splashing down on the stone balcony and on the leaves of the lemon trees.

To calm himself and to make the most of the time he must now spend closeted in his room, he decided to work on his Novella. He really did need to finish it before the great upheaval of the Elections, so that in January, when Parliament re-opened, he could emerge into the world of politics with his ancient name adorned with a halo of Erudition and Art. He pulled on his flannel dressing gown. And seated at his desk, with his usual pot of inspirational tea beside him, he slowly reread the beginning of the second chapter—and he was not at all pleased.

It was set in the castle of Santa Ireneia, on the August day on which Lourenço Ramires had fallen captive in the valley of Canta-Pedra, badly wounded and held prisoner by the Bastard of Baião. Tructesindo Ramires had been told the sad result of the battle by the captain of infantry, who, despite having one arm pierced by a lance, had galloped with desperate speed back to the castle. At this point, Uncle Duarte had slipped into a gentle almost sentimental lyricism, describing the Great Man pacing the *salle d'armes*, weeping and sobbing in his grief for his son, the flower of all the knights of Riba-Cávado, who had been laid low and bound hand and foot, at the mercy of Baião's men:

Irrepressible tears burst forth from him,
His armour heaves with his ardent sobs!

In the chapter's opening lines, Gonçalo had adopted the same harmoniously melancholy tone and described the old man sitting on a stool, head bowed, tears running down his white beard, his large, calloused hands hanging limp like those of some languid maiden, while his two greyhounds sat wagging their tails and watching him with a kind of yearning, almost human sympathy. Now, though, this tearful despair seemed to Gonçalo at odds with Tructesindo's indomitably violent nature. Uncle Duarte, who belonged to the Balsas family, was not a Ramires and therefore could not have felt the strength of the Ramires blood coursing through his veins, and, being a softhearted Romantic of 1848, he had immediately bathed in romantic tears the fierce face of a twelfth-century warrior, a companion of Sancho I! It was, however, Gonçalo's duty to restore the Lord of Santa Ireneia to an appropriately epic reality. Putting a line through that whole, false, somewhat vapid opening passage, he tried a different approach and filled the whole castle with alarm and rage. In his sublime, simple loyalty, Tructesindo did not even think about his son—revenge for that foul outrage could wait—but put all his efforts into hastening the preparations, so that he could ride to Montemor and bring the Princesses the succour denied them by that ambush in Canta-Pedra. However, when the Great Man was in the *salle d'armes* with his commander-in-chief, discussing the final details of the expedition, the sentinels sheltering from the August heat in the towers suddenly saw in the distance, beyond the woods on the river bank, the glitter of weapons and a party of horsemen advancing on Santa Ireneia. Burly Ordonho ran huffing and puffing up the steps to the barbican terrace and immediately recognised the standard of Lopo de Baião and the sound of his Moorish horns, which rang out long and sad over the silent fields. Then, cupping his mouth with his hairy hands, he cried:

'To arms, to arms! Baião is coming! Crossbowmen, to the battlements! And as many men as possible to the drawbridges!'

And scratching his head with the end of his pen, Gonçalo was still trying to think up some more authentic-sounding, suitably brave and Afonsine call to arms, when the door to the library opened very cautiously, with that irritating, stubborn creak that almost drove him to despair. It was Bento, in shirtsleeves:

'Could you possibly come down to the kitchen for a moment, sir?'

Gonçalo stared at Bento, blinking and uncomprehending:

'To the *kitchen?*'

'It's Casco's wife kicking up a terrible fuss. Apparently, her husband was arrested this afternoon. She turned up here in the pouring rain with her children, one of whom is still a babe in arms. She says she has to speak to you, sir. And she won't shut up, but kneels there, bathed in tears, along with her children, like a modern-day Inês de Castro!'

Gonçalo muttered, 'Oh really!' What a nuisance to have that distraught, screaming woman dragging her needy children to the very door of the Tower! And there he was on the eve of an Election campaign. His constituents would inevitably be touched by her plight—and he'd be the hardhearted aristocrat! He angrily flung down his pen:

'Oh really, Bento, tell the creature to go away and not to worry. The administrator will release Casco tomorrow. I'll go to Vila Clara myself before lunch to ask him to do just that. Tell her not to worry and not to distress her children. Go on, quickly!'

Bento stayed where he was.

'Rosa and I have already told her that, but she won't believe us. She insists on speaking to you, sir. She walked here in the pouring rain and one of the little ones is really ill and won't stop shivering.'

Moved by this story, Gonçalo thumped the desk so hard that the loose pages of his Novella scattered everywhere.

'Honestly, the things I have to put up with. And from a man who tried to kill me too! And now, to top it all, I'm the one who has to deal with the tears and the hysterical scenes as well as with his sick child! This place is just impossible! One day, I'll sell this house and the land and emigrate to Mozambique or to the Transvaal, some-where—anywhere—where one isn't bothered by such petty mat-ters. Anyway, tell the woman I'll be right down.'

Bento wholeheartedly approved of this decision:

'Yes, sir, if you wouldn't mind, especially if it's to give her good news. It would be such a consolation to the poor woman.'

'I'm coming, Bento, I'm coming. Don't you start nagging me too. Really, it's impossible to get any work done in this house. Another wasted evening!'

He strode off to his room, slamming doors as he went, intending to slip two ten *tostão* notes in his pocket to console the little ones. When he reached into the drawer, however, he stopped, feeling suddenly embarrassed. What a brutish idea, to try and buy the children off with money, when he'd been the one responsible for having their father taken away, handcuffed and thrown into a dun-geon! Instead, he picked up a box of dried apricots that Gracinha had sent him the previous day, a speciality of the Convent of Santa Brígida in Oliveira. And slowly closing the door behind him, he already regretted the unthinking severity of his actions, ruining a couple's peace of mind. Out in the corridor, with the rain hammering down on the roof and cascading into the courtyard, he was even more troubled and pained by the idea of that poor woman, half mad with anxiety, tramping down the dark road, dragging her drenched and exhausted children through the storm. By the time he went into the kitchen, he was shaking like a criminal.

Through the glass door, he could hear Rosa and Bento comforting the woman with friendly, almost cheerful words, but her wailing and her loud laments for her 'dear husband' only rang out all the more shrilly, as if to repel and stifle all attempts at consolation. When Gonçalo timidly pushed open the door, he almost recoiled in fear and horror from the strident grief aimed at him and his mercy! On her knees on the flagstones, her thin hands clasped above her head, and dressed entirely in black—which somehow looked still blacker and more mournful against the red sheet hung up to dry before the fire—the woman burst forth with a tumult of pleas, crying out:

'Ah, kind sir, have pity! My husband's been arrested and they're going to send him into exile, sir, off to Africa. And my poor babies, sir, will be left without a father! For their souls' sake, sir, for the sake of their happiness, sir, please, please help me. Oh, I know he was wrong, but he was desperate, sir. Have pity on the little ones, sir. My poor husband's in prison, sir. Please, sir, I'm begging!'

His eyes moist with tears, and still clutching the box of dried apricots, Gonçalo, managed, despite the knot that had formed in his throat, to stammer out:

'Calm down, woman, he'll be released tomorrow. Calm down. The order's as good as given. He'll be out in no time.'

On one side, bent over the dark sobbing figure, Rosa was saying, 'Isn't that what we told you, Maria! He'll be out tomorrow!' And on the other side, Bento was impatiently slapping his thigh and saying, 'Stop your screaming, woman. The Nobleman has given you his word. Your husband will be freed tomorrow!'

With the scarf all awry on her head and one plait unravelling, she would still not calm down, but continued her sobbing and, in-between sobs, kept shouting:

'I'll die if he isn't freed! Forgive me, sir, please, sir, forgive me.'

Gonçalo found this stubborn, endless litany of woes sheer torture, like a nail being hammered in again and again, and finally, he stamped his foot and roared:

'Listen, woman, and look at me, will you! Stand up, go on, stand up! And look me in the eye.'

Stiff and erect, her hands behind her back as if she, too, were being threatened with handcuffs, she stared at the Nobleman with deep, dark, terrified eyes, and the dark circles around them seemed to fill her gaunt, sallow face.

'That's better,' exclaimed Gonçalo. 'Now, tell me, do you think I would lie to you when you are so upset? Well, then, calm down, stop screaming, and I promise you, on my word of honour, that tomorrow morning, your husband will be freed.'

And Rosa and Bento cried out in triumphant unison:

'Isn't that what we told you, you silly woman? If the Nobleman has given you his word, then tomorrow you're sure to have your husband back!'

She slowly wiped away her now silent tears with one corner of her black apron, but she was still not entirely convinced and kept her wide, dark eyes fixed hungrily on Gonçalo. Would he really send orders first thing in the morning? Bento was the one who finally persuaded her, saying, almost violently:

'How can you be so impudent, woman? Are you doubting the Nobleman's word?'

She let go of her apron, bowed her head and sighed:

'In that case, sir, thank you, and may it be for the good of all.'

Gonçalo was now looking around for the two children she had brought with her all the way from Bravais through the pelting rain. The baby was sleeping beatifically on the lid of a trunk, where Rosa had carefully covered him with blankets and eiderdowns. However, the boy, who was seven, was sitting huddled in a chair by the fire, drying off like the sheet hanging next to him, his little face aflame with fever, his head drooping with sleep and exhaustion, as he gasped and groaned at the terrible hacking cough sapping his strength, all the while thrusting one small hand through a hole in his grubby shirt to scratch his still grubbier chest. Gonçalo put the box of apricots down on the trunk, and touched the boy's hand.

'This child has a fever, and yet you brought him here, all the way from Bravais, on a night like this?'

From the low chair on which she had slumped down, the woman murmured nervously, without looking up:

'I wanted them to plead with you too, so you'd see that they, poor things, had lost their father!'

'You're mad, woman! And do you intend to go back to Bravais now, in the rain, with the children?' She sighed:

'I have to. I can't leave my mother-in-law on her own. She's eighty years old and crippled ...'

Then the Nobleman despondently folded his arms at the thought of that journey, in which, all because of his vengeful demands, the lives of two children had been put at risk. Rosa, however, thought that the baby would not be harmed if held tight in his mother's arms and protected by a thick blanket. The boy, on the other hand, with that cough and a high fever ...

'He'll be staying here,' Gonçalo declared. 'What's his name? Manuel. Right, Manuel will stay here. And don't worry, Senhora Rosa will take care of him. What he needs is a good glass of eggnog and something to make him sweat out that fever. He'll be back in Bravais in a few days' time, fully recovered and fatter too, so don't worry!'

The woman sighed again, filled by a terrible debilitating weariness. And giving in to a long, doleful habit of submission and putting up no further resistance, she said:

'Of course, if you say so, sir.'

Bento peered out into the courtyard and announced that the rain was clearing up. Gonçalo immediately urged her to go back to Bravais:

'But don't be afraid. I'll send one of my men with a lantern to light your way and an umbrella to shelter the baby. No, listen, you can wear my waterproof cape! Bento, run and fetch that new cape I bought in Lisbon.'

And when Bento brought the raincoat, with its long cape, and placed it over the woman's shoulders, she was at first intimidated by the expensive material, which rustled like silk, but then a burst of laughter filled the kitchen. Like the rain, the tears had passed, and the encounter had turned into a friendly visit, ending with a cheerful loan of clothes. Rosa clasped her hands together, as pleased as punch:

'Now you look like a proper lady. If it was broad daylight out there, how the people would stare!'

The woman smiled openly at last, but said dully:

'I don't know what I must look like really ... a real sight probably.'

Gonçalo accompanied the little party across the courtyard, where the rain was dripping gently from the acacia trees, and even as the lad's lantern was merging with the damp depths of the now quiet night, he again called out, 'Make sure the baby's well wrapped up!' Back in the kitchen, stamping his damp slippers on the flagstones, he felt little Manuel's hand, but the boy had dropped asleep now, breathing hoarsely, curled up against the back of the chair.

'The fever's lessened, but he could still do with a mustard bath to sweat it out. And before you put him to bed, give him some hot milk, almost boiling hot, with a drop of brandy in it. He could also do with a good scrub down. They're so dirty these people! But that can wait until he's better. And now, Rosa, send me up something to eat, something substantial, because I've still had no dinner, and it's been quite a night!'

Back in the library, once he had changed his slippers and had a rest, Gonçalo wrote a letter to Gouveia demanding with touching urgency that Casco be freed. And he added, 'This is the first request I make as deputy for Vila Clara (yes, congratulations are due!)—I have just received a telegram from our friend André, announcing that it's all settled and that the ministry has agreed, etc. So we need to talk! Would you do me the honour, sir, of coming to dine at the Tower in the vast shadow cast by Tító and accompanied by Videirinha? Those two worthy gentlemen are indispensable if we are to enjoy our food in harmony. And please, my friend, may I rely on you to invite them to our banquet, and save me having to send out any further eloquent messages ...'

Once the letter was sealed, he again languidly took up the manuscript of his Novella. And, chewing the end of his pen, he continued to search for an appropriately medieval tone for the scene in which Ordonho and the guards first spot the Bastard's horsemen approaching from the river, weapons gleaming beneath the harsh August sun.

However, since finishing that letter to Gouveia, which he had written as 'the new deputy for Vila Clara', his imagination kept sidling restlessly, stubbornly away from the ancient Solar de Santa Ireneia and flying off to Lisbon, the Lisbon of São Fulgêncio. And the terrace of the barbican tower, and burly Ordonho breathlessly bawling out orders, kept dissolving like a soft mist to be replaced by the more appetising and more fascinating image of a room in the Hotel Bragança with a balcony overlooking the Tejo. It was a great relief when Bento summoned him to supper; seated at the table, he could allow his imagination free rein to wander Lisbon and the corridors of the Teatro de São Carlos, to drift over the trees in the Avenida, through the ancient palaces owned by his relatives in São Vicente and in Graça, and through the more modern drawing rooms of bright, cultivated friends, pausing occasionally to linger over other delightful visions, a smile of silent delight on his face. He would definitely need to hire a carriage by the month. And for the sessions in Parliament, he would always wear pearl-grey gloves and a flower in his buttonhole, and for convenience's sake, he would take Bento with him, in a smart new tailcoat.

Bento came in bearing a tray with a bottle of cognac. He had given the letter to Joaquim, with instructions to set off at six in the morning for the administrator's house and to wait by the prison until Casco was released.

'And we've put the little one to bed in the green room, near to mine, because I'm a light sleeper, and if he starts crying, I'll be sure to hear him. For the moment, though, he's sleeping peacefully.'

'So he's sleeping, is he?' said Gonçalo, quickly drinking his glass of cognac. 'Let's have a look at the young gentleman.'

And taking a candlestick, he followed Bento up the narrow stairs to the green room, smiling as they tiptoed along. In the corridor outside the bedroom, Rosa had lovingly folded up the boy's ragged clothes—the torn waistcoat and the baggy trousers with just one button—and placed them neatly on a faded damask green couch.

In the room itself, lined with old green flock wallpaper, the whole of one wall was obscured by the vast mahogany bed, once reserved for important guests. At the head of the bed, on either side of the turned bedposts, hung portraits of two of his ancestors—a vastly overweight bishop pictured leafing through a manuscript, and next to him, leaning on his sword, a handsome Knight of Malta with a reddish beard and a large lace bow over his gleaming cuirass. On the high mattress, little Manuel lay snoring, not coughing now, but quiet and snug beneath the thick covers, his skin moist with a cooling, healthy perspiration.

Still on tiptoe, Gonçalo carefully tucked the sheet in more tightly. Then, concerned about the old, ill-fitting windows, he made sure that no treacherous draughts were coming in through the cracks. He ordered Bento to fetch an oil lamp, which he put on the washstand, placing a vase in front of it to dim the light. He took another slow look around the room, to ensure that all was quiet, dark and comfortable. Then he left, still on tiptoe and still smiling, leaving Casco's son to be watched over by those two noble Ramires men—the bishop with his worthy treatise and the Knight of Malta with his pure sword.

When he returned from the old fountain at the bottom of the garden—where, after lunch, he had spent the hottest hours of the day, leafing through a copy of *Panorama* beneath the cool of the trees and accompanied by the sound of babbling water—Gonçalo found on the desk in the library, along with the post from Oliveira, a letter that greatly surprised him, an enormous letter, written on a sheet of lined foolscap paper and bearing a wax seal. Instead of a signature, there was a flaming heart drawn in blue ink.

He quickly read the pencilled words, written in a large, clear, round hand:

Esteemed Senhor Gonçalo Ramires,

Recently, the district's gallant governor, our very own bold André Cavaleiro, has frequently been seen riding past the Casa dos Cunhais, looking tenderly up at the windows and at the honourable Barrolo coat of arms. Since it seems unlikely that he was studying the arquitecture (which is not in the least remarkable), the more serious-minded among us have concluded that the worthy governor was waiting for you to appear at one of the windows that overlook the square or Rua das Tecedeiras, or, more likely, on the belvedere in the garden, in order to resume your old and broken friendship. That is why you were so right to go to his office yourself and propose a reconciliation and open your generous arms to an old friend, so that he no longer wastes his precious time on those endless sorties, with his eyes fixed on the house of that noblest of families, the Barrolos. We therefore send you our heartfelt congratulations on taking so wise a step, which should quieten the impatience of the passionate Cavaleiro and redund to the benefit of the public as a whole!

Turning the sheet of paper over his hands, Gonçalo thought:

'It's from the Lousada sisters!'

He looked more closely at the writing and eyed various turns of phrase, noticing that the writer had written 'architecture' with a 'qu' and omitted the 'o' from 'redound'. Then he furiously tore up the letter, muttering in the silence of the library:

'The evil cows!'

Yes, there was no doubting that it had come from the odious Lousada sisters! And this terrified him all the more, because this gossip, issued by such ardent spreaders of gossip, would be sure to have reached every house in Oliveira, even the prison, even the hospital! And now the whole town would be laughing and lapping up the scandal and treacherously linking André's prowlings around the Casa dos Cunhais with his own visit to the governor's office, which had so astonished the denizens of the arcade. In the minds of Oliveira's inhabitants, then, and inspired by the Lousada sisters, he, Gonçalo Mendes Ramires, had been the one to lure Cavaleiro from his office, humbly leading him to Largo d'El-Rei and flinging wide the doors of the Casa dos Cunhais—which Cavaleiro had, until then, stalked and ogled to no avail—and thus he had calmly and brazenly sold him his sister's favours! The shameless hussies deserved to have their grubby skirts pulled down in the middle of the square one morning after mass and have their wrinkled buttocks furiously flayed until their blood ran over the flagstones!

Worse, appearances seemed to be treacherously conspiring

against him! André's persistent stalking of Gracinha, constantly trotting on his horse along the streets around the house, had only been noticed and commented on now, in August, on the eve of Gonçalo's very public reconciliation with the governor, a mysterious event which had aroused the curiosity of the whole of Oliveira. Sanches Lucena could not have chosen a worse moment to die! Months before, not even the Lousada sisters' malicious tongues could have linked his reconciliation with André to an amorous siege that had not yet begun or had, at least, not been much talked about. Three or four months later, André, realising that the house remained impenetrable to him, would surely have given up riding round the square with a rose in his buttonhole! Alas, the moment when André's prowlings around the door to his desire had become most obvious had coincided with Gonçalo welcoming and embracing the prowler and opening that door to him! This gave the gossip spread by the Lousada sisters a firm foundation, to whose substance and solidity everyone could attest, and their slander, thus supported, now stood there like a great Eternal Truth! Ah, those wretched women!

What to do now? Should he keep his relationship with Cavaleiro strictly within the bounds of politics, avoiding any slippery intimacies that would make Cavaleiro a favoured guest at the Casa dos Cunhais, just as he used to be at the Tower? Since Gonçalo's reconciliation with André, Barrolo—his brother-in-law and shadow—had also resumed his friendship, as quickly and naturally as the shadow follows the branch. But how could he insist that Barrolo's renewed friendship with Cavaleiro should remain confined to politics, as if within a leper colony? 'I am once again André's good friend and so are you, Barrolo, but never invite him to your table or open your door to him!' No, that would be a ridiculous imposition, an utterly impertinent demand, and one that, in a small town like Oliveira—given their inevitably frequent encounters and Barrolo's easy hospitality—would snap as surely as a piece of frayed twine. And what a grotesque position he would be in then, standing erect outside the house, like the Archangel Michael, flaming sword in hand, to prevent Satan, the governor, from entering in! Then again, having the whole town whispering in corners, mingling Gracinha's name with that of André, and with his own name mentioned as the friendly thread that had bound them together—that was too horrible!

Impatient with these difficult, thorny snares set to entrap and injure him, he ended up thumping the table in disgust:

'What a confounded nuisance! But then that's what life is like in these small, tittle-tattling towns.'

In Lisbon, who would care if the governor were frequently to be seen riding through a particular square or if a certain Nobleman of the Tower had become reconciled with the governor? No, enough was enough! He would go proudly forward, as if he were living in Lisbon, ignoring the idle talk and the malicious prying eyes. He was Gonçalo Mendes Ramires of the House of Ramires! A name and a house that had endured for a thousand years! He was far superior to Oliveira and to all its Lousadas, and not, praise God, just because of his name, but because of who he was. André was his friend and would be welcome in his sister's house—and to hell with Oliveira!

He did not even allow the Lousada sisters' grubby letter to spoil his quiet morning's work, for which he had been preparing since breakfast, rereading passages from Uncle Duarte's poem and perusing articles from *Panorama* about siege warfare in the twelfth century. Finally, forcing himself to concentrate, he sat down and dipped his pen in the brass inkwell that had served three generations of Ramires. And as he read through the pages he had written, the castle of Santa Ireneia had never seemed so heroic, so sovereign in its stature, raised up on such a high hill of History, dominating the Kingdom that spread out all around it, with towns and cultivated fields springing up thanks to the labours of its castellans.

And on that Afonsine morning of broiling August sun, when the Bastard's standard and his troops' glittering weapons had suddenly appeared beyond the woods by the river, the Solar de Santa Ireneia did, indeed, seem bold and fearless! The battlements were filled with crossbowmen, crossbows at the ready. From the towers and parapets rose the thick black smoke from the barrels of boiling pitch ready to be poured over any of Baião's men who attempted to climb the walls. The commanding officer ran along the battlements, reminding his men of their tactics, checking the bundles of arrows and the boulders to be hurled at the enemy. Old servants, cooks and labourers huddled beneath the thatched porches in the vast courtyard, all anxiously making the sign of the cross or tugging at the tunic of some sentry hurrying past, eager for news of the advancing host. Meanwhile, the enemy's horsemen had calmly crossed the river on the rough wooden bridge and reached the poplar trees and the granite cross erected long ago on the boundary of the estate by Lourenço Ramires the Butcher. And in the peace of that scorching morning, the slow, sad, Moorish tones of the Bastard's horns sounded out more clearly still.

However, as Gonçalo was scouring the *Dictionary of Synonyms* for suitably resonant words to describe the long-drawn-out sound of those horns, he actually heard low, deep notes coming from the Tower among the lemon trees. He stopped writing and heard the words of the *Ramires fado* rising up from the garden—like an offering, like a serenade—to his balcony thick with honeysuckle:

> *Seeing you there so alone,*
> *Tower of Santa Ireneia ...*

It was Videirinha! Gonçalo rushed to the window. A bowler hat bobbed among the trees, and a laudatory cry rang out:

'Long live the deputy for Vila Clara! Long live the illustrious deputy Gonçalo Ramires!'

From the guitar came the triumphal chords of the national anthem. Standing on the tips of his patent leather boots, Videirinha was shouting, 'Long live the illustrious House of Ramires!' And beneath the bowler hat, trembling with excitement, João Gouveia, with not a thought for his sore throat, was bawling out, 'Long live the illustrious deputy of Vila Clara. Hurrah!'

Overcome by laughter, Gonçalo held out one majestic, eloquent arm:

'Thank you, my dear fellow citizens! Thank you. You do me immense honour in coming as you do, the three of you, the glorious administrator, the inspired pharmacist, and ...'

Then he noticed. Where was Tító?

'Did Tító not come? Didn't you tell him, João?'

Pushing his hat back on his head, the administrator, who was sporting a cravat of scarlet satin, declared Tító to be an utter brute.

'We had agreed that all three of us would come. He was even supposed to bring a few fireworks to let off when we sang the national anthem. We arranged to meet by the bridge, but the rotter never turned up. It was all arranged, down to the last detail, and if he isn't here, that's because he's a traitor.'

'Well, come up anyway!' cried Gonçalo. 'I'll get dressed in a jiffy, and to sharpen our appetites, I propose a glass of vermouth and a stroll through the estate as far as the pine wood.'

Standing very erect, guitar aloft, Videirinha immediately set off along the broad garden path shaded by the vine trellis, with João Gouveia marching along behind him, holding his parasol as if it were a flag. When Gonçalo went back into his room, calling for Bento and for some hot water, the heroic notes of the Ramires *fado* were already filling the bean-patch down below, beneath the open window where a towel had been hung out to dry. Videirinha was singing the Nobleman's favourite verses, the ones in which his ancestor Rui Ramires, ploughing the seas of the Gulf of Oman in a carrack and meeting three mighty English Ships of the Line, stands on the forecastle, all dressed in red, one hand on his gold-and-jewel-encrusted leather belt, and proudly orders them to surrender:

> *Nonchalant, one hand on his belt,*
> *Standing next to the Royal Banner,*
> *He calls to the ships: Strike your sails now*
> *In honour of the King of Portugal!*

Quickly doing up his braces, Gonçalo joined in that hymn of praise—*Nonchalant, one hand on his belt, standing next to the Royal Banner* ... And as he tunelessly bellowed out these stirring words, he was thinking that, with such ancestors, he was quite right to scorn Oliveira and all its ghastly Lousadas. Then the slow thunder of Tító's voice echoed down the corridor:

'Where's our new deputy for Vila Clara? Is he already donning his uniform?'

Gonçalo ran to his bedroom door, beaming:

'Come in, Tító! Deputies don't wear uniforms, man! But if they did, why, I would certainly put it on today, complete with sword and tricorn hat, in honour of such illustrious guests!'

Tító entered slowly, his hands in the pockets of his olive-green velvet jacket, his broad-brimmed hat pushed back on his head, revealing his honest, bearded face, ruddy with health and sun:

'When I said "uniform" I meant "livery"—a lackey's livery.'

'What do you mean by that?'

In a still louder voice, Tító said:

'Well, what else will you be, man, but subject to the orders of vile, bald, old São Fulgêncio? If he tells you to pour him his tea, you'll do it, and when he tells you to vote, you'll vote, and do it that very instant. Ramires, vote this way and Ramires will do precisely as he's told. You'll be nothing but a valet, a valet in fine livery.'

Gonçalo shrugged impatiently:

'You're like a monster from the deep, a prehistoric creature from the jungle! You understand nothing of social realities! In society there are no absolute principles!'

But Tító would not be put off:

'And what about Cavaleiro? Is he now a *talented* young man? Is he now an *excellent* governor?'

Irritated and blushing scarlet, Gonçalo protested. When had he ever denied that André was talented or good at his job? Never! He had merely made fun of his dandyish ways and his glossy moustache. Besides, public service sometimes obliged one to make alliances with men who did not share the same tastes or even have the same aims!

'It seems that you, Senhor António Vilalobos, have come here today in the guise of a fierce moralist, a veritable Cato with whom one cannot even dine! It has always been the custom among stern philosophers to flee the banqueting hall where licentiousness reigns and to protest by eating their supper in the kitchen!'

Tító calmly turned his majestic back.

'Where are you off to, Tító?'

'To the kitchen!'

And when Gonçalo laughed, Tító, at the door, turned like a great tower and faced his friend:

'I'm serious, Gonçalo. Election, reconciliation, submission, and you in Lisbon doing the bidding of São Fulgêncio, and, in Oliveira, arm-in-arm with André, somehow it all seems so wrong. But if Rosa is on her usual splendid form, then let's speak no more of sad things!'

And Gonçalo was still gesticulating and protesting when he heard the sound of the guitar in the corridor and Gouveia's marching feet; and the words of the *fado* ringing out again, more softly this time, more adulatory in tone:

> Ancient house of the Ramires,
> Pride and flower of Portugal!

VI

Cavaleiro's house in Corinde dated from the late eighteenth century; plain and inelegant, its vast, smooth, yellow façade was punctuated by fourteen windows, and the house itself was almost surrounded by flat, cultivated fields. There was, however, a noble avenue of neatly aligned chestnut trees leading to the front courtyard, which was adorned with two marble fountains. The gardens were still filled with the splendid abundance of roses that had made them so famous, and which, in the days of André's grandfather, Judge Martinho, had merited a visit from the Queen herself, Maria II. The rooms inside were kept scrupulously clean and tidy, thanks to the care lavished on them by the old housekeeper, a poor relation of Cavaleiro's, Senhora Dona Jesuína Rolim.

Gonçalo had ridden there from the Tower, and as he walked through the anteroom, he immediately spotted the painting—depicting a smoke-filled battle at sea—which, long ago, he'd accidentally pierced while playing at sword-fighting one afternoon with André. Beneath this painting, a melancholy clerk from the governor's office sat waiting on a wicker sofa, his red briefcase resting on his knees. From a distant door at the far end of the corridor, André—having been informed by a servant of Gonçalo's arrival—called out gaily:

'Come in, Gonçalo. I'm in the bedroom. I've just this minute finished my bath and I'm not yet dressed.'

Still in his underwear, he folded Gonçalo in a generous, congratulatory embrace. Then, while he was dressing, among chairs piled high with the contents of his luggage—ties, silk socks, bottles of cologne—he talked about the heat, the tedious journey, and how deserted Lisbon had been.

'Absolutely ghastly!' exclaimed Cavaleiro, heating up a curling iron over a spirit lamp. 'Almost every street in the Baixa is being dug up and is consequently nothing but rubble and dust. Plus, the

Hotel Central was infested with mosquitos and the city is full of blacks! Lisbon is becoming more like Tunis every day! Nevertheless, we managed to fight the good fight!'

Perched on a divan, between a pile of coloured shirts and another of long underwear, all bearing a flamboyant monogram, Gonçalo was smiling:

'So, my friend, it's all arranged, is it?'

Seated at his dressing table, Cavaleiro was engaged in the meticulous task of curling the ends of his moustaches. And only once he had applied a large amount of brilliantine to them, tamed his rebelliously wavy hair, and studied himself in the mirror from every possible angle, did he assure an increasingly anxious Gonçalo that the Election was definitely his.

'But you know, when I arrived in Lisbon at the Ministry of the Interior, I found that the position had already been promised to Pita, Teotónio Pita, the excellent fellow who writes for *A Verdade*.'

Gonçalo jumped to his feet, causing the pile of shirts to topple over.

'And what happened then?'

Cavaleiro had left José Ernesto in no doubt as to his annoyance at having the constituency handed out as if it were a cigar, without consulting *him*, the governor in charge of said constituency. And when José Ernesto, in turn, got on his high horse, declaring that the Government came first, Cavaleiro had wagged a stern finger at him and said, 'Well, Zezinho, my dear friend, either I have Ramires as the next deputy for Vila Clara or I resign—and that is that!' There was much alarm and shouting and general uproar, but José Ernesto finally had to give in and they ended up having supper together in Algés with his uncle Reis Gomes, where, later that night, over a game of bluff, the ladies won fourteen *mil réis* off him.

'In short, Gonçalinho, we need to keep our eyes open. José Ernesto is a loyal fellow, an old friend, and he knows me well, but there will inevitably be certain compromises and pressures. And now for the really funny part. Do you know who the Regenerationists are putting forward as your opponent? Guess ... Julinho!'

'Julinho? You mean Júlio the amateur photographer?'

'The very same.'

'Good heavens!'

Cavaleiro gave a pitying shrug:

'He'll get about ten votes from his nearest neighbours and take photos of all the local tavern-keepers in their shirtsleeves, but he'll still be Julinho. No, it's not him I'm worried about, it's the political rabble in Lisbon.'

Gonçalo was disconsolately twirling his moustache:

'I imagined it was all somehow more solid, more settled than that, but with all these possible plots, maybe it still won't work out and I might not be elected!'

Still standing before the mirror, Cavaleiro was now smoothing his morning coat, which, after first carefully buttoning it up, he then unbuttoned to reveal his olive-green waistcoat and a puff of pale silk cravat, complete with sapphire pin. Then, drenching his handkerchief with perfume, he said:

'What matters is that you and I are allies again, fully reconciled. So don't worry, my dear Gonçalo—let's go and enjoy a good lunch! Don't you think this morning coat, courtesy of our friend Amieiro, fits rather well?'

'Oh, yes, it's magnificent!' said Gonçalo.

'Good, let's go down into the garden and you can revisit our old haunts and pick a Corinde rose for your buttonhole.'

And out in the corridor flanked by Indian vases and lacquered trunks, he linked arms with Gonçalo, his lost friend now recovered, and said:

'Well, here we are again, treading the noble floorboards of Corinde, as we did years ago. And nothing has changed, not so much as a curtain or a servant! One of these days, I must visit the Tower.'

Gonçalo burst out ingenuously:

'Oh, the Tower has changed enormously!'

And a sudden embarrassed silence descended, as if between them there had arisen the sad image of the old garden, in the days of love and hope, when André and Gracinha—accompanied by the beaming, tutelary presence of Miss Rhodes—went looking near the damp walls of the pond for the last violets of April. In silence they descended the spiral staircase, where, as children, they'd slid down the banister, and in a vaulted room below, lined with wooden benches, all bearing the Cavaleiro coat of arms, André stood before the French doors opening onto the garden and made a glum, despairing gesture:

'I don't spend much time in Corinde—not, you understand, because my work as governor keeps me in Oliveira, but because this old house has grown colder and somehow bigger since my mother died. I wander around in it as if I were lost. And when I do stay here, my walks in the garden or along the Rua Grande are very sad affairs. You remember the Rua Grande, don't you? Ah, Gonçalo, I'm heading for a very lonely old age!'

His sympathy restored, Gonçalo reassured him, saying:

'Oh, I get very bored at the Tower too.'

'But you have a very different nature from mine. I'm a natural melancholic.'

With some difficulty, he slid back the stiff bolt on the door of the French windows. Then, wiping his fingers on his perfumed handkerchief, he said:

'I think I would only enjoy Corinde now if it were surrounded by great bare hills and huge rugged rocks. Sometimes I feel that what I long for is the hermitage of St Bruno.'

Gonçalo smiled at these rather precious ascetic longings, uttered by lips adorned by carefully curled moustaches, glossy with brilliantine. And out on the terrace, leaning on the ivy-clad balustrade, after praising the lush, immaculate garden, he said mockingly:

'Well, yes, to a disciple of St Bruno, all this perfection must be truly offensive! But for a sinner like myself, it's an utter delight! The garden at the Tower is an absolute jungle.'

'Yes, Cousin Jesuína loves flowers. Haven't you met her? She's a relative of my mother's, and she's in charge of the house now, poor old thing, but she takes such care of the place ... If it weren't for her, the pigs would be rooting around in the flowerbeds. Without women, my friend, there is no order!'

They went down the curved steps and past the blue ceramic pots overflowing with geraniums, asters and lilies. Gonçalo recalled one

St John's Eve when, clutching a bundle of fireworks, he had taken a terrible tumble down those same steps. And slowly, as they strolled about the garden, they both summoned up memories of their former friendship. The trapeze was still there from the days when they'd both cultivated the heroic religion of fitness, gymnastics and cold baths. On that bench, beneath the magnolia tree, André had read him the opening stanza of his poem, *The Arzila Border*. And what about the target where they'd practised with pistols in preparation for the future duels they'd believed would be inevitable in the campaign they both intended to wage against the Old Constitutional Syndicate? Alas, after André's mother died, the whole of that wall adjoining the laundry room had been demolished so as to extend the hothouse.

'Besides, all that target practice proved useless,' added Cavaleiro. 'Soon afterwards, I myself joined the Syndicate. And now you're joining it too, through the door I opened for you!'

Plucking a leaf of lemon verbena and crushing it between his fingers to savour the scent, Gonçalo, with a frankness made more piercing and heartfelt by these disinterred memories, suddenly blurted out:

'And as you well know, I passionately want to go in through that door, but are you sure I'll be elected? Won't some obstacle get in our way? Pita is a very clever fellow.'

Cavaleiro hooked his thumbs in the armholes of his waistcoat and murmured:

'The cleverness of the Pitas is no match for the strength of the Cavaleiros.'

They went down three brick steps to the other unshaded garden, where the celebrated rose trees—the pride of Corinde and once the delight of a Queen—had been gloriously blooming since May. Cavaleiro's easy disdain for Pita made it clear that the position was guaranteed, and a dazzled Gonçalo, treading as respectfully as if he were visiting a museum, showered the rose garden with compliments.

'It's so beautiful, André, really wonderful. The roses are absolutely sublime. And those cabbage roses are quite extraordinary, and these yellow ones too. Perfect. And look at this little charmer, blushing from the roots of its white petals. And that scarlet one over there! Divine!'

Folding his arms, Cavaleiro said in a mocking, melancholy voice:

'Yes, but such is my social and sentimental solitude that, despite having all these roses blooming around me, I have no one to whom I can send a bouquet! I'm reduced to giving them to the Lousada sisters!'

The Nobleman flushed even more scarlet than the roses he'd been praising:

'Not the Lousada sisters! Those shameless creatures!'

Glancing at his friend, André's lustrous eyes were suddenly filled with an uneasy curiosity:

'Why shameless?'

'Why? Because they are! It's their nature, the will of God! They're as shameless as these roses are red.'

Reassured, Cavaleiro went on:

'Oh, you're speaking in general terms. They're certainly full of malice. That's why I heap them with roses. And when I'm in Oliveira, I make sure to take a very respectful cup of tea with them once a week!'

'Well,' muttered the Nobleman, 'you'll never tame them.'

Then Mateus appeared on the steps, a napkin over his arm, his bald head gleaming in the sunlight. It was time for lunch. Cavaleiro picked a 'triumphant rose' for Gonçalo and 'an innocent rosebud' for himself. And thus adorned, they were proceeding on up to the terrace, surrounded by the glow and perfume of the roses, when Cavaleiro suddenly had an idea:

'What time are you heading off to Oliveira, Gonçalinho?'

The Nobleman hesitated. To Oliveira? He had no plans to go there that week.

'Why? Do I need to go to Oliveira so very urgently?'

'Of course, my boy! We have to talk to Barrolo tomorrow and reach some agreement, because we need the votes from his Murtosa estate! We can't afford to rest on our laurels, you know. Not because of Júlio, but because of Pita!'

'I see,' said Gonçalo, startled. 'I'll set off to Oliveira today, then.'

'In that case, we can go together, on horseback. It's rather a pleasant ride through Freixos, and there's always plenty of shade. You might perhaps send orders to the Tower, though, to have them bring you some fresh clothes.'

No, there was no need. Gonçalo always kept plenty of clothes at his sister's house, everything from slippers to a tailcoat. And he'd ride into Oliveira just as the philosopher Bias rode into Athens, armed only with a walking stick and infinite patience.

'Excellent!' cried André. 'We will make our official entrance into Oliveira this very evening. Let the campaign begin!'

The Nobleman twiddled his moustache rather anxiously, thinking of the mischievous titters such a flagrantly fraternal entrance would evoke from the Lousada sisters and from the whole town. And when Cavaleiro told Mateus to have his horse, Rossilho, and the Nobleman's horse ready for half past four, Gonçalo rather exaggerated his worries about the heat and the dust. Wouldn't it be better to leave in the cool of the evening, at, say, seven? (That way, he hoped to arrive in Oliveira unnoticed, under cover of dusk.) André, however, protested:

'No, because then we'd arrive in the dark. We need to make a solemn entrance, when the band is playing in the square. What if we leave at five o'clock?'

Gonçalo bowed to this implacable fate.

'Fine, at five o'clock, then.'

In the carpeted dining room, with its age-blackened paintings of flowers and fruits concealing the imitation damask wallpaper, André occupied his grandfather Martinho's venerable armchair. The glittering china, the fresh roses arranged in a Royal Saxe vase were all evidence of Cousin Jesuína's meticulous touch; she, however, having woken that morning with a stomach ache, had not even got dressed and was taking lunch in her room. Gonçalo praised the elegance and orderliness, so rare in the house of a bachelor, and regretted that he had no Cousin Jesuína at the Tower. André smiled modestly, unfolding his napkin and hoping that Gonçalo would tell the Barrolos about the comfort and luxury of Corinde. Then, spearing an olive with his fork, he began:

'Yes, as I was saying, my dear Gonçalo, after spending a day or so in the capital, I went on to Sintra ...'

Mateus opened the door a crack to remind His Excellency that the clerk was still waiting.

'Well, let him wait!' roared His Excellency.

Gonçalo reminded him that the worthy man might be getting impatient, might be hungry ...

'Let him eat, then!' cried His Excellency.

Gonçalo was taken aback by André's brusque scorn for the poor clerk, sitting forgotten on the bench in the hall, his briefcase on his lap. However, he merely speared an olive himself and said:

'What were you saying about going to Sintra?'

'Dreadfully dull,' said André. 'The dust was terrible and the women mediocre. Oh, but I was forgetting, who do you think I met there, on the road to Colares? Castanheiro, our friend Castanheiro of the *Annals*, and wearing a top hat too. He immediately flung up his arms and cried desolately, "Will Gonçalo Mendes Ramires never send me his Novella?" It seems that the first issue of the journal is due out in December, and he needs to have your story by the beginning of October. He begged me to urge you on, to remind you of the Ramires' glorious past. You really should try and finish the book. It would actually be rather useful if you were to publish a serious, erudite, very Portuguese piece of work just before your entry into Parliament.'

'It certainly would!' said Gonçalo brightly. 'And I only have the last chapter to write, but it's a chapter that requires more preparation, more research. To finish the Novella I need peace of mind and the certainty that I *am* going to win this wretched Election. It isn't that fool Júlio who worries me, it's the conspiratorial rabble in Lisbon. What do you think?'

Cavaleiro laughed and again reached out his fork for the olives:

'What do I think, Gonçalinho? I think you're like a small, anxious child, who's afraid there won't be enough rice pudding left when the dish reaches him. But don't you worry, little one, you'll get your fair share of pudding. I must say, though, José Ernesto was very stubborn. Apparently, he owes Pita several favours. Pita's newspaper, *A Verdade*, has been fiercely pro-Government. And ever since Pita found out that I've snatched Vila Clara from him, he's been incandescent with rage, not that I care. I won't lose any sleep over Pita's little tantrums or jibes, but José Ernesto admires Pita, he needs Pita, and he's committed to repaying Pita with a seat as a deputy. On my last day in Lisbon, he said to me—and I had to laugh, "It seems that the deputies for Vila Clara are in the habit of dying; so if, according to that excellent custom, your Ramires should suddenly die, then Pita will replace him."'

Gonçalo fell back in his chair.

'Me? Die suddenly? The brute!'

'He meant die as far as the constituency is concerned,' said Cavaleiro, laughing. 'For example, if you and I should quarrel, or if, tomorrow, we should have some disagreement—but that's just not possible!'

Mateus brought in a steaming tureen of chicken soup.

'Dig in!' exclaimed André. 'And let's have no more talk of constituencies or Pitas or Júlios or damned politics! Tell me about the plot of your Novella. It's historical, isn't it? Set in the Middle Ages? In the time of João V? If I were ever to attempt to write a novel, I would choose that really delicious period of history: Portugal under the Habsburgs.'

The clock on the Church of São Cristóvão in Oliveira, which was always fast, was striking a quarter to seven when André Cavaleiro and Gonçalo rode down Rua Velha into the main square, Terreiro da Louça (now renamed Praça Counsellor Costa Barroso).

Every Sunday, on the bandstand that the aforementioned Counsellor Costa Barroso had had built when he was mayor, on the spot previously occupied by the stocks, the regimental band or the local musical society transformed the square into the sociable heart of that otherwise quiet, stay-at-home town. However, on that particular afternoon, the bazaar sponsored by the Bishop had just opened in the Convent of Santa Brígida, and, consequently, there was only a scattering of women sitting on the stone benches or on the chairs underneath the acacia trees outside the almshouses. The Lousada sisters were absent from their usual reserved seats, chosen for their panoramic view of the whole square—the houses on either side of the church and the convent, Rua Velha and Rua das Velas, the stall selling lemonade, and even another small retreat, modestly screened by ivy. The only familiar faces were those of Dona Maria Mendonça, the Baroness das Marges, and the two Alboim sisters, who were chatting together, their backs to the square, next to the wrought-iron railings on what had once been the city wall, from which one could see the fields, the new seminary, the pine forest and the River Crede's glittering, meandering curves.

However, among the gentlemen strolling idly up and down the path known locally as The Ride and enjoying the coronation march from Meyerbeer's *The Prophet*, there was renewed astonishment (even though they were all aware of the famous reconciliation that had taken place in the governor's office) when the two friends, both wearing straw hats and long gaiters, rode in on their horses— Gonçalo's was a graceful bay, its tail cropped short English-fashion, while André's was darker and heavier, with a proudly arched neck and a thick tail so long that it brushed the flagstones. Melo Alboim, the Baron das Marges and the local delegate stopped in their tracks, open-mouthed, and were joined by one of the Vila-Velha brothers, then by the landowner Pestana, and finally by plump Major Ribas, who, uniform unbuttoned, rocked from side to side, joking about that 'new' friendship. The notary Guedes knocked over his chair as he sprang to his feet, indignant but respectful, baring his bald head in the lowest of bows and clutching his hat in one trembling hand. And emerging from behind the ivy-clad screen, still doing up his trousers, old Cerqueira, the lawyer, stood aghast, his spectacles perched on the end of his nose, his fingers still poised over his trouser buttons.

Meanwhile, the two friends continued gravely past the line of houses, which were dominated by Dona Arminda Vilegas' mansion, with the elaborate Vilegas coat of arms carved on the architrave, and its ten fine wrought-iron balconies opulently adorned with yellow damask curtains. On the corner balcony, Barrolo and José Mendonça were sitting on wickerwork stools, smoking. On hearing the slow clip-clop of hooves and unexpectedly seeing his brother-in-law, Barrolo almost fell off the balcony.

'Gonçalo! Are you going to our house?'

And not even waiting for a response, he again shouted, waving his arms about:

'We'll be right there. We dined here this evening—Gracinha's upstairs with her Aunt Arminda. We'll be there in two ticks!'

Cavaleiro waved and smiled at Captain Mendonça, for Barrolo, in his excitement, had already plunged through the damask yellow curtains. And, leaving a wake of astonishment behind them as they rode across the square, the two friends continued on down Rua das Velas, where, much to the Nobleman's gratification, a policeman stood to attention and saluted.

Cavaleiro accompanied Gonçalo to Largo d'El-Rei. Opposite the house, a man wearing a red beret was grinding out the wedding chorus from *Lucia di Lammermoor* on a barrel organ and gazing up at the deserted windows. Joaquim the porter, ran out from the courtyard to take the reins of the Nobleman's horse. Without a word, the organ-grinder smilingly held out his beret. And after throwing him a handful of change, Gonçalo hesitated before murmuring, embarrassed and blushing:

'Would you like to come in and rest for a moment, André?'

'No, thank you, but I'll see you tomorrow in my office at two o'clock, along with Barrolo, to sort out those votes. Goodbye, my friend! We've had a most enjoyable ride and given everyone something to talk about!'

And giving the house one last lingering look, he rode off down Rua das Tecedeiras.

In his room (which was always there ready for him, with the bed made), Gonçalo was just finishing his ablutions and brushing his hair when Barrolo came rushing down the corridor, eager and breathless, followed by an equally breathless Gracinha, nervously untying the scarlet ribbons on her hat. Ever since the afternoon when Barrolo had, 'with his own eyes', witnessed Gonçalo talking to André on the balcony of the governor's office, he and Gracinha had been burning to know the reasons—the secret story—behind that surprising reconciliation. Gonçalo's hasty return to the Tower in the carriage, without even stopping at the Casa dos Cunhais; Cavaleiro's sudden departure for Lisbon; the silence that had fallen, heavier than an iron lid, on the whole matter; all these things had left them anxious and terrified. At night, Gracinha would kneel at her prayer stool and, as she mumbled her way through her usual prayers, would find herself murmuring distractedly to Our Lady, 'Oh dear, whatever's going to happen?' Barrolo hadn't dared to ride over to the Tower, but the balcony at the governor's office kept invading his dreams, far larger than life and growing ever larger, until it filled the whole of Oliveira, pressing against the windows of the Casa dos Cunhais, where he managed to keep it at bay with a broom handle. And now here were Gonçalo and André serenely trotting into town, both wearing straw hats, like old friends returning from a ride!

Standing at the door of Gonçalo's room, Barrolo flung wide his arms and bellowed:

'What *has* been going on?! People are talking of little else. You, out riding with André!'

Still panting, her face as red as the ribbons on her hat, Gracinha could say only:

'And you don't visit, don't even bother to write. We were so worried.'

And still holding his towel and without even inviting them in, the Nobleman explained the 'mystery':

'It was all very unexpected, but perfectly natural too in a way. As you know, Sanches Lucena died, leaving the post of Vila Clara's deputy vacant. And since the candidate for the post really has to be a local man with property and influence, the Government immediately wrote to me, by telegram, to ask if I wanted to stand. And since I basically have nothing against the Historicals and am good friends with José Ernesto and would like to enter Parliament, I said Yes.'

Barrolo slapped his thigh triumphantly.

'So I was right, damn it!'

The Nobleman went on, still drying his hands:

'I accepted, although, of course, with certain very important conditions ... but, yes, I accepted. As you both know, it is important in such a situation for the candidate to get on well with the governor. Initially, I didn't wish to renew our friendship. However, urged on by the powers-that-be in Lisbon, who were most insistent, and for certain other overriding political reasons, I agreed to make that sacrifice. Given the difficulties in which the country finds itself, we must all make sacrifices, and this was mine. Besides, André was extremely kind and affectionate. And so here we are, friends again. Political friends, but friends too. I had lunch with him today in Corinde and since it was such a lovely afternoon, we rode back here together via Freixos. So harmony has been restored, and the Election is guaranteed.'

'Come here and let me embrace you!' roared Barrolo, beside himself with joy.

Gracinha had sat down on the edge of the bed, her hat in her lap, gazing silently, tenderly up at her brother, her eyes simultaneously smiling and tearful. Detaching himself from Barrolo's embrace, the Nobleman added as he distractedly folded up his towel:

'The Election is guaranteed, but we still have work to do. You must talk to Cavaleiro too, Barrolo, and I've already arranged for us to be at his office at two o'clock tomorrow. You have to be reconciled with him as well, because we need the votes from your Murtosa estate ...'

'Of course, my boy! Whatever you want—votes, money ...' And absentmindedly spraying his jacket with eau de Cologne, which dripped onto the floor, Gonçalo added:

'The moment I made my peace with André, you did too, Barrolo.'

Barrolo was so delighted, he almost leapt in the air:

'Of course! Besides, I've always liked Cavaleiro immensely, indeed, I've often said to Gracinha, "Why all this fuss about something as trivial as politics?"'

'Well,' said the Nobleman, 'politics separated us and politics has brought us together again. Such is the fickle nature of Time and Empire.'

And with that, he seized Gracinha by the shoulders and gave her a resounding kiss on each cheek:

'And how's Aunt Arminda? Has she recovered from her scalding? And has she gone back to reading the adventures of *Leandro the Handsome?*'

Gracinha was positively aglow, still smiling the same slow smile, which wrapped her in sweetness and light.

'Aunt Arminda is much better and able to walk again now. She asked after you, by the way. But Gonçalo, you must be hungry!'

'No, not at all, I had a huge lunch at Corinde. But since you dined old-fashionedly early with Aunt Arminda, you'll doubtless have a little supper later. So I'll join you then. Now all I need is a good strong cup of tea!'

Gracinha raced off, eager to serve her beloved hero. And as he and Barrolo walked to the stairs, with Barrolo gazing adoringly up at him, the Nobleman of the Tower was bemoaning the sacrifices he'd have to make:

'It's true, my boy, it's a real bore. But, damn it, we must all do our bit to drag our country out of the hole it's in!'

Still dazzled, Barrolo murmured:

'And yet you said not a word to a soul. Such modesty!'

'On another matter entirely, Barrolo, tomorrow, when you meet André, you must invite him to supper.'

'Naturally!' cried Barrolo. 'We'll lay on a feast!'

'No. We want a nice quiet, intimate little supper, with just us, André and João Gouveia. You can send a telegram to João. Oh, and the Mendonças too. But it's to be a very discreet affair, just so that we can talk and seal our reconciliation in the most sociable, elegant way possible.'

The next day, at the governor's office, Barrolo and Cavaleiro shook hands as simply as if they'd spent the previous evening playing billiards and chatting in the club on Rua das Pegas. They then spoke briefly about the Election, and when Cavaleiro idly mentioned the votes from the Murtosa estate, Barrolo almost choked in his impatience to offer them up to him:

'Anything you want, you just have to ask—votes, money, whatever. I'll go over to Murtosa, lay on a good spread, open a barrel of wine, and the whole parish will go to vote and there'll be fireworks to celebrate ...'

Cavaleiro laughed and tried to restrain such bounty:

'No, no, my dear Barrolo! We are preparing a very sober, very quiet Election campaign. Vila Clara will elect Gonçalo Mendes Ramires deputy simply for being the best man for the job. There's no competition really, Julinho is a mere shadow. Therefore ...'

But a radiant, jigging Barrolo could not be put off:

'No, André, I'm sorry, but there must be wine, revelry, fireworks and general merrymaking!'

Anxious to restrain Barrolo's chatter and the affectionate way he kept slapping Cavaleiro on the back to underline their renewed intimacy, Gonçalo pointed to André's desk:

'But you have things to do, André. Look at all that dreadful paperwork. We mustn't take up any more of our illustrious governor's time. To work!

To work, my brother, for work
Equals André, virtue and valour!'

He picked up his hat and gestured to his brother-in-law, who, cheeks aflame with delight, stammered out the invitation that would place a sociable, elegant seal on their reconciliation:

'Cavaleiro, perhaps we could best continue our conversation if you were to give us the great pleasure of dining with us on Thursday at half past six. Whenever Gonçalo is here, we always dine a little later than usual.'

Blushing, Cavaleiro thanked him discreetly and ceremoniously:

'The pleasure will be all mine. I would consider it an immense honour ...'

And accompanying them to the door of the anteroom, where he held aside the heavy scarlet baize curtain embroidered with the royal coat of arms, he asked Barrolo to present his deepest respects to Senhora Dona Graça.

Damp with emotion, Barrolo was mopping the sweat from his brow and neck as they went down the stone steps. And once out in the courtyard, he gave vent to his feelings:

'He's such a fine fellow, that André! A really honest lad. I've always liked him. To be frank, I couldn't wait for all this silliness to be over. And as regards our own household, he'll be such a fine addition to the company and to conversation.'

On Thursday, out on the terrace after lunch, where they were taking their postprandial coffee, Gonçalo advised Barrolo 'so as to emphasise the easy intimacy of the occasion', not to wear a tailcoat. 'And you, Gracinha, nothing décolleté, but something bright and simple.'

Lounging on a wicker chair, with a small white cat asleep on her lap, Gracinha smiled hesitantly and continued leafing through a copy of *Friendship's Offerings.*

After all the shock and turmoil of Sunday, she had affected a mute indifference not only to the reconciliation that was still causing tremors in the town, but also to the Election, and now to that evening's dinner party. These last few days, though, she had been so touchy and irritable that Barrolo had kept recommending she take his mother's favourite remedy for 'nerves', namely, rosemary leaves boiled in white wine.

Gonçalo could see how troubling she found the imminent triumphal return of André, the old André, into her marital home, the Casa dos Cunhais. And to calm his own anxieties, he reminded himself (as he had in the cemetery in Vila Clara) of Gracinha's essentially serious nature, her pure, lofty mind, her proud, heroic little soul. That morning, still caught up in his nervous excitement about the Election, his one fear was that Gracinha, out of embarrassment or caution, might greet Cavaleiro coldly, might cast a chill over his renewed fervour for the House of Ramires and his political patronage. He said again in the same jocular tone:

'Did you hear me, Gracinha? Wear a white dress, a cheerful dress, that'll put a smile on our guests' faces.'

Still immersed in her reading, she murmured:

'Yes, of course, especially with this heat ...'

Barrolo slapped his thigh. It was just such a shame he didn't have there in the house—to drink a toast to their reconciliation—a particularly famous Port wine from his mother's cellar, a wonderful, ancient wine from the reign of João II.

'João II?' snorted Gonçalo. 'It will be well and truly corked by now!'

'Or was it João VI? Anyway, it was some king or other, yes, a unique wine from the last century! Mama only has eight or so bottles left. And this would definitely have been the right occasion to open one.'

The Nobleman took a slow sip of coffee:

'The other thing André used to love was crème caramel.'

Gracinha abruptly put down her book, and Gonçalo, struck dumb by her reaction, watched her brush the drowsing cat off her lap and stride silently across the terrace and disappear among the tall yew trees in the garden.

And that evening, when the Nobleman took his place at the oval table next to cousin Maria Mendonça, the first thing he saw, prominently displayed between two large compotiers, was a generous dish of crème caramel. Even though this supper was supposedly an intimate affair, the table was set with the finest china and with Uncle Melchior's famous gold-plated cutlery, and two Royal Saxe vases overflowed with white and yellow carnations, the heraldic colours of the Ramires.

Dona Maria had not seen her beloved cousin since Gracinha's birthday, and in the ceremonious silence during which they all unfolded their napkins, she said with a smile and a grave bow:

'I haven't yet congratulated you, cousin Gonçalo.'

'Shh, cousin, not a word. It's been decided that we won't even mention the subject today—besides, it's far too hot for politics.'

She sighed softly, as if she were fainting, 'Ah, yes, the heat, this terrible heat!' Ever since she'd arrived wearing a black dress, which was, she said, 'her Sunday best', she had not stopped commenting on Gracinha's white dress.

'It really suits her. She looks so lovely!'

It was a simple dress of white crepe, which only emphasised Gracinha's almost virginal grace and made her appear still younger. And it was true, she had never looked more captivating, so pale and delicate, her green eyes shining like washed emeralds, her thick hair wavier and glossier than ever, a slight, transparent blush on her cheek; she had, in short, all the cool freshness of a newly watered flower, a flower brought back to life, despite the shyness that made her fumble slightly when she raised a golden spoon to her lips. And beside her, so much larger and more robust, his shirtfront bulging out like a cuirass and adorned with two sapphires, with a full-blown white rose in his lapel, sat André Cavaleiro—declining the soup (oh, no, he never drank soup in summer!)—who dominated the table and yet was clearly rather moved as well, dabbing at his glossy moustache with a handkerchief so strongly perfumed that it drowned out the scent from the carnations. Yet he was the one who set the tone of the conversation with his cheerful complaints about the heat, the dreadful Oliveira heat. What a burning Purgatory it was after his two days in Paradise, in the delicious cool of Sintra!

Dona Maria Mendonça turned her sharp eyes sweetly on the governor: How was Sintra? Busy? Were there a lot of parties in the evenings in Seteais? Had he met her cousin, the Countess de Chelas?

Yes, Cavaleiro had spoken briefly to the Countess when he visited the Queen in Pena.

'Ah, and how is the Queen?'

'Oh, as charming as ever.'

The Countess had, he thought, looked a little thin, but she was always so friendly, so intelligent, so very much the *grande dame*—wasn't that so? He turned to Gracinha with the slightest, gentlest inclination of his head, and she, flustered and blushing more furiously still, stammered something about never having met the Countess de Chelas. Dona Maria Mendonça immediately put the blame for this on the inertia of her Barrolo cousins, always hidden away in their house in Oliveira, never venturing forth to Lisbon in the winter to meet their relatives and get to know them.

'I blame cousin José, who loathes Lisbon.'

Barrolo didn't loathe Lisbon at all. If he could transport to Lisbon all his comforts, his bedroom, his stables, the excellent water from the spring in the orchard, and the gorgeous verandah overlooking the garden, then he'd go there like a shot!

'But the thought of being holed up in one of those mean little rooms in the Hotel Bragança ... And then there's the mediocre food and the constant noise to contend with. Gracinha never sleeps well in Lisbon. And the mornings there are so tedious. There's never anything to do in Lisbon in the morning!'

Cavaleiro smiled at Barrolo, as if charmed by his wit and intelligence. Then he confessed that, despite living (thanks to the State) in a very comfortable mansion and also enjoying excellent water from the wonderful São Domingos well, he regretted that his political duties and party loyalties kept him tied to Oliveira. His one hope was that the Government would fall and thus free him up to spend three divine months in Italy.

Seated on the other side of Gracinha was Gouveia, usually so shy and silent in the presence of ladies. However, suddenly, prompted by friendship and conviction, he exclaimed impetuously:

'Your hopes will, I'm afraid, be dashed, André! There's no stopping São Fulgêncio! You've got another three or four years of him yet!'

And leaning closer to Gracinha, in an attempt at friendliness that made his cheeks blaze, he said again:

'No, there's no stopping São Fulgêncio. Our André will be with us for another three or four years.'

Languidly closing his thick-lashed eyes, André protested:

'Oh, João, don't be so cruel!'

Even if he had to desert his party (and what would the loss of one rusty spear matter to such a powerful army?), he was already dreaming of that winter escape to Italy, indeed, he was already planning it. Might he pour Senhora Dona Graça a little white wine?

Barrolo effusively reached out one arm to stop him:

'André, I want you to taste that wine very carefully. It's from my vineyard in Corvelo. I think it's very special. But take your time!'

Cavaleiro tasted it as devoutly as if he were taking communion. And bowing his head appreciatively to Barrolo, who positively glowed with pleasure, he said:

'Delicious, absolutely delicious!'

'It is, isn't it? I actually prefer this wine to any of the French wines, however fine. Even our saintly friend, Father Soeiro, likes it!'

Obscured behind one of the tall vases of carnations, Father Soeiro had been silent up until then; now, though, he blushed and smiled, saying:

'Alas, these days, I have to take it with a lot of water, Senhor José Barrolo. My tongue may crave it, but my rheumatism says No.'

José Mendonça, who had no fear of rheumatism, always attacked that lovely Corvelo wine with great gusto.

'What do you think of it, João Gouveia?'

João Gouveia was fortunate enough to have known that wine for years! And in Portugal, he had certainly never found a white wine to compare for freshness, bouquet or savour!

'And I've been downing it with such enthusiasm, friend Barrolo, that this lovely cut-glass decanter is almost empty!'

Barrolo was thrilled. His only disappointment was that Gonçalo would never drink 'that nectar'. No, Gonçalo hated white wine.

'Today, though, I have one of those thirsts that can only be quenched by a good, slightly sparkling *vinho verde*, with ice. This Vidainhos wine is one of Barrolo's too. I certainly don't despise the family's wines, no—this Vidainhos, for example, I consider to be utterly sublime.'

Cavaleiro immediately asked to taste that sublime *vinho verde* from the Vidainhos vineyard in Amarante. In response to urgent signals from Barrolo, the butler presented Cavaleiro with a slender glass, especially made for that sparkling wine. However, Cavaleiro, stroking the cool glass without actually drinking from it, returned to the idea of holidays and journeys, as if to emphasise how weary and bored he was with Oliveira. And did Senhora Dona Graça have any idea where he'd go after that winter escape to Italy, if, God willing, the Government were to fall? To Asia Minor.

'It's a journey I would tempt our Gonçalo to make too. It's so easy now that we have railways! From Venice to Constantinople is a mere step! Then from Constantinople to Izmir it's just one or two days on board an excellent steamer. And from there you can join a caravan via Tripoli and ancient Sidon to Galilee, yes, Galilee. What do you think, Gonçalo? Wouldn't that be wonderful?'

Father Soeiro, his fork halfway to his mouth, recalled timidly that in Galilee, Senhor Gonçalo Ramires would be setting foot on land that had once very nearly belonged to his family:

'One of your ancestors, Gutierres Ramires, who accompanied Tancredo on the First Crusade, turned down the lordship of Galilee and of Oultrejordain.'

'Well, that was a great mistake,' cried Gonçalo, laughing. 'That was very wrong of him! What could be more amusing now than for me to be Lord of Galilee! Senhor Gonçalo Mendes Ramires, Lord of Galilee and Oultrejordain! What a joke!'

Cavaleiro protested earnestly:

'Why a joke?'

'Don't you believe him!' said Dona Maria Mendonça, eyes flashing. 'Deep down, for all his joking, Cousin Gonçalo is profoundly, terribly aristocratic!'

The Nobleman of the Tower set down his glass, having first taken a long, appreciative sip.

'Yes, of course I'm an aristocrat, and I would feel rather unhappy to have been born, like a weed, from other nameless weeds. I like knowing that I'm the son of my father Vicente, who was the son of his father Damião, and so on back to some Suevian king ...'

'Recesvinto,' said Father Soeiro respectfully.

'Yes, back to King Recesvinto. The trouble is that the blood of all those ancestors is no different from the blood of my porter's ancestors. And if I go back beyond Recesvinto, as far as Adam, then I have no special ancestors at all!'

And while everyone was laughing, Dona Maria Mendonça leaned towards him and whispered behind her open fan:

'You can speak as scornfully as you like, Gonçalo, but I know of a certain lady who greatly admires the House of Ramires and its representative.'

Gonçalo lovingly filled his glass again, watching carefully lest the bubbles should overflow.

'I'm glad to hear it. But, as Manuel Duarte would say, "Can you be more precise, please?" Who does she really admire, me or the Suevian king, Recesvinto?'

'Both.'

'Goodness!'

Then, again setting down his glass, he asked more seriously this time:

'Who is this person?'

Oh, she couldn't possibly tell him that. She wasn't yet old

enough to play the role of go-between bearing little *billets-doux*. Gonçalo didn't need a name, he said, only her qualities. Was she young? Was she pretty?

'Pretty?' cried Dona Maria. 'Why, she's one of the most beautiful women in Portugal!'

Amazed, Gonçalo blurted out a name: 'Dona Ana Lucena!'

'Why her?'

'Because she's the only extremely beautiful woman living in the area who you know well enough to be her confidante.'

Dona Maria smiled, adjusting the two roses brightening up her black silk bodice.

'Possibly.'

'Well, I'm immensely flattered, but, like Manuel Duarte, I need you to be more precise. If, on her side, her intentions are honourable, then, dear God, no! However, if they are entirely dishonourable, then I promise to do my duty as best I can.'

Scandalised, Dona Maria covered her face with her fan. Then, peering over the top, her bright eyes shining, she said:

'Her honourable intentions would suit you best, because they'd come with two hundred *contos* in tow!'

Gonçalo gave an admiring whoop:

'Oh, cousin Maria! There isn't a more intelligent woman in all Europe.'

Everyone was eager to hear Dona Maria's latest witticism, but Gonçalo silenced them, saying:

'We can't tell you. It concerns a marriage.'

Then José Mendonça recalled the latest snippet of piquant gossip, which had been doing the rounds of Oliveira since the previous day:

'Speaking of marriage, what do you make of Dona Rosa Alcoforado's marriage?'

First, Barrolo, then Gouveia, and even Gracinha, all declared it to be 'utterly dreadful'. That perfect young woman, with her lovely rosy complexion and her golden hair, bound in matrimony to Teixeira de Carredes, a patriarch with numerous grandchildren. A complete disgrace!

Cavaleiro did not, however, see the marriage as quite such a disgrace. Teixeira de Carredes, as well as being refined and intelligent, was a very young old man, with barely a wrinkle—indeed, that interesting contrast between his dark moustache and his thick, curly, white hair made him almost handsome. And despite her rosy complexion and golden hair, there was something rather limp and listless about Senhora Dona Rosa. She wasn't very bright either and somewhat slovenly too, with her hair all over the place and her clothes always creased.

'Forgive me for saying so, but the person making a bad marriage is poor Teixeira de Carredes.'

Dona Maria Mendonça stared at the governor with amusement and surprise:

'Well, if you don't admire Rosinha Alcoforado, who do you admire?'

He gave a swift and gallant response:

'Well, ladies, apart from your good selves, there's no one I admire! As regards feminine beauty, this is the most impoverished district in Portugal!'

Everyone protested. What about Maria Marges? And young Reriz from Riosa? And Melozinho Alboim, with those magnificent eyes of hers? Cavaleiro refused to be convinced, and demolished each and every candidate with caustic remarks aimed either at their dull complexion, their ugly gait, or their provincial tastes and manners, thus, without actually saying so, condemning them all for lacking Gracinha's beauty and grace, and throwing at her feet a pile of weary, crumpled ladies. She noticed this subtle adulation of his, and her eyes lit up with a flame that burned more tenderly even than the blushes covering her cheeks. Hoping to disperse all this accumulating adulatory incense, she mentioned another beauty who was the pride of the district:

'There's Viscount de Rio-Manso's daughter, Rosinha Rio-Manso. She's really lovely!'

Cavaleiro quickly demolished her as well:

'But she's only twelve years old! She isn't even a full-blown rose yet, but a mere rosebud!'

Almost humbly, Gracinha mentioned Luísa Moreira, the daughter of a shopkeeper, who always drew admiring glances at Sunday mass at the cathedral and in the main square.

'She's a very beautiful young woman and has a fine figure.'

Cavaleiro triumphed again, commenting languidly:

'Yes, Senhora Dona Graça, but her teeth are all crooked and crowded together. Have you never noticed? A most unpleasant mouth. And quite apart from her teeth, there's her brother, Evaristo, with his dull face and his dandruff and his grubby clothes and his Jacobinist views! No woman with a brother like that could possibly be beautiful!'

Mendonça brought up another curious piece of Oliveira news:

'Speaking of Evaristo, is he still planning to start a new republican newspaper, *O Rebate?*'

The governor gave a dismissive, superior shrug and said he had no idea. João Gouveia, though, his face flushed and glowing after drinking both white wine and red, told them that *O Rebate* would be published in November. He even knew the patriot who'd be providing the 'readies'. And the paper's campaign would begin with five forthright articles on the Storming of the Bastille.

Gonçalo expressed his astonishment at the spread of republicanism in Portugal, even in old-fashioned, royalist Oliveira:

'When I was studying for my university entrance exams, there were only two republicans in Oliveira—old Salema, who taught Rhetoric, and me. Now there's a party, a committee and two newspapers. I've even seen the Baron das Marges reading that republican rag, *A Voz Pública*, in the Café da Arcada.'

Mendonça did not fear the advent of the Republic and said jokingly:

'That's a long way off, and, meanwhile, we still have time to eat that crème caramel.'

'Delicious,' murmured Cavaleiro.

'Yes,' said Gonçalo, 'we still have time for the crème caramel. But if revolution should break out in Spain or if the young king dies before he comes of age, which he will of course ...'

'Oh, the poor thing and his poor mother too!' said Gracinha, touched by such a possibility.

Cavaleiro immediately reassured her. Why should the young king die? The republicans were spreading grim rumours about the health of that excellent boy, but he knew the truth; fortunately for Spain, there was sure to be an Afonso XIII and even an Afonso XIV. As for our own republicans, well, that's a matter for the municipal guard. Portugal's masses, though, would remain royalist to the end. Only at the top end of society, among the bourgeoisie and the intellectuals, do you find a light, rather grubby scum, which could easily be skimmed off with a sabre or two.

'I'm sure that you—a perfect housewife—will know that when cooking stock, you have to skim off the scum with a spoon, well, in the case of republicans you'd need a sabre. And that, very simply, is how Portugal will deal with the matter. Indeed, I said as much to the King just recently.'

He raised his head haughtily, and his shirtfront, swelling like a stout cuirass, glowed, ready to defend the Monarchy. And in the respectful silence that followed, two champagne corks popped behind the screen, in the pantry.

As soon as the butler had hurriedly filled the glasses, the Nobleman of the Tower said with a gravity belied by his smile:

'To your health, André. And I drink not to the governor, but to my friend!'

Amidst a caressing murmur of voices, all glasses were raised. João Gouveia raised his with particular enthusiasm, crying, 'To my old friend, Andrezinho!'

Cavaleiro very lightly clinked glasses with Gracinha. Father Soeiro murmured grace. And throwing down his napkin, Barrolo asked:

'Shall we have coffee here or in the drawing room? It will be cooler there.'

In the large drawing room, with all its red velvet, the chandelier glowed in solitary splendour; and wafting in through the three open windows came the calm, hot night air and the hushed Oliveira silence; and outside, in the square, a few people, notably two ladies, their heads covered by white woollen shawls, stared up at the bright lights and jollity spilling out from the Casa dos Cunhais. On the balcony, André and Gonçalo lit their cigars and breathed in what little coolness there was, and Cavaleiro said earnestly:

'As I always say, Gonçalinho, one dines sublimely at your brother-in-law's house!'

Gonçalo invited him to come for dinner at the Tower the following Sunday. He still had a few bottles of Madeira from his grandfather Damião's days, on which, with the help of Gouveia and Tító, they could launch an heroic assault.

A delighted Cavaleiro promised he'd be there and took his cup of coffee—no sugar—from the heavy silver tray, so heavy that the butler was almost bent beneath its weight.

'Your duty now, Gonçalo, is to stick close to the Tower. Your role is to be a strong presence in the area: the Nobleman of the Tower standing firm on his territory—for standing there, he will be elected to Parliament. Yes, that is your role.'

A beaming Barrolo slipped in-between the two friends and put his arms affectionately about their waists:

'And Cavaleiro and I will stay here, working away!'

From the deep sofa on which she had installed herself, Maria Mendonça, however, was demanding that Gonçalo join her in order 'to talk business'. Meanwhile, next to a console table, João Gouveia and Father Soeiro, stirring their coffees, were agreeing on the need for strong government. And Gracinha, with cousin Mendonça, was riffling through the sheet music lying on the piano lid, looking for the Ramires *fado*. Mendonça was a pianist of fluid brilliance and had composed not only waltzes, a hymn to Colonel Trancoso, the hero of Machumba, but even the first act of an opera—*A Pegureira, The Shepherdess*. When they failed to find Videirinha's *fado*, Mendonça, cigar in mouth, launched into one of his own waltzes, *The Pearl*, which had a lazy, amorous rhythm reminiscent of the waltz from Gounod's *Faust*.

Then André Cavaleiro, who had come slowly back into the room, tugged at his waistcoat, smoothed his moustaches and, half-grave, half-playful, advanced on Gracinha saying:

'Would Your Excellency do me the great honour of this dance?'
He opened wide his arms. Gracinha, scarlet-cheeked, accepted,
and was immediately swept away as Cavaleiro led her, with long,
sliding steps, across the carpet. Barrolo and Gouveia hurriedly
shifted the armchairs to clear a space, and the waltz proceeded with
Gracinha's dress leaving a soft, white wake behind her. Small and
light, she seemed entirely lost, as if she had melted into the sheer
masculine strength of Cavaleiro, who bore her off, turning slowly,
his head bent, breathing in the scent of her magnificent hair.

From the edge of the sofa, her keen eyes sparkling, Dona Maria
Mendonça expressed her amazement:

'Goodness, how well the governor waltzes!'

Beside her, Gonçalo was nervously twisting one end of his
moustache, astonished by this renewed familiarity, taken up by
Cavaleiro with such serene confidence and by Gracinha with such
abandon. They turned and they spun, their arms about each other.
Cavaleiro's lips curved into a smile and he murmured something
to her. Gracinha was breathing hard, her patent leather shoes
gleaming beneath her skirt, which had wrapped itself about Cavaleiro's trousers. And as they brushed past an ecstatic Barrolo, he
applauded affectionately, crying:

'Bravo! Bravo! Bravissimo!'

VII

As he was coming back in to lunch after a stroll in the orchard, Gonçalo was still casually leafing through the *Gazeta do Porto* when he saw Casco, José Casco from Bravais—wearily sunk in thought, his hat on his knees—sitting on the stone bench next to the kitchen door, where Rosa was changing her canary's millet. Hoping to avoid him, Gonçalo quickly hid behind his newspaper, but then he noticed the man's scrawny figure emerging out of the shade of the vine trellis and walking hesitantly, almost fearfully, towards him across the dazzlingly bright courtyard. Emboldened by Rosa's presence, Gonçalo stopped and attempted a smile, while Casco, turning the hard brim of his hat round and round in his trembling hands, finally blurted out:

'If you would be so kind as to let me have a word with you, sir.'

'Ah, it's you, Casco! I didn't recognise you. How can I help?'

Reassured, he folded up his newspaper, rather enjoying the submissive attitude of the ruffian who, dark and erect as a pine tree, had so terrified him when they'd met in the solitude of the woods. Barely able to speak, Casco kept tugging awkwardly at the thick embroidered collar constraining his neck, until, finally, he opened his heart and sobbed out his request, only just managing to hold back the tears filling his eyes:

'Please, sir, forgive me! Ah, I don't even know how to begin to ask your forgiveness!'

Gonçalo interrupted him, generously, gently. Hadn't he warned him? One achieves nothing by threatening people.

'You know, Casco, when you ambushed me that night, I had a revolver in my pocket. I always carry one with me ever since the night in Coimbra, in the Choupal, when two drunks attacked me. Now imagine if I'd taken out my revolver and fired! That would have been terrible, wouldn't it? Fortunately, I realised in time that I risked getting carried away, risked killing you, which is why I

fled, so as not to fire my revolver. Anyway, that's all in the past. I'm
not a man to hold grudges, and I've forgotten all about it. And now
that you've calmed down and are in your right mind, you should
forget it too.'

Head bowed, Casco was still clutching the brim of his hat. Without looking up, without daring to, his voice hoarse and broken
with sobbing, he said:

'I realise that, sir, and I curse my own stupidity, my madness.
Especially after what you did for my wife and for my little boy!'

Gonçalo smiled and shrugged:

'Nonsense, Casco! Your wife turned up here on a filthy night,
and the little boy, poor thing, was ill with fever. How is little Manuel, by the way?'

Out of the depths of his humility, Casco answered:

'God be praised, sir, he's strong and healthy.'

'Good. Now put on your hat, man, and off you go. You have
nothing to thank me for, Casco. But bring your little boy over to
see me one day. I liked him. He's a bright lad.'

Casco, however, would not leave. He remained glued to the spot,
until, finally, with a sob, he said:

'I just don't know how to put it, sir. That day in prison was the
end of everything. I have a very quick temper, I did something
foolish, and I paid for it. And thanks to you, sir, I paid very little.
But when I was released, when I found out my wife had come to
the Tower that very night, and that you'd even given her a cape to
wear, and wouldn't let the little one leave ...'

He stopped, overcome with emotion. And when Gonçalo, who
was equally moved, clapped him cheerily on the back, saying,
'That's enough of that, let's talk no more about it, such a trifling
thing ...' Casco burst out in a loud, grieving, broken voice:

'You don't know what that boy means to me, sir. Ever since God
sent him to me, I've felt such love for him inside, sir. You know,
that night I spent in the village gaol, I didn't sleep a wink. And God
forgive me, sir, but I didn't give a thought to my wife, nor to my
dear old mother, not even to the little bit of land I work, no, that
was all forgotten. All night I did nothing but moan, "My little boy!

My poor little boy!" Then, when my wife—who was waiting for me outside—when she told me you'd kept him at the Tower, and laid him in the best bed and sent for the doctor, and when Senhor Bento told me later how you'd go up and see him at night to make sure he was warm enough, and even tuck him in, poor love ...'

Suddenly—giving free rein to his emotions, amid cries of 'Oh, sir, sir!'—Casco grasped Gonçalo's hands and showered them with kisses, drenching them with his tears.

'Stop it, Casco! Don't be ridiculous. Stop it, man!'

Gonçalo had turned quite pale as he tried to shake off that furious show of gratitude, until both men stood face to face, Gonçalo with his eyes full of tears, and Casco sobbing and distraught. Holding back one last sob, Casco was the first to recover and to reveal what it was that had brought him there, the idea that had clearly moved him deeply and now filled his face with a look of unbending determination:

'Sir, I'm not good with words, and I don't know how best to say it, but if, in the future, for whatever reason, you should need a man's life, mine is yours for the taking!'

Gonçalo held out his hand to Casco, as simply as a Ramires of yesteryear would have done when receiving the homage of a vassal.

'Thank you, José Casco.'

'It's agreed, then, sir, and may Our Lord bless you, sir!'

Much troubled, Gonçalo ran up the steps into the house, while Casco walked slowly across the courtyard, head held high, like a man who has paid his debts.

And up in the library, Gonçalo was thinking in some alarm, 'In this sentimental world of ours, this is how one quite gratuitously earns the devotion of others! After all, who wouldn't prevent a feverish child from going out into the dark night, in the wind and the rain? Who wouldn't put him to bed, make him a hot drink and tuck in his blankets to keep him well wrapped up? And because of that hot drink and that bed, his father comes rushing here, trembling and weeping, to offer me his life! How very easy it is to be a king—and a popular king at that!'

And this certainty made him still more determined to take

Cavaleiro's advice and immediately begin his visits to influential voters, the adulatory visits that would, come Election time, ensure him an imperious, unanimous victory. Immediately after lunch, pushing aside the plates still on the table, he made a list of those local worthies, based on a scribbled note provided by João Gouveia. There was Dr Alexandrino, old Gramilde from Ramilde, Father José Vicente from Finta, and a few lesser figures; and Gouveia had marked with a cross, as being the most powerful and most difficult, the Viscount de Rio-Manso, who held sway over the vast parish of Canta-Pedra. Gonçalo knew all the other men of property and wealth (to all of whom his father had once been in debt), but he had never met the Viscount de Rio-Manso, an elderly Brazilian gentleman and the owner of the Quinta da Varandinha, where he lived alone with his eleven-year-old granddaughter, the lovely Rosinha, known locally as Rosebud, the wealthiest heiress in the whole province. That very afternoon, in Vila Clara, Gonçalo asked João Gouveia to provide him with a letter of introduction to the Viscount.

Gouveia hesitated, then said:

'Good grief! On the one hand, you don't need a letter—you're the Nobleman of the Tower! You just arrive, go in and start a conversation. On the other hand, at the last Election, Rio-Manso supported the Regenerationists, so we're not exactly the best of friends. And he's rather a grumpy old soul. Nevertheless, Gonçalinho, you really need to begin the hunt for popularity!'

The Nobleman initiated the 'hunt' at the club that very night, accepting an invitation from the honourable Romão Barros (a tedious and ridiculous man) to attend the lavish feast he was holding at his estate to celebrate his saint's day. And he spent one whole week and the next in Vila Clara, buttering up the voters, to the point of buying a couple of hideous cotton shirts from Ramos, ordering a sack of coffee beans from Telo the grocer, offering his arm in Largo do Chafariz to the odious wife of that drunken sot Marques Rosendo, and playing billiards, his hat pushed back on his head, at the billiards club in Rua das Pretas. João Gouveia did not approve of these excesses, advising him, rather, to make 'proper, formal visits to seriously influential people'. Yawning, Gonçalo continued to procrastinate, feeling an overwhelming reluctance to expose himself to old Gramilde's ill-tempered, slanderous tongue or Dr Alexandrino's forensic solemnity.

August was drawing to a close, and sometimes, in the library, Gonçalo would sit, disconsolately scratching his head and pondering the blank sheets of foolscap where the third chapter of *The Tower of Dom Ramires* had run aground. But what could he do? In that heat and with all the worry about the Election—how could he possibly reimmerse himself in that Afonsine era?

In the cooler evenings, he'd get on his horse and ride through the various parishes, still following Cavaleiro's advice, always making sure his pockets were filled with boiled sweets to throw to the children. However, in a letter to his beloved André, he had already confessed that his popularity still showed no signs of increasing. 'No, my friend, I simply have no talent for it! I can chat familiarly with the men, address the old ladies standing at their front doors by their first names, joke with the little ones, and, if I meet a young girl driving an oxcart and notice she has a torn skirt, then I can give her five *tostões* to buy herself a new one. But I've done these perfectly natural things perfectly naturally ever since I was a boy—without ever gaining any noticeable influence. I need you, as the much-loved Authority, to give me a shove with that powerful, skilful arm of yours...'

And yet one afternoon, when he met old Cosme from Nacejas at the Tower—and later, on a Sunday, came across Adrião Pinto from Levada saying his prayers at Bica-Santa—both highly respected men, who took an active role when it came to Elections—and asked them each for their votes quite openly, almost jokingly, he had been surprised by the promptness, even fervour, with which they agreed. 'Of course I'll vote for you, sir. That goes without saying. Even if it meant voting against the Government. You're like a father to us!' And in Vila Clara, talking to João Gouveia, Gonçalo commented that he saw in these passionate words 'the political intelligence of country folk':

'They're obviously not saying that just because they like me! They know I'm the kind of man who will speak up for them and fight for the interests of the land. Sanches Lucena was just a very rich, but very silent deputy. These people want a deputy who will make a noise and do battle and take a stand. They're voting for me because they recognise in me an intelligent being.'

Looking thoughtfully at the Nobleman, Gouveia had replied:

'Who knows? You've never put it to the test. Perhaps it really is simply because they like you.'

On one such outing, on a scalding hot Friday, with the sun still high, Gonçalo was riding through the hamlet of Veleda, on the Canta-Pedra road, where the hovels built along the road suddenly end, and in the square opposite the church stands the bright, white-washed façade of Pintainho's famous tavern, the tavern where, during local festivals, the crowds flock to enjoy the shady garden and the celebrated rabbit stew. Earlier that day, after a morning spent shooting partridge in Valverde, Titó had turned up at the Tower at lunchtime, declaring loudly that he was absolutely starving. It was a Friday, and Rosa had prepared hake with tomatoes followed by baked cod, all of it delicious. For the rest of the afternoon, though, Gonçalo had been tormented by thirst, made worse by the dust on the road, and so, when he reached the tavern, he stopped outside the door and shouted for Pintainho.

'Coming, sir!'

'Pintainho, bring me some nice cool sangria, will you. Quickly. I'm dying of thirst.'

Pintainho, a plump old fellow with yellowing hair, hastened to bring him a tall glass of the desired beverage, with a slice of lemon bobbing about in the sugary foam. And Gonçalo was still, with ineffable delight, savouring the sangría, when, from a ground-floor window came a long, slow whistle, high and trilling, the kind of whistle muleteers use to encourage their mules to drink from streams. Startled, Gonçalo stopped drinking. A big, strapping lad appeared at the window; he had a pale complexion and fair side whiskers, and, resting his fists on the windowsill, his head proudly lifted in a gesture of brazen defiance, he was staring boldly at him. In a flash, the Nobleman recognised him as the hunter who, on another afternoon, in Nacejas, next to the glass factory, had looked at him with equal arrogance, before pushing past him with his rifle and, afterwards—standing outside the house of that young woman in the blue jacket—had waved at Gonçalo mockingly as he rode off down the hill. It was the same man! As if he had not even noticed the insult, Gonçalo quickly finished his sangría, tossed a coin to a highly embarrassed Pintainho and spurred on his horse. Then from the window came a chuckle, jeering and contemptuous, which struck the Nobleman on the back like the lash of a whip. He broke into a gallop. Further on, reining in his horse in the safety of a quiet lane, he wondered, still trembling, 'Who is that shameless creature? And what did I ever do to him?' At the same time, his whole being was racked with despair at the wretched fear that assailed him, that shrinking of the flesh, that creeping of the skin, which always, in the face of some danger or threat, or some figure emerging out of the shadows, drove him furiously to run, to escape! Because his soul, thank God, was not a cowardly one! No, it was his body, his treacherous body, which startled and alarmed, fled, ran off, dragging with it his soul, which, inside was bellowing with rage.

Still mortified, he went into the house, envying his labourers' courage and thinking dark thoughts about that brute with the fair side whiskers, whom he would definitely report to Cavaleiro and have locked up in prison! However, as he was walking down the corridor, such thoughts were banished by Bento, who appeared, bearing a letter 'brought by a lad from Feitosa'.

'From Feitosa?'

'Yes, sir, from the estate of Senhor Sanches Lucena, God rest him. The lad said it was from the ladies ...'

'The ladies? What ladies?'

With no black edge to it, the letter was clearly not from the lovely Dona Ana. It was from Dona Maria Mendonça, who signed herself, 'Your loving cousin, Maria Severim.' He read it in an instant, immediately intrigued by this new surprise and completely forgetting the incident at Pintainho's, 'My dear cousin. I have been staying for the last three days with my friend Ana, and since it's nearly two months since her tragic loss and she can now go out (and, indeed, needs to because she has not been at all well), I will take the opportunity to go for a ride with her in the surrounding countryside, which people say is very pretty and which I hardly know at all. On Sunday, we intend visiting Santa Maria de Craquede and the tombs of your ancestors. I'm sure I will find it most moving. However, as well as the tombs in the cloister, there are, it seems, some still older tombs, which were plundered at the time of the French invasion, and which are now in some kind of underground chamber, which one can only enter with special permission and with a key. I am therefore asking you, dear cousin, to give orders that, on Sunday, we can go down into that chamber, which everyone declares to be terribly interesting, because it still contains remnants of bones and weapons. If there were a lady resident at the Tower, I would come there myself and ask you personally, but a lady cannot possibly visit such a dangerous bachelor as yourself alone. So get married soon! Good news from Oliveira. Your etc ...'

Gonçalo looked at Bento, who was awaiting some explanation for the look of astonishment on the Nobleman's face.

'Are there other tombs at Santa Maria de Craquede, in some kind of underground chamber?'

It was Bento's turn to be astonished:

'Tombs? In an underground chamber?'

'Yes. As well as those in the cloister, it seems there are other still older ones underground somewhere. I've certainly never seen them, at least, not as far as I can remember. Then again, I haven't visited Santa Maria de Craquede for years. Not since I was a boy. Do you know anything about them?'

Bento shrugged.

'Would Rosa know?'

Bento shook his head doubtfully.

'So you don't know anything either! Right, tomorrow morning early, go to Santa Maria de Craquede and ask the sacristan if such a chamber exists. And if it does, then tell him that, on Sunday, he is to show it to two ladies, to Senhora Dona Ana Lucena and Senhora Dona Maria Mendonça, my cousin. And tell him to make sure it's all swept out and clean!'

Reading the letter more carefully, he noticed in one corner, a postscript written in a smaller hand, 'Don't forget, on Sunday, our visit will be between five o'clock and half past five in the afternoon.'

Gonçalo thought, 'Is this a rendezvous?' And in the library, throwing down his hat and whip on a chair, he concluded that it clearly was! Maybe that underground chamber did not even exist, and Maria Mendonça, in her shrewdly intelligent way, had invented it, thus providing her with a convincing excuse to write to him and announce that on Sunday, at half past five, the lovely Dona Ana and her two hundred *contos* would be waiting for him in Santa Maria de Craquede. So his cousin hadn't been joking when they spoke in Oliveira. Did Dona Ana really like him? A thrill of voluptuous curiosity ran through Gonçalo at the thought that such a beautiful woman should desire him. Yes, but she doubtless desired him as a husband, because if she wanted him as a lover, she would hardly resort to using the services of Dona Maria Mendonça; and his cousin, despite her toadying attitude towards her rich female friends, would certainly not offer her services so brazenly, like a procuress in a play. But, damn it, he really could not marry Dona Ana! No!

And yet he felt a sudden eagerness to know more about Dona Ana's life. Had she been strictly faithful to old Sanches all those years? Yes, perhaps, at least in Feitosa, in the solitude of those great walls, because no rumour about her had ever surfaced in that provincial place so greedy for malicious gossip. But in Lisbon? Those 'esteemed friends' of which poor Sanches used to boast, Dom João something-or-other, the high-ranking Arronches Manrique, or Filipe Lourençal and his cornet? Someone must, at some point, have approached her—perhaps that same Dom João, impelled by a sense of traditional duty to his name. But what about her? Who could tell him about Dona Ana's love life?

Later, after supper, he suddenly remembered Gouveia. One of Gouveia's sisters, who lived in Lisbon and was married to a certain Cerqueira (a producer of magic shows and a clerk in the local hospital), used to send her brother intimate reports about any well-known people from Oliveira and Vila Clara who also spent time in Lisbon. His dear friend Gouveia would be sure to have gleaned from his sister a detailed history of what Dona Ana got up to during her winters in Lisbon, in the bosom of that 'select circle of friends'.

On that night, however, Gouveia was not to be found at the club. And Gonçalo was about to walk rather glumly back to the Tower, when he spotted him in Largo do Chafariz along with Videirinha, both of them seated on a bench beneath the dark Judas trees.

'Perfect timing!' cried Gouveia. 'We were just about to go to my house for a cup of tea. Would you care to join us? You usually enjoy my tea and toast.'

Despite feeling tired, the Nobleman accepted. And as they walked along, Gonçalo linked arms with Gouveia and told him he had received a letter from a friend in Lisbon containing some extraordinary news. Dona Ana Lucena was to be married.

Astonished, Gouveia stopped and pushed his hat back on his head: 'Who to?'

Having invented the letter, Gonçalo invented a fiancé as well.

'Oh, some distant relative of mine apparently, Dom João Pedroso or Pedrosa. Sanches Lucena often mentioned his name. They used to meet in Lisbon.'

Gouveia struck the paving stones with his walking stick.

'That's impossible! What can she be thinking of? Dona Ana can't possibly be arranging to get married just seven weeks after her husband's death. Lucena only died in mid-July. He hasn't even had time to get used to being in his grave!'

'Very true!' murmured Gonçalo.

And he smiled, basking in that sweet, flattering wave, thinking that, just seven weeks after she had been widowed, she'd been unable to resist trampling roughshod over decency and mourning and invite him to a rendezvous in the church at Craquede.

The lie, however nonsensical, had worked, because when they went up to Gouveia's small green living room, the friends were still full of amazement. Videirinha was gleefully rubbing his hands:

'It would be funny, though, wouldn't it, if Senhora Dona Ana, only a few weeks after receiving the old man's two hundred *contos*, should hook up with some handsome young man?'

Yes, when he thought about it, Gonçalo also found the news of the marriage unlikely, especially with poor Sanches still almost warm in his grave.

'There must have been some flirtation, perhaps an exchange of glances with that Dom João fellow, which is presumably what lies behind the rumour. In fact, someone did tell me, ages ago now, that someone of that name, as befits a Dom João, had made so bold as to woo her ...'

'Lies!' said Gouveia, leaning over the oil lamp to light his cigarette. 'All lies! I happen to know, and from an excellent source too— all right, from my sister—that while in Lisbon, Dona Ana never did anything to give rise to any gossip. She was always very proper indeed. Some rogue may well have made eyes at her, perhaps that same Dom João you're talking about or some other friend of her husband's, as is only natural, but she never so much as looked at another man. She was like Caesar's wife, my friend, above suspicion.'

Sitting on the sofa, idly twirling his moustache, Gonçalo was lapping up these revelations. And standing in the middle of the room, Gouveia pulled a smug, knowing face and said:

'Not that this surprises me! These terribly beautiful women are often very cold-hearted creatures. Beautiful as marble statues, but as cold as marble too. No, Gonçalinho, if you want feeling and soul and everything that goes with it, then go for small, thin, dark women. The pale, stately Venus types are best left in the museum to be looked at.'

Videirinha ventured a word of doubt:

'But a lovely woman like Dona Ana, given her background and being married to an old fellow like that ...'

'Some women like old men because their own hearts are equally old!' declared Gouveia, wagging his finger authoritatively, philosophically.

Gonçalo's curiosity was not yet satisfied. And what about when she was at Feitosa? Had no one ever mentioned some hidden affair? Apparently, Dom Júlio ...

The Nobleman was again inventing, and again Gouveia rejected that 'lie':

'Not in Feitosa or in Oliveira or in Lisbon. Besides, as I say, Gonçalo, the woman is made of marble.'

Then he added admiringly:

'But what marble, eh? You cannot imagine how beautiful that woman looks when she's décolleté!'

Gonçalo was astonished:

'And where have you seen her décolleté?'

'Where? In Lisbon, at a ball in the Palace. In fact, Lucena got me the invitation. Oh, yes, I cut quite a dash there, but it was all a terrible bore really, even rather embarrassing, with the hordes bunched around the buffet, shouting and furiously grabbing pieces of turkey ...'

'Yes, but what about Dona Ana?'

'Oh, Dona Ana was just gorgeous! You can't imagine. Dear God, what shoulders, what arms, what breasts! So white, so perfect! It was enough to drive a man mad! At first, because there were a lot of people there, and she was standing hidden modestly away in a corner, no one noticed, but once they discovered her, the crowds ran to gaze at her, open-mouthed. Who can she be? How lovely she is! Everyone there fell in love with her, even the King!'

And for a moment, the three men fell silent, pondering the vision he had conjured up—that superb body appeared before them, almost naked, filling the humble, ill-lit room with the glow of her white flesh. Finally, Videirinha drew his chair closer, ready to offer his own titbit of information:

'Well, I happen to know that Senhora Dona Ana is extremely clean and loves bathing ...'

And when the others laughed at the confidence with which he said this, Videirinha told them that a servant from Feitosa went to Pires' pharmacy every week to buy three or four bottles of Pires' home-made eau de Cologne.

'Pires would gleefully rub his hands and say that they must water the gardens at Feitosa with eau de Cologne. But then we found out from her maid that, every day, Senhora Dona Ana takes a long bath, not just to wash in, but for pure pleasure. She stays in the tub for a whole hour and even reads the newspaper while she's there. And she pours half a bottle of eau de Cologne into every bath. Now, that's what I call luxury!'

Gonçalo grew suddenly bored with all these revelations from Gouveia and Videirinha about that lovely woman's décolletage and the baths she took, the very woman who was waiting for him among the ancient tombs of the Ramires. He put down the newspaper he was fanning himself with and cried:

'Anyway, moving on to more serious business. What have you heard about Dr Júlio, Gouveia. Is he preparing for the Election?'

The maid came in bearing a tray of tea. And sitting around the table, eating Gouveia's famous toast, they talked about the Election, about the reports from the local councillors, about the expected lack of support from Rio-Manso, and about Dr Júlio, whom Videirinha had met in Bravais going from door to door, begging for votes, accompanied by a lad carrying the doctor's camera on his back.

After tea, tired and sated with 'revelations', Gonçalo lit his cigar in readiness for the walk back to the Tower.

'Aren't you coming with me, Videirinha?'

'No, I can't tonight, sir. I have to leave for Oliveira in the coach at the crack of dawn.'

'What on earth are you going to Oliveira for?'

'I have to change some beach shoes and a swimming costume bought by Pires' wife, Dona Josefa. I'm to take them to Emílio's along with some new measurements.'

Gonçalo flung up his arms in despair:

'What a country! A great artist like Videirinha having to go all the way to Oliveira to change Dona Josefa's beach shoes! When I'm deputy, Gouveia, we must find a good government position for our Videirinha. An easy job, with plenty of free time, so that he won't forget how to play his guitar!'

Videirinha blushed with pleasure and anticipation, then ran to fetch the Nobleman's hat.

On the walk back, Gonçalo's thoughts immediately, irresistibly flew to Dona Ana, to her décolletage and her languid baths, where she'd lie reading the paper. Damn it! Dona Ana was, without a doubt, magnificently beautiful, perfumed and honest, but, as a wife, she had just one drawback—her butcher father. And then there was her voice, the voice that had so horrified him when he heard it at Bica-Santa. And yet Mendonça assured him that, in private, those heavy, affected tones became soft, almost sweet. And when you come to know someone over a period of time, you can get used to even the most grating of voices—indeed, he himself no longer noticed how nasal Manuel Duarte's voice was. Yes, the only stubborn stain was her butcher father. However, in this Humanity born of one man, who—if he traces his thousands of ancestors all the way back to Adam—doesn't have one who was a butcher? If a nobleman like himself (born of a line of kings from which whole dynasties have sprung) were to rummage around in the past, he'd surely stumble upon at least one Ramires who had been a butcher. Regardless of whether the butcher running a busy shop appeared in the first generation, or was, in the dense past centuries, merely a vague, vanishing figure among his ancestors of thirty generations ago, still there he was, with knife and chopping-block and slabs of meat, and bloodstains on his sweaty arm!

And this thought stayed with him all the way home, and lingered on afterwards, when he was standing at the window in his room, finishing his cigar and listening to the chirping of the crickets. Even after he went to bed and his eyelids were growing heavy, he could still hear his own impatient footsteps trudging back into the past, into his family's dark past and its tangled history, in search of that Ramires butcher. He had already got as far as the Visigothic Empire, over which his bearded ancestor Recesvinto had reigned with a golden globe in his hand. Panting and exhausted, he had traversed cultivated cities peopled with cultivated men, had penetrated forests where the mastodon still grazed. Among that sodden undergrowth, he'd already encountered entirely unfamiliar Ramires men, groaning beneath the weight of dead animals or bundles of wood. Others emerged from smoke-filled caves, baring greenish teeth to smile at their distant grandson passing by. Then, having crossed bleak, silent wildernesses, he had reached a misty lake. And there on the slimy banks, among the bullrushes, a monstrous man, as hairy as a wild beast, was crouched in the mud, using a flint axe to chop up bits of human flesh. A Ramires. A black hawk flew across the grey sky. And there Gonçalo stood, waving at Santa Maria de Craquede and at the beautiful, perfumed Dona Ana through the mist from the lake and bawling out over all the Empires and Ages, 'I've found my butcher ancestor!'

On Sunday, Gonçalo woke up with 'a brilliant idea'! He wouldn't rush to Santa Maria de Craquede and arrive at five o'clock on the dot (the time stipulated by his cousin Maria in her postscript), thus revealing his eagerness to meet the very lovely and very rich Dona Ana Lucena! Instead, at six o'clock, when the ladies would have finished their pilgrimage to the tombs, he would turn up nonchalantly as if, on returning from a ride around the cool surrounding countryside, he had suddenly remembered and stopped at the ruins for a chat with his cousin.

However, at four o'clock, he began getting dressed and took such pains over it that Bento—weary of all the cravats his master had tried on, crumpled up and tossed onto the sofa—could hold back no longer:

'Please, sir, wear the white silk one! That's the one that suits you best. And in this heat, it's cooler too.'

After much thought about which flowers to choose for his buttonhole, he settled for a yellow carnation and a white one, the heraldic colours of the Ramires. Outside, as soon as he had mounted his horse, he began worrying that the ladies (not finding him at the church) might truncate their visit, and so he set off at a fast trot along the shortcut via Portela. Further on, when he reached the old royal road, he urged his horse into an impatient gallop, which left him covered in white dust.

He only resumed a more leisurely pace when he reached the railway line, where two men and a cart carrying firewood were waiting at the crossing, which was closed to allow a train laden with barrels to pass slowly by. One of those men, carrying a saddlebag over his shoulder, was the rather striking beggar who regularly touted around the local villages his majestic and highly remunerative beard, the vast beard of a river god. Gravely raising his broad-brimmed hat, he bade the Nobleman a friendly 'God be with you, sir'.

'Off to earn your fortune in Craquede?' asked the Nobleman.

'No, I sometimes wait here for the Oliveira train to pass, sir. The passengers enjoy seeing me standing on the embankment. They always rush to the windows for a look.'

Gonçalo smiled, and it occurred to him that a meeting with the old man always seemed to precede an encounter with the beautiful Dona Ana. 'Who knows?' he thought. 'Perhaps it's fate! That's exactly how the ancients used to depict Fate, with long hair and a long beard, with a sack containing all human destinies over his shoulder.' And then at the far side of the silent pine forest, which was turning gradually golden in the slowly declining sun, he saw her carriage stopped under an oak tree, with the uniformed coachman dozing on the driver's seat. The royal Oliveira road runs past the Craquede monastery, which had been scorched by heavenly fire in the furious storm that terrified all of Portugal in 1616 and which was given the name of St Sebastian. Between the stout trunks of the ancient chestnut trees grows lush green grass, and the new church, freshly whitewashed, can be seen gleaming whitely through the branches. Connected to the church by a crumbling, ivy-clad wall and taking up the whole of the east side of the square, rises the old monastery chapel, its façade slightly yellowed and weathered by the elements, but still filling the bright sky with its magnificent portal, its long-vanished doors, the remnants of its rose window and the empty grave niches that once contained the images of the chapel's founders, Froilas Ramires and his wife, Estevaninha, Countess de Orgaz, nicknamed Queixa-Perra. Two single-storey houses occupied the opposite side of the square, one pristine, with the window frames painted a strident blue, and the other derelict, nearly swallowed up by a herbaceous border gone to seed, almost roofless and currently full of splendid sunflowers. A pensive silence filled the trees and the proud ruins, a silence not broken, but rather lulled into sleep by the whispering flow of a fountain, which was reduced by the heat to a slow thread of water that barely filled the stone basin shaded by the pale, sparse foliage of a very tall weeping willow.

The footman had been sitting on the edge of the basin, crumbling some tobacco into his pouch, but when he spotted the Nobleman, he leapt gaily down and ran over to take the reins of his horse. And Gonçalo, who hadn't visited the ruins since he was a boy, was walking along a path through the grass, absorbed and entranced by the kind of romantic solitude usually found only in legend and in verse, when, from beneath the archway of the main door, two ladies appeared, returning from the old cloister. With her usual impulsive vivacity, Dona Maria Mendonça immediately waved at him with her checkered sunshade, which matched her dress, the sleeves of which puffed out exaggeratedly from her shoulders, emphasising her elegantly slender figure. Beside her, in the bright sun, Dona Ana was a svelte, silent, black figure, dressed entirely in black wool and black gauze, which almost concealed the splendid whiteness of her sensual, serious face, softened by her black veil.

Gonçalo had run towards them, doffing his straw hat and pretending to be surprised and saying how pleased he was to see them. Dona Maria, though, was already scolding him, thus ruining any attempt on his part to pretend that this was a chance encounter.

'You're most unkind,' she said.

'Why, cousin?'

'I told you in my letter that we were coming, yet you failed to be here at the appointed hour to do the honours, as you should have.'

With his usual easy laugh, he denied point-blank that this was his duty. The house did not belong to him, but to the Good Lord! Therefore, it was up to the Good Lord to 'do the honours' and welcome those two sweet pilgrims with some delightful miracle.

'Anyway, did you enjoy your visit? Did you, Dona Ana, enjoy the ruins? They're very interesting, aren't they?'

With a gravity rendered still graver by the thick black cloth of her veil, she murmured:

'Actually I've been here before. I came one afternoon with poor Sanches, God rest his soul.'

'Ah.'

At the mention of the poor dead man's name, Gonçalo's smile vanished completely, in a polite show of sadness. However, Dona Maria Mendonça, gesticulating with her thin arms as if to drive away that inopportune shadow, said:

'Oh, you've no idea, cousin. The whole cloister is just delightful. And then there's that rusty sword hanging over the tomb. It's always the really ancient things that make the strongest impression. And to think, cousin, that there lie our forefathers!'

Gonçalo's smile flashed into life again, happy and welcoming, as always happened when Dona Maria tried to elbow her way greedily into the House of Ramires. And he said affably, 'Forefathers, you say? Mere handfuls of vain dust! Isn't that so, Senhora Dona Ana? Can one really imagine cousin Maria, so lively, so sociable, so witty, being descended from a sad heap of dust inside a stone tomb? No, it's quite impossible to make a link between so much being and so much *non-being*!' But when he saw Dona Ana smile, as if in agreement, and then lean heavily on the pearl handle of her parasol with her two strong black-gloved hands, he said almost urgently:

'Ah, but you are perhaps tired, Senhora Dona Ana.'

'No, no, I'm not tired. We were about to make a brief visit to the chapel. Besides, I never get tired.'

And it seemed to Gonçalo that the beautiful creature's voice did not roll off her tongue quite so slowly and affectedly, but had grown more refined, somehow mellowed and softened by the gauze and wool of her heavy mourning clothes, just as loud, coarse daytime noises are attenuated by the night and the trees. Dona Maria, however, said that *she* was extremely tired. She found nothing more exhausting than visiting antiquities, not to mention the sheer emotion she felt at the thought of such ancient heroes.

'Let's sit down on that bench over there, shall we? It's too early to think of going home just yet, don't you agree, Ana? And it's so pleasant here in this cool, quiet place.'

It was a stone bench, next to a crumbling wall almost overgrown with ivy. The grass around it was particularly dense and dotted with the few daisies and buttercups that had been spared by the August sun. The delicate scent from a jasmine plant growing up among the ivy sweetened the serene afternoon air. And on the branch of a poplar tree, opposite the door to the chapel, a blackbird sang twice. Gonçalo carefully dusted off the bench with his handkerchief. And sitting at one end, next to Dona Maria, he also praised the cool and quiet of that small corner of Craquede. And yet he had never even considered coming to enjoy a bucolic picnic in that holy refuge, which, after all, almost belonged to him! Now, though, he would definitely come back to smoke a cigarette and think peaceful thoughts beneath these peaceful oak trees, close to his long-dead ancestors. Then he asked:

'And what about the underground chamber, cousin?'

'Oh, there is no such chamber, well, there is, but it's full of junk, and there are no tombs, no antiquities. The sacristan said straight away that there was no point in getting our dresses all dirty. By the way, Ana, did you give the sacristan a tip?'

'Yes, I gave him five *tostões*. Was that enough, do you think?'

Gonçalo assured her that she had been positively munificent. If he had known she was going to be so generous, he would have grabbed a bunch of keys, slipped on a black surplice, and shown them round himself.

'That's precisely what you should have done!' exclaimed Dona Maria, her eyes sparkling. 'And we would certainly have given you five *tostões* for your trouble. You would have been far more instructive than the sacristan, who just mumbled away and didn't know anything. Idle fellow! And I so wanted to know about the open tomb, the one with the cracked lid. All the fool would say was that it was a very ancient story involving the Nobleman of the Tower.'

Gonçalo laughed:

'Well, as it happens, cousin Maria, I do know that story, thanks to Videirinha's Ramires *fado*.'

Dona Maria Mendonça threw up her hands at this rank indifference to the heroic traditions of his family. Fancy only knowing about their history because it had been set to music in a *fado*! Cousin Gonçalo should be ashamed of himself!

'But why, cousin, why? Videirinha's *fado* is based on documents authenticated by Father Soeiro. All the historical filling for the *fado* was provided by him. Besides, cousin, in the past, it was the custom for history to be perpetuated in verse and sung to the sound of the lyre. Anyway, would you like to know about the open tomb, according, that is, to Videirinha?' I'm happy to reveal all, but only to Senhora Dona Ana, who does not share your scruples.'

'No!' cried Dona Maria. 'If Videirinha's account is historically accurate, then tell it to me as well. I am family after all!'

Gonçalo cleared his throat in mock dramatic fashion and smoothed his moustache with his handkerchief:

'Well, here's what happened. That tomb was inhabited by one of my ancestors, once he was dead, of course. I can't remember his name now, Gutierres or Lopo or something. I think it was Gutierres. Anyway, he was ensconced in there at the time of the Battle of Las Navas de Tolosa, about which I'm sure you've heard, cousin, you know, the five Moorish kings and all that. Now quite how Gutierres found out about the battle, Videirinha doesn't say, but the moment he caught a whiff of the carnage from inside his tomb, he burst forth, strode across this courtyard like a man possessed, dug up his horse, which had been buried in the forecourt where those oak trees are growing now, leapt on its back fully armed, and then—a dead knight on a dead horse—galloped off to Spain, reached Las Navas, drew his sword and lay waste to the Moors. What do you make of that, Dona Ana?'

He had directed this tale at her, looking for some sign of attention and interest in her beautiful eyes. And, despite herself and her self-imposed melancholy, she could not help but smile sweetly, carried away by his account and murmuring only, 'How very amusing!' Dona Maria, though, was so entranced that she almost took flight from the stone bench on which she was sitting. 'How lovely! How poetic! What a delightful legend!' And urging Gonçalo on to provide further amusing details of this chronicle, she said:

'Go on, cousin, tell us more. Did that ancestor of ours come back to Craquede?'

'Who do you mean, cousin? Gutierres? No, he was no fool! As soon as he was free of that dull old tomb, he never again appeared in Santa Maria de Craquede. The tomb was left as empty as it is today, and he continued to have a high old heroic time of it in Spain! Imagine, a dead man miraculously escaping from his grave, from that narrow, cramped, eternal posture!'

He suddenly fell silent, thinking of Sanches Lucena lying
equally cramped in his narrow lead coffin, in his splendid vault
in Oliveira. Dona Ana lowered her eyes, her face still more hidden behind her veil as she dug the tip of her parasol into the grass.
And in order once again to disperse that impertinent shadow, the
quick-thinking Dona Maria asked another question, again to do
with the nobility of the Ramires family:

'I keep meaning to ask, do you know if you still have relatives in
France? No, perhaps you don't.'

As it happened, Gonçalo did know the answer to this, even
though Videirinha had not included it in his *fado*.

'Well, tell us then, but make it a more cheerful tale this time!'

It wasn't such a prodigiously funny story, but one of the Ramires
ancestors, Garcia Ramires, had accompanied the Infante Dom Pedro, the son of King João I, on one of his famous journeys abroad.
Cousin Maria must know the one he meant, the man who was said
to have travelled to the four corners of the earth. Well, on their
return from Palestine, the Infante Dom Pedro and his noblemen
stopped for a whole year in Flanders, with the Duke of Burgundy.
They held lavish parties there, indeed, one banquet lasted seven
whole days and is mentioned in the compendiums of the History of
France. And where there is dancing, there is love. Their ancestor,
Garcia Ramires, lacked neither imagination nor daring. He it was
who, in the Valley of Jehosaphat, outside the walls of Jerusalem,
had thought of erecting a sign so that the Infante and his fellow
pilgrims would know each other on the Last Day of Judgement.
And he, of course, being a big, handsome lad, with a thick, dark,
very Portuguese beard, ended up marrying a sister of the Duke of
Cleves, a splendid woman, the niece of the Duke of Burgundy and
Brabant. Later, thanks to these connections, another Ramires lady,
a widow, also got married in France, to the Count of Tancarville.
And those same Tancarvilles, Grand Masters of France, owned the
largest castle in Europe, and ...'

Dona Maria clapped and laughed:

'Bravo! Excellent! Since you always claim to know nothing
about your noble past, how come you know every detail of these

important marriages? What do you think, Ana? The man's a walking chronicle!'

Gonçalo feigned embarrassment and confessed that he had only taken an interest in that heraldic history for the basest of reasons: money!

'Money?'

'Yes, cousin Maria, for the love of money, filthy lucre.'

'Tell us more. Ana is eager to know.'

'Are you, Senhora Dona Ana? Well, it happened during my second year at Coimbra. My friends and I had reached a point where we had not a penny between us, not even enough to buy cigarettes! Not even enough for our essential jug of cheap red wine and statutory three olives. Then one of these friends, a very witty fellow called Melgaço, came up with the stupendous idea that I should write to my French relatives in Cleves, the supposedly immensely wealthy Tancarvilles, and ask them straight out for the loan of three hundred francs.'

Genuinely amused, Dona Ana could not hold back her laughter: 'Oh, how funny!'

'Except that it didn't work, Senhora. There are no longer any Cleves or Tancarvilles! All those great feudal families died out, merged with other families, even with the French royal family. And despite all his genealogical knowledge, Father Soeiro never did manage to find a near enough relative who could lend me, a poor relative from Portugal, those three hundred francs.'

Dona Ana seemed almost moved by the great nobleman Gonçalo's penury.

'So you were left with nothing. Who would have thought it? But it's a very funny story all the same, those tales from Coimbra always are. Dom João da Pedrosa used to tell us such stories in Lisbon.'

Dona Maria Mendonça, however, used that student anecdote to reveal another unexpected proof of the grandeur of the Ramires family, and immediately, skilfully, unfolded it to Dona Ana:

'You see, all those great houses of France, so rich and powerful, died out, disappeared, whereas our little Portugal carries on in the House of Ramires!'

Gonçalo broke in, saying:

'Where it has reached its end, cousin! Now don't look at me like that. It's over because I have no intention of marrying.'

Dona Maria drew back her thin torso as if her cousin's marriage depended on certain other tender influences, as if her great bouffant sleeves might obstruct the flow of any romantic effluvia that needed to make themselves felt with no Maria Mendonças in the way on that narrow bench. And she smiled almost languidly:

'Not marry? But why, cousin, why?'

'I have no talent for it, cousin. Marriage is a very delicate art that requires vocation and a very particular genius. The Fates did not endow me with that genius. And were I to embark on such an enterprise, I would certainly run it completely into the ground.'

As though her mind were on other things, Dona Ana had slowly picked up the watch attached by a ribbon to her belt. Meanwhile, Dona Maria, rejecting the Nobleman's arguments, was saying:

'Nonsense! You really love children ...'

'I do, I adore children, even little babies. Children are the only truly divine beings our poor humanity can know. The other angels, the ones with wings, never appear. The saints, once they've been sainted, laze about in Paradise and no one so much as claps eyes on them again. So, in order to imagine what Heaven might be like, we really only have children. Yes, you're right, cousin, I do like children very much, but then I like flowers too, but I'm certainly no botanist and have no gift for gardening either.'

And with a promising sparkle in her eyes, Dona Maria said:

'Don't worry, you still have time to learn!'

Then, to Dona Ana, who was still lost in contemplation of her watch, she said:

'Is it getting late? If you like, we can go into the chapel. See if it's open, will you, cousin.'

Gonçalo ran over and obligingly pushed the chapel door open. Then he accompanied the two ladies through the tiny paved nave and past slender pillars painted in the same rough whitewash as the walls, which were bare apart from a few lithographs of saints in pinewood frames. The two women knelt before the altar, and cousin Maria buried her face in her hands, as if in a cup of mercy. Gonçalo gave the slightest of bobs and mumbled a hasty Hail Mary. Then he returned to the courtyard and lit a cigarette. Walking slowly across the grass, he was thinking how much widowhood had improved Dona Ana. Beneath her mourning clothes, as if in a penumbra that dissipates the gross inelegance of things, all her defects were melting away, the defects that had so horrified him on that afternoon at Bica-Santa: her affected way of speaking, her prominent bosom, her ostentatious air of a wealthy bourgeois woman living in the lap of luxury. And she had not once addressed him in that falsely formal way. There, in the melancholy courtyard of Craquede, she certainly seemed to him both interesting and desirable.

The ladies came down the two steps from the chapel. A blackbird fluttered about in the poplar trees. And as Dona Ana looked around to find him, Gonçalo caught a gleam in her serious eyes.

'Do forgive me for not offering you any holy water on the way out, but the font has run dry,' he said.

'Goodness, cousin, what an ugly church!' exclaimed Dona Maria

Dona Ana ventured shyly to say:

'Yes, after the ruins and the tombs, it doesn't seem very religious somehow.'

Gonçalo thought this comment rather subtle and astute. And walking slowly, pleasurably along beside her, he was aware of an equally subtle perfume being given off by her every move, every rustle of her skirt, and it was certainly not the ghastly eau de Cologne cooked up by Pires in his pharmacy. In silence, they walked beneath the shade of the chestnut trees back to the carriage, where the coachman stood smartly to attention and doffed his hat. Gonçalo noticed that he had shaved off his moustache since their last encounter. And the two immaculately harnessed horses gleamed and glistened.

'So, cousin, are you staying long in these parts?'

'Yes, for another two weeks. Ana is so kind that she asked me to bring the little ones too—you can't imagine the fun they've been having in the garden.'

Still grave-faced, Dona Ana murmured:

'They're such fun, such good company. I, too, love children.'

'Oh, yes, Ana adores children,' added Dona Maria fervently. 'She's so patient with them, she'll even play tag.'

As they neared the carriage, Gonçalo thought how sweet it would be to take another still slower turn about the courtyard with Dona Ana and her subtle scent in the peace of that late afternoon, as the sky above the already dark pine trees was becoming tinged with lovely shades of pink. However, the footman was coming to join them, holding the Nobleman's horse. And, admiring and patting the horse, Dona Maria discreetly asked her cousin how far it was from Feitosa to Treixedo, the Ramires' other historic property.

'To Treixedo? A good five leagues and on very bad roads.'

Then he immediately regretted saying this, realising that Treixedo might provide an opportunity for another outing, another meeting.

'Although they have been doing some work on the road lately, and it's a lovely spot, up on a hill, with the remains of what was once a huge castle. There's a lake, and a garden surrounded by an ancient grove of trees. A delightful place for a picnic.'

Dona Maria hesitated:

'It is a bit far, but we'll see.'

And seeing Dona Ana waiting silently, Gonçalo opened the carriage door for her and took the reins of his horse from the footman. Pleased that the afternoon had gone so well, Dona Maria Mendonça shook her cousin warmly by the hand, assuring him that she 'had quite fallen in love with Craquede!' Dona Ana, shy and blushing, barely brushed the tips of his fingers.

When he was alone again, with his horse's reins looped over his arm, Gonçalo smiled. Yes, he had found Dona Ana most pleasing that afternoon. She had quite a different manner, a kind of grave simplicity, and there was a new sweetness about her potent beauty as rural Venus. And that remark of hers about the chapel being 'not very religious somehow' really had been most astute. Who knows, perhaps beneath that sensual flesh lay a delicate nature. Under the influence of another man—and not that fool Sanches—the butcher's splendid daughter might develop into a truly charming woman. Yes, that remark of hers about the tombs and their religious nature, emerging, as they did, out of Legend and History, had been very astute indeed.

And he was suddenly seized by a desire to visit the cloister, which he had not entered since he was a boy, when the Tower still had its own carriages and when, on pensive autumn afternoons, the romantic Miss Rhodes often chose to make a trip out to Craquede. He tugged at his horse's reins and led it through the doorway and across the open space that had once been the nave, but was now only rubble and shards and fragments of stone from the vaulted roof lying buried among the weeds. And through a gap in the wall to which part of the altar was still attached, he entered the ancient Afonsine cloister, or the one corner that remained of it, with its rough pillars and large polished paving stones, which the sacristan had carefully swept that morning. And ranged along the wall, where one could still see the stone ribs of what had once been arches, stood the seven vast Ramires tombs, blackened with age and with any carvings worn smooth; they resembled coarse granite chests, some heavily sunk into the paving stones, others resting on balls corroded by the centuries. Gonçalo was following a flagstone path, close by the arches, remembering when he and Gracinha would play boisterously among those graves, while in the cloister itself, among the fallen columns and the grass-grown ruins, Miss Rhodes would pick wild flowers. In the vault above the largest of the tombs, hanging from an iron chain attached to its hilt, was the famous sword, black with age, its blade all rusty with time. Above another tomb there burned a strange Moorish lamp, that had been kept alight ever since the remote evening when some monk had silently lit it with a funeral candle. When had that eternal flame been lit? Who lay in those granite coffers, from which time had erased dates and inscriptions, so that all of History would vanish with them, condemning those proud, strong men to obscurity, to mere anonymous dust? At the far end of the cloister was the open tomb and, beside it, in two pieces, the lid that Lopo Ramires had broken open in order to gallop off and join the battle at Las Navas de Tolosa and defeat five Moorish kings. Curious, Gonçalo peered inside. In one corner of the deep chest lay a pile of very clean, neat, white bones! Had old Lopo, in his heroic haste, forgotten those few bones, already detached from his skeleton? Darkness had fallen, and with it a melancholy shadow grew denser above the vaults in the cloister and covered that resting-place of the dead with a pall of dull grief. Gonçalo shuddered, afraid that another lid might split thunderously open and pale, fleshless fingers thrust themselves up through the crack! He desperately dragged his horse back through the gap in the wall and, once among the ruins of the nave, leaped into the saddle, trotted through the doorway and then galloped urgently across the courtyard, his fears only abating when, at the edge of the pine forest, he saw an old woman going through the iron level-crossing, driving along her donkey laden with grass.

VIII

Since his visit to Santa Maria de Craquede, Gonçalo had been feeling uncomfortably guilty about his own idleness and his long neglect of the Novella; then, at the end of that week, when he had just finished his morning bath, he received a letter from Castanheiro. It was a short missive, informing him that, if the three chapters of the Novella had not arrived in Lisbon by the middle of October, then, instead of *The Tower of Dom Ramires*, the first issue of the *Annals* would contain a one-act play by Nuno Carreira, entitled *In the House of the Temeraire*. 'It may be a drama and a work of fiction,' he went on, 'but it suits the erudite flavour of the *Annals*, because the Temeraire in question is Charles the Bold, and the whole powerfully imagined story takes place in the chateau of Péronne, where there are gathered not only Louis XI of France, but also our own poor Afonso V and his squire Pêro da Covilhã, as well as other notable historical figures. Imagine that! Obviously, the truly chic thing would be to have Tructesindo Mendes Ramires' story told by our own Gonçalo Mendes Ramires, but it would seem that this truly chic thing will not appear now because of its author's utter indolence. *Sunt Lacrymae Revistarum!*'

Gonçalo threw down the letter and called for Bento:

'Have some strong green tea and a few slices of toast brought up to me in the library. I'll lunch late today, at two o'clock, or possibly not at all!'

And pulling on the usual faded dressing gown he wore when he was writing, he decided to chain himself to his desk like a galley-slave until he had finished that difficult third chapter, which described Tructesindo's most barbarous and most sublime characteristics. Damn it, he must not miss this chance to publish his Novella—and at such an advantageous moment too, on the eve of his arrival in Lisbon, precisely when his political influence and social prestige needed a little extra gloss; after all, did Vigny not say that 'a steel-nibbed pen always adds lustre to a nobleman's coat of arms?' Fortunately, on that bright morning, when the fountains in the garden outside were singing loudly, he, too, could feel his literary gifts bubbling up inside him, happy to be given free rein once more. His visit to the cloister in Craquede had give his imagination a clearer vision of his Afonsine ancestors, as if, having seen the great tombs in which their great bones lay crumbling, he could finally grasp their way of living and thinking.

In the library, he dusted off the pages of his Novella and resumed writing with great gusto at precisely the point where he had got stuck: the terrifying moment when, among the glitter of many raised lances, old Ordonho saw the Bastard's banner approaching along the stream's edge, before crossing over the old wooden bridge, disappearing for a moment among the green leaves of the poplars, then proudly advancing again as far as the rough stone cross erected by Lourenço Ramires. With a cry of 'To arms, to arms, the Bastard's men are coming!' plump old Ordonho almost tumbled down the steps in his haste.

Meanwhile, Tructesindo Ramires, intent on preparing his troops to set off for Montemor, had already given his commanding officer his instructions, ordering him to sound the horns the moment the sun's rays struck the wall of the great well. And now, in the high-ceilinged hall of the castle, he was talking to his cousin and brother-in-arms from Riba-Cávado, Dom Garcia Viegas—both seated on the stone window seat where a jug of refreshing water and a mug stood between two pots of basil. Dom Garcia Viegas, a thin, agile old man, with a broad, dark, clean-shaven face and small, bright eyes, had earned the nickname 'Dom Garcia the Wise' for his sage wit and for the substance of his remarks, his infinite knowledge of war, and his ability to speak Latin more fluently than any priest. Summoned by Tructesindo, along with other relatives in the area, to join the Ramires' troops and set off to bring succour to the Princesses, he had immediately, loyally, ridden to Santa Ireneia with his small band of ten lancers, and, en route, had begun by sacking the estate of Palha-Cã, which belonged to the Severosa family, who had joined forces with the Royal hosts against the threatened Princesses.

So urgently had he ridden there, that all he had eaten since dawn in Palha-Cã were two slices of plundered sausage, and he had eaten those while still in the saddle. Thirsty after this furious ride and still cast down by the bitter news of his godson Lourenço Ramires' defeat, he was once again filling his mug with water when Ordonho burst breathlessly into the *salle d'armes*—the entrance to which was adorned with three boars' heads.

'Senhor Tructesindo, Senhor Tructesindo Ramires! The Bastard of Baião has crossed the stream and is advancing on us now with a great company of lancers!'

Jumping down from the window seat and shaking one hairy, furiously clenched fist, as if he already had the Bastard by the throat, Tructesindo cried:

'God's blood, he has at least saved us a journey! What do you say, Garcia Viegas, time to mount up and after them?'

Hard on Ordonho's stumbling heels came the captain of the crossbowmen, who, brandishing his leather cap, shouted from the doorway:

'Sir, sir! Baião's men have stopped at the cross, and a young gentleman, carrying a leafy branch, is standing before the barbican, as if he brought a message.'

Tructesindo stamped his armoured foot on the flagstones, indignant at such an embassy sent by such a villain. However, Garcia Viegas, who had just downed another mug of water, reminded him calmly and sagely of the rules of war:

'Wait, my cousin and friend! It is the custom both far and near always to hear any messenger bearing an olive branch.'

'So be it!' roared Tructesindo. 'Go forth, Ordonho, and hear what he has to say, and take with you two lancers!'

Ordonho bustled plumply down the blackened spiral staircase to the courtyard. Two liegemen newly returned from a patrol, spears on their shoulders, were chatting to the armourer, who was busily painting in yellow and red the shafts of some new spears and lining them up against the wall to dry.

'On the orders of Lord Tructesindo,' cried Ordonho, 'take up your spears and follow me to the barbican to hear a messenger!'

The two men immediately fell in and, flanked by them, Ordonho crossed the bailey, went out through the barbican gate—which was guarded by a group of crossbowmen—and into the large area of bare earth beyond the walls, with no grass and no trees, on which still stood the worm-eaten beams of an old gallows, as well as piles of wooden laths and stone blocks for repairs to the castle. Then, standing on the threshold, between his two liegemen, he thrust out his large belly and shouted to the young man waiting beneath the scalding sun, brushing away the flies with a green branch:

'Tell us who you are and why you have come and what credentials you bring!'

And when Ordonho nervously cupped one hand to his ear, the horseman casually tucked the branch in-between his cuisse and the bow of his saddle, likewise cupped the mouthpiece of his helmet with his two gleaming, chain-mailed hands, and bellowed:

'I am a knight from the Baião estate! I have no credentials because I bring no embassy. But Senhor Lopo, who is waiting by the cross, asks the noble lord of Santa Ireneia, Senhor Tructesindo Ramires, to come out onto the barbican walls and hear what he has to say.'

Ordonho merely waved in response and went back in through the vaulted door of the barbican tower, murmuring to the two men with him:

'The Bastard has doubtless come to demand a ransom for Senhor Lourenço Ramires.'

Both men snorted:

'How dare he!'

However, when Ordonho hurried, panting, back into the castle, he found Tructesindo already waiting, for, in his anger and impatience at the Bastard's delays, he had come down into the courtyard, fully armed. Over the long, dark green, woollen tunic, which he wore on top of his coat of mail, his long beard—tied in a thick knot, like the tail of a horse—gleamed whiter than ever. From one side of his silver-inlaid belt hung a curved dagger and an ivory horn, while from the other hung his long-bladed Visigothic sword, with its high, gilded hilt, on which glittered a rare gem brought long ago from Palestine by Gutierres Ramires the Traveller. On a leather cushion, his sergeant bore Tructesindo's gloves and his round helmet with its barred visor, like the one worn by King Sancho; another carried a vast, heart-shaped buckler, covered in scarlet leather and adorned with a crudely painted black goshawk unsheathing its furious talons. The standard-bearer, Afonso Gomes, followed behind with the standard rolled up inside a canvas cover.

With him had come Dom Garcia Viegas and other relatives: ancient and decrepit Ramiro Ramires, a veteran from the taking of Santarém, his limbs as gnarled with rheumatism as the roots of an oak tree, supporting his tremulous steps with a stick not a spear; handsome Leonel, the youngest of the Samora brothers from Cendufe, a celebrated singer of ballads, who had singlehandedly killed two bears in the heathlands of Cachamuz; red-bearded Mendo de Briteiros, a great burner of witches and blithe master of revels and dances; and the gigantic figure of the Lord of Avelim, entirely covered, like some mythical fish, in gleaming scales. The sun's rays were now almost touching the edge of the great well, marking the moment for the troops to set off to Montemor, and from beneath the great canopies covering the jousting fields, the stableboys were leading out the warhorses, their high saddles studded with silver, their haunches and chests protected by long, fringed leather blankets that reached to the ground. The castle rang with the news that, following the fateful battle at Canta-Pedra, the Bastard had immediately ridden to Santa Ireneia. Crouched in the narrow passageways linking the castle wall to the buttresses or among the piles of slings heaped up in the corridors, the kitchen boys, serfs and villeins sheltering in the barbican were peering anxiously at the Lord of Santa Ireneia with his powerful companions, and trembling at the thought of Baião's imminent attack and the terrible cast-iron firepots that the Christian troops had been using to such effect against the Saracen hordes. Meanwhile, his cap pressed to his chest, Ordonho breathlessly presented Tructesindo with the Bastard's message.

'The messenger is just a young man and carries no credentials with him, but the Lord of Baião is waiting by the cross and asks that you go up to the barbican wall and hear what he has to say.'

'Let him approach then,' declared Tructesindo, 'and as many of his knaves as care to follow him!'

With his usual acuity, Garcia Viegas the Wise said gently:

'Wait, my cousin and my friend. Do not do so until I have assured myself that Baião is not up to some trick or other.'

And handing his heavy beechwood spear to a squire, he went up the dark stairs leading to the barbican tower. Once on the battlements, he urged silence on the line of crossbowmen waiting, bows at the ready, and slipped into the lookout point, where he peered through the arrow slit. Baião's messenger had since galloped back to the cross, which was surrounded by a shifting forest of glittering spears. His message was clearly a brief one, for Lopo de Baião, on his sorrel horse covered with a gold-flecked coat of mail, emerged from among the dense throng of horsemen, his visor up and carrying neither lance nor spear, his hands gripping the scarlet leather reins but otherwise idle on the bow of his Moorish saddle. Then came a long note on the horn, and he advanced slowly towards the castle, as if he were leading a funeral procession. His yellow-and-black standard did not stir. Only six squires escorted him, also unarmed and wearing purple tunics over their coats of mail. Behind came four sturdy crossbowmen bearing on their shoulders a stretcher made from branches, on which a man was lying, apparently dead, his body protected from the heat and the horseflies by light acacia twigs. And behind them rode a monk on a white mule, clutching both the reins of his mount and—partially obscured by the hem of his hood and the tip of his black beard—a metal crucifix.

Through the arrow slit, and despite the layer of twigs covering the man on the stretcher, Garcia Viegas immediately recognised Lourenço Ramires, his beloved godson, whom he had taught jousting and falconry. Clenching his fists and speaking in a dull voice, he said, 'Stand ready, crossbowmen, stand ready!' He then went back down the dark stairs, so distracted by rage and grief that his helmet clanged against the archway of the door, where Tructesindo was waiting with his fellow knights.

'Cousin!' he roared. 'Your son Lourenço is there outside the walls, laid on a stretcher!'

With a cry of horror and a clatter of metal feet across the echoing flagstones, everyone followed Tructesindo through the barbican tower's postern to the stout wooden ladder leaning against the outer wall. And when the vast figure of Tructesindo reached the top of the ladder, a heavy silence fell, so complete that one could hear the slow, sad creaking of the waterwheel in the orchard and the growling of the mastiffs.

In the empty space beyond the postern, the Bastard was waiting, sitting utterly still on his horse, his handsome face—that Bright Sun—uplifted, and his long curly beard glinting like gold against his cuirass. He greeted Tructesindo gravely and humbly, bowing his helmeted head. Then he raised one ungloved hand and spoke thoughtfully and calmly:

'Senhor Tructesindo Ramires, on this litter lies your son Lourenço, whom I took prisoner in honest combat in the valley of Canta-Pedra and who, according to the laws laid down by our nobility, now belongs to me. I have brought him all the way from Canta-Pedra to ask you to put an end to these murders and these ugly disputes, which waste the blood of good Christians. Like you, Senhor Tructesindo Ramires, I am of royal birth, and I was knighted by Afonso of Portugal. The whole noble race of the Baião family takes pride in me. Give me the hand of your daughter Dona Violante, whom I love and who loves me, and issue orders for the drawbridge to be raised so that the wounded Lourenço may enter in and so that I may kiss my father's hand.'

The litter trembled on the shoulders of the crossbowmen, and a desperate cry rang out:

'Say No, father!'

Stiff and erect on the battlements, arms folded, old Tructesindo took up the cry; then, his voice echoing proudly and cavernously around the whole castle, he shouted:

'My son has answered for me, knave!'

As if his breast had been pierced by a lance, the Bastard shuddered, and his sorrel horse, startled by the sudden tug on the reins, stepped back, shaking its golden head. Then, however, the Bastard moved closer to the castle gate, and standing up in his stirrups, he uttered a yearning, furious cry:

'Do not tempt me, Senhor Tructesindo Ramires!'

'Begone, vile knave, son of a knavish mother, begone!' cried the old man proudly, his arms folded, his whole body as hard and still and stubborn as if it were made of iron.

Hurling one glove at the barbican wall, the Bastard then roared out this fiery, hoarse response:

'Then I swear by Christ's blood and by the soul of my whole family that, if you will not, this instant, give me the woman I love and who loves me, you will lose your son, from whom, with my own hands and before your eyes, and even if the whole of Heaven were to come to his aid, I will wrest what little remains of his life!'

A dagger already glinted in his hand, but in a superhuman impulse of sublime pride, Tructesindo rose up like another dark tower on the castle battlements and unsheathed his sword:

'No, coward, use this sword, use this one! The blade that pierces my son's heart should be pure, not sullied like yours!'

With his great strong hands, he furiously flung the sword into the air, where it whirled down, whistling and glittering, until it stuck fast in the hard ground, trembling and still glittering, as if itself filled with a heroic rage. At that same moment, the Bastard gave a roar that made his horse start, and, leaning down from his saddle, he plunged the dagger into Lourenço's throat, so hard and deep that blood spattered his pale face and his golden beard.

Then all took flight. The four crossbowmen dropped the litter bearing the now dead body and, like hares caught in a clearing, dashed back to the cross, hard on the heels of the monk racing along, crouched over his mule and clinging to its mane. The Bastard, the six horsemen, all giving the alarm, rejoined the troops gathered around the cross, where, for a moment, helmets gleaming, they wheeled about in tumult, before racing off down to the stream, over the old bridge, and into the woods, leaving behind them only a cloud of dust.

Meanwhile, a clamorous cry thundered round the walls of Santa Ireneia—bolts and arrows and slingshot whistled after the fleeing troops, but only one of the crossbowmen who had been carrying the litter fell and lay writhing on the ground, an arrow in his side. Knights and pages desperately pushed their way through the postern gate to retrieve Lourenço Ramires' body. And Garcia Viegas and the others raced up to the barbican wall, where Tructesindo was still standing, silent and erect, staring down at his dead son sprawled on the ground. Hearing their voices, he slowly turned, and all were struck dumb by his impassive face—whiter than his white beard, the dead white of a tombstone—with not a tear in his coal-dark eyes, which blazed and flickered like the fire in a furnace. With that same sinister serenity, he touched the shoulder of old Ramiro Ramires, who was trembling as he leaned on his spear, and in a slow, booming voice, he said:

'My friend, please tend to my son's body, for today, God willing, I will bring succour to his soul!'

He pushed aside these gentlemen, who were still dumb with shock and emotion, and went down the worn wooden rungs of the ladder, which creaked beneath the weight of that great nobleman, heavy-laden with anger and grief.

At that point, jostled by crowds of crossbowmen and serfs, the body of Lourenço Ramires was being carried through the barbican gates, borne along by handsome Leonel and by Mendo de Briteiros, both of whom were drenched in tears and muttering furious threats against the whole Baião race.

Stumbling and groaning, old Ordonho had picked up Tructesindo's sword, which he embraced and kissed as if to console it. At the edge of the moat, a hazel tree spread its light shade over a rough wooden platform supported on logs, where, on Sundays, along with the commander of the crossbowmen, Lourenço used to organise archery contests, with contestants later generously rewarded with honey cakes and jugs of wine. They laid the body on this platform, quickly withdrawing and earnestly making the sign of the cross. Fearing for that helpless, unconfessed soul, a knight from Briteiros ran to the castle chapel in search of Father Múncio. Others, running round the walls to the old bastion, desperately shouted and waved up at the ruined tower in which the physician lived, perched like an owl. However, with one sure thrust, the Bastard's dagger had slain brave Lourenço, the very flower and model of all the knights in Riba-Cávado. And what a sorry, broken sight he was: his face smeared with mud, his throat thick with black blood, his chain-mail tunic wrenched open at the shoulders and embedded in his butchered flesh, and the leg that was wounded at Canta-Pedra, bare and exposed, all swollen and purple and sticky with more mud and blood.

Tructesindo approached, slow and stiff. And the blazing coals of his eyes burned still more fiercely when he walked through the grieving silence towards his son's body. He knelt down beside the platform, clasped one limp, cold hand in his, and pressing his face to that other blood-and-mud-caked face, he whispered, as one soul to another, a few secret words, not words of farewell, but some supreme promise, which concluded with a lingering kiss planted on his son's forehead, where a sliver of sunlight danced, glimmering down through the leaves of the hazel tree. Then, starting to his feet and reaching out one arm as if to summon up all the strength of his race, he cried:

'And now, gentlemen, to horse, and let us exact a cruel revenge!'

From the courtyards around the keep came the clatter of weapons being hastily snatched up. In response to the commands barked out by the infantry captains, the lines of crossbowmen and archers and slingsmen raced from the battlements to the courtyard to form into ranks. Stableboys were hurriedly loading the mules with wineskins and boxes of provisions, and in the low kitchen doorways, foot soldiers and servants were downing one last beaker of wine. In the outer bailey, the knights in their armour, with the help of their pages, were heaving themselves up onto the high saddles of their horses, and were then immediately flanked by their squires and men-at-arms, who handed them their spears and whistled for the hounds.

Finally, the standard-bearer, Afonso Gomes, removed the standard from its cover and shook it free, so that the goshawk's wings flapped dark and wide, as if taking furious flight. The shrill command of the officer in charge rang around the whole courtyard— *Ala! Ala!* Standing on a stone pillar next to the postern, Brother Múncio was holding out his thin, tremulous hands and blessing the host. Then Tructesindo, mounted on his black horse, received his sword from old Ordonho, the sword he had so boldly, so cruelly thrown down. And raising the gleaming blade up to the towers of his castle as if to an altar, he boomed:

'Walls of Santa Ireneia, may I never see you again if, in three days' time, from sunrise to sunset, there is still blood flowing in the accursèd veins of that traitor Baião!'

Then the gates were flung open and, gathered round the standard, the knights rode out, while, in the belltower, beneath the calm splendour of that August afternoon, the big bell began to toll the death knell.

That evening, sitting in his armchair on the balcony, Gonçalo re-read that chapter of blood and fury, over which he'd been toiling all week, and decided that it was 'an impressive piece of writing'.

Then he felt a desire to garner the praise it merited straight away and to show the three finished chapters to Gracinha and Father Soeiro before submitting them to the *Annals*. It could prove useful too, because Father Soeiro's archaeological knowledge could perhaps provide some new, suitably Afonsine touches that would further resurrect Santa Ireneia and its formidable owners. He decided to set off in the morning for Oliveira, and once Father Soeiro had studied the Novella minutely, he would entrust it to Dona Arminda Viegas' steward for him to copy out in his exquisite hand, famous throughout the district and equalled only (when it came to capital letters) by the Ecclesiastical Council's scribe.

He was already brushing the dust off an old morocco leather briefcase in which to transport his Great Work, when the door opened and Bento came in, weighed down by a wicker basket covered with a lace cloth.

'A present, sir.'

'A present? Who from?'

'From Feitosa, sir, from the ladies.'

'How delightful!'

'And there's a letter pinned to the lace.'

Filled with curiosity, Gonçalo tore open the envelope! However, despite the imposing wax seal, all the envelope contained were a few pencilled lines written on his cousin Maria Mendonça's visiting card, 'Yesterday, over supper, I mentioned to Ana your love of peaches, especially when poached in wine, and she is therefore taking the liberty of sending you this little basket of Feitosa peaches, which, as you know, are famous throughout Portugal. Fondest wishes.' Gonçalo immediately assumed that, tenderly hidden away beneath the peaches, he would find a note from Dona Ana!

'Oh, peaches! Leave them over there on a chair, will you.'

'Hadn't I better take them straight to the pantry, sir?'

'No, leave them on that chair!'

As soon as Bento had closed the door, Gonçalo spread the lace cloth out on the floor and emptied onto it the beautiful peaches, whose perfume filled the whole library. At the bottom of the basket, however, he found only a few vine-leaves. Then he decided that the peaches, arranged by her on vine-leaves that she herself had picked from the vine trellis and covered with a cloth that she herself had chosen from the cupboard, constituted, in their perfumed silence, a little love note. Still crouching down, he ate one of the peaches as he put the others back in the basket to take to Gracinha.

The next day, at two o'clock, when Torto's pair of horses were harnessed to the carriage, and Gonçalo had just pulled on his gloves in readiness for the journey to Oliveira, he received an unexpected visit—from the Viscount de Rio-Manso. Removing his gloves, the Nobleman thought, 'What can that grumpy old man want?' In the living room, perched on the edge of the green velvet sofa and rubbing his knees, the Viscount explained that he had been passing the Tower on his way back from Vila Clara and, overcoming his usual shyness, had decided to present his respects to Senhor Gonçalo Ramires, not just to carry out that most pleasurable of duties, but also (since learning that His Excellency was standing as deputy for the constituency) to offer his support and the votes that he commanded in the parish of Canta-Pedra.

Somewhat embarrassed, Gonçalo kept twiddling his moustache, smiling and astonished. The Viscount of Rio-Manso was not in the least surprised at his astonishment, because Senhor Gonçalo Ramires had doubtless always known him to be a resolute Regenerationist. He, however, belonged to the generation, now growing rather few in number, who placed the duty of gratitude above politics; and quite apart from the sympathy naturally due to Senhor Gonçalo Ramires (given his reputation in the area as a talented, affable and charitable young man) he also owed him a personal debt of gratitude, which had as yet gone unpaid, not out of indifference, but out of shyness.

'Can't you guess what that debt might be, Senhor Gonçalo Mendes Ramires? Don't you remember?'

'No, really, sir, I don't ...'

Well, one afternoon, when Senhor Gonçalo Mendes Ramires was riding past his estate, his granddaughter had been playing on the terrace (at the spot where a magnolia tree overhangs the railings) and the ball she'd been playing with had rolled away into the road. Senhor Gonçalo Mendes Ramires had immediately dismounted, laughingly picked up the ball, and then, in order to return it to her, had remounted and brought his horse up alongside the railings— and he had done all this with such simplicity and charm!

'You don't remember?'

'Yes, yes, I do now ...'

On the terrace, right next to the railings, stood a large flowerpot full of carnations. After joking with the girl (who, he was pleased to say, had not appeared in the least intimidated), Senhor Gonçalo Mendes had asked her for a carnation, and she had duly picked one and handed it to him very gravely, like a proper lady. He had been watching from his bedroom window, thinking, 'Well, well! Fancy a great aristocrat like the Nobleman of the Tower being so very kind!' There was no reason now for him to laugh or blush. It really had been a great act of kindness, and in his eyes, as the girl's grandfather, it had seemed extraordinary. And it hadn't only been the ball either.

'Do you really not remember, sir?'

'Yes, it's coming back to me ...'

The very next day, Senhor Gonçalo Mendes Ramires had sent from the Tower a beautiful basket of roses, along with a playful little note, 'In gratitude for a carnation, these roses for Senhora Dona Rosa.'

Gonçalo almost leapt out of his chair in his amusement:

'Ah, yes, I remember now!'

Ever since that afternoon, he had always longed for an opportunity to show Senhor Gonçalo Mendes Ramires his gratitude and friendship. Alas, he was extremely shy and lived a very retiring life. That morning, however, in Vila Clara, he had learned from Gouveia that His Excellency was standing as deputy for the constitutuency. And despite his Election being more or less guaranteed — given Senhor Ramires' influence and that of the Government — he had immediately thought, 'Now's your chance!' So here he was, offering Senhor Ramires his help and his votes in the parish of Canta-Pedra.

Genuinely touched, Gonçalo murmured:

'I find such a spontaneous offer deeply moving.'

'It moves me still more to know that you'll accept my offer. But let's talk no more of my poor offer of help and my poor votes. This is a most venerable house you have here.'

And when the Viscount mentioned that he had long wanted to take a closer look at the famous Tower, older even than Portugal itself, they both went down into the orchard. Resting his parasol on his shoulder, the Viscount gazed up in silent awe at the Tower; and despite his own liberal views, he could not but acknowledge what great prestige attached to such a long lineage; he was equally warm in his praise of the orange trees. Then, since he knew that Pereira had rented the land around the Tower, he said how he envied his having such a careful, honest tenant. The Viscount's carriage was waiting at the main gate, drawn by two groomed and glossy mules, on which Gonçalo, in turn, complimented the Viscount. Opening the carriage door, he asked the Viscount to kiss Senhora Dona Rosa's little hand for him. Touched, the Viscount expressed his hope, nay, his ambition, that on a day of his choosing, the Nobleman would visit Canta-Pedra and dine with them, in order to become better acquainted with the little girl with the ball and the carnation.

'I would consider that a huge honour! And I volunteer to teach Senhora Dona Rosa, assuming she does not already know, how to play the old Portuguese game of péla.'

The Viscount pressed one hand to his heart, all smiles and laughter.

Going back up the steps, Gonçalo was murmuring to himself, 'What a delightful man! And how generous too, repaying roses with votes. It's often the case that one small act of kindness can win you a friend! I will definitely go and dine at Canta-Pedra next week. Such a sweet man!'

And in this happy state of mind, he placed in the carriage the morocco leather briefcase containing the manuscript, along with Dona Ana's sentimental basket of peaches. Then he lit a cigar, jumped onto the driving seat, took up the reins, and urging the two white horses into a lively trot, set off for Oliveira.

In Largo d'El-Rei, before getting down from the carriage, he immediately asked the porter, Joaquim, for news of his master and mistress and was told that both were, praise be, extremely well. That morning, Senhor José Barrolo had ridden over to visit the Baron das Marges, and would only be back that night.

'And how's Father Soeiro?'

'I believe Father Soeiro is at Senhora Dona Arminda's house.'

'And Senhora Dona Graça?'

'She set off a little while ago now for the gazebo, wearing a hat. I think she was going to the church.'

'Fine. Take this basket of peaches and tell the other Joaquim to put it on the table just as it is. And have someone send some hot water up to my room.'

The wall clock in the parlour lazily groaned out five o'clock. The house was bathed in a bright, restful silence. And after all the dust and jolting of the road, the coolness of his room seemed even sweeter, with its four windows open to the recently watered garden and the courtyard of the neighbouring church. The first thing he did was to stow his precious morocco leather briefcase in a drawer. A maid with big round eyes came in carrying a large jug of hot water, and, as he usually did, the Nobleman joked with her about the handsome cavalry sergeants, whose tempting barracks overlooked the laundry room in the garden, where the female servants spent all day passionately soaping and scrubbing away. He then took some time changing out of his dusty clothes and whistling tunelessly as he leaned on the balcony that gave onto the silent Rua das Tecedeiras. The church bell rang out prettily. And bored with his solitude, Gonçalo decided to go down into the garden and surprise Gracinha at her prayers in the church.

Downstairs, in the corridor, he met Joaquim, the pantry boy:

'So Senhor Barrolo won't be dining here this evening?'

'No, sir, he's gone to dine at the house of the Baron das Marges. It's their little girl's birthday today, and he'll only be back late
tonight.'

In the garden, Gonçalo dawdled a while longer over the flower
pots, putting together a boutinière of dainty flowers. Then he
walked round the greenhouse, smiling at the fine door Barrolo
had had installed, a glass and ironwork confection emblazoned
with a monogram in brilliant colours, and strolled on along the
avenue that led to the fountain, all silence and shade beneath the
intertwining branches of the tall laurels. Further on, surrounded
by stone benches and scented, flowering trees, the slender fountain sang drowsily in the middle of the round pond, ringed, on
its broad edge, with several large white ceramic pots all bearing
the family's intricate coat of arms. The pond had obviously been
cleaned out either the day before or that very morning, because in
the clearer than clear water, the fish seemed to swim more vigor-
ously than usual—sudden orangey-pink flashes against the white
stone bottom—whenever Gonçalo startled them by plunging his
cane into the water and stirring it about. And from the edge of the
pond, he could already see, at the far end of another dahlia-lined
avenue, the faded pink gazebo, an eighteenth-century imitation of
a Greek temple, with a chubby Cupid poised on top of the domed
roof, and small rococo windows set between the bas-relief ribbed
columns thick with flowering jasmine.

As usual, Gonçalo plucked a few leaves from a lemon verbena
plant and crushed them between his fingers to enjoy the scent; then
he continued slowly on to the gazebo, past the dahlia beds. His
fine patent leather shoes made not a sound on the newly sanded
path. And thus, silent as an indolent shadow, he approached the
gazebo, where one of the windows stood ajar, with the green-slat-
ted blind inside closed. Right next to that window were the stone
steps that led down from the long, elevated terrace on which the
garden was built to the hidden Rua das Tecedeiras and the church
almost opposite. Still in no hurry, Gonçalo was just about to make
his way down those steps when, through the blind, he heard a
whisper coming from inside the gazebo, an anxious whisper. Smil-

ing, he thought that one of the maids had perhaps taken refuge in that miniature temple of love with one of those terribly handsome cavalry sergeants, but, no, that was impossible. Only minutes before, Gracinha had walked past that window and gone down those steps on her way to church! Then another idea pierced him like a sword—and it was so painful that he drew back in terror from the spot where that perverse thought had assailed him. And yet he was gripped, too, by a desperate curiosity that propelled him forwards, and he pressed his ear to the shutter as cautiously as a spy. Silence had descended on the gazebo, and Gonçalo was afraid the pounding of his heart might give him away. Then the murmuring began again, sounding more urgent this time, more alarmed. Someone was pleading, stammering, 'No, no, this is madness!' And someone else was insisting impatiently, ardently, 'Yes, yes, my love, yes!' And he recognised both those voices—as clearly as if the slats on the blind had been opened and the gazebo flooded with all the vast brilliance of the garden—Gracinha and Cavaleiro!

Seized by terrible embarrassment, horrified both by the thought that they might find him there right next to the gazebo and by the shameless secret that lay hidden therein, he retraced his steps, making as little noise as possible on the soft sand, creeping back down the dahlia-lined path, then around the shaded fountain, before plunging once more into the darkness of the laurel hedges, walking stealthily round behind the greenhouse and back into the quiet of the house. The murmuring voices from the gazebo were still repeating over and over in his head, fainter now and more submissive, 'No, no, this is madness!' 'Yes, yes, my love, yes!'

He raced through the deserted rooms like a ghost pursued; he slipped silently down the stone steps and out through the street door, looking all around him, afraid that Joaquim the porter might be there. In the square, he stopped in front of the railings around the sundial, but the whisper from the gazebo was everywhere, like a wild wind, scouring the flagstones, whirling about the moss-covered roof of the rope-maker's shop. 'No, no, this is madness!' 'Yes, yes, my love, yes!' Then Gonçalo felt a desperate need to escape as far away as possible from that square, that house, that town, from the shame enveloping everything. But he had no carriage? It occurred to him that he could hire one from Maciel, whose stables were furthest from the centre, beyond the last houses on the road to the seminary. And so, keeping close to the low walls of those poor streets, he ran all the way there and, when he arrived, demanded that a closed carriage be prepared for him as quickly as possible.

While he was waiting on a bench at the stable door, a cart trundled by, piled high with furniture, cooking pots and a large mattress bearing a vast stain. Gonçalo suddenly remembered the divan in the gazebo—a huge mahogany affair, upholstered in a striped fabric—and how its soft springs creaked. Then the murmuring began again, growing louder and louder, rolling like a rumble of thunder over the hovels nearby, over the seminary, over the whole of an astonished Oliveira. 'No, no, this is madness!' 'Yes, yes, my love, yes!'

Gonçalo sprang to his feet and shouted into the dark stables:

'Damn it, how long does it take to prepare a carriage?'

'Just coming, sir.'

The clock on the poorhouse was striking seven when he flung himself into the carriage, wound down the stiff blinds and sat there invisible and crushed, feeling that the world had been shaken, that even noble souls had been laid low and that his Tower, as old as the Kingdom itself, had cracked open to reveal within a hitherto unseen pile of detritus and soiled skirts.

IX

S tanding at the kitchen door, a crumpled envelope clasped in his hand, Gonçalo was scolding Rosa:

'I told you not to write to Graça, but, no, you must have your own way! I thought we'd decided what to do with the little one without going whining to Oliveira. The Tower is fortunately large enough to accommodate another child!'

Crispola had died. The poor widow and near neighbour of the Tower, with her small troop of children to take care of, two boys and three girls, had been gradually wasting away in her humble bed since Easter. And now Gonçalo, who had kept the family well supplied with food, was finding homes for the children, who were already, thanks to him, appropriately dressed in mourning. The oldest girl (also called Crispola), who was always to be found skulking in the kitchen anyway, naturally became Rosa's 'paid assistant'. Gonçalo also took on the older son, a tall, bright twelve-year-old, as errand boy, complete with yellow-buttoned uniform. The other boy, a rather limp, snivelling child, nevertheless had a great gift for and love of carpentry, and with the help of his Aunt Louredo, Gonçalo had found a place for him in Lisbon at a school run by Salesian monks. One of the other girls was taken in by Manuel Duarte's mother—a delightful woman who lived on a beautiful estate near Treixedo— who adored Gonçalo, considering him to be her Lord and she his vassal. However, he had as yet found no safe haven for the smallest and weakest of the girls. It had been Rosa who'd said that Senhora Dona Maria da Graça would be sure to take the child. Gonçalo had retorted brusquely, 'We don't need to trouble the town of Oliveira for a crust of bread!' Rosa, though, had got carried away, feeling that the fair, frail little girl needed the protection of a real lady, and so, in Bento's careful hand, she had written Gracinha a very long letter, giving the whole sad story of Crispola and lauding to the skies her master and his charitable ways. And it was Gracinha's belated but deeply felt response, telling them to send her the poor child straight away, that had so angered the Nobleman.

Ever since that dreadful afternoon at the gazebo, Gonçalo had been overwhelmed by a strange, almost prudish feeling of repugnance regarding any communication with the Casa dos Cunhais! It was as if the gazebo and the vile deed that had taken place within its pale pink walls had contaminated the garden, the house, Largo d'El-Rei, and the whole town of Oliveira, and these scruples now made him recoil from that contaminated region, where his heart and his pride could not breathe. Soon after his flight from the Casa dos Cunhais, he had received an anxious letter from Barrolo, 'Whatever got into you? Why didn't you stay? I was quite worried when I returned that night from the Marges estate and found you gone. Gracinha has been in a terrible state about it. We only found out by chance about your departure from one of Maciel's coachmen. We've started eating the peaches today, but we really don't understand what's going on!' Gonçalo responded abruptly with a one-word note, 'Business.' Then he remembered that he had left the manuscript of his Novella in the drawer in his bedroom there, and early one morning, he despatched one of his servants with a more or less secret message to Father Soeiro, containing a request 'to hand the briefcase to the bearer, well wrapped up, with not a word to my sister or her husband'. Between the Tower and the Casa dos Cunhais he wanted only separation and silence.

And in the days that he spent shut up in the Tower (not even risking going into Vila Clara, terrified that they were whispering his now sullied name in the tobacconist's and the grocery store) he trembled with a kind of amorphous anger that hit out at everyone. At his sister who—trampling on modesty, family pride, and a justifiable fear of the Oliveira gossips as easily and frivolously as she might tread on the faded flowers of a rug—had run to the gazebo, to that moustachioed male, as soon as he waved his perfumed handerchief at her! At Barrolo, the chubby-cheeked fool, who spent his foolish days celebrating Cavaleiro, parading him about Largo d'El Rei, choosing from his cellars the finest wines with which Cavaleiro could heat his blood, plumping up the cushions on all the sofas so that Cavaleiro could better savour his cigar and the gracious presence of Gracinha! And, finally, at himself, for he, out of his base desire for a seat in Parliament, had destroyed the one safe wall between his sister and the man with the glossy hair, namely, his enmity, his high-walled enmity, which he had always, ever since his days in Coimbra, kept solidly reinforced and white-washed! Ah, they were all horribly guilty!

Then, one afternoon, bored with being alone, he finally got up the courage to walk into Vila Clara. And he realised that no one there knew anything, not in the club, in the tobacconist's or in Ramos' shop, and that Gracinha's love affair might as well have been taking place in darkest Tartary. Once reassured, his easy-going soul abandoned itself to the pleasure of weaving subtle excuses for all those guilty of that sad fall from grace. With no children, with dull, ineffectual Barrolo as a husband, with no intellectual interests and too indolent even to take up sewing or embroidery, poor Gracinha had given in—and who wouldn't?—to the credulous, primitive passion that had sprung up in her soul, taken root there and awoken in her not just the only joy she had known in the world, but (more importantly) the only joy that had caused her to shed bitter tears! Poor dim Barrolo, on the other hand, was like the hawthorn bush in the song, incapable of producing any edible fruit, or even, in his case, any intelligent thoughts. And then there was Gonçalo himself, poor, forgotten Gonçalo, irresistibly seduced by the fateful Law of Increase, which had led him, as it leads all those greedy for fame and fortune, to rush through whichever door happens to open, oblivious to the dung heap blocking the way. None of us can really be judged guilty by a God who made us such fickle, fragile creatures, so dependent on forces over which we have even less control than the wind or the sun!

No, the only irredeemably guilty party was that rogue with the mane of wavy hair! In his behaviour towards Gracinha, he had always, ever since he was a student, revealed himself to be an out-and-out egotist—with an egotism that could only be punished as Gonçalo's ancestors would have punished their enemies, with a slow and very painful death, after which his corpse would be thrown to the crows. When, in the long, idle summers, it had suited him to conduct a bucolic courtship beneath the trees at the Tower, he had courted her. When he felt that a wife and children would get in the way of his free and easy life, he had betrayed her. As soon as his former beloved belonged to another man, he had resumed his languid siege of her in order to enjoy the pleasures of romance without the responsibilities of fatherhood. And as soon as her husband had opened his door to him, he had not hesitated for a moment, but had brutally pounced on his prey! Ah, how would Tructesindo have treated such a villainous villain? He would doubtless have roasted him over a roaring fire or, in the castle dungeons, have filled his lying throat with the finest molten lead.

Whereas when he, Tructesindo's descendant, met Cavaleiro in the streets of Oliveira, he could not even refuse to doff his hat to him and cut him dead! The slightest diminution in that disastrously renewed friendship would be tantamount to revealing the shameful incident in the gazebo! The whole of Oliveira would be gossiping and laughing, 'Did you see? The Nobleman of the Tower invited Cavaleiro into his sister's house and, a few weeks later, again broke off his friendship with him. Something truly scandalous must have happened!' How pleased the Lousada sisters would be! No, he must treat Cavaleiro with such free and frank affection that its very freedom and frankness would entirely cover up the whole vile business, concealing what lay pulsating beneath the surface. An agonising pretence, imposed by the need to protect the honour of his name and keep the sordid affair safely hidden away among the dense trees in the garden and in the still more private penumbra of the gazebo! And outside, in broad daylight, he'd be seen in the squares of Oliveira, affectionately arm-in-arm with Cavaleiro!

The days continued to roll by, and Gonçalo could find no peace of mind. What made him still more bitter was feeling forced into this ostentatious intimacy with Cavaleiro both by his desire to protect his name and by the needs of the upcoming Election. Sometimes his pride rebelled, 'What do I care about the Election!

What's some grubby seat in Parliament worth?' However, blunt reality soon silenced him. The Election was the only crack through which he could escape from his rural hole, and if he broke off his friendship with Cavaleiro, that villain—so practised in villainy— would, with the support of the conniving horde in Lisbon, immediately produce another candidate for Vila Clara. Gonçalo was, alas, one of those spineless individuals who depends on others. And where did that sad dependence come from? From poverty, from the meagre rent he earned from his two estates, which would be a fortune for a simpler man, but which to him—given his upbringing, his tastes, his duties as a nobleman, his sociable ways—meant poverty.

And these thoughts slowly and insinuatingly led him to another thought—to Dona Ana Lucena and her two hundred *contos*. Finally, one morning, he bravely faced up to a troubling possibility—should he marry Dona Ana? Why not? She had clearly indicated her interest, almost her consent. Why couldn't he marry Dona Ana?

True, her father had been a butcher and her brother a murderer, but, among his many ancestors, going all the way back to the ferocious Suevians, he'd be sure to find at least one butcher, and throughout those heroic centuries, the Ramires' main occupation had, it must be said, largely consisted of murdering people. Besides, both the butcher and the murderer—both dead now, remote shadows—belonged to a dying legend, for, by marrying, Dona Ana had risen from the populace to the bourgeoisie. Gonçalo had not met her in her father's butcher's shop or in her brother's hide-out, but at Feitosa, already a wealthy woman, with a steward, a chaplain and numerous lackeys, just like a Ramires of old. No, really, it was pure childishness to hesitate further, given that, along with those two hundred *contos*—good clean money, good rural money—that beautiful, serious-minded woman would also bring her body. With her pure gold and his name and talent, he would not need Cavaleiro's false hand of friendship in order to rise in politics. And what a full and noble life that would be! His ancient Tower restored to the sober splendour of earlier days; the finest agricultural care lavished on the ancient fields of Treixedo; fruitful journeys made to educational lands. And the woman who would provide these riches would not—as happens with so many marriages of convenience—sour those pleasures with her ugliness, her bony body or her flaccid skin. No, after the day's social glories, no monster would await him in the bedroom at night, but a Venus.

And so, one afternoon, succumbing to these tempting thoughts, he sent a note to his cousin Maria in Feitosa, asking if they could meet, alone, for a stroll nearby, because he wanted to have a serious, intimate little chat with her. Three long days dragged by, and the longed-for letter from Feitosa did not arrive. Gonçalo concluded that clever cousin Maria—sensing what that little chat would be about, but with no certain news to give him—was playing for time, avoiding having to answer. He had an awful, desolate week, ruminating on the melancholy of a life that seemed so utterly hollow and rife with uncertainty. Pride and a complicated kind of shame wouldn't allow him to return to Oliveira, to the room where, through the trees, he'd inevitably see the dome of the gazebo topped by its plump Cupid, and it almost made him shudder to think of kissing his sister on the same cheek that had received that man's slobbering kisses! A tomb-like silence had fallen on the matter of the Election, and a different, more acerbic repugnance prevented him from writing to Cavaleiro. João Gouveia was holidaying on the coast in his white shoes, picking up seashells on the shore. And Vila Clara was simply unbearable in the middle of that scorching September, with Titó in the Alentejo, where he had gone to tend his ailing brother, the heir to Cidadelhe; Manuel Duarte was at his mother's estate, directing the grape harvest; and the club was completely deserted, except for the innumerable, drowsily buzzing flies.

To fill those idle hours, more out of duty than love of Art, he returned to his Novella, but with a marked lack of enthusiasm or inspiration. He had reached the point when Tructesindo and his knights were setting off in angry pursuit of the Bastard of Baião. This was a difficult episode, requiring plenty of noise and dazzling medieval colour. And he, in his current mood, felt so limp and dull! Fortunately, his uncle's poem was full of beautiful descriptions of landscapes and interesting details of war.

When he reached the banks of the stream, Tructesindo found that the rickety bridge had been destroyed, and the meagre flow blocked by the broken supports and worm-eaten planks. As he fled, the Bastard had very sensibly demolished the bridge so as to delay the vengeful cavalcade pursuing him. Tructesindo's men rode along the narrow bank, skirting the rows of poplar trees in search of the ford at Espigal and making very slow progress indeed! When the last of the mules had clambered up onto the further bank, evening was already coming on, and the fading light reflected in the small pools among the stepping stones was sometimes tinged gold and sometimes rosy pink. Dom Garcia Viegas the Wise immediately advised the party to split up, with the foot soldiers and the mules making their silent, stealthy way to Montemor, thus avoiding any dangerous encounters and leaving the lancers and mounted crossbowmen to continue their furious pursuit of the Bastard. Everyone praised his tactical skills, and the cavalcade, able to move more speedily now without the slow columns of halberdiers and slingsmen, gave their horses free rein and galloped across the barren fields and along the craggy paths as far as Três-Caminhos, a desolate spot where three roads meet, and where the only living thing was the ancient oak tree which, before it had been exorcised by St Froalengo, used to be the regular meeting-point—by the light of sulphurous torches, on the darkest Saturday in January—for the Great Coven of all the witches in Portugal. Tructesindo ordered his men to halt beside the tree, and standing up in his stirrups and sniffing the air, he gazed along the trifurcating paths that vanished into harsh, lugubrious hills covered in brush and gorse. The Bastard and all his evil had clearly passed that way, for, behind a rock, next to three scrawny goats nibbling at the coarse vegetation, lay the ragged body of a poor young goatherd, arms flung wide, his poor starved chest pierced by an arrow, and all to prevent him from telling which way the men from Baião had gone. But which of the three paths had the Bastard taken? On the loose earth, whipped up by the hot southerly wind blowing in from the hills, the soil bore no trace of fleeing hoofprints. Nor, in such a desolate place was there a hovel or hut where, hidden away, some villein or old crone might have seen which path those men had chosen. And so the standard-bearer Afonso Gomes commanded three horsemen to gallop off and reconnoitre the three paths, while the knights, without dismounting, unbuckled their helmets, wiped away the sweat pouring down their bearded faces and let their horses go over to the tiny thread of water trickling through a sparse bed of reeds. Enclosed in his black armour, Tructesindo did not move from beneath the shade of the oak tree, motionless on his equally motionless horse, his hands folded on the pommel of his saddle and his helmeted head bowed as if in grief or prayer. And beside him, their collars bristling with spikes, their red tongues lolling from their mouths, his two mastiffs lay stretched out on the ground, panting.

After a long wait, during which they all grew increasingly restless and irritated, the scout who had set off along the path heading east suddenly reappeared in a cloud of dust, brandishing his lance. Less than an hour's ride away, he had spotted men on a hilltop, in an encampment surrounded by a stockade and by ditches.

'What standard were they flying?'

'One bearing thirteen roundels.'

'God be praised!' cried Tructesindo, shuddering and stretching as if waking from sleep. 'That's the standard of Dom Pedro de Castro, the Castilian, who joined the Leonese troops to bring succour to the Princesses.'

The Bastard wouldn't have dared to take that path. However, already galloping back along the western path came another scout, who reported that in a pinewood he had come across a band of Genoan pedlars, who had been there since dawn, because one of them had fallen ill with a fever. And? Along the edge of the wood, the only people to have passed all day (so swore the Genoans) was a company of clowns on their way back from the fair at Grajelos. All that remained, then, was the middle path, as stony and steepsided as the dried-up bed of a rushing stream. And at Tructesindo's shouted command, that was the path they took. The gloomiest of evenings was coming on, and still the path stretched ahead through heather and rocks, wild and dark and endless, with not a hut or a wall or a hedge or a beast or a man to be seen. Farther on, they came to a flat, arid plain, pitch-dark and deserted, that seemed to reach out mutely to the remote horizon, where one last strip of coppery, blood-red sky was slowly fading to nothing. Next to some thornbushes buffeted by strong gusts of wind from the south, Tructesindo stopped his men.

'It would seem, gentlemen, that we have embarked on an entirely vain and futile pursuit. What do you think, Garcia Viegas?'

Everyone gathered round, the panting horses steaming beneath their chain-mail coats. Garcia the Wise raised one arm:

'Gentlemen! Clearly the Bastard crossed this plain to reach Vale-Murtinho where he can spend the night in the stronghold of Agre-del, which is owned by a relative of his.'

'Then what should we do, Dom Garcia?'

'All we can do, my friends, is to do likewise and rest for the night. Let us go back to Três-Caminhos, and from there, if we're all in agreement, ride up to Dom Pedro de Castro's encampment, where we can ask for shelter. Such a great nobleman is sure to be far better provided for than we are with those things so necessary to all men, Christians and pagans alike, namely, bread, meat and three good draughts of wine.'

'An excellent plan!' they all cried. And they trotted wearily back down the shallow, stony ravine to Três-Caminhos, where two crows were now feasting on the body of the dead goatherd.

Shortly afterwards, at the far end of the path to the east, they spotted the encampment high up on the hill, lit all around by fires. The commanding officer of Santa Ireneia gave three slow blasts on his horn to announce the arrival of a nobleman. From within the stockade came answering calls, clear and welcoming. Then the commanding officer galloped over to the ditch to inform the sentinels posted among the warning beacons that friends in the form of the Ramires troops were at hand. Tructesindo had stopped along the dark path, made darker still by the thick pine trees swaying and moaning in the wind. Two knights in black hooded tunics immediately ran down the hill, declaring that Dom Pedro de Castro was waiting for the noble Lord of Santa Ireneia, ready and delighted to do all he could to help. Silently, Tructesindo dismounted, and along with Dom Garcia Viegas, Leonel de Samora, Mendo de Briteiros, and a few more of their closer relatives—all having downed lances and bucklers and removed their chain-mail gloves—walked up the hill to the stockade, where the gates stood wide open, revealing, in the sombre, flickering light of torches, clusters of infantrymen, and among the metal helmets, the occasional yellow bonnet of a camp-follower or the cap and bells of a jester. As soon as old Tructesindo appeared at the stockade, two infantrymen, brandishing their swords, shouted:

'All honour to the noblemen of Portugal!'

The harsh clamour of trumpets mingled with the slow roll of the drums. And the throng silently parted to make way for old Dom Pedro de Castro, the Castilian—a survivor of many a long war and the owner of vast estates—preceded by four knights bearing blazing torches. He was wearing a silver-embroidered leather corselet, and his back was bent as if worn down by too many battles and too many ambitions. Unhelmeted and unarmed, he rested one hairy, thickly-veined hand on the ivory pommel of his staff. In his thin, weathered face, his sunken eyes glinted, friendly and curious, while his nose was as hooked as a falcon's beak and marked on one side by a deep scar that ran down into his curly, pointed, almost white beard.

He opened wide his arms to Tructesindo, and with a grave laugh that brought his hawkish nose still closer to his pointed beard, he cried:

'God be praised! This is indeed a happy night that brings you, my cousin and my friend, to us! I could not have expected such an honour or such a pleasure!'

Gonçalo worked for three whole mornings on this difficult chapter, and when he finished, he threw down his pen with a weary sigh. He was starting to grow bored with this interminable Novella, which was beginning to resemble a loose skein of wool, the ends of which he could not cut because they were too entangled in the dense poem written by his uncle Duarte, in whose footsteps he was now somewhat reluctantly trudging. He could not even console himself with the certainty that he was writing something real and convincing. All those Tructesindos, Bastards, Castros, Garcia Viegases the Wise, were they really proper Afonsine men, cut from solid, historical cloth? They were perhaps merely hollow puppets, crudely got up in the wrong armour, inhabiting unlikely encampments and castles, making not a single authentic gesture or speaking a single authentic word!

Next morning, he could not summon up the necessary courage to resume his breathless pursuit of the Bastard's fleeing horde. Besides, he'd already sent off the first three chapters of the Novella, and thus assuaged Castanheiro's anxieties, but all that week idleness weighed heavily on him, as he slouched indolently from one sofa to another, or along the box-lined paths in the garden, smoking and feeling glumly that Life was vanishing before him like so much smoke. A financial problem was adding to his nervous mood—the lender of a promissory note for six hundred *mil-réis* taken out in his final year at Coimbra (and which had been renegotiated time and again and increased time and again), a man called Leite in Oliveira, was now sternly demanding to be paid. His tailor in Lisbon was also pestering him with a terrifyingly large bill, which filled two whole sheets of paper. What most depressed him, though, was the solitude of the Tower. All his jolly friends had escaped to the beach or to their country estates. The Election had run aground, like a ship in the mud. His sister was doubtless in the gazebo with that Other Man. Even his cousin Maria had ungratefully ignored his timid request for a little chat. And there he was in his great hot house, drained of all energy and immobilised by a growing inertia, as if he were bound by ropes that grew tighter each day, rendering him more parcel than man.

Sitting one afternoon in his room, feeling sluggish and gloomy, lacking even the energy to talk to Bento, he had just got ready to go out for a ride to Vilaverde to pass the time, when Crispola's little boy (now, in his yellow-buttoned uniform, well and truly settled in at the Tower) knocked urgently at his bedroom door. A lady had stopped at the gates, in a carriage, and was asking the Nobleman to come downstairs.

'Didn't she give a name?'

'No, sir. She's a thin lady, sir, drawn by two horses with nets on them ...'

Cousin Maria. He raced excitedly to meet her, grabbing an old straw hat from the hatstand in the corridor, and once downstairs, it was as if he were contemplating the Goddess of Fortune in her light chariot.

'Cousin Maria, what a surprise! And a very pleasant one too!'

Leaning out of the carriage window (it was the blue caleche from Feitosa), Dona Maria Mendonça, smiling from beneath a new hat adorned with sprigs of lilac, hurried to apologise for her silence. His letter had taken ages to arrive, the fault of their dreadful postman, who was always slow and often drunk. Then she'd spent a few very busy days in Oliveira with Ana, who was preparing her house in Rua das Velas for the winter.

'And finally, since I owed a visit to poor Venância Rios in Vila Clara—she's been ill, poor thing—I thought the simplest and most satisfactory solution would be to call in at the Tower. So what is it you want to discuss?'

Gonçalo gave an embarrassed smile:

'Nothing very serious, but ... I do need to talk to you. Why don't you come upstairs?'

She had opened the carriage door now, saying that she preferred to remain outside. And they both strolled over to the old stone bench shaded by the poplars flanking the Tower's mighty door. Gonçalo dusted off one end of the bench with his handkerchief.

'Yes, cousin, I do need to talk, but it's a very awkward matter. Perhaps I should simply attack the subject head-on.'

'Attack away.'

'Right, here goes. Do you think I'd be wasting my time if I were to turn my attentions to your friend, Dona Ana?'

Perched lightly on the edge of the bench, carefully furling her black silk parasol, Maria Mendonça took a while before answering, then murmured only:

'No, I don't think you'd be wasting your time.'

'You don't?'

She looked at Gonçalo, enjoying his evident confusion and impatience.

'Please, cousin, do say more!'

'What do you mean "more"? I told you all I had to tell you in Oliveira. And I'm still far too young to be delivering *billets-doux*, but what I will say is that Ana is pretty, rich, and a widow ...'

Gonçalo leaped up from the bench, waving his arms about in despair. And when Dona Maria also got up, they continued on together along the strip of grass beneath the poplars. In a voice that emerged almost like a disconsolate moan, he said:

'Pretty, rich *and* a widow! I hardly needed to write you a letter, cousin, in order to find out such "great" secrets! Damn it, be a good girl and tell me honestly. You must know. You've probably even discussed it with her. Be frank now. Does she like me, at least a little?'

Dona Maria stopped and, scraping at the yellowing grass with the tip of her parasol, murmured:

'Of course she does.'

'Bravo! Now, if, at some future date, once these first early months of mourning are over, I were to declare myself ...'

She shot Gonçalo a sharp look:

'Goodness, cousin, you're going at quite a gallop, aren't you? Are you in love?'

Gonçalo took off his old straw hat, slowly ran his fingers through his hair, and then, with great sadness in his voice, admitted:

'No, cousin, more than anything, it's a need to establish myself in life. Don't you agree?'

'Of course I agree, and I was the one who pointed you in that direction. Anyway, it's gone five o'clock and I must get on—the servants are waiting.'

Gonçalo protested and asked pleadingly:

'Stay a while longer. It's still early. Just one more thing. Tell me honestly. Is she a good girl?'

Dona Maria had turned as she reached the end of the line of poplars and was about to get into the caleche.

'She has a bit of a temper, but that just makes life interesting. Otherwise, yes, she's a very good girl. And she's a wonderful house-keeper! You can't imagine how beautifully she runs Feitosa, the orderliness, the cleanliness, the regularity, the discipline! She over-sees everything—even the wine cellar, even the stables!'

Gonçalo rubbed his hands, a radiant smile on his face:

'Well, if, in a year's time, the big event were actually to happen, I intend to shout it from the rooftops that it was cousin Maria who saved the House of Ramires!'

'That is precisely what I'm working for, to save our coat of arms and our name!' she exclaimed, jumping lightly into the caleche, as if eager to escape after that overly frank confession.

The footman had climbed into his seat. And as the horses, now slightly rested, were setting off at a trot, she called out:

'Guess who I met in Vila Clara? Titó!'

'Titó?'

'He's just returned from the Alentejo and he'll be coming to dine with you tonight. I didn't bring him with me, for fear of compromising him ...'

With that, the caleche rumbled off, and their friendly exchange of smiles and waves was made still friendlier by the new warmth born of that sentimental conspiracy.

Gonçalo immediately strode gaily off to Vila Clara to find Titó, already toying with the idea of gleaning from that close friend of Feitosa further information about Dona Ana, her character and her habits. Cousin Maria, out of love for the Ramires family (and especially, poor thing, anything that redounded to the benefit of the Mendonças!), was clearly idealising the bride-to-be. Titó, how-ever—the most honest man in all Portugal, who loved the truth with the old-fashioned devotion of a latter-day Epaminondas—would present her to him unadorned, but without malice. For be-neath that thundering voice and that appearance of bovine indo-lence, Titó possessed a very keen and penetrating intellect.

It did not take them long to find each other. And despite their very brief separation, they embraced with loud enthusiasm.

'Senhor Gonçalão!'

'Tító, my friend! You've been greatly missed. How's your brother?'

His brother was better, but completely exhausted. Tító put it down to far too much probing of parchments and of young ladies for an old man of sixty. He had told him so, 'João, if you carry on this way, always grappling either with old documents or young girls, you'll kill yourself!' But how were things there? What about the Election?

'The Election will be held in early October. Otherwise, things have been deadly dull, with Gouveia at the beach, Manuel Duarte away at the grape harvest, and me bored rigid, with no energy and not even much of an appetite.'

'Well, I'm coming to dine with you tonight, and I've invited Videirinha too.'

'Yes, so I heard from cousin Maria. She visited me at the Tower earlier today. She's staying at Feitosa with Dona Ana.'

For a moment, he babbled on about the close friendship between cousin Maria and Dona Ana, sorely tempted to tell Tító, right there in the street, about the possibility of a budding romance. His courage failed him, though. He felt vaguely embarrassed, as if ashamed of seeming to be coveting everything left behind by poor Lucena—both his seat in Parliament and his widow.

As they walked from Vila Clara to the Tower, with the intention of extending their walk as far as Bravais, they talked instead about the Alentejo and Tító's brother João (who had told him many a tedious tale about the Ramires genealogy). However, when they reached the Tower, Gonçalo wanted to warn Rosa about those two unexpected guests, both past masters at wielding knife and fork. They went in through the orchard door, where a slow, feeble trickle of water was filling the irrigation ditches. When Rosa heard their jocular voices, she came bustling out, drying her hands on her apron. Only two guests? Why, there was more than enough food for four and with even bigger appetites too! That very afternoon, she had bought a basket of sardines from a woman come from the coast, nice plump ones too! Tító immediately ordered a huge sardine omelette. And the two friends were just crossing the courtyard when Gonçalo spotted Bento sitting on the bench near the vine trellis, crouched over a bowl and enthusiastically polishing an embossed silver knob that was attached to something wrapped in a rolled-up towel, like a sheath.

'What's that you've got there, Bento?'

Bento slowly unwound the towel to reveal a long, dark whip, with three sharp strands to it, each with a sharp tip, like the tip of a fencing foil.

'Have you never seen it before, sir? It was in the attic—I was rooting around in there, looking to see where the cat had left her latest litter of kittens, and behind a trunk I came across a pair of silver spurs and this.'

Gonçalo studied the solid silver handle, then gave the slender stock a flick, and the whip whistled through the air.

'It's certainly a splendid specimen, eh, Tító? Sharp as a knife. And old, very old, as old as my coat of arms. What on earth is it made from? Whaleskin?'

'No, that's hippopotamus hide. It's a highly dangerous weapon. It could kill a man. My brother João has one, only with a plain metal handle. Yes, you could kill a man with that.'

'Good,' said Gonçalo. 'Clean it up, Bento, and put it in my room! It'll be my personal weapon of war!'

At the orchard door, they also met Pereira, his cotton jacket draped over his shoulders. On St Michael's day, he would be officially taking over the lands around the Tower. Gonçalo introduced Tító to the celebrated farmer, joking that this was the man, the great man, who was preparing to transform the Tower's landscape into a marvel of wheatfields, vineyards and vegetable plots! Pereira scratched his sparse beard:

'And burying a lot of good money in the process, but then pleasure is worth more than any amount of money! And the landlord here deserves an estate that is a delight to the eyes!'

'Senhor Pereira,' boomed Tító. 'Don't forget to take special care of the melons. It's an absolute disgrace, you know—I've never once eaten a decent melon here.'

'Well, next year, God willing, you shall!'

Gonçalo embraced the highly capable farmer and hurried off down to the road, determined now to take advantage of the propitious solitude of the Bravais woods to confess all to Titó. However, as soon as they set off, he felt the same constraint, almost fearing what he might learn from stern Titó with his strict moral values. When their long walk to Bravais and back was over, Gonçalo still hadn't unburdened himself. By the time they returned, dusk had fallen, soft and warm, and they were deep in conversation about fishing for shad in the Guadiana river.

Videirinha was waiting outside the Tower, under the poplars, strumming his guitar. Since it was still quite close, without a breath of wind, they dined out on the balcony, by the light of two oil lamps. As soon as he had unfolded his napkin, Titó, red-faced and leaning back in his chair, declared that, thanks to the Lord of Good Health, his thirst remained undiminished! He and Videirinha performed their usual sterling feats with knife and fork and glass. As Bento was serving coffee, a bright new moon was rising on the far side of the dark garden, from behind the Valverde hills. Comfortably installed in a wicker chair, Gonçalo beatifically lit a cigar. All the tedium and uncertainty of those past weeks fell from his soul like so much ash, now quickly swept away. And feeling not so much the sweetness of the night as a sense of a newly unclouded life, he exclaimed:

'Ah, yes, gentlemen, what could be more delicious than this!'

After briefly smoking a cigar, Videirinha, took up his guitar again. On the far side of the garden, fragments of whitewashed wall, the occasional stretch of empty road, the water in the great fountain, all shone in the moonlight silvering the hills; and the stillness of the trees and of that luminous night seeped into the soul like a soothing caress. Titó and Gonçalo were enjoying the famous moscatel brandy, one of the Tower's most precious antiquities, and listening, silent and rapt, to Videirinha, who had withdrawn to the shadows at the back of the balcony. Never had he played more tenderly, more sweetly. Even the fields, the vaulted sky and the moon above the hills were listening intently to the mournful *fado*. Below, in the darkness, they could hear Rosa clearing her throat, the servants' muffled footsteps, a girl's occasional suppressed laughter, a hunting dog flapping its ears, and all those sounds were like the presence of people subtly drawn to that lovely song.

And as it grew later, the moon rose higher still in solitary splendour. Heavy with food, Tító had dozed off. And as always, to close the evening, Videirinha gave an ardent rendition of the Ramires *fado*:

> *Who can see you and not tremble,*
> *Tower of Santa Ireneia,*
> *So silent and so dark,*
> *Ah, so silent and so dark,*
> *Tower of Santa Ireneia!*

And then he launched into a new verse, which he had been lovingly working on that very week, based on an erudite note from Father Soeiro. It spoke in praise of Paio Ramires, Knight Templar, who was called upon by Pope Innocent, by Queen Blanche of Castile and by all the Princes of Christendom to arm himself and ride as fast as he could to free Saint Louis, King of France, held captive in the lands of Egypt ...

> *Now the world's hopes rest*
> *On brave Paio Ramires ...*
> *Gather together all your knights*
> *And save the King of France!*

Gonçalo took such an interest in that ancestor of his and his exploits, that he began accompanying Videirinho in a shrill, tremulous voice, one arm held aloft:

> *Yes, gather together all your knights*
> *And save the King of France!*

As the chorus rose to a crescendo, Tító opened his eyes, raised his huge body from the sofa, and declared that he was heading off home to Vila Clara:

'I'm just about done in! I've been travelling since four o'clock yesterday morning, when I left Cidadelhe, and haven't had a wink of sleep. I'm like that Greek king at the moment—I'd give a gold coin for a donkey!'

Enlivened by the brandy, Gonçalo also stood up, cheerful and resolute:

'Before you go, Tító, come inside for a moment, will you? There's something I want to ask you.'

He grabbed one of the lamps and went into the dining room, which was filled with the scent of some fading magnolia blossoms. There, he fixed Tító with a determined look—Tító having followed him sluggishly, still yawning and stretching—and asked him straight out:

'Listen, Tító, be honest with me now. You used to be a regular visitor to Feitosa. What do you think of Dona Ana?'

Tító started as if a mortar had exploded nearby and stared at Gonçalo in amazement:

'Why on earth would you ask me that?'

In his desire for reassurance, Gonçalo went on:

'Look, I have no secrets from you, and in recent weeks, there have been certain conversations, certain meetings. Anyway, to cut a long story short, if, in the fullness of time, I were to consider marrying Dona Ana, I think that she, for her part, would not refuse me. You used to visit Feitosa. You know her. What kind of girl is she?'

Tító had angrily folded his arms:

'You're going to marry Dona Ana?'

'Not this instant, no. I'm not heading off to the church tonight. All I want now is some information. And who could be in a better position to give me the kind of honest, trustworthy information I need than you, my friend and her friend too?'

Tító was still standing, arms firmly folded, looking at the Nobleman of the Tower sternly, frankly:

'You, Gonçalo Mendes Ramires, are seriously thinking of marrying Dona Ana?'

Gonçalo gave an impatient, irritated shrug:

'Oh, don't start talking to me about the nobility and Paio Ramires and all that ...'

In his indignation, Tító almost bellowed at him:

'Nobility has nothing to do with it! But a decent man like you cannot possibly even consider marrying a creature like her! All right, nobility does have something to do with it, but nobility of the soul and the heart!'

Taken aback, Gonçalo said nothing. Then, with a hard-won serenity, he said:

'You obviously know something I don't. All I know is that she's pretty and rich. I also know that she's honest, because there's never been a hint of gossip about her either here or in Lisbon. Those seem to me to be reasons enough to marry a woman. But you're saying that's impossible, which means you know something about her. Out with it.'

Now it was Tító's turn to fall silent, standing motionless before Gonçalo, as if tightly bound by ropes. Finally, with a great effort, he took a deep breath and said:

'You didn't invite me here to give testimony. Without any explanation, you suddenly ask if you can marry that woman. I, also without any explanation, say no. What more do you want?'

Gonçalo exclaimed angrily:

'What do I want? For heaven's sake, Tító! Imagine I *was* madly in love with Dona Ana, or had a genuine desire to marry her, neither of which is true by the way, but just imagine that it was. You wouldn't warn a friend off doing something he's really set on doing without giving him some reason, some proof.'

Caught, Tító bowed his head and desperately scratched it. Then, taking the coward's way out, he postponed entering into battle:

'Look, Gonçalo, I'm really exhausted. As you say, you're not heading off to the church right now, nor is she, given that her first husband is not yet cold in his grave. We'll talk tomorrow.'

He took two enormous strides over to the balcony, where he opened the door and called to Videirinha:

'It's late, Videirinha! Time to go home. I haven't slept since I left Cidadelhe.'

Videirinha, who was carefully preparing himself a glass of cold grog, hastily downed the contents and picked up his precious guitar. And Gonçalo did nothing to hold them back, silently rubbing his hands, furious with Titó's stubborn, unfriendly refusal to talk. Like shadows, his two friends crossed the room in which there slept a laquered spinet, silent and forgotten since the Ramires who had lived there in the eighteenth century. On the landing that led down to the green door, Gonçalo held up a candlestick to light their way. Titó lit a cigarette on the flame. His hairy hand was trembling.

'I'll be back tomorrow, Gonçalo.'

'Fine, if that's what you want, Titó.'

There was such exasperation in the Nobleman's brusque words that Titó hesitated on the narrow stairs, which he entirely filled with his great bulk, then continued on his lumbering way.

Out in the road, Videirinha was looking up at the bright, serene sky:

'It's a lovely night, sir!'

'It is indeed, Videirinha. And thank you for coming. You played superbly this evening!'

Gonçalo had just gone into the portrait room, where he set down the candle, when, from beneath the open balcony, Titó's great voice boomed out:

'Gonçalo, come here, will you?'

The Nobleman raced eagerly down to meet him. Beyond the poplar trees, on the moonlit road, Videirinha was tuning his guitar. And as soon as the Nobleman appeared framed in the lighted doorway, Titó, his hat pushed back on his head, blurted out:

'Oh, Gonçalo, you're angry with me. That's so silly. I would hate there to be any ill feeling between us. So here goes. You can't marry that woman because she once had a lover. And she may have had another either before or afterwards. There's no craftier, more two-faced woman alive. Don't ask me anything now, but believe me, she definitely had a lover. I, Titó, am telling you this, and you know I never lie!'

He then strode off along the road, his great shoulders hunched. Gonçalo did not move from where he was on the stone steps, before the silent poplars, which stood as motionless as him. In the soft silence of the night and the moonlight, a few words had been spoken, a few irreparable words, and the lofty dream he had built on Dona Ana and her beauty and her two hundred *contos* lay now submerged in the mud. He went slowly up the stairs and back into the portrait room. In one of the gloomy canvases lit by the tall candle flame, a face had stirred into life, a gaunt, yellowish face with proud black moustaches, leaning forward intently, as if watching. And far off, Videirinha was scattering his ingenuous verses over the sleeping fields, celebrating the glorious past of the illustrious House:

Now the world's hopes rest
On brave Paio Ramires …
Gather together all your knights
And save the King of France!

X

Pacing his room until late at night, Gonçalo brooded on the bitter certainty that, throughout his life (almost since his schooldays), he had suffered ceaseless humiliations. And they were all born of the simplest of intentions, as safe and sure for any other man as flying is for a bird, but for him they always ended in pain, shame or loss! At the start of his life, he had enthusiastically chosen a confidant, a brother, whom he had invited into the quiet intimacy of the Tower, and that man had, first, blithely stolen Gracinha's heart, then villainously abandoned her! Then he conceived the perfectly ordinary ambition to enter political life, but chance immediately forced him to bend the knee and accept the influence of that same man—who was now a powerful figure of authority—the man whom he, for long, embittered years, had loathed and mocked. And when he once again welcomed that man into the family home and flung wide the doors of the Casa dos Cunhais, trusting in his sister's honesty and unshakeable pride, his sister immediately, and without a struggle, surrendered to her former deceiver on the very first afternoon she found herself alone with him in the auspicious shade of a gazebo! Most recently of all, he had considered marrying a woman who promised to bring him great beauty and a great fortune, then a friend from Vila Clara happened past, whispering, 'The woman you have chosen, Gonçalinho, is a slut with a string of lovers!' True, he did not love that woman with a strong and noble love, but he had nevertheless decided to accommodate his uncertain fate very comfortably in those beautiful arms of hers; then, with crushing inevitability, came the customary humiliation. Destiny really did seem to be laying into him with extraordinary venom.

'But why?' murmured Gonçalo, glumly taking off his jacket. 'Why so much disappointment in such a short life? Why me?'

He fell into his vast bed as if into a tomb, and buried his face in his pillow with a sigh, a tender, pitying sigh for his star-crossed, hopeless fate. And he recalled Videirinha's presumptuous lines, which he had sung that very night:

> *Ancient house of the Ramires,*
> *Pride and flower of Portugal!*

How that flower had faded and how puny that pride seemed now! What a contrast between him, the last Gonçalo, holed up in Santa Ireneia, and those great ancestors of his, as set to music by Videirinha, all of whom, if History and Legend were to be believed, had led such triumphant, glorious lives! No, he had not even inherited from them the one quality they had all shown down the ages—spontaneous courage. Even his father had been a fearless Ramires, and when trouble famously broke out at the Riosa Fair, he had advanced, armed only with a sunshade, against three rifles, cocked and ready to fire. He, on the other hand ... yes, in the privacy of his darkened room, he could freely bemoan having been born with that most heinous of faults, an uncontrollable weakness of the flesh, which, whenever he was faced by a danger, a threat, a shadow, forced him to retreat, to flee. To flee from Casco. To flee from that rogue with the fair side whiskers who, on the road and, later, outside an inn, had insulted him for no reason, simply to demonstrate how brazen and bold he was. Such shameful, easily frightened flesh!

And what about his soul? In the silent gloom of his room, he could hear his soul whimpering too, for his soul was filled with the same weakness that made him susceptible to any influence, on which he was borne along like a dry leaf by whatever wind might blow. Cousin Maria could bat her clever eyes at him and advise him, from behind her fan, to set his cap at Dona Ana, and he, aflame with hope, would immediately build a presumptuous Tower of good fortune and luxury on Dona Ana's money and beauty. And what about the Election, that wretched Election? Who had propelled him into that Election, into that indecent reconciliation with Cavaleiro and all the ills that followed? Gouveia, and with just a few subtle arguments insinuated to him from over the top of his scarf as they walked from Ramos' shop to the post office! Even at home, he was ruled by Bento, who imposed on him tastes, foods, walks, opinions and cravats! Such a man, however intelligent, is an inert mass that the world is constantly shaping into various, contradictory forms. João Gouveia had made of him a servile candidate. Manuel Duarte could turn him into a vile drunk. Bento could easily encourage him to wear around his neck, not a silk cravat, but a leather collar. What a wretched fate! And yet a Man is worth only as much as his Will, and all of Life's pleasures lie in the exercise of that Will. For if a strong Will encounters only submission, then it has the delight of being serenely in control; if it meets with resistance, then there is the still greater delight of engaging in an interesting struggle. However, no strong, manly pleasure can ever be born of inertia, which allows itself to be led silently along, as mute and malleable as wax. But surely he, being descended from so many strong men famous for their Will, surely he must have some portion of that hereditary energy hidden away somewhere in his Being, warm and dormant like a hot coal beneath the ashes. Possibly. However, in his stunted, stultifying existence at Santa Ireneia, those embers would never reignite and become a fierce, useful flame. No, poor him! Even in his soul, where most men find true liberty, he would always be oppressed by his enemy Fate!

With another long sigh, he pulled the covers up over his head. He did not fall asleep, though; the night was nearly over, four hollow chimes had already rung out from the clock in the corridor. Then, in the bewildered, weary wake of that jumble of misfortunes, through his closed eyelids, Gonçalo saw looming out of the darkness, pale faces parading lowly past.

They were very ancient faces, sporting old-fashioned ancestral beards, faces scarred by brutal metal weapons, some flushed as if still in the heat of battle, others smiling as majestically as guests at an opulent gala, all clearly accustomed to commanding and vanquishing. Peering over his sheets, Gonçalo recognised in those faces the genuine features of old Ramires men, faces he had seen before in blackened portraits, or as with Tructesindo, a face he had imagined would suit the rigour and glory of his deeds.

Slowly but ever more clearly, faces emerged from among the dense, pulsating shadows, quick with life; their bodies were now becoming visible too, robust bodies encased in rusty chain-mail tunics or glittering armour or swathed in dark, dull cloaks that hung in many folds, or wearing magnificent brocade doublets on which jewelled necklaces and belts glinted; and all were armed, with weapons from every possible period of history, from a Gothic club made from the root of an oak tree and bristling with spikes to a ceremonial dress sword beribboned in silk and gold.

Unperturbed, leaning back against his pillow, Gonçalo did not for a moment doubt their marvellous reality! Yes, these were his Ramires ancestors, his formidable historical grandfathers—a majestic assembly of his entire race brought back from the dead—all hurrying from their scattered tombs to the nine-centuries-old house of Santa Ireneia to gather round his bed, the bed in which he had been born. He even recognised some of the most valiant of these ancestors, for, after repeated readings and rereadings of Uncle Duarte's poem and Videirinha's loyal *fado*, they were constantly in his imagination.

That man over there was clearly Gutierres Ramires the Traveller, wearing the same white tunic emblazoned with a great red cross that he would have worn when he raced from his tent to storm the walls of Jerusalem. That very fine-looking old man, holding up one hand, was, he felt sure, Egas Ramires, refusing to receive King Fernando and the adulterous Leonor in his chaste home. That other man—with the curly, reddish beard, singing as he waved the royal standard of Castile—could only be Diogo Ramires the Troubadour, still filled with the joy of that radiant, victorious morning after the Battle of Aljubarrota. In the uncertain light cast by the mirror he saw the soft, tremulous scarlet feathers on the helmet of Paio Ramires as he armed himself before going off to save Saint Louis, King of France. Swaying slightly, as if rocked by the humble waves of a vanquished sea, Rui Ramires was smiling at the English ships, which, prow to prow with his flagship, were submissively striking sail. And leaning on the bedpost, with his young, fair face, Paulo Ramires, standard-bearer to the King on the fateful fields of

Alcácer—his helmet gone, his metal cuirass sundered—was gazing down at him as gently as a loving grandfather ...

That look of attentive tenderness from the most poetic of the Ramires made Gonçalo feel that all his ancestors loved him, that they'd come from the darkness of their various tombs to watch over him and help him in his weakness. He gave a long groan, threw back the bedclothes, and opened his heart to them, painfully describing to his resurrected ancestors the vengeful Fate that weighed on him, how tirelessly it heaped upon his life sadness, humiliation and loss! Then the point of a weapon glinted in the darkness, accompanied by a muffled cry, 'My grandson, my dear grandson, take my never-broken lance!' Then the hilt of a bright sword brushed his chest and another grave voice spoke urgently, 'Grandson, my dear grandson, take this sword—consecrated at Ourique!' And then an axe with a glittering blade thudded onto his pillow, along with the haughty, confident words, 'This axe, which broke down the gates of Arzila, will never be defeated.'

Like shadows borne along by a transcendental wind, his formidable ancestors paraded past, all offering him their strong, proven weapons, ennobled throughout the ages in crusades against the Moors, in long-drawn-out sieges of castles and towns, in splendid battles against the insolent Castilians ... His bed was surrounded by the heroic glitter and clank of iron. And those forebears of his kept proudly shouting, 'Grandson, take our weapons and vanquish thine enemy Fate!' Gazing sadly at these flickering shadows, Gonçalo said only, 'Oh, my ancestors, of what use to me are your weapons, when I lack your soul?'

He woke very early, with, in his head, the tangled remnants of a nightmare in which he'd spoken with the dead, and then, with none of the indolence that usually kept him snugly between the sheets, he pulled on a dressing gown and flung open the windows. What a beautiful morning! A late September morning, soft and clear and fine; not a cloud in the vast, immaculate blue sky; and the sun already touching the woods on the distant hills with an autumnal sweetness. And yet, despite the bright, pure morning instilling him with hope and good cheer, Gonçalo remained plunged in yesterday's gloom, which lingered in his sad mind like mist in a deep valley. And with a sigh, he slouched glumly across the room in his slippers and rang the bell for Bento, who soon arrived with a jug of hot water so that he could shave. Accustomed to the Nobleman waking up in the best of moods, Bento—troubled by Gonçalo's silent, sluggish demeanour—asked if he'd had a bad night.

'Yes, dreadful!'

In a lively, reproving voice, Bento immediately put this down to his master having enjoyed so much of that muscatel brandy, which was very sweet and over-stimulating. A burly gentleman like Senhor Dom António could cope, but a more highly-strung man like his master should never touch the stuff, or, at most, only half a glass.

Gonçalo looked up, surprised to be confronted, at the very start of his day, by such a flagrant example of the dominion over him that everyone apparently felt entitled to impose—precisely what he had been complaining about throughout the whole of that long, bitter night! There was Bento telling him how much brandy he should drink. Indeed, Bento went on:

'You drank more than three glasses last night, which really won't do, but then I'm partly to blame for not taking the bottle away.'

Faced by such blatant despotism, the Nobleman rebelled:

'Will you stop laying down the law. I will drink however much brandy I want!'

At the same time, he dipped his fingers into the water in the jug to test the temperature:

'This water's lukewarm!' he exclaimed. 'How many times do I have to tell you: I need boiling-hot water for shaving.'

Bento gravely dipped his finger into the water too:

'The water's near enough boiling, sir. You don't need it any hotter than that for shaving.'

Gonçalo stared at Bento furiously. What? More objections, more laws?

'Go and fetch me some more water this instant! When I ask for hot water, I expect it to be boiling hot. Honestly! Stop telling me what to do. I don't want moral platitudes, I want obedience!'

Bento observed Gonçalo with growing amazement. Then, slowly, his dignity wounded, he picked up the jug and left the room. Gonçalo was already regretting his violent reaction: Poor man, it's not his fault that my life is such a directionless failure! Besides, in such an ancient household, it was both traditional and proper to have equally ancient servants, and Bento—the perfect embodiment of that blend of impertinence and loyalty—after long years of proven devotion, had earned the right to take such liberties.

Face still flushed and puffy, Bento returned with a jug full of steaming water. And to pacify him, Gonçalo said sweetly:

'Lovely day, eh, Bento?'

A still disgruntled Bento merely murmured:

'Hm, lovely.'

Gonçalo was quickly soaping his face, anxious to make peace with Bento, to restore his usual fond authority over him. Finally, still more gently, almost humbly, he said:

'Well, since it's such a lovely day, I think I'll go for a ride before lunch. What do you reckon? It'll be good for my nerves, and you're quite right, that brandy really didn't agree with me at all. Anyway, Bento, would you be so kind as to tell Joaquim to have my horse ready. A good gallop is sure to calm me down. But, first, I need some nice hot water for my bath. Hot water has a calming effect too, which is why I need it good and hot. You're behind the times in that respect, Bento. All the doctors agree that hot water, at sixty degrees Fahrenheit, is best for the health.'

And after a quick bath, as he was getting dressed, he confided his woes to Bento:

'Ah, Bento, Bento, I need more than a short ride to calm my nerves. I need a proper journey. My heart is heavy, and I'm tired of the same old places, Vila Clara, Oliveira, with all their gossip and backbiting. I need bigger places, more distractions.'

Now entirely reconciled and rather touched, Bento reminded his master that soon, in Lisbon, he'd find a very fine distraction in the form of Parliament.

'I don't even know if I'll get into Parliament, Bento. I don't know anything. Nothing seems to be turning out as I expected. Besides,

Lisbon isn't what I need either. I need a long, long journey—to Hungary, to Russia, to places where there are adventures to be had.'

Bento smiled rather loftily at this idea. And handing the Nobleman his grey velveteen overcoat, he commented:

'It does indeed seem that there's no shortage of adventures to be had in Russia, sir. According to the papers, they rule with the whip. But you know, sir, adventures can be found much closer to home. Why, your own father, may he rest in peace, had that set-to with Dr Avelino da Riosa just outside the gates here, when he lashed out at the doctor with a whip, and he got stabbed in the arm.'

Gonçalo was pulling on his leather gloves and looking in the mirror.

'Poor Papa, he didn't have much luck either. But speaking of whips, Bento, give me that hippopotamus-hide whip you found the other day. It could prove useful.'

On leaving the house, the Nobleman of the Tower set off, with no particular aim in mind, along the usual road to Bravais. When he reached Casal Novo, however, where two children were playing ball beneath the oak trees, it occurred to him that he could visit the Viscount de Rio-Manso. The company of that serene, generous old man would be sure to soothe him. And if he happened to be invited to lunch there, the famous garden where he'd first met 'Rosebud' would drive away all his sorrows, and he could even pay tender court to her.

All that Gonçalo could remember about the garden was that it overlooked a road lined with poplars, somewhere between the hamlet of Cerda and the scattered village of Canta-Pedra. So he took the old road that descends from the oaktrees in Casal Novo down into the valley, between the Avelã hills and the ruined monastery of Ribadais—the historic place where Lopo de Baião had defeated Lourenço Ramires. The rather wearisome, unlovely road wound along between hedges and stone walls, but the honeysuckle growing among the ripe blackberries gave off a wonderful scent; the cool silence was made still cooler and more delightful by the fluttering wings of passing birds; and such was the radiant blue of the clear sky that a little of its serene glow installed itself in

Gonçalo's soul. Feeling the gloom lifting somewhat, Gonçalo trotted along at a leisurely pace. When he passed through Casal Novo, he heard the Bravais church clock strike nine; and after skirting round a rather bare field, he paused idly to light a cigar next to the old stone bridge that crosses the stream there. The stream had almost dried up in the summer heat and was little more than a trickle of dark water, flowing under the broad leaves of the water-lilies and pushing through the thick, choking reeds. Ahead, in the shade of a clump of poplar trees, beside a grassy field, the stones of a washing-place gleamed whitely. On the other side, in an old boat that had run aground, a boy and a girl were deep in conversation, bunches of lavender forgotten in their laps. Gonçalo smiled at this idyllic sight, then was surprised to discover, on one end of the bridge, his own coat of arms, roughly carved, showing a huge goshawk reaching out its fierce talons. Perhaps those lands had once belonged to his family, or maybe one of his kindlier ancestors— to help the labourers and their beasts—had built the bridge over what would then have been a torrent. Perhaps it had been built by Tructesindo, in pious memory of Lourenço Ramires, who had been vanquished and captured on the banks of that same stream!

Beyond the bridge, the path wound past stubble-filled fields, and in that year of plenty, the stacks glowed big and golden. In the distant hamlet, wisps of smoke rose up from the low roofs of the houses and vanished instantly into the brilliant sky. And Gonçalo felt all his melancholy leaving his soul and disappearing, just like those wisps of smoke, into the lustrous blue above. A flock of partridges flew up from the stubble and Gonçalo galloped after them, shouting and wielding his strong whip, which whistled through the air like a thin blade.

Soon afterwards, the path curved, skirting round a stand of cork oaks before dipping down to become a stony, dusty track overgrown with brambles. At the far end of that track, the sun glinted on the freshly whitewashed wall of a one-storey house with a low front door set between two windows, with a newly patched roof and a courtyard shaded by a huge, dark fig tree. At one corner there was a low stone wall, then a hedge, and further on, an old wicket gate that opened onto a shady garden. The empty expanse in front of the house was strewn with masonry and wooden beams; the smooth, well-maintained road that began there seemed to Gonçalo to be the road to Ramilde. Up ahead, as far as a pine wood in the distance, there were only empty plains and fields.

Sitting on a bench by the door, with a rifle leaning against the wall, a well-built lad wearing a green woollen cap was pensively stroking the muzzle of his dog. Gonçalo stopped:

'Excuse me, do you happen to know the best way to the house of the Viscount de Rio-Manso?'

The lad raised his dark face with its faint, youthful down and made as if to doff his cap.

'You need to follow this road until you reach the quarry, then turn left, keeping close to the plain ...'

At that moment, however, a burly man with fair side whiskers appeared at the door; he was in his shirtsleeves and wore a silk cummerbund about his waist. With a start, Gonçalo recognised the hunter who had insulted him on the Nacejas road and, on another occasion, outside Pintainho's inn, had whistled jeeringly at him. The man shot the Nobleman a dismissive glance. Then, leaning in the doorway, he told the boy off:

'What are you doing giving him directions, Manuel? This road isn't intended for asses!'

Gonçalo felt himself turn pale, and felt the blood in his heart pounding furiously in a mixture of fear and rage. Yet another insult from the same man and, again, entirely unprovoked! He pressed his knees into his horse's flanks, ready to gallop away, then, trembling, he managed to stammer out:

'How dare you? This is the third time you've insulted me. I'm not the kind of man to get involved in public brawls, but I know your face now and, sooner or later, you'll get your comeuppance.'

The other man immediately snatched up a short staff and, with a defiant lift of his chin, stepped out into the road, in front of Gonçalo's horse:

'Well, here I am. Give me my comeuppance now, because you're not going any further, you piece of Ramires sh—'

A kind of mist came down over the Nobleman's horrified eyes. And suddenly, on a blind impulse, as if swept along on a furious wave of pride and strength that rose up from the very depths of his being, he let out a yell and made his horse rear. He didn't even know what he was doing, only that a staff had been raised threateningly against him. The horse again reared angrily, its head back. And Gonçalo caught a glimpse of the man's great dark hand grabbing the reins.

Then, standing up in the stirrups, he lashed out with his whip, which whistled through the air, catching the man on the side of his face and dealing him such a blow that the man's ear hung loose, spurting blood. With a cry, the man stumbled backwards. Gonçalo launched another attack, another stinging blow, which this time caught the man's mouth, tearing his lips and doubtless dislodging teeth and hurling him, screaming, to the ground. The horse's hooves trampled the man's broad splayed legs, and Gonçalo again leaned down and again struck him hard, slashing face and throat, until the man's body lay limp and as if dead, dark blood drenching his shirt.

A shot rang out! And startled, Gonçalo saw that the boy was holding the smoking rifle, but was clearly terrified and unsure what to do next.

'You cur!'

He urged his horse forward, his whip held high, and the terrified boy blundered across the space in front of the house, intending to leap over the ditch and escape across the fields!

'You cur! You cur!' Gonçalo was screaming.

Confused and frightened, the boy tripped on a stray beam, but he had already struggled to his feet and was running away when the Nobleman slashed at his neck with the whip—a neck immediately bathed in blood. Hesitantly, holding up his hands in self-defence, he was still unsteadily retreating when he fell and hit his head on the corner of a post, and more blood poured from that wound too. Then Gonçalo, panting, reined in his horse. Both men were lying motionless! Good God, could they be dead? Blood flowed from both bodies onto the dry ground. The Nobleman of the Tower felt a kind of brutal joy—but a horrified cry came from within the courtyard.

'Someone's killed my boy!'

An old man, head bowed, was running from the wicket gate to the door of the house, keeping close to the hedge. So effectively did the Nobleman spur on his horse to stop him that the old man collided with the horse's panting, sweating, foam-covered chest. And faced by that restless beast pawing the ground and by Gonçalo, still standing up in his stirrups, face aflame, whip at the ready, the old man fell to his knees in terror and cried out urgently:

'Please, sir, don't hurt me, for the love of your own dear father, Dom Vicente Ramires!'

Gonçalo kept him there for a moment frozen in that tremulous, supplicant pose, beneath the vengeful glare of his eyes, and he took proud pleasure in the sight of those calloused, pleading hands, begging for mercy and invoking the name of Ramires, which had once again become a name to be feared—its heroic prestige restored. Then, drawing back his horse, he said:

'That wretched boy fired at me! I'm not sure I can trust you either! Why were you running to the house? To fetch another rifle?'

The old man flung his arms wide, offering his bared chest as witness to the truth of what he said:

'Sir, I swear on my life and on my boy's life too, I don't even own a staff!'

Gonçalo was not convinced. If he rode off now down the road to Ramilde, the old man could easily run into the house, grab another rifle and shoot him treacherously in the back. Then with a presence of mind made keener by this encounter, he thought of a sure safeguard against any such ambush. He even smiled to think of Dom Garcia Viegas the Wise and his 'war tactics'.

'Walk ahead of me along the road!'

Still abjectly kneeling, the old man did not, at first, react. Then he beat his gnarled hands on his thighs, almost too overwhelmed with emotion to speak:

'Sir, sir, how can I leave the boy here unconscious?'

'The boy's only stunned. I've seen him move. It's the same with that other wretch over there. Come on, start walking!'

And at this irresistible command from Gonçalo, the old man,

having slowly brushed the dust from his trousers, began to walk along the road, head bowed like a captive, his long arms hanging loose by his sides, and muttering hoarsely to himself, 'Why this now? Ah, dear God, why me?' He would stop occasionally and stare up at Gonçalo, his dark eyes filled with fear and hatred. Then, urged on by another command to walk, he would walk. Further on, where a cross had been erected to the memory of the murdered Abbot Paguim, Gonçalo recognised a broad track that led to the Bravais road and which was known locally as the Caminho da Moleira. He forced the old man to go down that solitary lane, and the man was filled with dread, thinking that Gonçalo was leading him away from the busier roads in order to be able to kill him at his leisure. He began moaning, 'I'm going to die! Holy Mother of God, I'm going to die!' And he continued this moaning and groaning, tripping over his own feet, until they emerged onto a road with steep sides overgrown with gorse. Then suddenly filled with a new dread, the man spun round, his hands clutching his head:

'You're not arresting me, are you, sir?'

'Keep walking! Go on, run! We're going to trot now!'

The horse trotted, and the old man ran awkwardly ahead, panting like a bellows at a forge. After a mile, Gonçalo stopped, fed up both with his prisoner and with the slow pace. Besides, before the man could run home, grab a rifle and return to take his revenge, Gonçalo would have ample time to gallop back to the Tower! With furrowed brow, he boomed out:

'Halt! You can go home now, but, first, tell me the name of your house.'

'Grainha, sir.'

'And what's your name and the boy's?'

Mouth agape, the old man hesitated before answering:

'I'm João and my boy's name is Manuel, Manuel Domingues, sir.'

'You're lying, of course. And the other rogue with the side whiskers?'

The old man immediately blurted out:

'He's Ernesto de Nacejas, the local bully and skirt-chaser, and he's really led my poor boy astray.'

'Well, tell those two scoundrels who attacked me with a staff and a rifle that they're not going to get away with just a beating—they'll have to deal with the law too, and there'll be no escaping that. Off you go!'

Gonçalo stayed for a while in the middle of the road, and watched the man hurrying away, wiping the sweat from his brow and forcing his weary legs onwards. Then he galloped back to the Tower along the now familiar road.

And the wild joy he felt plunged him into daydreams and fantasies. He had the sublime feeling that he was galloping across the heights on a legendary warhorse so large and magnificent that he could touch the bright clouds. And below, in the cities, men recognised in him a true Ramires, like the ones in the history books, those who had demolished towers and changed the fate of kingdoms, and who'd left in their wake—the wake left by mighty men— a murmur of admiration and shock. And quite right too! For when he left the Tower that morning, he would never have stood up to so much as a determined boy brandishing a stick, but then, suddenly, outside that isolated house, when that brute with the side whiskers had hurled his filthy insult, something, quite what he didn't know, had surfaced inside him and overflowed, stiffening every sinew with skill and strength, and filling every vein with burning blood and every pore with a contempt for pain and his soul with indomitable courage. And now he was returning, like a new man, proud and virile, free at last from the shadow that had cast such a painful pall over his life—the limp, shameful shadow of his fear! Now he felt that if all the bullies in Nacejas were to come at him with staffs raised, that something-or-other deep inside his very being would once again be released, and with every vein pulsing, every nerve tensed, he would launch himself into the delicious clamour of battle! He was, at last, *a man*! When, in Vila Clara, Manuel Duarte or Titó, puffing out their chests, started recounting their various exploits, he would no longer withdraw into silence and roll a cigarette, not just because of his disheartening dearth of exploits, but, above all, because of the humiliating memory of past cowardices.

And on he galloped, gripping the handle of his whip, as if he were on his way to still more thrilling encounters. Once he had passed Bravais, seeing the Tower ahead of him, he galloped still harder. And strangely, it seemed to him that the Tower was more 'his' now, and that a new affinity, founded on glory and strength, made him still more the lord of his Tower!

As if to welcome Gonçalo in a more dignified fashion on his triumphal return home, the two heavy doors of the great gate—normally closed—stood wide open. He rode into the centre of the courtyard, shouting:

'Joaquim! Manuel! Come quickly!'

Joaquim emerged from the stables, his sleeves rolled up and with a sponge in one hand.

'Quickly, Joaquim! Saddle up Rossilho and go straight to a place on the Ramilde road called Grainha. I've just been involved in a terrible fight there! I think I may have killed two men. I left them lying in a pool of blood. Don't tell anyone you're from the Tower, because they might attack you! Just find out what happened and whether or not they're dead! Hurry, hurry!'

Stunned, Joaquim went back into the dark stables, and from one of the balconies above came astonished cries:

'Good God, Gonçalo! Whatever's happened?'

It was Barrolo. Without dismounting and seemingly unsurprised to find Barrolo there, Gonçalo immediately gave him a garbled account of the fight. An arrant scoundrel had insulted him, and another had fired at him. And both had ended up lying beneath his horse's hooves in a pool of blood.

Barrolo left the balcony and rushed down into the courtyard, waving his short, plump arms, wanting to know exactly what had happened. Trembling now with weariness and emotion, Gonçalo dismounted and explained in more detail. He had been riding along the Ramilde road and some lout had insulted him! He had gashed the man's mouth and lopped off one ear. Then the other fellow, a big lad, had fired off his rifle. Gonçalo had ridden straight at him and dealt him such a blow that he'd fallen backwards and hit his head and lay there as if dead.

'But dealt him a blow with what?'

'With this whip, Barrolo. It's a fearsome weapon. Titó was quite right. I would have been lost if I hadn't had it with me.'

Barrolo gazed open-mouthed at the whip. It really was stained with blood. Gonçalo also looked at the whip and at the blood. Human blood! Fresh blood, which he had caused to be shed! And his pride was mingled with such a feeling of pity that he turned quite pale:

'What a terrible thing!'

He then inspected his jacket and his boots, horrified at the blood spattering them. Dear God, he even had blood on his gaiters. In his anxiety to get out of his stained clothes and wash, he raced up the stairs, with Barrolo at his heels, mopping his brow and muttering, 'What a thing to happen and on the public highway too!' Gracinha suddenly appeared in the corridor, having come up from the kitchen; she, too, looked deathly pale, and Rosa, behind her, was clutching her head in dumb terror.

'What's happened, Gonçalo? Goodness, whatever's happened?'

Then, finding Gracinha at his side, in the Tower, at this magnificently proud moment, when he had just overcome real danger, Gonçalo forgot all about André, the gazebo, his own feelings of humiliation, and as he embraced her and kissed her beloved cheek, all his displeasure melted into tenderness. Clutching her to his breast, he sighed gently, like a weary child. Then, squeezing her poor, trembling hands, he gave a slow, fond smile, his eyes moist with confused emotions, confused joy, and said:

'It was awful, Gracinha, really horrible. Especially for a peace-loving fellow like me. Imagine.'

And as they walked together slowly down the corridor, he gave a fresh account to a breathless Gracinha and a horror-struck Rosa: the meeting, the vile insult, the bullet that missed him and the scoundrels soundly whipped, and the old man marching ahead of him along the Ramilde road like a captive, moaning and groaning. Pressing her hands to her bosom, Gracinha could only murmur:

'But, Gonçalo, what if one of them is dead?'

Barrolo, his face scarlet, roared out that such scoundrels richly deserved to be dead. And if they were only wounded, they deserved the ultimate punishment of being transported to Africa! They must send a message to Gouveia to tell him what had happened. Then the floor trembled with eager footsteps, and a frantic Bento appeared before Gonçalo, anxious and agitated:

'What happened, sir? They say there was a serious fight.'

And at the door to his study, where they were all gathered now, listening intently, the story began again, for the benefit of Bento, who drank it in, a slow, pleasurable smile gradually spreading across his face, his tear-filled eyes shining, as if he had shared in his master's victory. Finally, he declared loudly and triumphantly:

'It was the whip, sir. What saved you was the whip I gave you!'

It was true. Touched, Gonçalo embraced his old servant, who, overcome, cried out to Rosa, to Gracinha and to Barrolo:

'Our master did for them with that whip! You could easily kill a man with it! The rascals are dead. And it was the whip that did it, the whip I gave my master!'

Gonçalo was calling now for hot water to wash off the dust and sweat and blood. Bento rushed back along the corridor and down the stairs to the kitchen, all the while yelling, 'It was the whip that did it, the whip I gave my master!' Gonçalo went into his bedroom, accompanied by Barrolo, and set down his hat on the marble-topped chest of drawers with a great sigh of relief, the relief of finding himself, after such a violent morning, among sweet, ordinary things, treading his old blue carpet, running one hand over the mahogany bed in which he had been born, breathing the air coming in through the open windows, where the familiar branches of the beech trees were waving a greeting to him in the breeze. With what delight he approached the mirror with its gilt columns, and looked and looked at himself, as if at a new and much-improved Gonçalo, whose shoulders seemed broader, his moustache more curled.

It was only when he turned away from the mirror and saw Barrolo waiting there, that he was suddenly gripped by intense curiosity:

'But what are you two doing here at the Tower this morning?'

They had made the decision the previous evening, during tea.

Gonçalo didn't visit, didn't write, and Gracinha was worrying herself sick about it. He, too, had been alarmed by Gonçalo's sudden disappearance after leaving that unexplained basket of peaches. And so, thinking that the horses needed a trip out, he had said to Gracinha, 'Shall we go to the Tower tomorrow? In the phaeton?'

Barrolo paused.

'Besides, I need to talk to you, Gonçalo. I've been worried about something lately too.'

The Nobleman placed two cushions on the divan and sat down. 'What do you mean worried? About what?'

With his hands in the pockets of his flannel jacket, which fitted rather snugly around his plump thighs, Barrolo stared glumly down at the flowers on the carpet:

'It's such a bore really. One can't trust anyone ... not even one's friends!'

In a flash, Gonçalo imagined Cavaleiro and Gracinha at the Casa dos Cunhais making no secret of the feelings that had once overwhelmed them in the gardens of the Tower. And he expected poor Barrolo to open his heart, to bemoan his fate, dogged by suspicions or perhaps having witnessed certain intimate moments. The supreme emotion of the fight had swept into the shade all the cares that had so oppressed him only hours before: in the freshness of that new-found courage, all of life's difficulties suddenly seemed to him as easy to defeat as those two scoundrels; and he did not fear what his brother-in-law was about to tell him, confident that he could reassure and calm that gentle, submissive soul:

'So Barrolo, has something untoward happened?'

'I've received a letter.'

'Ah!'

Barrolo gravely unbuttoned his jacket and produced from his inside pocket a large wallet of shiny green leather, bearing a monogram in gold. And it was the wallet that he showed to Gonçalo first, with a proud smile.

'Nice, eh? A present from André, poor old chap. I think he may even have had it sent specially from Paris. The monogram is very chic, isn't it?'

Gonçalo was waiting, greatly alarmed. At last, Barrolo took a letter out of the wallet. It had clearly been crumpled up, then smoothed out again. The Nobleman only had to glance at the tiny writing on the sheet of lined paper to declare confidently:

'It's from the Lousada sisters.'

And leaning on one elbow, he read slowly and serenely, 'Dear Senhor José Barrolo, Despite the nickname, Barrolo the Dimwit, given you by your friends, you have lately shown great intelligence in allowing the governor, the noble André Cavaleiro, to resume his close friendship with you and your worthy wife. For your wife, the lovely Gracinha (who had, of late, appeared lacklustre to the point of drabness—something we were all rather concerned about), has suddenly blossomed again and the colour's back in her cheeks, ever since she has been able to enjoy the excellent company of the district's first gentleman. You have behaved as every zealous husband should, eager that your charming wife should be happy and healthy. Hardly to be expected in someone whom all of Oliveira considers to be its most illustrious fool! Our sincere congratulations!'

Gonçalo very quietly stuffed the letter into his pocket, a letter which, only days before, would have plunged him into a mood of infinite bitterness and anger:

'It's definitely the work of the Lousada sisters. And you actually believed such nonsense?'

Cheeks ablaze, Barrolo retorted:

'What do you take me for? I've always hated anonymous letters. And then there's that rude comment about my friends calling me a dimwit. Terrible, isn't it? Can you believe it? I can't. But it's created ill feeling between me and the other fellows. I haven't been back to the club since. A dimwit. Why? Because I'm a simple soul, frank and hospitable? If the lads at the club call me a "dimwit" behind my back, they're being most ungrateful. But I really can't believe it's true.'

He shambled disconsolately round the room, his hands behind his back, resting on his large posterior. Then, standing before the divan, where Gonçalo was watching him pityingly, he added:

'As for the rest of the letter, it's so stupid, so garbled, I didn't understand it at first. Now I do. They're saying that Gracinha and Cavaleiro are having an affair. At least that's what I think they mean. But it's utter nonsense. Even the bit about our "close friendship" is a lie. Since that last supper, the poor fellow has only visited three or four times, at night, for a game of cards, along with Mendonça. And now he's gone off to Lisbon.'

It was the Nobleman's turn to be surprised.

'Gone to Lisbon, you say?'

'Yes, he left three days ago.'

'Has he gone for long?'

'Oh, yes, he won't be back until mid-October, in time for the Election.'

'Ha!'

At this point, Bento burst into the room, still bubbling with excitement and carrying a jug of hot water and two lace-edged towels. Standing before the mirror, Barrolo was slowly rebuttoning his jacket:

'See you later, then, Gonçalinho. I'm going down to the stables to see the horses. Do you know, they made it all the way from Oliveira without a rest, and kept up a cracking pace too. They didn't even break sweat! You're going to keep that letter, are you?'

'Yes, I want to study the handwriting.'

As soon as Barrolo had closed the door, the Nobleman again launched into the delicious story of the fight, reliving every surprise, every detail, acting out his manoeuvres on his horse, snatching up the whip to demonstrate the resounding thwacks he had delivered, slicing through flesh and drawing blood. Suddenly, standing there in his underwear, he said:

'Bento, bring me my hat, will you? I think the bullet might have grazed it.'

Both of them studied and scrutinised the hat. Bento, so enamoured of the whole exploit, thought the crown of the hat was indeed slightly dented, almost singed.

'The bullet must have brushed right past it, sir.'

With the grave modesty of a strong man, the Nobleman dismissed the idea:

'No, I don't think so. When the rascal fired, his arm was already shaking. We should thank God for that, Bento, but I really wasn't in any great danger!'

Once dressed, Gonçalo walked about his room and reread the letter. There was no doubting that it came from the Lousada sisters. However, that malicious slander, aimed with grubby malice at poor, chubby-cheeked Barrolo, would cause no real harm, rather it would serve the almost beneficent purpose of cauterising a wound, like a fiery brand. What had shocked poor Barrolo more was the revelation that his ungrateful friends had given him that cruel nickname, which they apparently bandied about in the club and in the Café da Arcada to gales of equally ungrateful laughter. He had scarcely grasped the other dreadful insinuation—that Gracinha was blossoming again in the warmth of Cavaleiro's love, a suggestion that, with distracted, entirely innocent disdain, he had barely bothered to take in. However, the letter that had whistled past Barrolo like a stray arrow would strike Gracinha, would wound her in her pride, her highly impressionable modesty, showing the poor fool how her name and even her heart were already being dragged through the mud by the Lousada sisters' base calumnies! Such deeply humiliating knowledge would clearly not extinguish a feeling that had failed to be extinguished by far more personal and more painful humiliations, but it would speak to Gracinha's natural reserve and wary circumspection. And now that André had escaped to Lisbon, it would work away at her, in silence and solitude, without his tempting presence to spoil its soothing, healthy influence. And so that vile letter could work to Gracinha's advantage, like a dire warning nailed to a wall. Having been rancorously written by those two females with the intention of bringing grief and scandal to the Casa dos Cunhais, it might perhaps reestablish peace and gravity in that threatened household. Gonçalo was pleased to think that, on such a happy morning, such a piece of evil work might bring about good!

'Bento, where is Senhora Dona Graça?'

'She went up to her room a little while ago, sir.'

It was the room where she had slept before she married, a bright, cool room with a view of the orchard, and still furnished with her lovely marquetry bedstead, the famous dressing table that had belonged to Queen Maria Francisca of Savoy, and the sofa and chairs upholstered in pale cashmere on which, over long years, Gracinha herself had embroidered the black goshawk of the Ramires coat of arms. Whenever Gracinha came back to the Tower, she loved to spend time in her room, reliving the years before her marriage, rummaging around in the drawers, leafing through the old English novels kept in the small glass cabinet, and simply standing on the balcony, gazing out at the beloved grounds of the house, which stretched as far as the Valverde hills, and down into the green garden, so much a part of her life, where every tree spoke to her, where every verdant corner was like a corner of her own mind.

Gonçalo went upstairs and knocked on the closed door, asking, as he used to, 'May your brother come in?' She ran in from the balcony, where she had been watering the plants in their old glazed pots, plants that Rosa constantly, lovingly tended in Gracinha's absence. She immediately blurted out the thought filling her mind:

'Oh, Gonçalo, how wonderful that we should come to the Tower today of all days!'

'Yes, you're right, Gracinha, it really is extraordinarily lucky. And I didn't feel in the least surprised to see you either! It was as if you were still living in the Tower, and I had met you in the corridor. It was different with Barrolo—when I got off my horse, I was thinking, "What the devil is Barrolo doing here? How on earth did he get here?" Odd, isn't it? Perhaps it's because, after that fight, I felt rejuvenated, with new blood in my veins, and thought I was back in the days when we used to long for another war in Portugal, with us besieged in the Tower, with our standard flying and our "troops" hurling stone balls at the Spaniards.'

She laughed to remember those heroic imaginings. And with her dress tucked between her knees, she resumed her slow watering of the pots, while Gonçalo, leaning on the balcony, contemplating the Tower, was again assailed by the idea that there was now a closer relationship between him and that noble remnant of Santa Ireneia, as if his own long-unproven strength had finally become welded to the centuries-old strength of his race.

'You must be so tired, Gonçalo, after that very real battle of yours!'

'No, I'm not tired, but I am hungry, yes, very hungry and with a splendid thirst on me!'

She immediately put down the watering can, gaily shaking her hands to dry them.

'Well, lunch won't be long. I've been working in the kitchen with Rosa and making a Spanish-style fish stew. It's a new recipe from the Baron das Marges.'

'So it'll be as insipid as he is, then.'

'No, it's actually rather spicy. The Vicar-General gave him the recipe.'

And watching her as she sat at Queen Maria Francisca's dressing table, hurriedly pinning up her hair, he decided to take advantage of that moment of privacy and hastened, somewhat uncomfortably, to broach the subject troubling him:

'Anything happening in Oliveira?'

'No, nothing, it's just very hot.'

Running his fingers slowly over the delicately intertwining lilies and laurels on the mirror frame, he said cautiously:

'I've heard that your friends the Lousada sisters are still very active.'

Gracinha shook her head innocently:

'The Lousada sisters? No, they haven't been to visit at all.'

'They've been busy plotting though.'

And when Gracinha's green eyes grew wide with bewilderment, Gonçalo pulled from his pocket the letter, which now weighed on him like lead:

'Look, Gracinha, it's best if we talk plainly. This is the letter they wrote to your husband a few days ago.'

In an instant, Gracinha had devoured the terrible words. Waves of blood rushed to her cheeks as she desperately wrung her hands, crushing the letter as she did so.

'So, Gonçalo, does he ...'

Gonçalo immediately reassured her:

'No, Barrolo took no notice. He even laughed about it. And

I did too when he showed it to me. And the proof that we both consider it a lot of old nonsense is that I'm showing it to you now quite openly.'

Pale and dumb with terror, holding back the bright tears brimming in her eyes, she crumpled the letter in her clasped and trembling hands. Gonçalo felt for her deeply and, very gravely, very tenderly, said:

'You know what these small towns are like, Gracinha, especially Oliveira. You need to be very careful, very reserved. It's entirely my fault, though. I resumed a friendship that should never have been resumed. I am truly sorry. But, believe me, I have spent many a bitter day here at the Tower because of this false and dangerous situation, which I myself frivolously created out of mere foolish ambition. I didn't even dare come to Oliveira. Today, for some reason, after this morning's "adventure", it all seems to have disappeared, to have melted into a great shadow. My heart no longer burns as it did, which is why I can talk to you openly and calmly.'

She began to weep uncontrollably as if her poor weak heart would break. With renewed tenderness, Gonçalo embraced her bowed shoulders, shaken with sobs. And clasping her to his bosom, he whispered these words of advice:

'Gracinha, the past is dead, and for the sake of all of us and our honour, we need it to stay dead. Or that it should, at least, in your every gesture, appear to be dead. I'm asking you for the sake of our family name!'

Folded in her brother's arms, she said with infinite humility:

'He's left. He'd grown tired of Oliveira!'

Gonçalo stroked her head, which she, in her humiliation and distress, had again pressed to his bosom, as if seeking the merciful balm she sensed within.

'I know, I know, and that just shows me that you have been strong, but you must remain aloof and vigilant, Gracinha. For now, though, try to calm yourself. And let us never talk about this incident again. Because that's all it was, an incident, one that I provoked, fool that I am, out of sheer thoughtlessness and ambition. It's over and forgotten now. So calm yourself and rest. And when you come downstairs, make sure all your tears have dried.'

He slowly released her from his arms, to which she clung as if to her most certain refuge, her most longed-for consolation. Then he made to leave, overwhelmed by emotion and also fighting back tears. He was stopped by a timid, supplicant moan.

'Gonçalo, do you think ...'

He turned and embraced her once more and planted a slow kiss on her forehead.

'I think that if you follow my advice, you will show great dignity and great determination.'

Then he did at last leave, shutting the door behind him. On the narrow staircase, only dimly lit by a skylight, he was still wiping away the tears when he bumped into Barrolo, who was coming upstairs to find Gracinha and to hasten on lunch.

'Gracinha will be right down,' said the Nobleman quickly. 'She's just washing her hands. She'll join us shortly. But why don't we go to the stables before lunch? We owe my beloved horse, my saviour, a visit, don't you think?'

'Heavens, yes, we most certainly do!' cried Barrolo, enthusiastically heading back down the stairs. 'She's a big, bold beast, isn't she? But I bet she sweated more than my horses. Imagine! All the way from Oliveira and not a drop of sweat on them. Wonderful creatures! But then I do take excellent care of them!'

In the stable, they both stroked and patted Gonçalo's horse. Barrolo suggested giving her a large ration of carrots. Then, so that Gracinha would have plenty of time to calm herself, the Nobleman showed Barrolo into the orchard and the vegetable plot.

'You haven't been to the Tower for nearly six months, Barrolo! You must see the progress we've made, now that Pereira's in charge.'

'Oh, I'm sure. He's a great man, Pereira! But, you know, Gonçalinho, I'm really hungry!'

'Me too!'

It was striking one o'clock when they went out onto the balcony, where the table awaited them, beautifully laid and decked with flowers. Gracinha, sitting on the divan, was engrossed in reading an old *Gazeta do Porto*. Despite much splashing with cold water, her lovely eyes were still red, and to justify this and her rather exhausted air, she complained, blushing, of a headache. It was all the emotion and excitement of Gonçalo's exploit.

'I've got a headache too,' declared Barrolo, walking round the table. 'Mine comes from hunger though. Do you know, all I've had this morning is a cup of coffee and a boiled egg!'

Gonçalo rang the bell, but the person who came bursting in through the French doors, breathless and smiling broadly, was Joaquim, the stableboy, who had just returned from Grainha.

Gonçalo leapt to his feet:

'What news?'

'I went straight there, sir,' exclaimed Joaquim, his breast swelling with pride. 'And there were crowds of people. Everyone knows about it. A girl from Bravais saw it all, from inside the courtyard. Then she ran off and spread the word. But the old man, Domingues, who lives in the house, him and his son, they've both taken off. Apparently, the boy wasn't badly hurt at all. If he did fall over and faint or whatever, it was out of fright. Ernesto de Nacejas, though, he's in a really bad way. He was carried to the house of a friend who lives nearby, in Arribada. It seems he's got no ear and no mouth either. And he used to be the darling of all the girls in the neighbourhood too! Then he was taken to the hospital in Vila Clara, because his friend couldn't really do much for him. The crowd, though, they all side with you, sir. Old Domingues was a rogue, and as for Ernesto, no one could stand him anyway, and they were all afraid of him. So you've done everyone a favour, sir!'

Gonçalo glowed with pride. And it was a relief to know that no greater harm was done than the loss of the local Don Juan's good looks!

'So what's the crowd doing there? Just talking and looking around?'

'Yes, they won't go away. They keep pointing at the blood on the ground and the stones your horse kicked up. And now they're saying it was an ambush, that you were fired at three times, and that, afterwards, in the woods, three masked men attacked you, but that you gave them a good thrashing too!'

'So that's the legend growing up around me, is it?' said Gonçalo.

Bento came in, bearing a large, steaming dish of food. The Nobleman smiled, patted Joaquim on the back, and told him to give orders to Rosa to open two bottles of old Port wine for this family occasion. Then, resting his hands on the back of his chair, he murmured gravely:

'Let us, for a moment, think gratefully of God, for today he saved me from a grave danger.'

Barrolo bowed his head reverently. Gracinha sighed softly and said a brief prayer to herself. Then, as they were unfolding their napkins, and Gonçalo was praising the fish stew, Crispola's youngest son pushed open the French doors again, clutching 'A telegram from town'! Everyone stopped, forks in mid-air, wondering what it could be. There had been so many shocks and surprises that morning! But a triumphant, pleasurable smile was already spreading over Gonçalo's slender face:

'Oh, it's nothing. It's from Castanheiro, about the chapters from my Novella that I sent him. He's a good lad.'

And leaning back in his chair, he slowly read out the telegram, lingering over the words. 'Chapters of novel received. Read to friends. Great enthusiasm. A masterpiece. Well done.'

His mouth too full to speak, Barrolo applauded. And Gonçalo, not even noticing the plate of fish Bento had set before him, filled his glass with *vinho verde*, his hand trembling slightly. Then with a blissful smile on his lips, he said:

'What an excellent morning this has been. Extraordinary!'

Despite Gracinha and Barrolo trying to persuade him to go back with them to Oliveira, Gonçalo declined, eager to finish the final chapter of his Novella that week, before finishing his lazy round of visits to influential voters in the constituency. Thus he would conclude both the work of Art and the work of Politics, and God be praised, complete the task he had set himself for that very fruitful summer!

He returned to the manuscript of his Novella that very night, and in the wide margin, wrote the date and a note, 'Today, in the parish of Grainha, I had a terrible fight with two men, who attacked me with a staff and a rifle. I gave them both a sound thrashing.' Then he slipped easily into that redolently medieval passage, in which

Tructesindo Ramires, in his pursuit of the Bastard, entered Dom Pedro de Castro's encampment, lit by flickering, smoky torchlight. The old warrior gave a grave, warm welcome to his Portuguese cousin, who had once brought his mighty troops all the way from Santa Ireneia to Enxarez de Sandornim when the Castros had to do battle there with the Moorish hosts. Then, in the vast tent, full of glittering weapons and carpeted with the skins of lions and bears, Tructesindo, still struggling to control his grief, told him of the death of his son Lourenço, wounded in the Battle of Canta-Pedra and then slain by the Bastard of Baião's knife, outside the walls of Santa Ireneia, with the sun in the vault of the sky gazing down on such treachery! Old Castro indignantly thumped the table, on which lay a gold rosary and some large chess pieces; he swore on Christ's life that never, in his sixty years of battles and horrors, had he heard of so vile a deed. And clasping Tructesindo's hand, he ardently offered to help him in his quest for holy vengeance by lending him his entire army—three hundred and thirty lancers and a solid body of foot soldiers.

'By all that's holy, what an expedition this will be!' roared Mendo de Briteiros, his red beard aglow with delight.

Dom Garcia Viegas the Wise, however, realised that in order to take the Bastard alive, as befitted a revenge to be savoured slowly, he would be better served by a small, silent body of knights and just a few foot soldiers.

'But why, Dom Garcia?'

'Because the Bastard, having left his foot soldiers and all the pack-mules by the side of the stream, is clearly heading for Coimbra, where he can join the King's men. Along with his exhausted band of lancers, he will have spent the night at the castle of Landim, and, at first light, will certainly take the shorter way along the old Miradães road, which winds through the Caramulo hills. Now I happen to know that, beyond the place known as the Poço da Esquecida, there is a pass, where a few knights and some crossbowmen, strategically positioned among the scrub, will be able to catch Lopo de Baião like a wolf in his lair.'

Unconvinced, Tructesindo pondered this plan and ran slow pen-

sive fingers through his long beard. Old Castro was equally unconvinced, preferring to take on the Bastard in the open, where his
large number of lancers would not only have the advantage, but
could then gallop gaily on to lay waste to the Baião lands. Then
Garcia Viegas begged his cousins from Spain and from Portugal to
come outside with him into the bright torchlight where they could
see more clearly. And there, surrounded by curious knights and
lit by torches, Dom Garcia crouched down and, with the point of
his dagger, drew in the dust the route that his 'hunt' would take,
thus demonstrating to them the beauty of his plan. The Bastard
would set off from Landim at dawn. At moonrise, they, too, would
set off, with twenty knights from both the Ramires and the Castro troops, so that men from both parties could enjoy the fight.
Further on, they would post crossbowmen and archers among the
undergrowth, always assuming that Senhor Dom Pedro de Castro
would do the Lord of Santa Ireneia the great honour of lending
him such excellent aid and help keep the Bastard encircled. Ahead,
in order to grab the villain by the throat, would go Senhor Dom
Tructesindo, who, as Lourenço's father, should, in God's eyes, be
the avenger. And there, in that narrow pass, they would unhorse
him and bleed him like a pig, and since his blood was unclean, they
would find, a mere stone's throw away, plentiful water in which to
wash their hands, in the pond known as the Pego das Bichas—the
Pool of Leeches.

'An excellent plan!' murmured Tructesindo.

And shooting a fiery glance at his Spanish knights, Dom Pedro
de Castro roared out his approval:

'Christ's wounds, if my great-uncle Gutierres had had Senhor
Dom Garcia as his captain, the men of Lara would not have escaped
when they took the Boy-King with them all the way to Santo Es-
tevão de Gurivaz! It's agreed then, my cousin and my friend! To
horse at moonrise, ready for the hunt!'

And they withdrew into the tents, where a roast kid was already
growing golden over the fire for supper and, from among the carts
laden with grapes, the stewards were carrying in heavy wineskins
full of wine from Tordesillas.

It was with that supper in the encampment (which took place in solemn silence, because the guests' hearts were veiled in mourning) that Gonçalo finished work on his fourth chapter for the night, writing another note in the margin, 'Midnight. A full day. I fought and I worked.' Later, in his room, while undressing, he sketched out in his mind the brief, tumultuous battle in which the Bastard would be captured like a wolf in his lair, at the vengeful mercy of the men from Santa Ireneia. However, in the morning, before lunch, when he was just about to sit happily down to work, he received two telegrams, which provided a delightful distraction from his ardent pursuit of the Bastard of Baião.

Both telegrams were from Oliveira, one from the Baron das Marges, the other from Captain Mendonça, both congratulating the Nobleman on 'having escaped that terrible ambush and laid low those two scoundrels from Nacejas'. The Baron added, 'Bravissimo. You're a hero!'

Gonçalo was so moved that he showed the telegrams to Bento. The impressive news of his exploit had obviously spread as far as Oliveira.

'It was Senhor José Barrolo who told them!' said Bento. 'And just you wait, sir, just you wait. Even the people in Oporto will know about it soon!'

When the clock struck noon, the vast figure of Tító erupted into the corridor, accompanied by João Gouveia, who had arrived from the coast the previous evening, and, on hearing the news at the club, had immediately raced to the Tower to embrace him, first, as a friend, before appearing in his more official capacity at the trial. Then, still in Gouveia's embrace, Gonçalo asked very generously that no action should be taken against the bandits. The administrator refused point-blank, citing the Principle of the Law and the need to hand down a harsh punishment, so that Portugal would not revert to the barbarous days of João Brandão de Midões. He and Tító lunched at the Tower, and afterwards, Tító jokingly proposed a toast, which he gave in his usual bellowing tones, comparing Gonçalo to the elephant, 'normally so good and so long-suffering, but who suddenly turns and tramples on the world!'

Lighting a large cigar, João Gouveia demanded a detailed account of every lunge and scream, so that, in his role as administrator, he could gain a clear understanding of the matter. Using the balcony as his stage, Gonçalo recreated the whole heroic story, reenacting the blows he had dealt by whipping the divan (which ended up in shreds), and even imitating the way the braggart from Nacejas had fallen to the ground, half-fainting and drenched in blood. The administrator and Titó then visited the historic horse in the stables, and Gonçalo showed them his leather gaiters drying in the sun in the courtyard, washed clean of all bloodstains. At the door to the house, João Gouveia earnestly clapped the Nobleman on the back:

'You know, Gonçalo, you really should put in an appearance at the club tonight ...'

Gonçalo did as his friend advised and was greeted like the victor of some famous battle. In the billiard room, at old Ribas' suggestion, a great bowl of hot punch was brought in, and Comendador Barros, his face flushed, insisted that, on Sunday, a thanksgiving mass should be held in the church of São Francisco, which he would be proud to pay for, damn it! When Gonçalo left, accompanied by Titó, Gouveia, Manuel Duarte, and other club members, they found Videirinha, who didn't belong to the club, but who had been waiting for the Nobleman to appear, so that he could sing him the two new verses—written that very evening and lauding him above all the other Ramires of History and Legend!

The party sat down by the fountain. The guitar thrummed lovingly. And Videirinha's voice, which came straight from his soul, rose up through the mute leaves of the Judas trees:

The Ramires of other ages
Conquered with the lance,
This one uses a whip,
How strange is time's dance!

The famous Ramires of old
Whole generations apart
Relied for strength on their arms,
His strength lies in his heart.

On hearing this clever conceit, his friends cheered Gonçalo and the House of Ramires. And as the Nobleman, much moved, was walking back to the Tower, he was thinking:

'It's odd. All these people genuinely seem to like me!'

His excitement was even greater when, bright and early, Bento woke him up with a telegram from Lisbon. It was from Cavaleiro, who had learned of the attack from the newspapers and was sending him enthusiastic greetings and congratulations on the happy outcome and on his bravery.

Sitting up in bed, Gonçalo roared:

'Heavens above! Even the newspapers in Lisbon are talking about it, Bento! We're famous!'

Famous indeed! For during that whole delicious day, the telegraph boy, breathless and limping, kept coming to the door of the Tower with more telegrams, all of them from Lisbon: from the Countess de Chelas; from Duarte Lourençal; from the Marquis and Marchioness of Coja; from Aunt Louredo offering congratulations to her bold nephew; from the Marchioness of Esposende hoping that her dear cousin had given due thanks to God!—and lastly, from Castanheiro, exclaiming, 'Magnificent! Worthy of Tructesindo himself!' In the library, Gonçalo flung up his arms in amazement:

'What on earth have those newspapers been saying?'

And in-between the telegrams came visits from all the influential gentlemen of the district—a terrified Dr Alexandrino, fearing a return to the politics of Costa Cabral; old Pacheco Valadares de Sá, who was not in the least surprised by his noble cousin's actions, because the Ramires blood, like the blood of the Sás, had always run red-hot; Father Vicente from Finta, who, along with his congratulations, brought a small basket of some of his famous moscatel grapes; and finally, the Viscount de Rio-Manso, who, clasping Gonçalo to him, was moved to tears, almost proud that the fight should have broken out on the road when 'his dear friend and Rosa's dear friend' had been on his way to visit them. Blushing furiously and smiling broadly, Gonçalo patiently went over the incident and accompanied those gentlemen to the door, where, as they mounted their horses or got into their carriages, they all smiled up at the old Tower—standing firm and dark in the sweet light of that September afternoon—as if paying homage not only to the hero of the day, but to the centuries-old basis of his heroism.

And running up the stairs to the library, the Nobleman, still astonished, again wondered out loud:

'What on earth are those newspapers saying?'

He could not sleep in his eagerness to read them, and when Bento rushed into his room with the morning's post, Gonçalo sat bolt upright and threw back the sheets as if he were sweltering. Hastily leafing through the *Século*, he found the telegraphed report from Oliveira, describing the attack, the shots fired, and the Nobleman's immense courage, with only a whip to defend himself. Bento practically snatched the paper from the Nobleman's trembling hands and ran to the kitchen to announce the glorious news to Rosa!

That afternoon, Gonçalo hurried into Vila Clara, to the club, in order to devour the other newspapers from Lisbon and from Oporto. All carried the story and all joined in celebrating it. The *Gazeta do Porto* believed the attack was politically motivated and railed against the Government. The *Liberal Portuense*, however, lay the blame at the door of certain vengeful republicans in Oliveira for 'this appalling attack, which almost brought about the death of one of the greatest Noblemen of Portugal and Spain and one of the most prodigious talents of the new young generation'. The Lisbon newspapers focused on the 'remarkable courage of Senhor Gonçalo Ramires'. And the most ardent of all was *A Manhã*, which published a very wordy article (doubtless written by Castanheiro), recalling the heroic traditions of that illustrious House, describing the beauties of the Castle of Santa Ireneia and concluding thus, 'We now await, with renewed impatience, the publication of Gonçalo Ramires' Novella, based on the deeds of his ancestor Tructesindo in the twelfth century, and which is due to appear in the first issue of the *Annals of Literature and History*, the new magazine from our dear friend, Lúcio Castanheiro, that worthy restorer of Portugal's heroic consciousness!' Gonçalo's hands trembled as he read the papers, and João Gouveia, greatly impressed, stood eagerly devouring the articles over his shoulder, occasionally murmuring: 'You're going to get a huge number of votes, Gonçalinho!' On returning to the Tower that night, Gonçalo found a rather troubling letter. It was from Maria Mendonça and written on perfumed paper, the same perfume that had so sweetly emanated from Dona Ana at Santa Maria de Craquede:

'We only found out this morning about the terrible danger you were in, and we were *both* deeply moved. At the same time, though, I (and not only I) felt very proud of my cousin's magnificent courage. The courage of a true Ramires! I won't come to the Tower to embrace you (at the risk of compromising myself and provoking envy), because one of my little ones, Neco, has a bad cold. Fortunately, it's nothing very serious. Here, though, even the little ones are longing to see the hero, and I don't think anyone on either side would find it so very extraordinary were you to appear here the day after tomorrow (Thursday) at around three o'clock. We could take a turn about the garden and even have tea, in the good old-fashioned way of our ancestors. Won't you come?

Many, many regards from Ana, and from me, Yours etc.'

Gonçalo smiled thoughtfully, rereading the letter and breathing in its perfume. Cousin Maria had never so blatantly propelled Dona Ana into his arms. And Dona Ana was clearly allowing herself to be propelled, willingly and with her eyes closed. Ah, if it was only a matter for the bedroom, but, alas, it would also involve the church! And he could again hear Tító's booming voice on the steps outside the house's green door, with the moon bright above the dark trees, 'That creature had a lover, and you know I never lie!'

Then he slowly took up his pen and replied to Dona Maria Mendonça:

'Dear Cousin, I was deeply touched by your concern for me and by your congratulations. Let's not exaggerate, though! All I did was whip the bullies who attacked me. An easy enough task for someone who, like me, happens to own an excellent whip.

As for that visit to Feitosa, which would, of course, have been a delightful prospect, I regret to say that I cannot come either on Thursday or on any other day this month. I am extremely busy with my book, the Election and my move to Lisbon. The age of serious work has dawned for me, bringing to a close that sweet age of country walks and daydreams. Please give my deepest respects to Senhora Dona Ana, and my very best regards to you and wishes for a speedy recovery to dear Neco. I remain your devoted and grateful cousin, etc.'

He slowly folded the letter, and as he stamped his seal on the green wax, he was thinking, 'That rascal Tító has deprived me of two hundred *contos!*'

During the whole of that soft late-September week, Gonçalo worked hard on the final chapter of his Novella.

At last the vengeful morning dawned when, in the wild ravine that Garcia Viegas the Wise had proposed for the ambush, the knights of Santa Ireneia, joined by the finest of Castro's lancers, took Baião's men by surprise in their race to reach Coimbra. The fight was brief and inelegant, with no bold, skilful use of arms— more like a wolf-hunt than an attack on a nobleman. And that is precisely what Tructesindo wanted—with Dom Pedro de Castro's heartfelt approval—because this was not a matter of engaging an enemy in combat, but of capturing a killer.

Before day had broken, the Bastard had set off in haste from the castle of Landim, paying so little heed to his own safety that he sent ahead of him no scout to reconnoitre the paths. The larks were singing when, at a fast canter, he entered that ravine, which runs between steep, rocky, gorse-grown cliffs and is known as the Racha do Mouro—the Moor's Ravine—ever since Mahomet first created it so that the Moorish Governor of Coimbra could escape Fernando the Great's Christian troops, in hot pursuit of both him and the kidnapped nun riding on the saddle behind him. No sooner had the last of the Bastard's lancers entered the ravine than, from the far end, came the closed ranks of the knights of Santa Ireneia led by Tructesindo, his visor up and with no buckler, merely brandishing a javelin, as if he were out on a leisurely hunt. Bursting forth from the dense trees concealing them appeared Dom Pedro de Castro's men, lances at the ready, sealing off the one escape route as effectively as the iron grille of a drawbridge. From behind the hills, like water from a broken dam, flowed a whole dark company of rough foot soldiers! The fearsome Bastard was caught, lost! Yet still he furiously unsheathed his sword and whirled it about his head, crowning himself with glittering light. Then with a feral scream, he launched his horse at Tructesindo. However, from out of an obscure knot of slingsmen emerged a curling hempen cord, which wrapped about the Bastard's neck and hauled him from his Moorish saddle onto the boulders, his long sword breaking off at its golden hilt. And while the still astonished knights of Baião allowed themselves to be surrounded, a great wave of whooping foot soldiers, like mastiffs attacking a boar, dragged the Bastard over to the side of the ravine, where they stripped him of buckler and dagger, tore his tunic of purple wool, wrenched off the fastenings of his helmet, and spat in his face, on his proud, beautiful golden beard!

Then the same brute mob lifted him up and placed him, tightly bound, on the back of a strong pack-mule and laid him down between two narrow boxes of arrows, like a trophy from a hunt. Foot soldiers stood guard over that proud knight, the same Bright Sun who had lit up the House of Baião—now wedged in-between two wooden boxes, with cords binding feet and hands, in which was placed a branch from a thistle bush, as a symbol of his treachery.

Meanwhile, his fifteen knights lay scattered on the ground, overpowered by the furious onrush of lances that had felled them; some, in their black armour, lay as still as if they were sleeping, others were twisted and disfigured, their mutilated flesh bulging grotesquely from the gashes in their chain-mail tunics. Their squires were pitilessly driven at spear-point to the edge of a precipice, as if they were a filthy band of cattle thieves, and there they ended up having their heads chopped off with axes by the bearded Leonese troops. The whole ravine stank of blood like a butcher's yard. In order to identify the Bastard's companions, a group of knights went around unbuckling gorgets and lifting visors, furtively stealing the silver medallions, lucky charms or small bags of relics worn by all God-fearing men. In one neatly bearded face, smeared with blood and spit, Mendo de Briteiros recognised his cousin Soeiro de Lugilde, with whom, on St John's Eve, he had danced and sported at the castle of Unhelo, and now, sitting in his high saddle, he bowed his head and said a devout Hail Mary for that poor, unconfessed soul. Dark, melancholy clouds were casting a pall over that August morning. And standing apart, at the entrance to the ravine, beneath the shade of an ancient holm oak, Tructesindo, Dom Pedro de Castro and Garcia Viegas the Wise were all in agreement that the Bastard, that most ignominious of villains, should suffer an appropriately slow, painful and ignominious death.

Like someone laboriously pushing a plough through stony ground, Gonçalo spent the whole of that sweet September week describing the grim ambush. And on the Saturday, in the library, his hair still wet from his shower-bath, he sat at his desk, rubbing his hands, because with just two more hours of intense work, he would finish his Novella, his Great Work—and before lunch too! And yet he found the sordid end of that story almost repellent. In his poem, his Uncle Duarte had barely sketched it in, with the lofty, punctilious disdain of a poetically-minded nobleman, who, confronted by a scene of brutish violence, merely sings a brief lament, puts down his lyre and sets off instead down gentler paths. And when he took up his pen again, Gonçalo, too, genuinely regretted that his ancestor Tructesindo had not killed the Bastard in the heat of battle, with one of those marvellous blows with his sword, so easy to celebrate in prose—slicing through both knight and horse and resonating down the centuries.

But no, beneath the shade of the oak tree, those three knights were slowly concocting a truly ghastly revenge. Tructesindo had wanted to return to Santa Ireneia and build a gallows in front of the gates, on the very spot where his son's dead body had been thrown down, and there, after a sound whipping, hang the villain who had killed his son, thus giving him a suitably villainous death. Dom Pedro de Castro, however, advised a swifter, but still pleasurably vengeful death. Why ride all the way back to Santa Ireneia and waste that August day, when they could be on their way to Montemor to help the Princesses? Why not tie the Bastard to a beam, at Dom Tructesindo's feet, like a Christmas pig on a spit, and have a stableboy singe his beard and then another, with a kitchen knife, slit his throat and let him slowly bleed to death?

'What do you think, Dom Garcia?'

Dom Garcia Viegas the Wise unfastened his iron helmet and wiped the sweat and dust of battle from his deeply-lined face:

'Gentlemen and friends! We have much nearer at hand a far better punishment, with no need for long journeys, for just beyond these hills lies the Pego das Bichas. And we do not even have to go out of our way, because from there, via Tordeselo and Santa Maria da Varge, we can go directly to Montemor, as straight as the crow flies. Trust me, Tructesindo! I will arrange a death for the Bastard more painful and humiliating than any known since Portugal was a mere county ruled by the Asturians.'

'More humiliating for a knight than hanging, my friend?'

'You will see, my friends, you will see!'

'So be it! Sound the horns.'

At a command from the standard-bearer Afonso Gomes, the horns were sounded. A group of crossbowmen and Leonese attendants surrounded the mule on which the Bastard lay bound. And led by Dom Garcia, the small party set off for Pego das Bichas, with the lancers trotting along as blithely as if they were going on a country ride, all chatting, boasting and laughing about the morning's events.

Hidden among the hills, not two leagues from Tordeselo and its beautiful castle, was the Pego das Bichas. It was a place of eternal silence and eternal sadness. Uncle Duarte had written four perfect lines describing the desolation and harshness of the scene:

> No trilling bird sings on a swaying branch!
> No fresh flower grows beside the fresh stream!
> Only rocks and scrub and grim banks,
> And, in the midst, the Pego, dark and dead!

And when the first knights galloped to the top of the hill and saw it in the melancholy of that misty morning, all talk stopped, and they reined in their horses, taken aback by the sheer desolation of the place, a place for witches and ghosts and souls in torment. At the bottom of the steep bank, down which the horses skidded and slipped, lay an open expanse dotted with muddy pools, almost sucked dry by the summer heat, but still glinting dully among the large boulders and the low-growing gorse. At the far end, half a crossbow-shot away, was the Pego, a long, narrow pool, its surface utterly smooth and black, apart from some still blacker patches, like a sheet of tin grown rusty with time and weather and neglect. All around rose the hills, thick with tall, wild scrub, crisscrossed by reddish, gravelly tracks like trails of blood, and topped by rocky outcrops glinting white as bones. So heavy was the silence and the solitude that even old Dom Pedro de Castro—a man who had travelled far and wide—even he was alarmed:

'What an ugly place! I swear by Christ and by the Virgin Mary that, before us, no man redeemed by baptism has entered here.'

'But, Senhor Dom Pedro de Castro,' said Garcia Viegas the Wise, 'many a splendid soldier has been here, and even in the days of Dom Soeiro and your own King Fernando there was a famous castle built on these banks. Look over there!'

And he pointed to one end of the pool, where, emerging out of the black water were two sturdy stone pillars, burnished, like fine marble, by the wind and the rain. A wooden walkway built on slimy, half-rotten posts connected the bank to the larger of the pillars. Halfway up hung an iron ring.

Meanwhile, the foot soldiers had spread out along the bank. Dom Garcia Viegas dismounted, calling for Pêro Ermigues, the captain of the Santa Ireneia crossbowmen. And standing beside Tructesindo's horse, smiling and taking pleasure in everyone's surprise and bemusement, he ordered the captain to have six of his strongest men lift the Bastard down from the mule, lay him on the ground and strip him bare, leaving him as naked as he was when his whorish mother brought him into this grim world.

Tructesindo looked at Garcia Viegas, frowning:

'Surely to God, Dom Garcia, you're not simply going to drown the villain and sully this innocent water!'

Other knights also protested at such a peaceful and relatively benign death. Dom Garcia's beady eyes looked around, glittering with triumph and delight:

'Fear not, gentlemen! I may be old, but the Lord God has not yet deprived me of all my wits. He will neither be hanged nor have his throat cut nor be drowned. He will, gentlemen, be bled very slowly to death by the great leeches that fill this black water!'

Thrilled, Dom Pedro de Castro slapped one armoured thigh:

'Christ's blood! Having Senhor Dom Garcia in our company is like having Hannibal and Aristotle all rolled into one, for any advice we could possibly want, be it military or political!'

A murmur of admiration ran through the ranks:

'An excellent idea!'

And Tructesindo beamed and bellowed:

'Get to work, crossbowmen! And you, gentlemen, withdraw to the slope of the hill, where the view will be better, for what we are about to see will be a spectacle indeed.'

Six crossbowmen were already lifting the Bastard down from the mule. Others surrounded him, carrying coils of rope. And like butchers skinning a cow, the whole rough crew fell upon the unfortunate man, removing helmet, tunic, greaves, armoured shoes, and finally his thick, filthy undergarments. Held by his long hair and by his feet—into which sharp nails dug as they struggled to hold him fast, his arms gripped by other strong, hard arms—the Bastard still had energy enough to struggle and writhe and roar, spitting reddish foam into the anonymous faces of the rabble.

Among the dark crowd swarming over him, his naked body gleamed white, bound now by still thicker cords. Slowly, grown breathless and hoarse, his furious roaring faded away. And one after the other, the crossbowmen stood up, puffing and panting and wiping the sweat from their brows.

The knights of Spain and Santa Ireneia had, by now, dismounted and stuck their lances in the ground among the rocks and the gorse. Every inch of the slope was packed with men, like the stands at a jousting tournament. On one of the smoother rocks, in the sparse shade of two rather scrawny thornbushes, a pageboy spread out sheepskins for Senhor Dom Pedro de Castro and the Lord of Santa Ireneia. However, only Dom Pedro took advantage of this opportunity to rest, unbuckling his gold-inlaid corselet.

Tructesindo remained erect and silent, his gloved hands resting on the hilt of his long sword, his deep-set eyes fixed eagerly on the gloomy pool that would avenge his son by dealing out a foul and bestial death. And along the edge of the pool, foot soldiers and a few Spanish knights were stirring the muddy water with the tips of arrows or lances, curious to see the black creatures lying hidden in the depths.

Suddenly, at a shout from Dom Garcia, the moving spirit behind the spectacle, all the foot soldiers still gathered round the Bastard drew back to reveal his powerful body, white and naked on the black earth, a thick reddish pelt covering his chest, his manhood smothered in another thicket of reddish hair, and his entire body wound about with hemp cords to keep him immobile. So rigid was he kept by those bindings that not even his ribs rose and fell, only his eyes glowed red, bulging horribly with horror and rage. A few men ran to see the famous man of Baião in his ignoble nakedness. The Lord of Argelim said loudly and mockingly:

'I knew it! The body of a virgin, with not a mark on it!' Leonel de Samora scraped the point of his metal shoe along the poor wretch's shoulder:

'Regard this Bright Sun about to be extinguished in the blackest of waters!'

The Bastard closed his eyes tight shut, and two large tears rolled slowly down his cheeks. However, a loud cry rang out from the banks:

'Justice! Justice!'

It was the commanding officer from Santa Ireneia, who was pacing up and down, brandishing his spear, and roaring out:

'Justice! Let justice be done to that murderous dog by the Lord of Treixedo and Santa Ireneia! Justice for a dog, for the son of a bitch, who committed foul murder and who will die an equally foul death!'

He repeated this cry three times to the men crowding the slope.

Then he stopped and bowed humbly to Tructesindo Ramires and old Castro, as if bowing to the judges on their bench.

'On with it!' cried the Lord of Santa Ireneia.

Immediately, at a command from Dom Garcia, six crossbowmen, their legs wrapped in thick blankets, lifted the Bastard's body as if they were lifting a corpse on a sheet and carried it into the water, as far as the tallest of the granite pillars. Others, dragging coils of rope, ran along the slippery wooden walkway. With a shout of, 'Steady now! Steady! Raise him up!' the Bastard's strong white body was, with considerable difficulty, plunged into the water up to the groin, then propped against the pillar, to which he was tied with a long cable looped through the iron ring, leaving him hanging there, as securely as a furled sail tied to the mast. The crossbowmen then scrambled out of the water, immediately tearing off the blankets and rubbing their legs, terrified that some of the bloodsucking beasts might be clinging to them. The others returned along the walkway, pushing and shoving. Lopo de Baião was there on display for that slow, showy death, with the water up to his waist, with cords coiled about him up to his neck, like a slave bound to a post; and one thick lock of his fair hair was caught back on the iron ring, revealing his pale face, so that all could enjoy to the full the humiliating death of that Bright Sun.

The attentive hush of the gathered host waiting on the slopes of the hills made the misty silence of that desolate place still sadder. Not a ripple disturbed the surface of the water, stained black like a rusty sheet of tin. Among the rocky outcrops above, archers had been posted by Dom Garcia to keep watch on the barren lands around. A flock of jays flew past high up, cawing. From the lances stuck in the ground pennants fluttered in the breeze.

To rouse and chivvy the indolent leeches, some foot soldiers were throwing stones into the muddy water. A few of the Spanish knights were already complaining about the time they were wasting in that silent place. Others, to prove that the infamous creatures would never come, went and crouched on the edge of the pool, plunging their bare hands tentatively into the black water, then shaking them dry, laughing and mocking Dom Garcia the

Wise. Suddenly, though, a tremor ran through the Bastard's body; in their furious efforts to break free of their bonds, his powerful muscles squirmed and swelled beneath the cords, like wriggling snakes; through his bared teeth came roars and groans, insults and threats aimed at cowardly Tructesindo and at the whole Ramires race, whom he condemned, within the year, to burn in the fires of Hell. Indignant, one of the Santa Ireneia knights snatched up a crossbow and was about to shoot, when Dom Garcia stopped him:

'For God's sake, my friend, don't deprive the leeches of so much as a single drop of that fresh blood. See how they come!'

A shiver ran through the thick water; around the Bastard's submerged thighs, large bubbles rose to the surface, and from them a beast emerged, then another and another, glossy and black, undulating through the water and attaching themselves to the white skin of the belly, to which they clung, sucking and growing instantly plumper and glossier with the slowly flowing blood. The Bastard had fallen silent, and his teeth were loudly chattering. Even coarse foot soldiers turned away in disgust, spitting into the gorse bushes. Others, though, urged the creatures on, shouting, 'Go to it, ladies!' And gentle Samora de Cendufe protested at such a dull death! Why, a dose of leeches was what you might prescribe for someone with haemorrhoids! This is less like a sentence handed down to a Nobleman, and more like a prescription from a Moorish herbalist!

'What more do you want, Leonel?' said Dom Garcia cheerily, glorying in his triumph. 'This is just the kind of death that will be set down in books! This winter, there won't be a fireside in all the houses from the Minho to the Douro, where this story won't be told. Just look at our cousin Tructesindo Ramires! He must have witnessed many a fine scene of torture in his long life as a soldier, but see how he enjoys it, how he stares—how he marvels at it!'

On the hillside, next to his spear, which his standard-bearer had stuck in-between two rocks, and which stood as still as he did, old Ramires did not for a moment take his eyes off the Bastard's body, so filled was he with fierce delight, with sombre joy. He could never have expected such a magnificent revenge! The man who had bound up his son, had him carried on a litter, then slit his throat before his very eyes, was now shamefully naked and tied up like a pig, bound to a pillar, submerged in filthy water and being bled dry by leeches, while two armies, the very finest in Spain, watched and jeered! That blood, the blood of a hated race, would not be absorbed by the dry, churned-up earth after a day of battle, flowing from an honourable wound made through sturdy armour, no, it would vanish drop by quiet, obscure drop, drunk by those loathsome creatures emerging greedily from the mud and returning, sated, back to the mud, where they would vomit up the proud blood filling them. In a pool, into which he had plunged him, slimy creatures were quietly drinking the knight of Baião! What family feud had ever known a sweeter revenge!

With inexhaustible pleasure, the old man's cruel heart watched the leeches climbing up and wandering over that securely bound body, like a flock of sheep climbing the hill they graze upon. The man's belly had already disappeared beneath a black, viscous layer, pulsating and gleaming with warm, wet blood. A row of them were sucking away at his stomach, which was contracted in fear, and from which a slow fringe of blood seeped out. The dense reddish hair on the chest, as dense as a jungle, deterred many of the undulating beasts, which left a trail of mud behind them. A heaving tangle of them were draining blood from one arm. Those who were already swollen and glossy with blood let go and fell softly back into the water; but others hungrily took their places. Blood flowed weakly from the abandoned wounds, held back by the cords, from which it dripped like very light rain. Globules of wasted blood floated in the dark water. And yet even as he was being sucked dry, even as he was oozing blood, the wretch still kept growling out vile insults and threats of death and hellfire against the Ramires race! Then, with a gasp that almost broke the cords, his mouth horribly wide and desperate, he began to shout hoarsely, pleadingly, 'Water! Water!' And in his despair, his fingernails, which one cord had pinned against his sturdy thighs, were tearing at his flesh, digging into the open wounds already swimming with blood.

This furious tumult finally faded away into a long, weary groan, until he appeared to have fallen asleep, his beard shining beneath the sweat that covered it like a very heavy dew, his dreadfully pale lips parted in a crazed smile.

As for the crowd scattered over the hillside like spectators at a tournament, their initial barbarous eagerness to observe this new form of torture was beginning to wane. And it was nearly time for their midday rations. The commanding officers of Santa Ireneia and of the Spanish troops ordered the trumpets to sound. Then the whole of that stark wilderness sprang into life as the men set to work as if in an ordinary encampment. The mules carrying the stores of both sides had stopped behind the hills, on a brief scrap of pastureland, where a clear stream dribbled over the pebbles and in among the roots of the weeping alder trees. The famished foot soldiers raced over the rocks to the line of pack-mules where they received from the provisioners and other attendants their allotted slice of meat and large crust of black bread; sitting in the shade of the trees, they ate slowly and silently, scooping water from the stream with wooden bowls. Then they lay down on the grass or set off together up the other hillside, through the scrub, in the hope of finding some prey to hunt and kill. Beside the pool, the knights, sitting on thick blankets around the open saddlebags, were slicing off large chunks of pork meat with their daggers and taking long draughts from plump wineskins.

At the invitation of Dom Pedro de Castro, Dom Garcia the Wise was sitting beside him and eating from a large wooden bowl full of 'Pope's cake', a cake made from honey and fine flour, into which both were slowly dipping their fingers, which they then wiped clean on the lining of their helmets. Only Tructesindo was neither eating nor resting, still erect and silent before his standard, flanked by his two mastiffs, feeling it his cruel duty not to miss a single shudder or moan or dribble of blood in the Bastard's slow agony. In vain did Dom Pedro offer him a silver pitcher to quench his thirst after that long, hard excursion, praising his own Tordesillas wine as the equal of any from Aquila or Provence. Tructesindo did not even respond, and Dom Pedro de Castro, after throwing two loaves to the faithful hounds, began talking to Garcia Viegas about the Bastard's stubborn love for Violante Ramires, which had led to so much murder and mayhem.

'You and I are fortunate, Senhor Dom Garcia! We are too old and tired and spent to be bothered by such temptations. When I was fighting the Moors, a physician once told me that a woman is like a soothing, scented breeze, but one that leaves everything tangled and confused. You only have to see how the men in my family have suffered for them. Driven mad by jealousy, my father stabbed my own sweet mother Estevaninha. And she was a saint, the daughter of the Emperor! Passion can make a man do almost anything. Even die, like this man here, drained dry by leeches before a crowd of men eating and jeering. But what a very long time he is taking to die, Senhor Dom Garcia!'

'But he *is* dying, Senhor Dom Pedro de Castro, and with the Devil beside him to carry him off.'

Yes, the Bastard was dying. Bound now by blood-soaked cords, he was a monstrous sight, a scarlet and black ghost covered by the sticky, sucking, pulsating creatures and by the slow threads of blood that flowed from every wound, like water streaming down a blackened wall.

The desperate breathing had stopped as had his anger and any attempt to struggle against his bonds. Limp and inert as a bundle of clothes, his glazed eyes would occasionally open horribly wide and peer about him in uncomprehending horror. Then his head would droop, pale and flaccid, his lips hanging open, his mouth a black hole from which dripped a bloody drool, while from his swollen, closed eyelids there oozed a strange mucus, like tears thickened with blood.

The foot soldiers were returning from their meal and crowding the edges of the pool, staring in astonishment and making cruel jokes at the expense of that hideous body still covered with leeches. The young squires were collecting together blankets and saddlebags. Dom Pedro de Castro had gone down to the edge of the muddy water with Dom Garcia to have a closer view of the man dying this strange death. And a few other gentlemen, bored with the delay, were putting on their coats of mail and muttering, 'The man's dead! It's over.'

Then Garcia Viegas shouted to the captain of the crossbowmen:

'Ermigues, go and see if there's any life left in that blood-drenched thing!'

The captain ran along the wooden walkway and, grimacing, touched the livid flesh, then held the blade of his dagger to the man's mouth.

'He's dead!' he cried.

He was indeed dead. Within its tight bonds, the flesh was turning purple and the body was shrinking, shrivelled, drained, empty. The blood, no longer flowing, was coagulating into dark scabs, where a few shiny leeches were still stubbornly sucking. A few latecomers continued to make the ascent. Two huge creatures were flailing around in one ear. Another obscured an eye. Bright Sun was now nothing but a heap of putrescent ordure. Only the lock of fair hair, caught back in the iron ring, glowed like a flickering flame, like a remnant left behind by that ardent soul now flown.

With his dagger still unsheathed, the captain waved it in the air as he approached Tructesindo, crying:

'Justice is done, the justice you demanded—the murderous dog is now dead!'

Then Tructesindo shook one hairy, threatening fist and, in a raucous voice that echoed around the rocks and hills, declared:

'He is dead! And a similarly infamous death awaits any man who treacherously insults me or my family!'

Then, setting stiffly off up the hill through the gorse, he waved to his standard-bearer:

'Afonso Gomes, sound the horns. And if you so please, Senhor Dom Pedro de Castro, let us to horse once more—for you have been to me a good and loyal cousin and friend!'

Dom Pedro smiled and waved his hand:

'By the Holy Mother, it has been my pleasure and honour. Yes, to horse. For Senhor Dom Garcia Viegas promises us that we shall reach the walls of Montemor while the sun is still high in the heavens!'

The foot soldiers were already forming into ranks, and the rested horses, made skittish by those murky waters, were being led along the banks by the young squires. With the two standards unfurled—the black goshawk and the thirteen roundels—the cavalcade trotted away up the steep hill, sending loose stones skittering down. At the top, a few knights turned in their saddles to look silently back at the Bastard of Baião, left there to rot, tied to the pillar, in the solitude of the Pego das Bichas. But when the line of crossbowmen and slingsmen trooped past, they hurled shouts and jibes and vile insults at the 'murderous dog'. Halfway up the slope, a crossbowman turned and unleashed a furious arrow, which only pierced the water. Another followed, along with a stone; the barbed arrow stuck in the Bastard's side, just above a black knot of leeches. The captain bawled, 'Close ranks! March!' The train of pack animals advanced, beneath the crack of whips; the provisioners picked up large stones and flung them at the dead man. Then the peasants driving the carts marched past, in their brief leather kilts and carrying short spears, and the foreman picked up a lump of dung and threw it, hitting the Bastard's face and smearing his fine golden beard.

XI

Exhausted and with his Afonsine ardour beginning to wane, Gonçalo was just putting the final touch to that final insult, when the bell for lunch began ringing. At last! Thank heavens! His eternal Novella was finished! He had been working on that sombre resurrection of his barbarous ancestors for four months, four painful months, ever since June. At the bottom of the page, in large, bold letters, he wrote *Finis*. And then he added the date and the hour, which was fourteen minutes past noon.

However, leaving the desk where he'd laboured so hard, he did not feel as pleased as he had expected. Indeed, the torture inflicted on the Bastard had left him with a real distaste for that remote, bestial, inhuman, Afonsine world! If only he could at least console himself with the thought that he had brilliantly, truthfully reconstituted the moral being of those savage ancestors of his, but, no! He rather feared that he had merely succeeded in creating a few insubstantial souls with no historical reality, clothed in a lot of ill-fitting and archaeologically inexact armour. He wasn't even sure that leeches could climb out of a pool to cover a man's body and bleed him dry from thighs to beard, all the while watched by a crowd of people eating lunch! Then again, Castanheiro had praised the first three chapters. What the crowd loves most in Novellas are titanic rages and lots of blood, and soon, the *Annals* would have spread throughout Portugal the fame of that illustrious House, which had assembled armies, razed castles to the ground, laid waste to large areas in the name of family honour, and arrogantly insulted kings in the court and on the battlefield. His summer had, in that sense, proved most fruitful. And to crown it, there was the Election, which would free him from the melancholy of his rural hideaway.

Not wishing to delay the visits he still owed to his influential neighbours, and also wanting to clear his head, he got on his horse immediately after lunch, despite the heat which, since the previous day—and in the middle of October too!—had been bearing down on the village with all the blazing weight of an August noontide. At the bend in the Bravais road, he was greeted with an extravagant bow by a fat man wearing grubby white trousers, who was hurrying along, puffing and panting, beneath a red sunshade. It was Godinho, a clerk who worked for Gouveia. He had just delivered an urgent missive to the alderman in Bravais and was now on his way to the Tower with a message from the administrator.

Gonçalo guided his horse into the shade of an oak tree:

'What is it, friend Godinho?'

Gouveia wanted to let the Nobleman know that Ernesto, the braggart from Nacejas, had been treated in the Oliveira hospital and was making considerable progress. His ear had been sewn back on and his mouth was healing. And since they were now ready to proceed to the court case, the insolent rogue had been transferred to prison.

Gonçalo immediately protested, slapping his saddle:

'Please be so good as to tell Senhor João Gouveia that I don't want the man to be arrested. He was, indeed, insolent, but he got a sound whipping for his pains, and so we're even.'

'But Senhor Gonçalo Mendes ...'

'My friend, that is what I want, so please pass the message on to Senhor João Gouveia. I loathe revenge. It's simply not what I or my family do. No Ramires has ever gone in for revenge, well, it has been known ... but, nevertheless, tell Senhor João Gouveia what I've told you. I'm sure to see him at the club anyway. It's quite enough that the man has lost his looks, and I won't allow him to be humiliated any further. I hate brutality.'

'But ...'

'That is my last word, Godinho.'

'I'll be sure to give Senhor Gouveia your message.'

'Thank you, and off you go now. Isn't this heat terrible?'

'Dreadful, sir, dreadful!'

Gonçalo rode on, revolted by the idea that the poor braggart of Nacejas, even before his wounds had properly healed, with his ear only just sewn on, should be sent to a filthy cell in Vila Clara, to sleep on a pallet bed. He even considered galloping straight to Vila Clara to restrain João Gouveia's legal zeal. However, nearby, beyond the local washing-place, was the house of one of the district's influential men, João Firmino, a carpenter and a friend of his. So off he trotted, dismounting at the garden gate. Firmino had left early for Arribada, where he was working on Senhor Esteves' wine press, but Firmino's wife came bustling out of the kitchen, plump and glowing, with two very grubby children clinging to her skirts. The Nobleman tenderly kissed their sticky cheeks.

'What a delicious smell of fresh-baked bread, Senhora! Just out of the oven, eh? Well, give my best wishes to Firmino and tell him not to forget: the Election is next Sunday and I'm counting on his vote. And tell him it's not just a question of a vote, it's a matter of friendship too.'

The woman bared her magnificent teeth in a large, generous smile:

'Oh, you needn't worry about that, sir! Firmino has already sworn, to the alderman no less, that everyone here is going to vote for the Nobleman, and those who don't vote out of love will be beaten into voting.'

The Nobleman shook her hand, and she, from the garden steps, with her two little ones still clutching her skirts, and with that same rapt smile on her face, followed the trail of dust left by his horse, as if it were the retinue of some beneficent king.

And after other visits, to Cerejeira and Ventura da Chiche, he met with the same fervour, the same delighted smiles. 'Of course we'll vote for you, sir. That goes without saying. Even if it meant voting against the Government!' At Manuel da Adega's tavern, a group of workers were drinking and talking loudly, their jackets on the benches beside them; the Nobleman drank with them, laughing and genuinely enjoying the cheap wine and the hubbub. The oldest man, a swarthy, toothless grotesque, his face more shrivelled than a prune, enthusiastically thumped the bar, 'You have here the kind of Nobleman, boys, who when he finds a poor soul on the road with a bad leg, lends him his horse and walks more than a league with him, like he did with Solha. This is a Nobleman we can be proud of!' And loud cheers echoed round the room. When Gonçalo got back on his horse, they all gathered about him like ardent vassals, who, at a wave of his hand, would rush off to vote—or to kill!

At Tomás Pedra's house, Grandma Ana Pedra, very old and frail and almost crippled, burst into tears because her Tomás was away in the olive grove when the Nobleman had chosen to visit. 'It's like being visited by a saint!'

'Hardly, Senhora Pedra. I'm a sinner, a great sinner!'

Sitting very bent in a low chair, with strands of straggling white hair escaping from beneath her headscarf and down her gaunt, lined, hairy face, she slapped her bony knee:

'Certainly not, sir! Anyone who showed such charity to Casco's son deserves to be placed on an altar!'

The Nobleman went on his way, laughing, planting loud kisses on the small, grimy cheeks of children, clasping hands as coarse and gnarled as roots, lighting his cigarette at open fires, and chatting familiarly about aches and pains and who was in love with whom. Then, in the heat and dust of the road, he thought, 'It's odd, these people really seem to like me!'

At four o'clock, by which time he was exhausted, he decided to stop and take the cooler route back to the Tower via Bica Santa. And he had just passed the hamlet of Cerdal, when, on a sharp bend in the road, next to a grove of holm oaks, he almost ran into Dr Júlio, who was also on horseback and also making a tour of the district, wearing an alpaca jacket and bathed in sweat under his green sunshade. They both reined in their horses and greeted each other in friendly terms:

'Good to see you, Senhor Dr Júlio.'

'Likewise, Senhor Gonçalo Ramires.'

'Out electioneering?'

Dr Júlio shrugged and said:

'What do you expect, sir, since others got me into this. But you know how it will end. It will end with me, on Sunday, voting for you, sir.'

The Nobleman laughed, and both men leaned over to shake hands with genuine pleasure and respect.

'What do you think of this heat, then, Senhor Dr Júlio?'

'Horrendous, Senhor Gonçalo Ramires. And such a bore too!'
Thus the Nobleman spent that week visiting his electorate—'the
great and the small'. And two days before the Election, on a Friday
evening, when the weather had turned a little cooler, he set off for
Oliveira, where, on the previous day, André Cavaleiro had arrived
after his long and much-discussed sojourn in Lisbon.

At the Casa dos Cunhais, as soon as he had jumped down from
the caleche, he was infuriated to learn from João the porter that
the Lousada sisters were upstairs, visiting Senhora Dona Graça.

'Have they been here long?'

'A good half hour, sir.'

Gonçalo crept surreptitiously up to his room, thinking, 'The
shameless hussies! André returns to Oliveira, and immediately
they're on the snoop.' He had already washed and changed into his
grey suit when Barrolo appeared, breathless and beaming, in his
frockcoat and top hat, his cheeks even pinker than usual.

'Well, aren't you the dandy!' said Gonçalo.

'It's like magic!' cried Barrolo, after embracing Gonçalo, and
then embracing him again with unexpected fervour. 'I just this
minute sent you a telegram, asking you to come.'

'Why?'

Barrolo stifled a laugh, which lit up his plump face:

'Why? Oh, nothing. I mean, because of the Election—which is,
of course, the day after tomorrow! Cavaleiro arrived yesterday, in
fact, I've just come back from seeing him. I was at the palace with
the bishop, and then I went over to see Cavaleiro. He's looking
wonderful. He's trimmed his moustache and seems younger somehow. And he brings news, great news!'

Barrolo rubbed his hands so gleefully, his eyes and face shining
with such pleasure, that the Nobleman eyed him curiously:

'Listen, Barrolo, have you got some good news to tell me?'

Barrolo stepped back and roundly denied this, like someone
slamming a door shut. Him? No! He knew of no such news, only
that the Election was imminent, and the vote on his estate was going to be phenomenal!

'Ah,' murmured Gonçalo. 'And Gracinha?'

'Gracinha doesn't know anything either.'

'What do you mean, man? I simply wanted to know how she is.'

'Oh, she's with the Lousada sisters. The vile creatures have been here forever, talking about the bazaar being held at the new poorhouse, another of those wretched bazaars. Anyway, Gonçalo, are you staying until Sunday?'

'No, I have to go back tomorrow to the Tower.'

'Oh!'

'It's the day of the Election, man, and I need to be at home, in my own parish, with my parishioners.'

'That's a shame,' muttered Barrolo. 'Because then you'd have found out at the same time as the Election. And I would have put on a tremendous supper.'

'Found out what?'

Barrolo fell silent, still beaming, his cheeks ablaze. Then, swaying from one foot to the other, he stammered:

'Found out ... oh, nothing. The result, the count. And then feasting and fireworks! I'll be opening a barrel of wine at Murtosa.'

Then Gonçalo put his arm around Barrolo's shoulder and said cheerfully:

'Come on, Barrolinho, out with it. You've obviously got some good news to tell your brother-in-law.'

Barrolo slipped from his grasp, protesting loudly. What a persistent fellow he was! There was nothing to tell. André hadn't said a word.

'Fine,' concluded the Nobleman, certain that some pleasant mystery was in the air. 'Let's go downstairs, then. And if those bloodsuckers are still there, send in the butler to tell Gracinha, loud and clear, that I have arrived and wish to speak to her at once in my room. One shouldn't be polite to such monsters.'

Barrolo said hesitantly:

'The bishop seems to like them. And he was very charming to me just now.'

As they were going down the stairs, however, they heard the sound of the piano and Gracinha's lilting voice. Free of the Lousada sisters, she was singing an old patriotic song from the Vendée, which, when they were children, she and Gonçalo used to sing with great emotion, whenever they felt filled with a noble, romantic love for the Bourbons and the Stuarts:

> *Monsieur d'Charette a dit à ceux d'Ancenis:*
> *'Mes amis!'*
> *Monsieur d'Charette a dit à ceux d'Ancenis …*

Gonçalo slowly pushed aside the door curtain and completed the line, holding one arm aloft like a flag, '*Mes amis, le roi va ramener la Fleur de Lys!*'

Gracinha jumped up from the piano stool in surprise.

'We weren't expecting you! I assumed you'd spend the Election at the Tower. Is everything all right there?'

'Yes, everything's fine, but I've been terribly busy. I had to finish off my Novella, and then there were voters to be visited.'

Barrolo, who kept pacing about the room, interrupted them, wearing the same repressed smile:

'Do you know, Gracinha, ever since he arrived, he's been seething with curiosity. He thinks I have some good news, some important news to tell him. But I don't know anything, apart from the fact that the Election is on Sunday. Isn't that so, Gracinha?'

Gonçalo very gravely pinched his sister's chin:

'Come on, tell me.'

She smiled, blushing. She didn't know anything … only about the Election.

'Come on, out with it!

'Really, I don't know anything. It's just some nonsense of José's.'

Then, seeing her wan, wavering smile, which threatened to confess all, Barrolo could contain himself no longer and he exploded like a mortar. All right, yes, there was some big news, but André, who'd brought it with him from Lisbon, hot off the press so to speak, wanted to be the one to surprise Gonçalo.

'So I really can't tell you. I promised André. Gracinha knows, because I told her yesterday, but she can't tell you either, she promised too. Only André can tell you. He's joining us after supper, and then the bomb will burst, because it is a bomb, and a big one too.'

Despite his intense curiosity, Gonçalo merely shrugged and murmured:

'I know. It's an inheritance, isn't it? Well, here's fifteen *tostões*, Barrolo, for being the bearer of good news!'

During supper, though, and afterwards, in the living room, while they were drinking coffee and Gracinha was playing more old patriotic songs, Jacobite ones this time, in praise of the Stuarts, Gonçalo couldn't wait for Cavaleiro to appear. He wasn't even concerned that there might be a degree of bitterness and concealed contempt in that meeting. All his rage against Cavaleiro, ignited on that painful afternoon outside the gazebo and ruminated over at the Tower for many a long, tormenting day, had gradually dissipated after his touching conversation with his sister, on the morning of his historic fight at Grainha. Shedding pure, honest tears, Gracinha had sworn to remain reserved and withdrawn. In leaving Oliveira, André had also shown praiseworthy resistance to the emotions or the sheer vanity that had led him astray. Besides, he could not again break with Cavaleiro, since the very public reconciliation that had brought Cavaleiro back into the bosom of the family was still the subject of much gossip and speculation in Oliveira. And what was the point of all that anger and hurt? No amount of bluster on his part would wipe out the evil that had taken place in the gazebo, if, that is, it did take place. Thus all his anger at André had dissolved in his light, gentle soul, where feelings, especially those of the darker, heavier variety, always vanished like clouds in a summer sky.

However, when, at around nine o'clock, Cavaleiro came into the room, looking languid and magnificent, his moustache trimmer but more ornately curled, a strident red cravat puffing out above his puffed-up chest, Gonçalo felt a renewed aversion for all that hollow insolence, and when Cavaleiro folded him in an extravagantly tender embrace, he could only bring himself to pat his old friend rather feebly on the back. While André played with his pale gloves and leaned idly back in the armchair that Barrolo fondly brought over for him, and kept up a constant chatter about Lisbon and Cascais—such fun!—and about games of bridge and the

Parade and the King, Gonçalo was reliving that afternoon outside the gazebo, the coarse, pleading words spoken by those bold moustachioed lips, and he fell silent, as if turned to stone, nervously chewing on his burned-out cigar. Gracinha, on the other hand, remained calm and attentive, her cheeks pale and not aflame with blushes, with no tell-tale fumbling over words or gestures, she was merely rather serious, in a rehearsed and practised way. Then André remarked casually that he'd be going back to Lisbon after the Election, because his uncle Reis Gomes, José Ernesto and other cruel friends were loading onto his shoulders all the work involved in the new administrative reforms.

Although he and Gracinha were separated only by a small rug, it was as if, between them, a very deep ditch had been dug, into which their summer romance had plunged to its death, and on their faces there was not a flicker of that past passion. And Gonçalo, quietly content with this appearance, finally managed to get up out of the chair in which he had turned to stone, light his cigar on the candle on the piano, and enquire after mutual Lisbon friends. According to Cavaleiro, they were all longing for him to arrive.

'Oh, yes, I met up with Castanheiro too. He's absolutely thrilled with your Novella. It seems that, as an historical reconstruction, nothing can compare, not even the work of Herculano or Rebelo. Castanheiro actually prefers your epic realism to Flaubert's in *Salammbô*. Anyway, as I say, he's thrilled. And we, of course, are burning for that sublime work to be published.'

The Nobleman blushed deeply, murmuring, 'What nonsense!' Then he brushed past the armchair in which André was sitting and gently patted André's broad shoulder:

'You've been much missed, old man. I thought of you when I rode past Corinde the other day.'

Barrolo, scarlet-cheeked and bouncing restlessly about the room with a mute, eager smile ever on his lips, kept looking now at Cavaleiro and now at Gonçalo, until, at last, he could stand it no longer:

'Right, that's enough of a prologue, let's get to the big surprise, André. I've been bursting to tell him all evening. I promised to say nothing though, and I kept my word, but I can't hold it in any longer.

So let's get on with it. And you, Gonçalinho, prepare to give me those fifteen *tostões*.'

Gonçalo's curiosity bubbled into life again, but he merely smiled nonchalantly and said:

'Yes, apparently you have some very good news for me.'

Cavaleiro still didn't move from his armchair, but merely stretched his arms.

'It's a very simple matter, nothing could be more natural really. Senhora Dona Graça knows already, of course. It's not such a big surprise. As I say, nothing could be more legitimate, more natural!'

Impatient now, Gonçalo cried:

'Out with it, then. Speak.'

Cavaleiro droned indolently on. The really surprising thing was that no one had thought of doing something so very deserved, so very right, before. Wouldn't Senhora Dona Graça agree?'

Furious, Gonçalo roared:

'For heaven's sake, what is it?'

Cavaleiro rose slowly from the armchair, tugged at his shirt cuffs and, standing silently before Gonçalo, puffing out his chest, he began gravely, almost officially:

'My Uncle Reis Gomes and José Ernesto both came up with this most natural of ideas; they then told the King, and the King approved. Indeed, he approved so heartily that he wanted to claim the idea as his own and wished he had thought of it first. So now it is the King's idea alone. The King, then, thought, as did we, that one of the foremost Noblemen of Portugal, if not *the* foremost, should have a title that would confirm the illustrious antiquity of his House, and confirm too, the superior qualities of the person who now represents that House. That is why, my dear Gonçalo, I can today announce, almost on the King's behalf, that you are to be made Marquis de Treixedo.'

'Bravo! Bravo!' thundered Barrolo, applauding wildly. 'You'd better give me those fifteen *tostões* now, Marquis!'

Gonçalo's slender face flushed scarlet. He felt instantly that the title was a gift from Cavaleiro not to the head of the House of Ramires, but to Gracinha's complaisant, obliging brother. He also felt the inappropriateness of it, that an empty title, published in the Government lists, should be bestowed on the head of a family ten centuries old—the mother of whole dynasties, one of the founders of the Kingdom, more than thirty of whose menfolk had died in armed battle—as if he were a mere nouveau-riche shopkeeper who had bought a few votes. He nodded to Cavaleiro, who was expecting effusive cries of gratitude and embraces. 'Marquis de Treixedo, hmm. How elegant, how nice!' Gonçalo said. Then, with a smile that was, at once, amused and amazed, 'But on what authority does the King make me Marquis de Treixedo?'

Cavaleiro looked up, offended and surprised:

'On what authority? Well, the authority he has over us all, as King of Portugal, which, praise God, he still is!'

And Gonçalo, very simply, with no show of pomp or pride, and still smiling that faintly amused smile, said:

'Forgive me, Andrezinho. My ancestors had a house in Treixedo long before there were any kings of Portugal, long before there was a Portugal. I approve of exchanges of noble gifts between great Noblemen, but it is up to the oldest of them to begin. The King has an estate near Beja, I believe, called Roncão. Well, tell the King that I take enormous pleasure in making him Marquis do Roncão.'

Barrolo stood open-mouthed and uncomprehending, his fat cheeks sagging and deflated. From her place on the sofa, Gracinha, blushing furiously, glowed with pleasure at that show of pride which so chimed with her own and brought her still closer to her beloved brother. André Cavaleiro was clearly furious, but he bowed his head in ironic submission, merely murmuring, 'Fine! To each his own.'

Then the butler came in bearing the tea tray.

And on Sunday, it was the Election.

Still distrustful, still maintaining a superstitious reserve, the Nobleman wanted to spend the day very much alone, almost hidden away, and on the Saturday, while all his friends in Vila Clara, and even those in Oliveira, assumed he would be ensconced at the Casa dos Cunhais, and in constant, frantic communication with the governor, he, instead, got on his horse at dusk and trotted quietly off to Santa Ireneia.

Barrolo (still shaken by Gonçalo's absurd reaction, so insulting to Cavaleiro and to the King!) had been given the task of sending telegrams to the Tower as the votes came in, as soon as the governor was notified. And with noisy zeal, immediately after mass, a constant stream of tireless servants went to and fro between the Casa dos Cunhais and the former monastery of São Domingos. In the dining room, Gracinha, assisted by Father Soeiro, lovingly copied out in a very round hand all the telegrams sent by Cavaleiro, who occasionally added an affectionate note, 'Everything going swimmingly!' 'Victory is in sight.' 'Congratulations all round!'

The telegram boy hobbled incessantly back and forth along the road from Vila Clara to the Tower. And each time, Bento would burst into the library, crying, 'Another telegram, sir.' And Gonçalo, seated nervously at his desk with a huge pot of tea before him, the tray already filled with half-smoked cigarettes, would read out the telegram to Bento, who would then run, cheering, down the corridor, to carry the good news to Rosa.

And so it went on until around eight o'clock, when the Nobleman finally agreed to have some supper—knowing that he had scored a magnificent victory. What impressed him, on rereading the telegrams, was the affectionate enthusiasm of those influential people, some of whom he had barely spoken to, and who were transforming the Election process almost into an act of love. The whole parish of Bravais had marched to the church, in closed ranks like an army, with José Casco at their head, bearing an enormous flag, between two clamorous drums. The Viscount de Rio-Manso had ridden into the forecourt of the Ramilde church in his carriage, accompanied by his granddaughter dressed all in white, followed by an imposing line of *char-à-bancs* crammed with voters shaded from the sun by leafy branches. In Finta, every farm was deserted, with the women decked out in all their gold jewellery, the boys with a flower tucked behind one ear, hurrying to elect the Nobleman, accompanied by strumming guitars, as if on a holy pilgrimage. And outside Pintainho's tavern, opposite the church, the people of Veleda, Riosa and Cercal had erected an arch made of boxwood, with a sign written in red letters on a piece of cloth, 'Long live our Ramires, the finest of men!'

Then, while he was having his supper, one of the gardeners returned from Vila Clara in a state of high excitement, describing the joy in the streets, with bands playing, flags flying outside the club, and, above the door at the Town Hall, a picture of Gonçalo being cheered by the crowd.

Gonçalo quickly drank his coffee. Out of shyness and afraid of those celebrating crowds, he hadn't dared go into Vila Clara to see what was happening. Instead, he lit a cigar and went out onto the balcony to breathe in that sweet, festive night so full of noise and lights, and all in his honour too. When he opened the door, though, he almost drew back in alarm. The Tower was lit up! A glow emanated from inside the deep arrow slits, through the black iron bars, and around the very top, above the old battlements, there was a crown of lights. This was a surprise prepared, with delicious secrecy, by Bento and Rosa and the gardeners, who were all now standing in the darkness beneath the balcony, contemplating their work, which was lighting up the tranquil sky. Hearing muffled footsteps and Rosa clearing her throat, Gonçalo called gaily down from the balcony:

'Bento! Rosa! Is anyone there?'

There was a small explosion of laughter, then Bento's white jacket emerged out of the shadows.

'Did you want something, sir?'

'No, I just wanted to say thank you. This is your work, isn't it? The lights look lovely, so beautiful. Thank you, Bento. Thank you, Rosa! Thank you, boys! It must look really superb from far off.' Bento, however, was not satisfied with those dim lights. To really stand out, the Tower needed gas lights. It was so high, though, and the terrace at the top was vast.

Gonçalo felt a sudden desire to climb up to that vast terrace. He hadn't been inside the Tower since he was a student, and he had never liked the interior, so dark and entirely built of granite, as bare and silent and cold as a tomb, and on the ground floor, there were those iron trapdoors that led down to the dungeons. Now, though, the lights in the arrow slits were breathing warmth and life into that last remnant of the Castle of Ordonho Mendes. It would, he thought, be interesting to be up there among the battlements, higher than on his dining room balcony, and to absorb that scattering of sympathetic murmurings rolling in from the various parishes and rising up to him through the night like incense. He pulled on a jacket and went down to the kitchen. Greatly amused, Bento and Joaquim the gardener immediately grabbed a couple of large lanterns, and together the three of them went into the orchard, through the low, squat postern door, and began to climb the narrow stone steps, polished and worn smooth by many iron soles.

Any memory of precisely what position that tower had occupied in the complicated fortifications of Honra de Santa Ireneia had been lost centuries ago. It was definitely not (according to Father Soeiro) the barbican or the keep, where any treasure was kept, along with the archives and the precious sacks of spices from the Orient, so perhaps, obscure and nameless, it had merely defended one particular corner of the wall, on the side where the castle looked out over the cultivated fields and the elm trees growing along the banks of the stream. Having outlived the other loftier constructions and been incorporated into the beautiful palace that was later erected on the ruins of the sombre Afonsine castle, and which had dominated Santa Ireneia during the Avis Dynasty, it was still linked by a pale, elegant arcade to the Italianate palace into which Vicente Ramires had transformed the Manueline palace after his successful campaigns in Castile; alone in the orchard, but looming over the mansion that had slowly been built after the palace burned down during the reign of King José, and definitely the last part of the castle to have rung to the clank of weapons and the tread of Ramires soldiers, it connected all those different ages, and its eternal stones somehow maintained the unity of that long lineage. That is why the ordinary people referred to it vaguely as 'The Tower of Dom Ramires'. And still under the influence of the ancestors and the times he had revived in his Novella, Gonçalo felt a new respect for its vastness, its strength, its steep steps, its thick walls, so thick that, in the dim light of the little oil lamps with which Bento had brought them back to life, the arrow slits resembled corridors. He stopped on each of the three storeys, peering curiously, and yet almost familiarly, into the bare, echoing rooms, with their vast paved floors and dark, vaulted ceilings, their stone benches, the strange hole in the middle of the room, as round as a well, the smoke-stained walls and the rings that had once held the torches. Up above, on the vast terrace illuminated by the lines of lanterns fixed to the battlements, Gonçalo, turning up his collar in the cooler air, had the sudden overwhelming sense that, in a fatherly way, he somehow dominated the whole province, simply because of his Tower's sovereign height and age, older by far than the province and the Kingdom. He walked slowly round the battlements as far as the lookout point, where an oil lamp placed on a wicker chair placed opposite an arrow slit rather spoiled the feudal atmosphere. In the soft, slightly misty sky, a few dull stars were shining. Down below, the garden, the wide fields and the dense woods merged into the shadows. In the silence and darkness, though, sometimes as far away as Bravais, distant fireworks flickered. A yellowish, smoky glow heading towards Finta was probably a torchlit procession. A faint, tremulous light could be seen on the top of the tall church of Veleda. Other lights filtered through the trees, stippling the old archway of the monastery in Santa Maria de Craquede. Occasionally, the faint sound of drums rose up from the dark earth. And what the lights and torches and muffled drumming signified was that ten parishes were lovingly celebrating the Nobleman of the Tower, who received their love and homage atop his tower, surrounded by silence and darkness.

Bento and Joaquim had gone down to refill the guttering lamps in the arrow slits. Alone and having finished his cigar, Gonçalo resumed his slow patrol of the battlements, unable to shake off the thought that had been dogging him during the whole of that strangely troubling Sunday. He was popular! In all those villages caught in the long shadow of the Tower, the Nobleman of that Tower was popular! And this knowledge did not fill him with joy or pride—rather, in the quiet of the night, it filled him with confusion and regret. Ah, if only he had known, how he would have walked, head held high, arms outstretched, alone and confident and smiling, towards all that affection so freely given. But, no, he had always believed that those villages were utterly indifferent to him, despite his ancient name, that he was just the lad who had returned from Coimbra to live quietly off his rents and go for the occasional rural ride. He had never imagined that what he assumed to be their perfectly natural indifference would provide him with enough votes to enter politics, where he would earn with his intelligence what the old Ramires men had merely inherited—money and power. That's why he had so eagerly grasped Cavaleiro's hand, the hand of the governor who, as his good friend, could show him off and promote him as the right man, the Government's favourite, the best of the best, to whom the parishes should, one Sunday, give him their votes.

And in his impatience to gain that favour, he had smothered the memory of bitter injuries; before the astonished eyes of Oliveira he had embraced the man he had hated for years, whom he had mocked and criticised in public and in the newspapers; he had facilitated the resurrection of feelings that should have been left forever buried and had plunged the person he loved most, his poor, weak little sister, into moral misery and confusion. So many stupid, harmful blunders and to what end? To steal a handful of votes that ten parishes would have rushed joyfully to give him anyway, cheering and letting off fireworks, if he had merely asked them.

That was it. It was that lack of confidence, that craven lack of confidence in himself that had been the bane of his life since he was a schoolboy. It was that same wretched lack of confidence, which, only weeks before, had made him flee—trembling and cursing his own cowardice—from a shadow, a raised stick, a jeering laugh from a tavern window. Finally, one day, at a bend in the road, he had taken a step forward, raised his whip and discovered his own strength! And now he had gone among the people, shyly clasping the governor's powerful hand, because he thought himself so unpopular, only to find that he was, it seemed, hugely popular. How foolish he had been and how that ignorance had soiled his life!

Bento had still not returned, busily making sure that all the arrow slits were properly illuminated. Gonçalo threw down his cigar end and, hands in his jacket pocket, gazed absentmindedly up at the stars. The mist had thinned and almost vanished, bright lights were shining in that now much deeper sky. From the stars and the skies came the sense of the infinite, of eternity, that so pierces souls unaccustomed to looking at them. The wonder and horror of those eternal vastnesses, beneath which our low, dark human dust vainly struts its hour, fleetingly passed through Gonçalo's soul. In the distance, a last firework flickered, then was gone in the serene darkness. The little lights on the church in Veleda and the archway of Santa Maria de Craquede were also dying. The remote murmur of music had stopped too, submerged in the deep silence of the sleeping fields. The day of victory was ending, as brief as those lights and fireworks. And standing there motionless, Gonçalo was pondering the value of the victory he had so longed for and for which he had so abased himself. He was a deputy! The deputy for Vila Clara, like Sanches Lucena before him. And given that tiny, trivial result, all his desperate, unscrupulous efforts seemed not so much immoral as risible. A deputy! Whatever for? To have lunch at the Hotel Bragança, to take a cab up the hill to São Bento, and to sit at his desk inside that grubby convent scribbling a letter to his tailor, yawning at the inanity of the men and ideas around him, and, either in silence or else bleating, distractedly following all the other parliamentary sheep, having deserted the identical flock led by Brás Vitorino. Yes, perhaps one day, through low intrigue, by grovelling to some high-up personage or the high-up personage's wife, by smiling and making promises to newspaper editors, or giving some fiery speech, he might become a minister. And then what? The same cab going up the hill to São Bento, with the post boy behind him on his white nag, the ill-fitting uniform for official occasions, and the toadying smiles of amanuenses in the dark corridors of the ministry, and mud being flung at him from every opposition newspaper. Ah, what a dull, uninteresting life, in comparison with the other full, proud lives pulsating beneath those twinkling stars! While he, the new deputy for Vila Clara, was there in his overcoat, clutching his miserable little triumph, Thinkers were coming up with a complete explanation for the universe; Artists were producing works of eternal beauty; Reformers were perfecting social harmony; Saints were in their saintly fashion improving souls; Physiologists were easing human suffering; Inventors were improving the wealth of nations; magnificent Adventurers were dragging whole worlds out of their sterility and silence ... Ah, they were real men, who truly and deliciously lived life to the full, tirelessly shaping humanity into fairer, more beautiful shapes. Oh to be like them, those superhumans! Did such supreme actions require Genius, the gift which, like the ancient flame, descends from God onto the chosen one's head? No! Only a clear understanding of human realities and a strong will.

And the Nobleman of the Tower, stockstill on the top of his Tower, between the brilliantly starry sky and the pitch-black earth, thought long and hard about the Superior Life, until, swept away, as if all the energy of his long lineage were being channelled through the Tower directly into his heart, he imagined himself finally setting off to create a vast, fruitful life, in which he would enjoy the sheer joy of living, a new life that would add new lustre to the old lustre of the family name and gild it with pure gold, and one that would earn him the praise of his whole country, because he had done all he could to serve it.

Bento appeared at the door, carrying a lantern:

'Are you staying up here much longer, sir?'

'No, Bento, the party's over.'

At the beginning of December, *The Tower of Dom Ramires* appeared in the first issue of *Annals*. And every newspaper, even those supporting the opposition, praised 'this masterly study (in the words of *A Tarde*), which, while revealing the talents of both a scholar and an artist, continues, in a more modern and colourful style, the work of Herculano and Rebelo, namely, the moral and social recreation of our old, heroic Portugal'. After the Christmas celebrations, which he spent happily at the Casa dos Cunhais, helping Gracinha make cod rissoles from a sublime recipe given them by Father José

Vicente of Finta, his friends in Oliveira, the lads from the club and the Café da Arcada, held a banquet in honour of the new deputy for Vila Clara in the Town Hall, which they adorned with decorative box-trees and flags; among the guests was Cavaleiro, wearing his Grand Cross; and the Baron das Marges, who presided over the meal, saluted 'this excellent young man, who soon, from the seat of power, might well lift this valiant country out of the mire with the vigour and courage proper to his noble lineage.'

In the middle of January, on a wild, rainy night, Gonçalo left for Lisbon, and throughout the winter, his name was constantly being mentioned in the gossip columns of *Carnet-Mondain* and *High-Life*, in any reports of suppers, social gatherings, pigeon-shoots or hunting trips with the King, down to the smallest detail of his elegant life, so much so that the Barrolos took out a subscription to the *Diário Ilustrado* hoping to find out when he would next be seen strolling down the Avenue. At the club in Vila Clara, João Gouveia would shrug and mutter, 'The fellow's turned out to be nothing but a dandy.' However, towards the end of April, a piece of news shook Vila Clara, and alarmed the boys in the Café da Arcada in quiet Oliveira, and so shocked Gracinha—who was in Amarante at the time with Barrolo—that they both set off for Lisbon that very night, while at the Tower, it caused Rosa to slump down on the stone bench in the kitchen, her face bathed in uncomprehending tears, sobbing:

'Ah, my dear boy, my own dear boy—I'll never see him again!'

Without a word to anyone, almost secretively, Gonçalo Mendes Ramires had leased a huge tract of land in Macheque in Zambia, mortgaged his historic Treixedo estate, and was setting off with Bento for Africa at the beginning of June on the steamship *Portugal*.

XII

Four years passed as lightly and swiftly over the old Tower as a flight of birds.

One warm, late-September afternoon, Gracinha—who had arrived the day before from Oliveira accompanied by Father Soeiro—was reclining on the wicker sofa on the balcony of the dining room, still wearing a voluminous white apron lent to her by Bento, so large that it covered her all the way up to her neck. She had been wearing it as she came and went in the house, helped by Rosa and by Crispola's daughter, breathlessly tidying and cleaning, with such pleasure and vigour that she herself had been banging books together in the library, shaking off four quiet years of dust. Barrolo had been busy too, overseeing the work being carried out on the stables, which the valiant mare from the encounter in Grainha would soon be sharing with an English mare, a half-blood, bought in London. Father Soeiro had also been zealously dusting the archives. And even Pereira, their excellent tenant, had been chivvying along the two gardeners who were putting the finishing touches to the now immaculate vegetable garden, complete with a melon patch, a strawberry patch, and two new paths, both edged with rosebushes and sheltered by an arbour covered in dense vines.

To everyone's undisguised joy, the ancient Tower was being spruced up, because on Sunday, after four years in Africa, Gonçalo was finally returning home.

As Gracinha lay there on the sofa in her old white apron, smiling thoughtfully out at the silent garden, at the sky turning red over the Valverde hills, she was looking back over those four years, from the morning when, trembling and biting back tears, she had embraced Gonçalo in his cabin on board ship. Four years had passed, and nothing had changed in the world, not at least in her small world, which comprised the Casa dos Cunhais and the Tower, and life had rolled on, as uneventfully as a slow river flowing through some desert place. Gonçalo was somewhere in Africa, and his letters, though few and far between, were always cheerful and full of the enthusiasm of the empire-builder; and she was at home with Barrolo, and their day-to-day routine was so quiet and unvarying that the supper parties they gave were positively intoxicating—they'd get together with the Mendonças, the Marges, the Colonel from the 7th regiment and a few other friends, and later, in the living room, open up two card tables to play ombre or Boston whist.

And in the gentle flow of life, the dark torment of her heart had very gently, almost imperceptibly, dissipated. Even she could not understand now how a feeling—which, at the height of her passion, she used to justify to herself (indeed almost sanctify) as unique and eternal—could disappear like that, unobtrusively and painlessly, leaving only a faint sense of remorse, a vanished longing, as well as bemusement and confusion, so that all that remained of the fiery blaze was a very fine layer of ash. Events had rolled by, like a gusting wind over a field, and she had rolled along with them, borne aloft as indifferently as a dry leaf.

Immediately after the last Christmas spent with Gonçalo, André, who had gone with them to midnight mass and shared a New Year's Eve meal with them afterwards, returned to Lisbon to carry out the 'reforms' he was always complaining about. In the growing silence between them, there was now the chill of abandonment. And when André came back to Oliveira to his role as governor, she left for Amarante, where Barrolo's saintly mother had fallen ill, succumbing to a combination of anaemia and old age, which in May, carried her off to our Lord.

June had seen Gonçalo's emotional departure for Africa, and on the deck, among all the noise and the luggage, she had encountered André, who had arrived from Oliveira only days before and was full of cheerful talk about the marriage of Mariquinhas Marges. Barrolo had decided to have some major work done on their house in Largo d'El-Rei, and so they spent all that summer at their Murtosa estate, which Gracinha had chosen because of the lovely woods around the house and the tall convent walls. Barrolo blamed this new solitude for her melancholy, her thinness, and the way she would often stare wearily off into space while sitting on the mossy benches under the trees, a novel forgotten on her lap. In September, hoping to distract her and help restore her to health with some sea bathing, Barrolo rented Comendador Barros' elegant house on the coast. She did not once bathe in the sea or go down to the beach at the coolest time of day, the hour when everyone went to their beach huts or sat around on low chairs; only later, in the early evening, did she go for walks along the shoreline, accompanied by two huge greyhounds, a present from Manuel Duarte. One morning, at lunch, when he opened the newspaper, Barrolo started and cried out in astonishment. It was the unexpected fall of São Fulgêncio's government! André Cavaleiro had immediately sent a telegram offering his resignation. The same newspaper next informed them that Cavaleiro had left on 'a long and picturesque journey', the journey to Constantinople and Asia Minor he had spoken of during that supper at the Casa dos Cunhais. Gracinha opened an atlas and with one slow finger traced the route from Oliveira to Syria, over frontiers and mountains, already feeling that André had vanished over those bright horizons. She closed the atlas, thinking only, 'How people change!'

They returned to Oliveira on a rainy November Saturday and, sitting in the carriage, she felt the melancholy and chill of that grey sky seeping into her heart. On the Sunday, though, she woke to the lovely sun pouring in through her window. She wore a new hat to the eleven o'clock mass in the cathedral; then, on the way to Aunt Arminda's house, she glanced up at the governor's residence; another governor lived there now, Senhor Santos Maldonado, a fair-haired young man who played the piano.

The next spring, Barrolo, now obsessed with refurbishing things, decided to demolish the gazebo and build a much larger hothouse, complete with fountain and palm trees, and thus create 'a really elegant winter garden'.

The workers had begun to empty the gazebo, removing the old furniture that had been there since the days of Uncle Melchior: for two whole days, the divan lay in the garden, next to one of the box hedges, and Barrolo, who had no interest in that useless piece of junk with broken springs, did not even want it relegated to the attic along with other such detritus, and so he ordered it to be burned, along with some broken chairs, on a celebratory bonfire, on the night of Gracinha's birthday. That night, she had walked around the fire, watching. The faded fabric flared up instantly, while the heavy mahogany frame burned more slowly, giving off only a little light smoke, until all that was left were some smouldering embers, which gradually darkened into ashes.

One afternoon that same week, the Lousada sisters, their features grown darker and sharper, invaded the Casa dos Cunhais, and as soon as they were perched stiffly on the sofa, their bright, beady eyes glinting with malice, they launched into an account of the latest major scandal: Cavaleiro, in Lisbon, was conducting a brazen affair with the wife of the Count de São Romão, who owned land in Cabo Verde!

That night, she wrote a very long letter to Gonçalo, which began, 'We're all fine here, back in our usual routine ...' And life and its routine had indeed begun again, simple, continuous, uneventful, like a clear river flowing through some desert place.

Crispola's son peered round the French doors. He was the one who had stayed on at the Tower as an errand boy, but having long since grown out of that first yellow-buttoned jacket, he now wore the Nobleman's cast-offs and had a nascent fuzz of beard on his chin.

'Senhor António Vilalobos is downstairs with Senhor Gouveia and another gentleman, Videirinha, and they want to know if they can speak with you.'

'Senhor Vilalobos! Of course, have them come up. Show them out here onto the balcony!'

As Tító crossed the room, where two men from Oliveira were nailing down some new matting, he commented in loud, approving tones on 'the preparations for the party'. And when he appeared on the balcony, his face—now even more sunburned and thickly bearded—glowed with pleasure to find the Tower finally waking from the lassitude into which it had fallen, and which had made everything seem so sad and dim, even the fire in the kitchen stove.

'Forgive the invasion, cousin Graça, but we were just coming back from a walk to Bravais and we learned that you were here with Barrolo.'

'I'm delighted to see you, cousin António, and I'm the one who should apologise for receiving you in this rather dishevelled state, wearing this huge apron, but we've spent all day getting the house ready. And how have you been, Senhor Gouveia? I haven't seen you since Easter.'

Gouveia thanked Senhora Dona Graça. He had been quite well since Easter, apart from that wretched throat of his. He hadn't changed at all in those four years; he was still rather swarthy and thin, as if carved out of wood, and still very erect in his black frockcoat; the only change was perhaps his moustache, which had grown somewhat stained with nicotine.

'And what about the great man? When does he arrive?'

'On Sunday. We're all so excited. Won't you sit down Senhor Videirinha? Bring that wicker chair over here. We haven't quite finished sorting out the balcony yet.'

Immediately after the Election, Gonçalo had given Videirinha the promised easy and undemanding position, so that he would not neglect his guitar. He was a clerk at the administrator's office in Vila Clara, but still on familiar terms with his boss, who used him in all sorts of capacities, including that of nurse, and ordered him about rather abruptly, even when they were dining together at Gago's.

He shyly dragged the wicker chair nearer, placing it respectfully just behind his boss' chair. Then, removing the black gloves he always wore now to emphasise his new position, he explained that the train arrived at Craquede at ten forty, always assuming there were no delays. But perhaps, if Gonçalo had a lot of luggage, he would be getting off at Corinde.

'I doubt it,' said Gracinha. 'Anyway, José intends leaving early tomorrow morning to meet him at the junction in Lamelo.'

'We won't do that,' said Titó, who was leaning on the balustrade. 'Our little group will go to Craquede, which is more or less part of the family estate, there should be fewer people around when we cheer him off the train. So he's not staying long in Lisbon, then, cousin?'

'He's been there since Sunday. That's when he arrived from Paris on the Sud-Express. And he was given an amazing reception, really amazing. I received a letter yesterday from Maria Mendonça, a long letter describing ...'

'What? Maria Mendonça is in Lisbon?'

'Yes, she's been there since the end of August, staying with Dona Ana Lucena.'

João Gouveia immediately sat up in his chair, betraying a curiosity he had clearly long been wanting to satisfy:

'That's true, Senhora Dona Graça! It seems that Dona Ana Lucena has bought a house in Lisbon and is busy fitting it out. Is that what you've heard too, Senhora Don Graça?'

Gracinha had heard nothing, but it seemed only natural really, given that Dona Ana spent most of her time in Lisbon now and very little time at Feitosa with its lovely garden.

'She's obviously going to remarry!'cried Gouveia with great conviction. 'If she's furnishing a house, that means she intends to marry. It's only natural. She wants a position in society. After all, she's been widowed for four years now, and ...'

Gracinha smiled, but Titó, who was slowly scratching his beard, wanted to know more of Maria Mendonça's letter, describing Gonçalo's arrival.

'Indeed,' said Gracinha. 'She says she was there at the Rossio Station, and Gonçalo apparently looks really strong and healthy. But, cousin António, read the letter, read it out loud. It contains no secrets, and it's all about Gonçalo.'

She produced from her pocket a thick envelope, with a coat of arms on the wax seal. Cousin Maria, though, always wrote very quickly and in a terrible scrawl and sometimes the lines ran into each other. António might not be able to read it—and in fact Titó recoiled in horror at the sight of the four sheets of paper bristling with black lines, like a thorn bush. João Gouveia immediately offered to help, given his experience of deciphering reports written by village councillors. And if it contained no secrets ...

'No, there are no secrets,' Gracinha assured him, smiling.

'It's all about Gonçalo, like a newspaper report.'

Gouveia rather solemnly smoothed his moustache, then began: 'My dear Gracinha, Silva's seamstress says that the dress ...'

'No, no!' cried Gracinha. 'Start on the other page, at the top. Turn over.'

Gouveia commented in loud, jocular tones that one wouldn't really expect anything else in a letter between ladies; clothes were always the first thing to be mentioned, and yet there was Senhora Dona Graça assuring them that it was all about Gonçalo. These ladies and their fashions! She'd probably still be talking about clothes in the middle of the letter too. Then he began again on the next page, reading in slow, measured tones:

> You must be eager to know about the grand arrival of cousin Gonçalo. It was a truly brilliant occasion, like a reception given to royalty. More than forty of his friends came. And, of course, all the family were present, and if a revolution had broken out that morning, the Republicans would have been able to round up the cream of Portugal's oldest and best nobility right there in Rossio station. Among the ladies were cousin Chelas, Aunt Louredo, the two Esposende sisters (as well as Uncle Esposende, who, despite his rheumatism and the grape harvest, came all the way from his estate in Torres), and me. All the men had come, of course, and given that the Count de Arega, who is secretary to the King, and cousin Olhalvo, who is his majordomo, were both present, along with the Minister of the Navy and the Minister of Public Works, both of whom were at university with Gonçalo and are close friends, the other people at the station must have thought the King himself was about to arrive. The Sud-Express was forty minutes late, and so the scene at the station rather resembled a salon, with all the society people in attendance, with everyone in an excellent mood, and cousin Arega, who's always so charming and funny, issuing invitations to a supper (which he later gave) in honour of cousin Gonçalo. I went to the supper actually, and wore my new green dress, which looked very good ...

Gouveia cried triumphantly:

'Aha! What did I say? A dress. A green dress!'

'Keep reading, man!' roared Titó.

And the administrator, who was, in fact, genuinely interested, read on in lofty tones:

… my new green dress, which looked very good, apart from the skirt, which I found a little cumbersome. I think I was the first to spot cousin Gonçalo on the Sud-Express platform. You can't imagine how handsome he looked, and so much more manly too. The African sun hasn't burned his skin at all, it's still as white as ever. And he was so elegant, so well turned out! It just goes to show how civilised Africa is becoming, said cousin Arega, that must be the new fashion in loincloths in Macheque! As you can imagine, there were lots of hugs and kisses. Aunt Louredo even wept. Oh, and I was forgetting, the Viscount of Rio-Manso was there too, with his daughter, Rosinha. She caused quite a sensation, looking pretty as a picture in a dress by Redfern. Everyone asked me who she was, and the Count de Arega, of course, immediately wanted to be introduced. The Viscount wept too when he embraced Gonçalo. And to the amazement of the other people, we all trooped out of the station like a royal procession. But immediately there was a moment of drama. Suddenly, in the middle of that gathering of the crème de la crème, Gonçalo rushed off and fell into the arms of the little man wearing a cap with a badge on it, who was taking our tickets. The same old Gonçalo! Apparently, he had met the ticket collector when he arrived in Lourenço Marques, where the man had been trying to set himself up as a photographer. But I'm forgetting the best bit—Bento! You cannot imagine how magnificent Bento looked. He's let his side whiskers grow a little, and he was dressed like a fashion plate, in new clothes bought in London, and so dignified in his full-length travelling coat and yellow gloves. Bento was obviously pleased to see me at the station and, with tears in his eyes, he immediately asked after Senhora Dona Graça and Rosa. That night, José and I dined *en famille* with cousin Gonçalo at the Hotel Bragança, so that we could talk about the Tower and the Casa dos Cunhais. He had lots of interesting things to tell us about Africa. He's planning to write a book about it, and it seems that the estate is doing very well. In the few years he's been there, he's planted two thousand coconut palms as well as cocoa and rubber. And he has countless chickens. Apparently, a chicken in Macheque costs one *pataco*. Whereas here, in Lisbon, a chicken that's all skin and bone costs six *tostões*, and if it's got a bit of meat on it, then it's ten *tostões* if you're lucky. He's built a big house on the estate, near the river, with twenty windows and all painted in blue. And cousin Gonçalo says that he wouldn't sell the land even for eighty *contos*. To complete his happiness, he's found an excellent administrator. I'm not sure, though, that he's going back to Africa. I have my own plan for the future of cousin Gonçalo. You'll laugh when I tell you, and you'll never guess. In fact, I myself only had this inspired idea the night we dined at the hotel. The Viscount de Rio-Manso is staying at the Bragança too. When we went downstairs to the private room where we were to have supper, we met him and his granddaughter in the corridor. He immediately embraced Gonçalo again, like a fond father. And Rosinha blushed so deeply that even Gonçalo, despite being so excited and distracted, even he noticed and blushed a little as well. It seems that they know each other of old, something to do with a basket of roses, and that fate has, for years now, been slyly drawing them together. She really is a beauty. And so charming, so polite. She's only eleven years younger than him, and she would bring a huge dowry. About five hundred *contos* people say. There is the question of blood, of course, and hers, poor thing ... But as they say in heraldry, 'The king makes the shepherdess a queen'. And not only are the Ramires descended from kings, kings are descended from the Ramires. Now, moving on to less interesting matters ...

João Gouveia discreetly folded up the letter and handed it to Gracinha, praising Senhora Dona Maria Mendonça as an excellent reporter. Then, with a bow, he added:

'And if her predictions come true ...'

But Gracinha didn't believe it. These were Maria Mendonça's fantasies.

'Cousin António knows her well and knows what a matchmaker she is.'

'Yes, she even tried to marry *me* off,' boomed Titó, standing up.
'Imagine that, *me*! To Widow Pinho from the draper's shop.'

'Good heavens!'

However, Gouveia insisted with the air of a man of the world:

'But, Senhora Dona Graça, that would be far better than Gonçalo going back to Africa. I don't believe in those vast estates or in Africa. Indeed, I have a real horror of Africa. It's only ever brought us trouble. Best sell it off, I say. Africa is like those little, half-wild farms that people inherit from some aged aunt, in some back-of-beyond place, where you don't know anyone, where you can't even find a tobacconist's, just goatherds and fever all year round. Yes, best sell it off.'

Gracinha was slowly twining the belt of her apron round and round her fingers.

'What, sell something that cost so much to win, all those dangers at sea, all that loss of life and money?!'

Ready for a quarrel, Gouveia protested heatedly:

'What dangers? It was a simple matter of disembarking on the beach, planting a few wooden crosses and beating up some blacks. It's all lies, that stuff about the glories of Africa. You, of course, Senhora, are speaking as a noblewoman, the granddaughter of noblemen, whereas I am an economist. I'll go further ...'

His raised forefinger threatened more keen arguments.

To save Gracinha, Titó interrupted, saying:

'Listen, Gouveia, we're wasting cousin Graça's time. She has work to do. We can leave the question of Africa for later, after supper, when Gonçalo is here. Anyway, dear cousin, we will see you on Sunday in Craquede. The whole gang of us will be there. And I'll be the one letting off fireworks!'

But Gouveia, smoothing his bowler hat with the sleeve of his jacket, was still hoping to convert Senhora Dona Graça to reasonable ideas about colonial politics.

'We should sell it off, Senhora, sell it off!'

She smiled as if in agreement, then taking Videirinha's hand, who hesitated, his fingers stiff, she said:

'So, Senhor Videira, have you written some new verses for the *fado*?'

Blushing, Videirinha said that he had written a little something, another *fado*, to celebrate the Nobleman's return. Gracinha promised to learn it by heart and sing it at the piano.

'Thank you, Senhora. At your service, Senhora.'

'So we will see you on Sunday, cousin António. Hasn't it turned out to be a lovely afternoon?'

'Yes, on Sunday in Craquede, cousin.'

However, João Gouveia stopped as he was about to go through the French doors and struck his head with his hand:

'Forgive me, Senhora, I was forgetting. I received a letter from André Cavaleiro, from Figueira da Foz. He sends greetings to Barrolo and asks if Barrolo could let him have some of that *vinho verde* from Vidainhos. He wants to give it to another Africanist, the Count de São Romão. It seems the Countess would do anything for a good *vinho verde*!'

And the three friends filed out of the dining room, where Tító's booming voice was praising the colourful new matting. In the corridor, Videirinha peered into the library and saw the quill pens stuck in the old brass inkstand, which was waiting, gleaming, all alone, on the table bare of papers or books. Then Rosa appeared at the door to Gonçalo's room, her arms full of bed linen, a smile filling every line of her round, ruddy face, which was haloed by her large, very white chambray scarf. Tító patted her back affectionately.

'So, Rosa, time to start making those delicious specialities of yours again, eh?'

'God be praised, Senhor Dom António, I never thought I would see my beloved master again. In fact, I'd already decided that if I were buried here at Santa Ireneia before I saw the dear boy again, my soul would be sure to fly to Africa to visit him.'

Her little eyes sparkled, brimming with happy tears, and she continued resolutely down the corridor, carrying her bundle, which gave off a delicious scent of apples. Gouveia muttered, 'What a sad thought!' And the three friends went down to the courtyard where, to satisfy Tító's curiosity, they visited the stables.

'You see,' he said to Gouveia, who was lighting a cigar. 'Deny it if you like, but all this—furnishings, new stables, an English mare—was bought with African money.'

Gouveia shrugged.

'Let's wait and see what state his liver's in …'

At the main gate, Titó paused to pick a rose from the usual bush to adorn his velvet jacket, and, at that precise moment, Father Soeiro came in, returning from a walk to Bravais, carrying his large parasol and his breviary. They all fondly greeted the saintly, scholarly old man, who was a rare visitor now to the Tower.

'So, Father Soeiro, our man will be back with us on Sunday!'

Reverently, gratefully, the chaplain pressed one plump hand to his heart.

'God has been kind enough, in my old age, to grant me that one great favour, because I really wasn't expecting it. Such a harsh country for a man with such a delicate constitution …'

And in order to speak more of Gonçalo and to hear of their plans to meet him at Craquede, he walked with them to the bridge at Portela. João Gouveia was limping, tortured by the dreadful new boots he was wearing for the first time. The four friends rested for a moment on the fine stone bench that Gonçalo's father had ordered to be placed there, when he was Governor of Oliveira. From that pleasant spot, you could see the whole of Vila Clara—always so clean and white, albeit tinged with pink at that late hour—from the vast Convent of Santa Teresa to the new cemetery wall up on the hill, with its slender cypresses.

Far beyond the Valverde hills, towards the coast, the sun was setting among the clouds, as red as a piece of cooling molten metal, still lighting the windows of the town with glittering gold.

At the bottom of the valley, the tall ruins of Santa Maria de Craquede glowed brightly among the dense trees surrounding them. Beneath the arch of the bridge, the full river flowed noiselessly past, already drowsing in the shade of the poplars, where the birds were still singing. And at the bend in the road, behind the trees concealing the house, stood the old Tower, older than the village and the ruins and all the houses round about, encircled now by the dark flight of bats and gazing silently out over the plain and the sun on the sea, as it had every evening for the last thousand years, from the days of Count Ordonho Mendes.

A little boy carrying a long staff passed by, driving along two slow cows. Father José Vicente from Finta trotted by on his white mare and greeted Gouveia and his friend Father Soeiro, and gave thanks for the return of the Nobleman, for whom he had already prepared a fine basket of his moscatel grapes. Three hunters with a pack of hounds, crossed the road, and went down the lane that runs past the Mirandas' place.

A still, restful silence, as sweet as if it had come down from heaven, was descending upon all the houses in the countryside round about, where not a leaf was stirring in the transparently soft September air. The smoke from home fires drifted up, slow and light, from between sparse roof tiles. In the workshop of João the blacksmith, opposite the bridge, the forge glowed intensely red. The celebratory boom-boom of a drum could be heard over towards Bravais, growing louder and faster, keeping up a marching rhythm; then, when it reached a hilltop, it moved slowly off, growing fainter and fainter until it vanished among the trees in the depths of the valley.

Leaning back on the broad stone bench, his bowler hat on his knees, João Gouveia pointed in the direction of Bravais:

'I'm just remembering that passage from Gonçalo's Novella, when the Ramires are preparing to go to the aid of the Princesses and gathering their men together. It's just at this time of day, with the sound of beating drums, and it would have been right here too. "In the cool of the valley …" No, that's not it. "In the valley of Craquede …" No, that's not it either. Wait, normally I have a really good memory. Ah, I know. "And all around Santa Ireneia, in the sweet afternoon air, Moorish drums, their drumming muffled in the woods, *ba-da-dam, ba-da-dam*, or louder on the hilltops, *ra-ta-ta, ra-ta-ta*, were summoning all the mercenaries and foot soldiers who owed allegiance to the Ramires." Gorgeous!'

Tító was leaning forward, pensively scraping at the dust on the road with his stick, and standing immediately behind him, Videirinha turned to his boss Gouveia with a bright smile on his face:

'Perhaps even better is that part where the Ramires men set off in pursuit of the Bastard. I find that piece more poetic somehow.

When the old man swears on his sword and later, in the Tower, the death knell begins very slowly to toll. Wonderful!'

On the edge of the bench, pressed up against Tító, so that Gouveia could spread out in comfort, Father Soeiro, his hands resting on the handle of his parasol, said:

'Oh, yes, those are definitely very interesting passages indeed. There's such a rich imagination at work in his Novella, and there's considerable learning and truth too.'

Tító hadn't opened a book since reading Jussieu's *Fables* as a child, and so hadn't read *The Tower of Dom Ramires*, but he murmured as he scored a longer line in the dust:

'He's an extraordinary fellow, Gonçalo.'

Still smiling his rapt smile, Videirinha added:

'And so talented.'

'And he's certainly determined!' cried Tító, looking up. 'That's what saves him from his other defects. I'm one of Gonçalo's oldest and best friends, but I don't hide my views, not even from him—especially not from him. He's very frivolous, very inconsistent, but it's his determination that saves him.'

'And his kindness, Senhor António Vilalobos!' added Father Soeiro softly. 'And kindness, especially Senhor Gonçalo's sort of kindness, also saves. For example, there are some very serious, very pure, very austere men, veritable Catos, who have always done their duty and respected the law, and yet no one likes them or seeks them out. Why? Because they never gave, never forgave, were never fond of anyone or helped them. And beside them you put another man, frivolous, careless, who has faults and has made mistakes, who has even neglected his duty and broken the law, but he's also lovable, generous, devoted, helpful, always ready with a kind word, an affectionate gesture. And that's why everyone loves him, and may God forgive me, but I wonder too, if God doesn't prefer such men ...'

His small hand, which he had pointed up to the heavens, fell back onto the bone handle of his parasol. Then, blushing at the temerity of such a statement, he added cautiously:

'Not that this is exactly Church doctrine, but it's there in men's souls, in many men's souls.'

João Gouveia, his bowler hat slightly askew, got to his feet, drew himself up and buttoned his frockcoat, as he always did when about to make some conclusive statement:

'Well, I've studied our friend Gonçalo Mendes long and hard, and do you two know what he reminds me of, do you Father Soeiro?'

'Who?'

'You may laugh, but I stand by my idea. Everything about Gonçalo, his honesty, his gentleness, his kindness, yes, his immense kindness, as pointed out by Father Soeiro. His impulses and sudden enthusiasms, which immediately vanish like so much smoke, combined with great determination and real grit when he sticks to an idea. His generosity, his thoughtlessness, his chaotic business dealings, his truly honourable feelings, his scruples, which can seem almost childish. His imagination, which leads him to exaggerate to the point of lying, and yet, at the same time, his practicality and realism. His intellect, his quickwittedness. His constant hope that some miracle will happen, like the famous miracle of Ourique, which will solve all his problems. His vanity, the pleasure he takes in cutting an elegant figure, and his enormous simplicity and sincerity, which means he will gladly help a beggar in the street. An underlying melancholy, despite his talkative, sociable nature. A terrible lack of self-confidence, which makes him draw back, shrink from danger, until the day he decides not to, and then he becomes the all-conquering hero. Even the antiquity of his race, here in this old Tower, for a thousand years. Even that recent departure for Africa. Put it all together, the good and the bad, and do you know who he reminds me of?'

'Who?'

'Portugal.'

The three friends set off again along the road to Vila Clara. In the clear sky, a tiny star was twinkling over Santa Maria de Craquede. And Father Soeiro, with his parasol under his arm, walked slowly back to the Tower in the sweet, silent evening air, saying his 'Hail Marys' and praying to God for peace for Gonçalo, for all men, for all the fields and houses sleeping in the dark, and for the lovely land of Portugal, so full of grace and love, praying that it should always be blessed among nations.

FINIS

Afterword

This apparently simple novel becomes more complex the deeper one goes. At first sight, it is, in part, a parody of the historical novel, sending up the mock-medievalism of, say, Sir Walter Scott or Alexandre Herculano, as well as the phoney nostalgia for the past that fills Videirinha's *fados* and Father Soeiro's reverence for the Ramires family history. Then there is the strangely modern business of that novel-within-the-novel, which is both the author's creation and Gonçalo's creation, with Gonçalo by turns despairing of and feeling exhilarated by the writing process; and behind that lies Eça's own evident delight in the very mock-medievalism he is parodying. Then again, the novel is a reflection on Portugal and its woes, and depicts Portugal as stagnating in the present and obsessed with its past glories, but also as a place and a people of which the author is at once wryly dismissive and very fond.

Out of all this ambivalence comes one of Eça's most engaging antiheroes: Gonçalo Mendes Ramires. As we and he are repeatedly told, Gonçalo, The Nobleman of the Tower, is the last male heir to one of Portugal's noblest families—if not *the* noblest—which dates back to before Portugal's existence as a nation, and his family's history is intricately intertwined with the nation's history, with one illustrious ancestor even sharing a wet nurse with the first king of Portugal, Afonso Henriques, and another fighting at the fateful Battle of Alcácer-Quibir alongside King Sebastião and, like him, disappearing among the Moorish hordes. And, as with the real Portuguese aristocracy, the Ramires family eventually sank into moral and economic decline.

Gonçalo is full of contradictions, being cowardly, lazy, lacking in self-confidence and yet also rather proud and instinctively, impulsively generous. He occasionally throws an aristocratic tantrum (for example, when handed an unlaundered napkin by Bento his servant) and is appalled by the smelliness of the lower orders, yet he much prefers the company of his servants Bento and Rosa, Videirinha the pharmacist's assistant, and his rather disreputable friend, Tító, taking little interest in his aristocratic connections. When, at his friend Castanheiro's bidding, Gonçalo decides to write a Novel, or, rather, Novella, he immediately, and lazily, resorts to plagiarism, basing his prose work on a poem written by his late uncle about one particularly 'glorious' episode in the family's history. While writing about these manly ancestors of his, he himself quails in the face of any danger, even when finding himself alone in a cemetery as dusk is coming on. The turning point for Gonçalo and the novel is when he finally confronts his own cowardice and tackles Ernesto, a local bully boy who, for reasons we never discover, is intent on humiliating Gonçalo.

Here again, we are faced by more ambivalence. Is Gonçalo's violent attack on Ernesto, which leaves Ernesto permanently disfigured, really as heroic as his family and friends affirm? Or is it as unnecessarily brutal as the unspeakably cruel death dealt out to the Bastard in the Novella? And does Ernesto represent the political bully Portugal was facing at the time?

A little history. When Eça began writing the novel, Portugal was going through a period of great political instability and suffering from a general sense of inferiority as regards other more industrialised European countries. Having lost its largest colony, Brazil, earlier in the century, it was doing little to exploit its remaining colonies, notably those in Africa. In 1890, when Eça began writing the novel, Portugal was engaged in a bitter territorial dispute with Britain. Portugal had laid claim to an area of land linking its largest African colonies Angola and Mozambique (on the western and eastern sides of Africa respectively) with the intention of creating a swathe of exclusively Portuguese territory. Portugal referred to this project as the *Mapa Cor-de-Rosa*, the Pink Map. Britain, of course, protested because Portugal's ambition got in the way of its own very similar ambition to impose British influence from Cape Town to the Mediterranean, Cecil Rhodes' so-called Cape-to-Cairo project (perhaps by naming the romantically inclined governess Miss Rhodes, Eça was getting in a sly dig at that British bully). A brief skirmish between Portuguese and British troops resulted in Lord Salisbury issuing a memorandum known as the British Ultimatum on 11 January 1890, demanding that Portuguese military forces be withdrawn from the disputed territories. In response, there were demonstrations all over Portugal, the British consulate was stoned and economic sanctions against Britain called for. The current borders were only finally established following the signing of a treaty between the two countries in 1891. This whole affair was deeply humiliating for the Portuguese, although Eça himself, in an article published in February 1890, argued that Portugal was in no position to challenge the British, and that continued expressions of Portuguese resentment would work against Portugal's own interests: 'It is far more important for Portugal to have life, heat, energy, an idea, an aim, than to possess the land of Mashona ... If we have no life, how can we carry life to Africa?' Gonçalo's defeat of Ernesto could be seen as a bit of wishful thinking, with Portugal (represented by Gonçalo) defeating the bully Britain (represented by the suspiciously fair-haired Ernesto). Then again, Cavaleiro's seduction of Gonçalo's sister Graça—in which Gonçalo openly connives in order to achieve his political ambitions—could be seen as symbolic of Portugal's shameful defeat by Britain.

The other characters are, in a way, fairly familiar types—the innocent younger sister, the complaisant husband, the adulterous wife, the utter cad, the bureaucrat, the social climber, etc—and they remain utterly unchanged throughout the novel. Gonçalo and his actions, on the other hand, are always complex and contradictory. His much-celebrated 'defeat' of Ernesto is hardly heroic since he launches his attack while safely seated on his horse and armed with a particularly vicious whip, apparently an heirloom from some distant, equally vicious ancestor. His other great triumph, being elected deputy, can hardly be seen as an untarnished success either, given that the electoral system is both far from democratic and deeply corrupt. Despite all Gonçalo's declared ambitions to use his position as deputy to bring about radical change, he becomes instead a familiar figure in the society columns and does nothing of any use at all. He then gives up the post after barely a year, sets sail to Africa on a ship named *Portugal* and rents a large estate in precisely the part of Africa where the British-Portuguese dispute arose, and where he apparently makes a great deal of money. We do not see or hear from Gonçalo himself on his return from Africa, but have only a second-hand account from Maria Mendonça and the gushing reactions of his friends and relatives. In the almost royal welcome Gonçalo receives on his return from Africa it is hard not to see an oblique reference to the longed-for (and completely impossible) return of King Sebastian, who was killed in an ill-judged battle in 1578 in Morocco and his body never found, a disappearance that gave rise to Sebastianism, the belief that Sebastian would one day return and save Portugal. We the readers see Gonçalo as a rather spoiled young man coming back from Africa, having made his wealth out of exploiting African labour (he is suspiciously pale for a man who has purportedly been labouring beneath the burning African sun), and who, given his track record, is highly unlikely to save anything, let alone Portugal.

The final scene of the novel is set in exactly the same location as earlier in the book, when Videirinha accompanies Gonçalo back to the Tower. Gonçalo may have escaped to Africa, but back in Portugal absolutely nothing has changed. And when, on the final page, Gouveia describes Gonçalo in all his fickle, feckless splendour, suggesting that Gonçalo reminds him of Portugal, are we to believe him or indeed to believe that Eça agrees with this assessment? Neither Maria Mendonça nor Gouveia have shown good judgement as regards flighty Dona Ana and dastardly Cavaleiro. And the praise heaped on Gonçalo's Novella does seem excessive. After all, we the readers know that it is only a very slender, largely plagiarised Novella, not the Great Historical Novel Gonçalo originally intended to write. And then there is that last elegiac paragraph, in which Father Soeiro prays:

> ...for peace for Gonçalo, for all men, for all the fields and houses sleeping in the dark, and for the lovely land of Portugal, so full of grace and love, praying that it should always be blessed among nations.

The words are so tender and yet, given what has gone before, it is hard not to read them as ironic or as both things at once. Eça spent most of his working life outside of Portugal, although he went back as often as he could, and Portugal is the subject of all his novels. Perhaps Gouveia is right in a way: Gonçalo may not represent Portugal exactly, but Gouveia's description of him does perhaps represent Eça's own ambivalent view of Portugal, part loving, part despairing.

About the author

José Maria de Eça de Queirós was born on November 25, 1845, in the small town of Povoa de Varzim in the north of Portugal. His mother was nineteen and unmarried. Only the name of his father—a magistrate—appears on the birth certificate. Following the birth, his mother returned immediately to her respectable family in Viana do Castelo, and Eça was left with his wet nurse, who looked after him for six years until her death. Although his parents married later—when Eça was four—and had six more children, Eça did not live with them until he was twenty-one, living instead either with his grandparents or at boarding school in Oporto, where he spent the holidays with an aunt. His father only officially acknowledged Eça as his son when the latter was forty. He did, however, pay for his son's studies at boarding school and at Coimbra University, where Eça studied Law, and was always supportive of his writing ambitions. After working as the editor and sole contributor on a provincial newspaper in Évora, Eça made a trip to the Middle East. Then, in order to launch himself on a diplomatic career, he worked for six months in Leiria, a provincial town north of Lisbon, as a municipal administrator, before being appointed consul in Havana (1872–74), Newcastle-upon-Tyne (1874–79) and Bristol (1879–88). In 1886, he married Emília de Castro with whom he had four children. His last consular posting was to Paris in 1888. He served there until his death in 1900 at the age of only fifty-four.

He began writing stories and essays as a young man and became involved with a group of intellectuals known as the Generation of '70, who were committed to reforms in society and in the arts. He published four novels and one novella during his lifetime: *The Crime of Father Amaro* (three versions: 1875, 1876, 1880), *Cousin Bazilio* (1878), *The Mandarin* (1880), *The Relic* (1887) and *The Maias*

(1888). His other novels were published posthumously: *The City and the Mountains, The Illustrious House of Ramires, To the Capital, Alves & Co., The Letters of Fradique Mendes, The Count of Abranhos* and *The Tragedy of the Street of Flowers.*

About the translator

Margaret Jull Costa has translated the works of many Spanish and Portuguese writers, and her work has brought her many prizes, among them the Portuguese Translation Prize for *The Book of Disquiet* by Fernando Pessoa in 1992; the translator's portion of the 1997 International IMPAC Dublin Literary Award for *A Heart So White*; the 2000 Weidenfeld Translation Prize for José Saramago's *All the Names*; the 2008 Pen/Book-of-the-Month Club and the Oxford Weidenfeld Translation Prizes for *The Maias* by Eça de Queiroz; the 2011 Oxford Weidenfeld Translation Prize for *The Elephant's Journey* by José Saramago; the 2012 Calouste Gulbenkian Translation Prize for *The Word Tree* by Teolinda Gersão; and, most recently, the 2015 Marsh Award for Children's Fiction in Translation for Bernardo Atxaga's *The Adventures of Shola*.

In 2013 she was invited to become a Fellow of the Royal Society of Literature and in 2014 was awarded an OBE for services to literature. In 2015 she was given an Honorary Doctorate by the University of Leeds.